SINKING ISLANDS

SINKING ISLANDS

a novel

Cai Emmons

 Red Hen Press | *Pasadena, CA*

Book Design by Mark E. Cull

Library of Congress Cataloging-in-Publication Data

Names: Emmons, Cai, author.
Title: Sinking islands : a novel / Cai Emmons.
Description: First edition. | Pasadena, CA : Red Hen Press, [2021]
Identifiers: LCCN 2021005996 (print) | LCCN 2021005997 (ebook) | ISBN
    9781597093248 (trade paperback) | ISBN 9781636280080 (epub)
Classification: LCC PS3605.M57 S56 2021 (print) | LCC PS3605.M57 (ebook)
    | DDC 813/.6—dc23
LC record available at https://lccn.loc.gov/2021005996
LC ebook record available at https://lccn.loc.gov/2021005997

The National Endowment for the Arts, the Los Angeles County Arts Commission, the
Ahmanson Foundation, the Dwight Stuart Youth Fund, the Max Factor Family Foun-
dation, the Pasadena Tournament of Roses Foundation, the Pasadena Arts & Culture
Commission and the City of Pasadena Cultural Affairs Division, the City of Los Angeles
Department of Cultural Affairs, the Audrey & Sydney Irmas Charitable Foundation, the
Meta & George Rosenberg Foundation, the Albert and Elaine Borchard Foundation, the
Adams Family Foundation, Amazon Literary Partnership, the Sam Francis Foundation,
and the Mara W. Breech Foundation partially support Red Hen Press.

First Edition
Published by Red Hen Press
www.redhen.org
Printed in Canada

To my son, Ben, a man of many superpowers.

And for all the inspiring teachers and mentors I've had over the years,
including Stefan Vogel, David Cole, Adrienne Kennedy, Seymour
Sarason, Chang-rae Lee, Peter Ho Davies.

SINKING ISLANDS

PART ONE

Fire Lady

1

Before they left the island it was Analu's habit to canoe along the shore at sunset. The sea was unusually calm then, a quiet mutter beneath the keel. Skipjacks and big-eyes swarmed to the water's surface, sensing Analu's proximity, puckering their lips for insects and to kiss the fading day. The sun would plummet suddenly, becoming dense and heavy, losing the will to hold itself up. As dusk deepened, the island's lights poked the dark, but eventually the stars, tossed across the sky like rice, won out in brilliance, and he felt lifted, a tiny insignificant thing, invisible as salt in the sea. It comforted him to feel such loneliness, it was that very loneliness that linked him to everything, the departed sun, the stars, the moon, his dead children.

But on the last evening before their departure he and Nalani sat on the beach together, legs pressed into the cool sand, thinking the same thoughts and different ones, wondering how it would be. They had no way of knowing, not really. There were the occasional bulletins from people who had gone before them, one family to Indonesia, one to New Zealand. It wasn't as they expected, they said, but how it was they couldn't quite say, which left Analu wondering if he and Nalani were making a big mistake.

The island had become for him a winking hologram of beauty and sadness, back and forth, even now as twilight bellied down, emptying the world of malice, promising the possibility of peace and the passing of grief, even at this beautiful hour as the smell of excrement wafted over them and trash fluttered in their sightlines, and when they walked home they would find Tamati beneath his favorite coconut tree, snoring loudly, reeking of alcohol. A sudden scream, brief but unsettling, rose from the cluster of houses where Penina, their eleven-year-old daughter and Analu's mother, Vailea, awaited them.

Vailea did not want to come with them. She could not, she said, leave the island. She didn't want another life. Her feet were bad from the diabetes. She didn't like to walk too far. *You go. Leave me here. Your sisters will care for me.* What would happen in the next flood when the waters would rise higher, which surely they would, everyone said so? They might rise to Analu's house, flooding the sewage system along the way. Dysentery always followed the floods. And death. Heni and Ipo both went that way, Heni at three, Ipo at nine months, their bodies drained. Beautiful daughters, but so fragile. Penina was their strong one. They were leaving mostly for her. *No,* Vailea insisted, *I won't go.* And it made Analu sometimes wish that the waters would rise more quickly, as they did in the Bible, an irresistible tsunami of water, netting them all like fish, so they could go together, willingly, in joyous surrender.

He and Nalani waited until the fish surfaced to say goodnight, and the village exhaled quiet, and all they heard was the geckos clicking, the rustling of curlews and noddies, the whisper of fronds. All the things that might sadden them were in the past, so the island had only one face—it was a sweet thing, dear to them. Holding hands, they made their way home.

2

Penina, concealed by the dark, stood on a rocky promontory watching her parents make their way up the beach and enter the trees. How old they looked, how bent and sad. For them, leaving the island was a terrible thing. They wouldn't have been leaving if it weren't for her, and while she felt guilty for that, she was also really happy to be going. She loved the island as much as they did, but she was also keen to see the world beyond. She'd seen glimpses of that world when Kimo's internet was working. The cities and cars and mansions. People making music and movies and dancing wildly, everyone with a cell phone and wearing fancy clothes. There were elephants and tigers in that other world, cows and horses and hummingbirds, and even polar bears. Ice cream all the time. So, so much!

She marveled at her cousins. Same blood, but so different. They had no interest in leaving. They didn't believe the island was sinking, despite what many people said. How could they keep thinking that, when they saw the water rising every year? Maybe she thought differently because her sisters had died. But even if the island wasn't sinking, how could you not want to see other things, know other things? To her, that was crazy. Sure, the island was special, but there was so much more, and she was ready to see as much as she could. ·

She leapt from rock to rock until she reached the sand, still warm under her toes. She slipped out of her clothes and waded in until the water draped her shoulders then rose to her chin. Her hair swarmed across a surface shimmering with starlight. The water lapped her lips and she lapped back. The salty taste of her own blood. She stroked out and rolled onto her back so she and the stars blinked at each other.

Alone and together. Blink, blink. *I see you, I don't. I see you, I don't. I am the luckiest girl in the world. Goodbye stars. Goodbye water. Goodbye sky. Goodbye island.* What a good place to be born—the best really—but now her future was out there in the world beyond.

Tomorrow it would all finally begin after so much back and forth, so much yes and no, so much planning. They would get on a plane—she and her mother and father and grandmother, a small plane her father said, but she didn't care big or small—and they would rise into the sky. Close to the clouds. Close to the sun. They would look down and see their homely island becoming smaller and smaller, diminishing to a tiny pinpoint in the gargantuan sea. Then, like magic, it would be gone.

3

The heat is cranked too high and the amphitheater is steamy with the breath of three hundred geeky, satin-cheeked undergraduates, mostly men, freshmen and sophomores, superlative students, loveable for their eagerness, but bloated with hubris. She usually likes the chance to work with undergraduates, who aren't yet jaded. She can look into their formless, bud-like faces and see them as puttering children exploring things on their own terms, still oblivious to the world's demands and conventions.

But today, on the first day of the term, Dr. Diane Fenwick returns to teaching unrestored by the break. Her situation on campus has become nearly unbearable. She's no dope, she knows she's being shunned. In the hallways and on the quad other faculty members refuse to look at her, sometimes pointedly turning their backs. Even Newt Goldberg, a chemist known for being aggressively friendly, no longer hails her from his office. She hasn't done anything "actionable" in terms of her tenure, but she's made the mistake of sharing with a few people the crack in her belief system—prompted by seeing what Bronwyn can do—and now no distinguished scientist wants to be associated with a colleague who is even entertaining the idea that human beings might influence the Earth's forces. Surely such a person must have lost her mind. And without a mind you certainly do not belong at a major research institution. It's her own damn fault for thinking a few others might be open-minded.

She and Joe went to Maine for Christmas, despite the record cold and daunting snow. They brought bundles of wood for fires, and they sat on the couch in front of the blaze, quilts weighting their laps, reading, talking, sometimes simply sitting and contemplating the flame's whimsy. They ate simple meals of soup and bread and cheese and wine. And once or twice a day they layered up and went outside, carving a foot path through the deep snow out to the end of the point where they admired the ocean for the way it appeared so different each day, every hour even, sometimes smooth and onyx, other times austere and erratic, potentially annihilating.

But through all this nearly ideal time with Joe, questions simmered. What can she really do without Bronwyn? Her presence is necessary for any research that might explore this new way of thinking. And Diane is finally realizing that Bronwyn is gone for good. For the last year, since their life-changing trip to Siberia, Diane has been biding her time, completing several research papers, floating her new ideas to people she thought might be interested, but mostly waiting for Bronwyn's return. But who is she kidding? Bronwyn isn't coming back. What Diane thought would be a "rest" has turned into an entire life in some other place. Diane doesn't even know where, as Bronwyn hasn't been in touch. It's time to move on, forget Bronwyn, who seems to have forgotten her. Not the easiest thing to do when they've been joined at the hip for so many years, Diane not only a mentor, but also a surrogate mother.

She shouldn't be letting these bleak thoughts waylay her. She's never been one for self-pity. Here she is, back at work, lecturing in front of a class again: "Introduction to Atmosphere, Ocean, and Climate Dynamics." Usually she's a lively teacher, full of surprises, but now she hears herself speaking as a preoccupied actor might recite lines. She used to read the Harry Potter books to her nieces and nephews like this, perfect vocal inflections while her mind was entirely elsewhere, a sin she is quite sure she has never committed in the classroom before. Her PowerPoint cedes to whiteness, a field of frozen tundra on which she sees Bronwyn collapsed, exactly as she appeared in Siberia when the helicopter was descending to rescue her.

Diane gasps quietly and turns away from the screen, sealing off the image. She stares out at the students, pausing to get her bearings. The note taking ceases, the clicking keys of the laptops gives way to silence.

Such expectant faces out there, young but already devoted to science. Their glasses wink at her over the blue apples of their laptops. She hates to say anything to dent their beliefs. She brings up the next frame—Bernouli's equation, critical to the understanding of fluid mechanics. The symbols are assembled as usual, staunchly sure of themselves. There is no reason to question an equation that has for years proven its reliability. And yet, now nothing is exempt from questioning.

"That's enough for today. See you on Wednesday."

A hand shoots up. "But what about the equation?"

"We'll get to Bernouli soon enough."

She shuts down her computer and averts her gaze as the students stream past her. She has not exactly humiliated herself, but she holds herself to high standards as a professor and can't remember ever dismissing a class early. She hurries back to her office, head down. Newt Goldberg's door is open, as usual, but he doesn't look up as she passes.

She closes her own office door and collapses into the desk chair. It is only January, but winter has already outstayed its welcome. Drifts along the streets and sidewalks are so calcified with black particulates they no longer resemble snow. Even in the places where the snow has not been disturbed, cycles of melting and refreezing have left a crust, a perfect landing pad for dust and soot, which makes the city's pollution unpleasantly visible.

She fires up her computer, wondering if one more email to Bronwyn is in order. Her inbox is full, much of it missives from the university's administration that don't require a response. One from the Dean says *chat?* in the subject line. She stares at the word chat. Not the kind of formal subject heading for an email he'd be sending university-wide.

No, it's meant for her, her alone. *Let's have a chat soon, Diane,* he says. *I'd like to learn more about your radical revision of belief.* He doesn't say more, he doesn't need to.

4

Sometimes Analu thinks he began to worry too soon. Maybe the island has another hundred years after all, two hundred years. Maybe forces will shift and it won't sink at all. But when these thoughts come to him, as he rides the bus to work at the retirement community west of Sydney, or as he watches his mother dozing on the small square of concrete that is their patio, he reminds himself of why they left, closing his eyes and forcing himself to see again how it was when the water rose. The water had a will of its own. After the storms it covered more than half the island. It circled the trees so they stood like gangly teenagers, stranded, panicked, unsure what was next. Sandbags and buckets did little to help, the water had its own pathways, its own schedule; once it left the sea it became a trickster, muscular and despotic, all its winking blue beauty gone. It pushed past the doorways of the houses and settled in kitchens and bedrooms for weeks, sullen and brown and concealing. If you dug under the pools you never knew what you'd find. People discovered their decaying shirts and shorts in other people's yards. Ruined packages of bread drifted through bedrooms. What looked like a lost shoe turned out to be a floating turd. Plastic wrappers, soggy foliage, fruit looking like pus—it was best not to touch anything.

Then, done with its pillaging, the water would withdraw, and each time, as Analu looked at the sad wreckage left in the water's wake, he saw the island's future, its torturously slow but inevitable disappearance. These floods, he's always known in his heart, and he still knows, are the beginning of the island being repurposed for something else. Death is afoot, he senses, far and wide.

A few weeks before they were scheduled to move, Analu developed extreme doubts about leaving. He walked alone to the south side of the island to visit the abandoned resort. It was situated on the lowest-lying part of the island, a beautiful sandy point. The island residents had always understood this point as a place to visit, not to live. But a developer from China, a rich man who the islanders called Mr. Dung—a man who wore comically wide dark glasses and a wide-brimmed straw hat ribboned with American hundred-dollar bills—had come to the island with big plans to construct a hotel. He told the island council they would benefit from the tourism. Each room for the hotel would be a separate cabana stretching out over the water with transparent glass flooring that would allow a person to recline in a lounge chair, and sip a cocktail in shade or full sun, and watch the fish swimming beneath. The resort was designed to encourage visitors to immerse themselves in the landscape, to imagine they were part fish themselves. Analu's brother-in-law, Kimo, who is on the island's council, showed Analu the plans. They included pictures of people, mostly white, a few Chinese, wearing bathing suits and the foolish smiles of monkeys.

Materials arrived by boat and plane. Workers stayed in makeshift huts on the island's south side. Mr. Dung appeared every few weeks in a private plane and stayed for a day or two, huffing orders. The project moved slowly, hampered by the usual challenges of working in a remote location, coupled with poor planning and incompetence. The workers were weakened by the island's heat and took frequent breaks under the trees. Two months into construction a huge cyclone hit and flooded the entire area. Three weeks later, a second cyclone came in. After more than two months of waiting, the water didn't entirely recede, and Mr. Dung abandoned the project, leaving a vast submerged concrete slab, some of the workers' temporary huts, and jumbles of construction trash: wheelbarrows, and hunks of concrete, and plastic water bottles, and bottles of sunscreen, and lost or cast-off cellphones. Human life, thought Analu.

It was midday and a breeze was just coming up and stirring the water. Analu wandered around the area, wading knee-deep out onto the rough slab in his bare feet. He had the strange sensation of walking on a massive gravesite, and wondered if something illicit might be buried under the concrete, if that had been the point all along and the resort had only been a cover for more suspect activities. He stood still, the sun ironing his back and shoulders, and stared down at his callused feet, toes spread wide and magnified by the water. A few small fish arrived to investigate his ankles. At the edge of his vision he saw a pair of petrels resting on an outcropping of rock. They seemed to be eyeing him, and he eyed them back, and after they'd taken each other in, the petrels took off in silent flight. They flew out over the sea, carrying his gaze with them. They swooped low and shot straight up again, releasing shrill calls.

Analu squinted. The arc of the petrels' flight widened. They didn't shut up. What were they so angry about? What did they want him to see? Something kept them plunging down again. Analu's vision sharpened and homed in on some disturbance in the water. There was something strange there. Flecks of shimmering color. Red, yellow, silver, layering over one another, emerging, sinking, then breaching the surface again. Something alive? A school of fish he'd never seen before? It hurt his eyes to look in one place too long.

He scanned right, then left. My god, the thing was huge, hundreds of feet wide. But what—? For a moment he was more afraid than he'd ever been. The petrels had flown off. Frightened as he was?

In a moment understanding arrived. Plastic. It was one of those rafts of plastic flung together by the ocean currents, stitched into a new unwieldy floating thing. He'd heard about this, these islands of trash, but he'd never seen one. They were supposed to be farther out at sea on the ocean gyres.

Everything seemed like a mirage now, nothing clear. He glanced down at his feet, at the cement slab beneath them. He cursed Mr. Dung. This island of plastic had to have something to do with him. It was made from the soda bottles his workers had cast on the beach, their abandoned flip-flops. Analu is not a man given to hatred, but if he were, Mr. Dung would be one of his first targets—the way he came to the island thinking it was *his*.

Analu retreated to the beach. He found a rock and hurled it out as far as he could, aiming for the plastic. But the noxious island floated and sparkled mockingly out of reach, and the rock fell short and disappeared into the ocean with a meek plink.

Of course they would leave, Analu thought. There was no future here.

5

Felipe is two blocks from the theater when he spots Giovanna and Manuel, Giovanna always easy to spot with her bright platinum hair. Felipe breaks into a jog. He hates being late, but last night a brief but heavy rain filled his roof buckets, so this morning he had to funnel the water into jugs and bring them inside and cover them securely to keep the mosquitos out. It was a good haul, but time-consuming, and it's made him late.

"No rehearsal," Giovanna says, pointing to a sign on the door. "Rafael is having a water emergency."

"Aren't we all?" Felipe says.

"Water *crisis*," Manuel suggests.

"Someone stole all his rain buckets. He's furious. He wants us to run lines," Giovanna says. "I don't have a key. Do you guys have keys?"

"We don't have to do it here," Manuel says.

"I have a key," Felipe offers.

The theater is a former church, and its tall stained glass windows, blacked out during performances, celebrate daylight, tinting the dust motes to gauzy pale blues and reds. Since the drought began dust has veiled everything in São Paulo, inside and out.

Felipe, a former dancer and still limber at thirty-eight, leaps onto the stage and perches on its lip while Giovanna switches on the house lights. Without the director, Rafael, it is Felipe's job to infuse them all with energy. It's not contractual, it's simply what Felipe does wherever Felipe goes—he uses his energy as a match to ignite the people around him, his roundabout way of being a leader and getting others to collaborate as if it's their idea. But these days, since the "hydric collapse," it's hard for Felipe to find energy for himself, let alone sowing it among others. The drought has dragged on for months, years really, squeezing the verve from everyone. The city officials, having long ignored the exigencies of water management in a country that owns twelve percent of the world's fresh water, are now grasping for solutions and promising quick fixes they can never deliver. Paulistanos are disgusted. A pessimism has taken over the city's public discourse and apocalyptic predictions have run rampant on social media. Walking the streets Felipe feels anarchy breeding in fetid alleyways and hot apartments. Even the music people play is more aggressive.

Felipe loves doing theater. He's given up so much in his life first to dance, then to act—he has no family at almost forty years old and he still lives in a one-room apartment—and he's always believed that theater could be a force in the world to alter thought and behavior. But now his theories are being put to the test. Everyone in São Paulo is suffering. The water is turned on only a couple of days a week for a few hours, and even that is unpredictable. People can't flush their toilets, bathe, do laundry or dishes. Even water for cooking and drinking is scarce. When the water flows everything else stops, decisions have to be made quickly. The thirst has made everyone edgy. Water skirmishes are breaking out all over the city, some flourishing into small-scale riots. People play tug-of-war over full buckets, argue about who owns the rainwater coming down on apartment rooftops or in the alleys between buildings. They shit into plastic bags and send the bags out with the garbage so as not to defile their dry toilets and fill their apartments with fetor. And the water people collect in buckets sometimes goes uncovered, breeding mosquitoes, then malaria, dengue fever, zika, chikungunya. A simple satisfying hand washing is hard to come by.

Felipe, curious, once visited the Jaguari Reservoir with his friend Isabella. The shoreline, along with much of what was once the reservoir's bed, was so parched it had contracted into a puzzle of polygons separated by deep fissures, reminiscent of a moonscape. The remaining water, abloom with algae, was neon green. It wasn't water you'd want to depend on for much, certainly not water you'd want to drink.

Knowing all this, Felipe's idea about the force of theater has been dwindling a little. In recent months audiences have shrunk dramatically, despite positive reviews. Felipe has been talking to Rafael about taking their work into the streets, writing and performing a series of "water plays" in public spaces. Rafael, while open to talking, is dubious. He's asked Felipe to write some of these little plays first and they'll go from there.

So, on nonperforming evenings, Felipe leaves his friends early and sits alone in his hot apartment waiting for inspiration. He doesn't consider himself a writer and doesn't know how to launch an idea—or else he begins an idea but can't sustain it. So he waits and waits. *Hello, Muse, where are you?* As he waits he begins to feel silly, doomed—no one will care anyway. Art is for people with full stomachs and comfortably filled pocketbooks and water on demand, which would not describe most Paulistanos at this moment. He thinks of the political playwright Bertolt Brecht and wonders if Brecht would think theater has any role to play now.

Besides, Felipe asks himself: *What do I have to say in the first place?* He has considered dramatizing the ways the water shortages are causing suffering, but everyone knows about that already—they want to escape the scarcity, not see it dramatized. What they really want is solutions and he, a dancer and actor by training, hasn't the slightest idea about solutions to a massive mismanaged drought.

Felipe opens his script, *Our Country's Good,* by British playwright Timberlake Wertenbaker. The play, set in the first penal colony in Australia, centers on the production of a play by the convicts. Felipe plays the convict John Arscott, who despairs about the possibility of freedom and only feels alive when he escapes into his character. If any play could make a case for theater as a humanizing force, this is it, but right now Felipe is having trouble immersing himself.

"Let's bail," he says, leaping down from the stage.

Manuel and Giovanna look at him strangely.

"If you say so, Captain," Giovanna says. "Your call."

"I think we're fine with lines. And anyway, we're here tomorrow with the whole cast," Felipe says. "I'll find out what's up with Rafael. Also, I need to work on my play."

Manuel rolls his eyes. He doesn't believe Felipe will come through with any plays.

Felipe walks home past the Café de Rosa where he has been able to get, with a little flirtatious begging, the best glass of water in the city. He sits in the shade of the restaurant's back patio, away from the noise and fumes of the street. He's the only one back here. Luana, the waitress who has come to know him, brings him the glass full of cool water without asking what he wants. She sets it down with a wink and he slips some bills into the pocket of her apron.

After she leaves he notices a dead spider belly-up on the water's surface. He laughs to himself, thinking how even last year he would have objected, asked for a new glass. Now he fishes the spider out, flicks it to the ground, and drinks, allowing himself only a few sips at a time to make it last. After the first few sips he takes out his phone and holds up the glass so it snares some golden light, making the water look beautifully smoldering. He snaps a photo. Perfect, grade-A water, pure and full-bodied, with more complex notes than his favorite Cabernet—and certainly more satisfaction. He has never before appreciated the flavor of good water. These days it's hard to find water that isn't brackish and redolent of some rank odor—heavy chlorine, or iron, or sulfur or, god forbid, sewage. He's quite sure he'll find this image reassuring in the days to come.

Back at his one-room apartment Felipe is restless. The light feels wrong. He's accustomed to actors' hours. Usually in the mornings, if he isn't in rehearsal, he's sleeping. Theater is a demanding taskmaster. He's one of ten regular players in his repertory company and he's often cast in two shows at a time. Exhaustion is a way of life, but he's gotten good at not allowing it to gain purchase.

Making himself sit at the table that serves as dining table and desk, he breaks out his computer and opens an empty Word file. His brain is inert. He thinks of the glass of water he drank earlier, how he was able to taste every drop, each a delicate generous bead. Sometimes he imagines the city's reservoirs going entirely dry, nothing left at all. He envisions a mass exodus from São Paulo, people booking planes to more water-blessed places in Brazil and beyond. Where would he go if it came to that? The rest of his family, his parents and three sisters, moved to Rio years ago. At the time he couldn't comprehend moving away from the place you were born and raised, and he still can't. He is Paulistano through and through. He loves this city, parched as it is; it is still lively, still a city of inventors and artists. This is the only place he's ever known. It saddens him to think of a great city like this collapsing from lack of water—and all the associated disease and starvation. But it could happen, couldn't it? Shouldn't he try to write about that?

He's tempted to call his best friend Isabella, but he hates interrupting her at work. They used to dance together, but not long after he turned to acting she became an attorney, and now she keeps business hours.

He pulls his shades so the apartment light turns sepia and rummages in a duffle bag he keeps in the closet. He pulls out a silk slip. Stripping off his shorts, he slides into the slip. It's a deep pink, the color of certain orchids, and it's been worn to exquisite softness. He lies on the bed and strokes the fabric covering his thighs, his buttocks. He closes his eyes, thinking of his childhood summers when school would be out and they'd go to the beach, he and his sisters and his mother and father. How free they were then, how oblivious to peril. No one worried about water, whether there was enough and if it was clean. Back then, no one worried about anything.

6

Vailea draws her tongue along the edge of the canyon left by the extraction of two teeth. The pain blinks on and off like a warning light. The space is enormous. She has never known her mouth to be so big. Analu took her to the dentist yesterday. The dentist peered into her mouth and, disgusted by what he saw, his eyes, above a blue mask, grew roundly pregnant. He shot her full of painkillers and extracted two bottom teeth, important teeth whose loss has changed the entire landscape of her mouth. He wants her to come back again next month and have more teeth pulled. She told him no, she would not be back. Enough has changed; she needs to keep her mouth as it is.

This day will be a long one, though she has gotten used to long days, days filled with the thickness of waiting. Analu and Nalani have gone to work, Penina to school. Vailea will spend the day as she spends most of her days—outside on her chair watching the sun travel across the small fenced patio, daydreaming of the island. Beyond the fence everything moves too fast—double time, triple time, why so fast? Even the insects and birds seem speedy here in Australia, as if there is so much to be done. The sun does not have the gentle touch of the island sun. Here it is like sharp metal, sizzling and shriveling everything until the skin feels like hunks of fatty cooking pig. There is no relief to be gotten from a sea breeze or a quick dip in the water. Sometimes she retreats inside to the three-room apartment, but she doesn't like the tight seal of the windows, or the way the doors snap closed like the jaws of a crocodile. At night it feels as if she's closed in a glass jar, running out of air. And from inside there is no way to keep track of the snake who often creeps under the fence to sleep in the sun. Vailea has never seen such a snake—the island has none—and she doesn't trust it. It is fat and black with green spots and almost as long as Vailea is tall. She suggested to Analu that they kill the snake, but Analu is a gentle man, and he sees the good in other creatures, and he does not think the snake is doing them any harm. Still, when the snake is around Vailea never takes her eyes off it. You can't predict harm. Harm comes unexpectedly and then it is too late. She thinks about how she might get rid of the snake herself, using a kitchen knife or a broom while the snake sleeps. But she worries the snake might be faster than she, and she pictures it rearing up to sink its teeth into her face.

Sometimes many hours pass when she and the snake sleep at the same time. When she wakes she chides herself for letting her guard down. Today, her tongue visits and revisits the new terrain of her mouth, and the snake moves each time her tongue moves. She stills her tongue to urge the snake back to sleep.

The day always takes a turn at three thirty or four when Penina comes home from school, and time does backflips. Penina has become a little Australian in the nearly two years they've been living here. She wears tight skirts and short shorts. Everything about her is *rush-rush, hurry-hurry, I need, I want.* She is still a sweet girl—at almost thirteen just beginning to tip into womanhood—but her island self is gone, dissolved like mist. Vailea tries to remember how her own girls, Analu's sisters, were at this age. Some things are hard to remember. They were all terrible flirts. The middle daughter popped out babies starting at sixteen, the oldest loved to make things with her hands, the youngest liked to sing. They are all in their forties now, some of their children parents themselves. Those years of active mothering blur together, but she knows it was good. She has been blessed.

The dentist told her those teeth no longer belonged in her mouth. That is what Vailea wants to say to the snake: *You don't belong here. There isn't room here for both of us.*

That's island thinking, Analu told her. *We aren't on an island any more. There's plenty of space for everyone.*

Penina arrives home a little later than usual. She comes outside to greet her grandmother. She wears a tight purple skirt that shows the two moons of her buttocks.

"Momu," Penina says in greeting. She has a boy with her, his name is Dinh. She's never brought a boy home. Vailea smiles at Dinh. He's a friendly boy, smaller than Penina.

The young people go inside and Vailea listens to them chatting. Penina's voice twitters up and down the scale like a small perturbed bird. They speak English, but Australian English which sounds foreign. Music plays. Vailea understands it must be from Dinh's phone. It is quiet, but frantic and angry. Vailea thinks if she had to listen to such music for very long it might alter the easy flow of her blood.

She rises slowly and shuffles inside, and the young people look up at her in alarm. The music stops abruptly. She laughs. "Just me," she says. She pours sodas for them, and they accept them gratefully. "Can I fix you something to eat?"

"We're fine," Penina says. "Momu? Will you tell Dad I need a phone?"

"Why do you need a phone?"

"Everyone has a phone," Penina says.

Vailea laughs. The logic of young people.

"I need it for school," Penina says.

Vailea swishes warm salt water around her mouth as the dentist told her to do. The dentist was so sure of the things he said. How could he be so sure? She spits into the sink. There is still blood, diluted to pale pink, and the pain still blinks on and off, though less insistently.

Penina and Dinh are focused on the phone again, riveted by the tiny screen.

"Wait—what happened?" Penina says. "Play it again. It looked like she put that fire out!"

"She did," Dinh says. "That's why they call her the Fire Lady."

"Is she a witch?"

"Like a witch, maybe."

"How did she do it?"

"Beats me."

Penina makes a face, and she and Dinh laugh with their whole

bodies, and Vailea thinks if she can't have water nearby, laughter is
the best replacement.

7

Diane hesitates outside the Mirabelle Café, wondering if it's too late to text Ted Hagopian an excuse—a nasty bug, blindsided by something at work, or—instead she pushes through the front door. Ted sits near the back, wearing his customary jeans and moccasins and Red Sox cap, always so undeniably himself. He's one of her favorite people, an adorable gnome of a man, and in all the many years she's known him he has never failed to set her at ease. After Siberia he was the first person she confided in about Bronwyn's amazing capability, and he has stood by her ever since, though she knows he harbors doubts. His field is philosophy, human consciousness in particular, but he's ready to speculate about anything. Sometimes he can be a little oblivious to social cues, but once he focuses on a conversation he becomes rooted there, a rare quality these days. She's hoping he'll have advice for her about how to handle the Dean.

Seeing her, he removes his cap—as if to announce *here's my brain*—and his gray curls seem to fibrillate. Diane hasn't seen him for a while (he keeps to his department and she to hers, both are busy), and seeing him now she realizes she's missed him. He isn't the sort to abandon you even when you aren't making sense.

The place is mobbed with young people, student types who always appear so curiously idle and enviably carefree, though perhaps she herself conveys the same to strangers. She certainly knows youths are rarely carefree. She threads a path to the back, eyes on Ted, her thick winter coat and oversized handbag slapping the edges of tables, rotating cups, setting off ceramic chitters, so she's aware of herself as a disturbance. She's begun to carry with her an aspect of Bronwyn, some intimation of blurred boundaries.

Ted, centered in mind more than body, gives her a brief, emblematic hug, its awkwardness underscored by the several inches of height she has on him. They settle, order coffee, deplore the weather. Diane speaks too quickly.

"I've been summoned by the Dean. I knew this would happen eventually."

Ted's forehead, wide as a delta, is brindled with consternation. "Really, when?"

"Soon."

"He called?"

"Emailed. With veiled urgency."

"Did he say why?"

"Well, we know why."

"But it's up to him to state his case."

She scours the café for other faculty, a new habit she can't control. Transparent is how she feels, as if everything she might say is already laid out there on the table, exposed, a slab of skinned meat, an egg cracked open, about to be dissected, judged for possible impurities and toxicities.

They fall silent and drink their coffee in mutual recognition of the difficulty of her situation. The café's din rises around them, kids on phones mostly. *So, I'm like . . . and he's, like . . . Dude, dude . . . Okay, text me . . .* She thinks of Matt and Bronwyn shacked up somewhere, who knows where, leading some life she can't begin to picture. Fifty-five and she already feels very old and irredeemably confused.

"I thought you'd have some sage advice."

"Hold your cards close. Talk about the other research you've been doing—you're always articulate about that. You don't have to mention Bronwyn. How much can he know anyway?"

"Who knows who he's been talking to."

"He's probably hoping you'll give yourself away. Make some silly claim."

For God's sake. "You think I'd do that, make a *silly claim*?" She tries to hold his gaze, but he's reaching for his cap which he screws over his curls.

"I said *he* might expect that. No matter, he can't fire you."

"Being fired isn't what worries me. You have no idea how bad it's gotten. No one will talk to me, forget working with me. I'm the kid on the playground with cooties. No—Ebola!"

"No one can deny your reputation."

"I need to move on from that."

"Meaning?"

She shrugs, all the hope and indignation she brought here leaking away. What was she expecting from Ted? "You have to admit, even you don't really believe me."

"Of course I—"

"No, you've been nice, you've stood by me, you've been a good friend, but even you think I'm likely to say something silly."

"I don't *disbelieve* you, Diane. I just don't understand. I haven't seen what you've seen. You'd be the same way in my position."

She leaves the café regretting the meeting, wondering what support or advice she'd really expected from him. Whatever it was, she failed to get it. Much to her chagrin there are two engineering faculty at a table near the exit, Ken Kurlish and Pujit Chatterjee. Pujit smiles, but Ken's face falls into an instant deep freeze, and her shame quickly transmutes into indignation again. She isn't a lunatic. If only she could get additional data from Bronwyn herself, study Bronwyn while she's at work.

She plods home under clouds lined up precisely as militia, wondering when the city of Cambridge became so ugly. Joe is in the kitchen making spanakopita. The TV is on in the living room. The scent of cheese and spinach roils through the house.

"A fracking earthquake in Oklahoma," Joe reports. "Five point two."

"Ted was no help at all. It was awkward for both of us. He hasn't ever really believed me though he hasn't said so straight out." She sighs. "So I'm on my own."

Joe lays down his butter brush and fixes her squarely in his sightline, daubing her with one of the soft, naively reassuring looks she loves him for. "You've always been on your own. As well as one step ahead of everyone else. That's how you've gotten to where you are."

"I hate being thought of as a fool. One more hysterical woman."

"Can you try to ignore them all, just carry on as you always have?"

"That's exactly what I've been doing for the better part of the past year. You see what it's brought me to, what shape I'm in."

He comes around the island and seizes her shoulders almost roughly. "Embrace the crazy woman if you have to. Be her gladly. The crazy women get things done. You know that. They're the ones with power."

How fervently she wishes that were true.

8

The sun is a brash tambourine in the Eastern sky. A rare winter morning when the view south across the bay is not sullied by sleeves of fog. Sea and snow-capped Olympics are both clear, and visible in the same line of vision, one of the reasons she loves this place. She stands on the chilly winter sand in bare feet, binoculars in hand, listening to the polished pebbles at the end of the beach chortling with each outgoing wave. Three seals pop up in quick succession maybe twenty yards out, staring at her as if to say *good morning,* then they submerge again, reappearing a minute later much closer. An eagle rides a thermal, rising to a pinpoint against the blue as if to display his strength and grandeur, then descending abruptly to the ocean's surface to grasp something in its talons. Instead of rising in flight again the eagle begins to swim, hunching its broad wings at regular intervals like someone swimming the breaststroke. She feels her own scapula rising and falling in sympathy. What work it must be, especially in water this cold. How vigorous he looks, how determined, how nearly human. There is so much to be learned from birds—no, from *all* animals.

She tracks the bird's progress through her binoculars to where it arrives on the western bank. Standing on a rock it assumes its recognizable eagleness again, talons locked on a large fish. It glances around, suspicious, protective, unsure where to settle, then it half flies, half hops with intricate footwork from rock to rock along the shoreline. Finally it stops and rips into the fish. She's seen this two or three times before—eagles swimming when their prey is too heavy to transport in flight—but it still has the power to amaze her.

A blur at the edge of her vision. The awareness of being watched.

A man, lanky and dressed in black, stands in the field of the adjacent property, partly obscured by a row of bare blackberry bushes. Strange. There's no dwelling there, the land is used for grazing. She's accustomed to seeing cows in the field, not people. In the year she and Matt have been on the island, the only people she's seen at this end of the dirt lane are her elderly landlady, Ruth, and Ruth's husband, Hal, who live in the house at the top of the property. They are lovely, discrete people who never intrude. And it's highly doubtful, given their age, that they've seen the fire video.

She glances away from the man then back again, trying to determine if he has a camera. Not as far as she can see, at least not a camera that's raised. The direction of his gaze is hard to gauge. Maybe he bushwhacked down from the road to get a closer view of the eagle. She looks away again and when she looks back, he's gone. If he was coming to find her wouldn't he have made an overture? She pats her hair. Of course it hasn't reverted to red. She shouldn't be so paranoid.

Still her heart twitches, broomlike, and she wishes Matt were here. He's on assignment for a couple of days in Eastern Oregon, covering a group of armed ranchers occupying public land to protest the overreach of the federal government. The online publication he writes for is headquartered in Seattle. Mostly their situation on the island suits them both. It's remote enough that she is unlikely to be recognized— especially having dyed her telltale red hair black—and he is reasonably close to an urban hub that provides solid employment and the regular hit of stimulation he needs. He's occasionally annoyed by the lack of reliable cell and internet service at the cabin, which means that he often goes to the island's center to work, but for her the querulous reception is just fine. She has always preferred, even before the fire video and the growing pressure from Diane, to be intermittently reachable. A year and a half ago, when the video went viral, she began to feel like public property. She was bombarded by emails and phone calls and people said things without restraint. *Bitch. Witch. Kook.* But the reverential ones were often just as bad. Some thought if she could stop rain, put out fires, arrest tornados, then surely she could heal human bodies, cure cancer, bring the dead back to life. She's always known that all humans have a propensity for occasional irrational thinking, and see-ing patterns where they don't exist, but all those whacky missives and phone calls have made her think the norm favors the irrational.

The communications didn't stop when they moved away from New Hampshire, but she learned to ignore them, erase them, and gradually they ebbed: the solicitations for interviews, the requests for interventions, the insults, the venomous lectures from irascible climate change deniers.

Still, a few of the things that were said have stuck with her and still have a needling power. *If you really can do what some people say you can do, you should get out there and do something! But for God's sake act wisely.* Of course, of course, but what does *acting wisely* mean? She and Matt have discussed this so often there is nothing left to say. Until she knows what *acting wisely* means, she won't do another intervention.

And yet, the skill, the power, the gift—whatever it is she does to alter the Earth's forces—takes up space in her gut like an extra organ, dormant, but not atrophied. Sometimes it feels like a hernia of the soul, protruding, demanding attention and action. And when news reaches her these days, as inevitably it does, of apocalyptic slow-moving hur-ricanes, and tornado swarms that refuse to die for hundreds of miles, or temperatures that scorch for weeks or months without remorse, she can't sleep, feeling at once too powerful and not powerful enough. Her discomfort is intensified by the guilt about Diane. They could not see eye to eye about Bronwyn's skill, and the pressure Diane was exerting was becoming unbearable. She wanted to study Bronwyn to gener-ate data as if Bronwyn was some kind of lab rat. When she and Matt moved to the Northwest she stopped answering Diane's emails. It's childish of her, she knows, this tendency to flee from difficult relation-ships, but it has been a matter of self-preservation. Now it's in her court to break the silence.

As she stows her binoculars a flash of sensation zings up her left pinky finger, from the amputated tip up through a tendon in her hand. Not pain exactly, simply a periodic reminder of what was lost during her last intervention in Siberia. Immediately after the amputation, she was destabilized and found it challenging to walk in a straight line. It made her wonder: if losing this tiny body part could alter so much, how will we all feel when large parts of the Earth disappear, forests and glaciers and fish and birds? Now she's fine and grateful she didn't lose more. The occasional zings and twitches and cold sensitivity are easily borne. Matt often jokes that she's like Lubov, their humorous Tiksi hostess, who had also lost a finger to frostbite. He addresses the smooth truncated pinky tip as if it has a personality and will of its own, along with a special understanding of Bronwyn. "Hey, Lube, any news from the front?" he asks, trying to coax Bronwyn from one of her withdrawals. How can she possibly share with him the content of her premonitions: nature's dire imbalances, the looming storms and opportunistic diseases.

The lanky person in black is back again, a woman she now sees, who stretches her arms overhead as her lean hips sketch figure eights. There's something unnatural about this person. The black clothes maybe. The fact that she's probably trespassing. The odd hip motion. Bronwyn retreats inside. She refuses to let herself become paranoid. And anyway, it's time for her shift at the Dockside Café.

9

If it hadn't been for the tornados, Patty would never have left Kansas, but the season when her husband Rand and her minister Earl were both taken by tornados, that changed everything. Before that she hadn't given much thought to tornados. They were a fact of life in Kansas—like hurricanes in Florida, or earthquakes in California—but before now she'd never known anyone who'd been killed by a tornado.

Before she left for California she visited the Jobsville, Kansas cemetery every day. The visits kept her organized and grounded at a time when she had no idea what to do with herself. Life had lost its ballast. She got by well enough on Rand's social security and the small nest egg he'd left, but there wasn't much to fill her days. The craftwork she used to do—knitting, crocheting, needlepoint—no longer satisfied her. Baking seemed senseless when there was no one in the household to eat what she baked. She saw her closest neighbors Bill and Cora frequently, and she was fond of them, but she hated being a third wheel.

The cemetery was a four-acre plot at the top of a drumlin dotted with oak trees that were often overtaken by crows, enormous black birds aggressive as rats. She spent the most time at Earl's grave, because he was always more of a talker than Rand. He wasn't garrulous in a bad way, he just loved conversation. He had a booming voice that surged up from underground, ignoring the confines of coffin and earth and stone marker. He was always an outside-the-box thinker. Even if he had known she didn't believe in God, he wouldn't have minded. She could never bring herself to tell Earl or Rand about her disbelief when they were alive, especially not Earl. Most people in Jobsville thought of Patty as highly religious. And in some ways she guesses she is. She has always tried to be kind. She likes people, almost everyone really, and she feels the sorrow of others intensely, sometimes too intensely, Rand used to say. She always went to church because she likes church-going people, their hopefulness and the way they value being together. Also because she likes to sing. Oh, how she loves to sing. Hymns. Pop songs. Spirituals. Advertisement ditties. Singing was one of the greatest lures of church.

But *God* has never sat well with her. Who or what is *God* anyway? And where does he—or she—operate? Does *God* have a body? Skin? Any definition at all? Or is *God* like water or air, or like some Disney movie fairy flitting here and there? For Patty's money, all this *God* business is hocus-pocus.

So, she has always tried to avoid saying *God*, unless she's singing. She made that contract with herself long ago—she wouldn't use the word in conversation, but it's all right to say it when she sings. Since she has a carrying voice and their congregation was small, it would have been obvious to everyone if she were to omit *God* in the hymns.

She made a point of spritzing Earl's gravestone with citrus cleaner and wiping it down with a cloth. Earl never minded much about cleanliness, but she felt it was always easier to communicate when there was no dirt in the way. It wasn't the same with Earl gone. Not the same at all. The congregation had no money, had never had much money, and Earl never expected to be paid a cent. He survived on whatever the forty or fifty congregants could pull together. They would never find another minister like him. He wanted to preach because he had such a passion for it, and because he found everything about life to be wondrous. He not only tolerated people in the congregation, he found ways to cherish every last one of them, making their little band of worshippers all feel they had a place in the world. Without him—and of course without Rand—Patty had grown restless.

The last time she visited the cemetery, just before she left for California to live with her sister Barb, she tried to explain to Earl why she was leaving.

"I hate to go, but I get shaky in the knees when I think about another tornado season coming through here. If I stay there's a good chance I'll fall apart."

She waited for Earl to respond and sure enough his voice came through, full and strong. The crows seemed to take note, lowering their screeching.

Patty, you're not going to fall apart. I have faith in you. You were put on this earth to do something big. It's time you realized that. You're a talented woman.

"Oh, Earl. The only talent I have is singing."

Singing is good, but you can do even more than singing.

"What though?"

You never know. You need to stay open to what it might be. You remember that gal who came here a while back and stopped the tornados?

Of course she remembered, it wasn't the kind of thing you could ever forget. The tornado was a terrible troublemaker, and that young woman stood squarely before it and insisted it vacate the neighborhood. Her bravery made a deep impression on Patty.

"Oh, Earl, I can't do that. I'm just a big fat old woman."

Earl was laughing. Definitely laughing. *Patty, you've got to get over that view of yourself. You're not an old woman, you're an old soul, and you still have important work ahead of you. Find that girl and see what she's up to.*

"I can't go see her if I'm not invited. It's impolite."

He was laughing again. *Bold. Not impolite. She'll understand. You, Patty Birch, you don't have an impolite bone in your body.*

"Oh Earl." She laughed along with him, flattered, happy. What would she do without Earl?

The smell of the city has become intolerable. Everywhere he goes, the stink of human body odor, human waste. On the buses, in the streets, in the theater. It's unavoidable. The stench winds its way to your nostrils and sets up camp there, lingering long after you arrive home and crawl into bed. It brings on strange apocalyptic dreams. Even Felipe's fellow actors smell bad. Sometimes on stage in the middle of a performance, he catches a whiff of someone, and he misses a beat, skips a line, blows his timing. And every once in a while he understands he also smells bad, in clothes and costumes worn too many times without being laundered, and in a body that can't be coaxed to sweat less. It makes him feel ashamed of himself, as if he's no better than a barnyard animal wallowing in his own stink. It doesn't matter to him that it's the same for everyone, that it has become a communal joke. He has always taken supreme care of his body, keeping it fit and fragrant and smartly dressed. As every actor and dancer knows—your body is your instrument.

He and Isabella sit in an outdoor café on Rua Libero Badaro with prawns and *caipirinhas*. It is almost ten, dark. The city always looks best these days in the dark.

"The theater is closing in two weeks," he tells her. "We haven't had more than fifty audience members for any show in the last month. It seats five hundred. We can't afford it."

"What will you do?"

"I have no idea. I won't find another sweet gig like this one. I'll have to start auditioning again. And find some other job to tide me over."

"You could start over somewhere else."

"I can't do that. This is my home."

"There are so many beautiful places to live. Paris. New York. Prague is stunning. I wouldn't call Tokyo beautiful, but it certainly is interesting. And Sydney, Australia."

"Are you trying to get rid of me?"

"Don't be crazy. You know as well as I do that this city's future is pretty darn bleak. Go somewhere else for a while. You might like it."

Isabella caught the traveling bug in high school when she went to the US as an exchange student. She stayed with a family in Boston who took her all across the country: New York, Chicago, San Francisco, Los Angeles. After that, she developed the yen to travel everywhere. Now, though she talks about wanting to move somewhere else permanently, she's signed a three-year contract with her law firm and knows it's advisable to stay a few more years to build experience and credibility.

Felipe shakes his head vigorously. "I'm meant to be here."

"How do you know when you haven't been anywhere else?" Her grin is lopsided and playful. She still has the most beautiful dancer's body imaginable, tall and lean and supple, but her face is almost homely, asymmetrical with a lower jaw that protrudes slightly and a cauldron of a mouth. Felipe adores this unlikely face of hers, the way it imperfectly tops her perfect body.

"But you're so fed up. What's stopping you, really? Why not LA? I know a guy who works in film there. He could put you up. You don't have to stay, but at least check it out."

"I'm not going anywhere. This is my home. Anyway, my English isn't so good."

Isabella who, even remade as an attorney, never tires of dancing, gestures to the night sky, the pointed tip of the prawn's tail becoming an extension of her slender arm. "Your English is good enough." She shakes her head. "Grumpy old man already, eh?"

He remembers dancing with her another lifetime ago. They were a good pair, their bodies perfectly matched; their spirits matched too. They slept together for six months or so, and he enjoyed everything about her. Now he can't remember why they broke up. Is he really a grumpy old man? He has already made a new life once—he can't imagine doing it again.

Diane is heading to the Dean's office for the "chat" about her "radical revision of belief." She laughed when she first got his email, but now she's furious, and hopes she can keep her fury in check for the duration of this meeting. She's done some roleplaying with Joe to make sure her approach remains airtight, and though Ted was not a great deal of help, he was right to advise her to not divulge much—nothing really. The Dean, like most scientists and academics, has a strong ideological immune system characteristic of those with high IQs. He's a skeptic and resistant to fundamental paradigm changes. She herself was always that kind of person until Bronwyn changed her. She entertains no expectations about changing the Dean's mind, winning him over to the idea that a woman like Bronwyn, or any person, can influence the Earth. She will admit nothing, turn the questions back on him to make him appear the ridiculous one. Why flaunt her new understanding of the world until she can prove it irrefutably?

Still, despite her preparation, she cannot claim to be relaxed, and as she heads down the long corridor that leads to the Dean's office she's acutely aware of the skew of her spine. She can't seem to straighten it. It's as if she's acquired the apologetic stoop of an exceptionally tall person. Then, catching her reflection in a window, she sees her posture is perfectly straight after all, though in her conservative blue suit and pumps, instead of her usual bohemian attire—worn because Joe suggested and she agreed that such an outfit might help her case—she scarcely recognizes herself.

The Dean sits behind his vast black-lacquered desk, gray hair blown into a pompadour, appearing much more powerful than a mere academic dean. He has had a career as a respected chemist, but now he's mainly a figurehead. Several weeks back from some South Pacific island where he was vacationing at a resort built right over the water, his tan has begun to morph into an unhealthy yellow. He clears his throat and they exchange the usual pleasantries, then he opens his phone and shoves it across his desk so she can admire pictures of the resort where he vacationed, fish passing beneath the glass deck like occult mantelpiece ornaments.

"Well, it's not Siberia," she says, expecting him to smile, but he doesn't acknowledge the remark.

"Diane—" He pauses to clear his throat. "I'm sure you're aware of the rumor that's been circulating about you for a while now. People are saying you believe it's possible for human beings to change the weather."

"You believe that?" She's careful not to smile. There's no need to be obsequious.

"Of course not, but word has it that you do."

"Are you expecting me to combat a rumor? Can you give me something specific to address?"

"Diane—"

"Dr. Fenwick."

"Dr. Fenwick, there must be some reason this rumor has arisen. It can't be spontaneous combustion. I'm trying to get to the bottom of it. Did something happen to you?"

An involuntary smile skitters around the corners of her mouth, but she prevents it from taking over her entire face. Does he expect her to confess to a mental breakdown? A religious conversion?

"You've always been a highly respected member of our faculty. I can't believe you really think the laws of nature can be suspended."

"Did I say that?"

"Well, that's what—"

"What other people are saying? Surely you can do better than that. Anecdotes don't make for good science, as I'm sure you know."

"There's no need to condescend to me, Dr. Fenwick. If there's any truth to the claims being made, I simply want to remind you of Feynman's statement: 'The first principle is you must not fool yourself—and you are the easiest person to fool.'"

"I'm well aware of that quote."

"Look, Dr. Fenwick, I have the reputation of an esteemed institution to protect. And if I were you I might think a little more about grooming my own reputation."

"I'll take that under advisement, sir. And you might want to inform yourself of PEARS, a program at Princeton a few years back." As soon as she mentions this she regrets it—it couldn't be more perfect fodder for him. The PEARS Institute, begun by a respected engineering faculty member, was researching psychokinesis and how human beings may affect machines. The results over a number of years were inconclusive, and eventually they closed the institute, though they never fired its director. Still, this failed experiment hardly works in her favor. What a fool she was to mention it.

She leaves his office fuming under her cordial smile. She is, no doubt, on some kind of notice, surveillance even. Taking a circuitous route home, she winds through side streets ankle-deep in slush. She arrives home hoping Joe will be out. She hates to admit it, but the Dean has succeeded in making her feel foolish, and she isn't ready to discuss it, even with Joe.

She enters the house quietly and hurries upstairs to her study, listening for Joe in his downstairs study. She doesn't hear a thing, but often, when writing, he maintains such silence the house appears empty.

She sheds her coat and sits at her desk. There are decisions to make but, angry as she is, she can scarcely lay them out rationally. If she resigns now how can she continue her research? The platform from which she applies for grants would be gone. Her funding has already been drying up; her stellar grant-getting record suddenly not so stellar. Furthermore, she hates to do anything rash that could be construed as succumbing to pressure.

Her thoughts turn to Bronwyn. She was angry when Bronwyn disappeared without warning, but as the months passed, now more than a full year, the anger has dissipated and she feels only hurt. The two of them share so much history—too much to have had it cauterized so abruptly. What Diane wishes she could convey to Bronwyn is that they are a *team*, and they should be addressing Bronwyn's power *together*, starting their own institute perhaps, collaborating for the sake of the world. They're a team because life threw them together years ago, back when Bronwyn was in college and she appeared in one of Diane's atmospheric science classes. Since then Diane has taught her in grad school, been her research mentor, her surrogate mother, her friend. And, when Bronwyn discovered her exceptional ability, she revealed it to Diane, she *wanted* Diane's approval and blessing. So Diane isn't foisting this notion of collaboration on Bronwyn, Bronwyn sought it herself.

Diane stares at her own reflection in the dark screen of her computer. Recently she's let herself go. Her hair hasn't been cut for almost three months, and its tufts orbit her face like a child's drawing of the sun. A scroll of flesh spills over her skirt's waistband. She turns away and flings off her suit jacket. Life is too complicated to pay attention to everything at once. A little denial is the only thing that makes it possible to keep the entire enterprise moving forward.

She rises to lower the heat in her study. They've been trying to keep the inside temperature at a consistent sixty-five degrees this winter, wear sweaters when necessary, but consistency is hard to find in a winter like this where days of single-digit or subzero cold are followed by spates of spring-like temperatures.

The midafternoon light flickers like a faulty lightbulb. She sits at the computer again, weary in a way she's never felt before, filled with a melancholy that reverberates through her bones. She's always loved being a pioneer, a person who travels against the tide, rallying alone for truth until others have come on board as collaborators. She's always liked a battle, even the ones she's had to wage solo. But now there are too many wars to wage, too many elements of the climate to change, too many people to convince of one thing or another.

12

Patty is sure California is the perfect place for some people, but she's a homebody at heart, a Kansas homebody, and she might be too old at almost sixty-one, to love another place. She misses the wide-open spaces of Kansas, the way the light poured over the fields and hills, the changing colors of the sky. Most of all she misses talking to Earl. His voice is weakened by Southern California's exhaust and asphalt. It comes through occasionally, but often only a word or two, like a staticky radio making no sense. She still feels his presence, but she misses the way it used to be, his voice booming as if he was still alive, bringing no-nonsense advice, accompanied by jovial humor.

It's time for her to move out of her sister Barb's place. Four months, going on five, is too long for her to have stayed. Barb encouraged her to come in the first place, but Patty has outstayed her welcome. Barb hasn't said anything, but the message is clear from the looks Barb gives her, the sighs. Once Barb walked in on her when she was trying to talk to Earl. Patty has made sure not to let that happen again. She doesn't want to have to defend her sanity to her own sister.

Barb is a doer. On weekends when she's not at the bank where she's a manager, she works on home improvement projects—currently the bedroom wallpaper—and makes regular visits to her fitness club. In the last five years she has gone from a size fourteen to a size eight. She looks at Patty, her younger sister, as if she's a lost soul, a hopeless case. Patty can feel those thoughts coming at her like dozens of little needles: *overweight, aimless, unwilling to change.* Patty can see why Barb could think these things, but Barb is wrong. Patty is just taking some time. A year and a half might seem like a long time to regroup after the death of your husband and your minister, but Patty doesn't think it's right for Barb, who still has a husband, to weigh in on this.

The house is a small ranch house in West Covina, a place Barb and her husband moved to after their kids left home. Patty is sleeping in the spare room, which is small but fine. She's only inside during the hot part of the day. The rest of the time she spends in the fenced succulent garden out back. Around the square of fake grass, cactuses grow like tiny trees, gnarled and spikey, not what Patty would call pretty, but interesting. Some look more like fairytale animals than plants. She admires them because they've made do with limited resources, exactly what Patty herself is trying to do now.

Patty's favorite times out there are early morning just after Barb and Everett have gone to work, and then in the mid to late afternoon when the day's heat has passed. The winter light can be lovely, thick like sweet pink syrup, and the cactuses occasionally send out star-shaped red or orange blooms, as if they're raising their hands and have things to say. When things align just right out there she feels heavenly. She sings whatever comes to mind. Lively show tunes, or melancholy love songs, or even hymns. Last night she was singing hymns and thinking of Earl, knowing he was present despite his silence, when a neighbor pounded on the fence.

"Excuse me," said the irascible voice of a man she couldn't see. "Are you going to stop your braying soon? You've been at it for over an hour."

Patty was so stunned, so hurt by the word braying, it took her a moment to speak.

"I'm sorry. I'll stop."

Braying? Like a donkey? No one had ever made such a comparison. People everywhere have always raved about her rich soprano. In church she was called "Patty Solo."

She skulked inside, went to the spare room, and lay on the bed. Had her voice changed, or was the man just being rude? She heard Barb and Everett coming home, bustling back and forth from bedroom to kitchen, chatting. A knock on her door. "Patty, are you in there?"

The door opened and Barb stood on the threshold. Patty held her breath.

"Dinner's almost ready." Barb paused. "I have to tell you something." She hovered awkwardly, glanced down the hallway. "Our neighbors aren't happy about you singing. I know you have a beautiful voice, but they feel it imposes on them. They called it noise pollution—their words, not mine. I've always loved your singing, you know that. They only used that term in case they have to take legal action."

"I understand," Patty said.

"You do?"

Patty nodded. "I'm going to look for my own place."

13

Analu chooses to walk, too ashamed to take the bus. It is midday and the sun is directly overhead, and it is hotter than yesterday, which was already very hot, and hotter than the day before that. This Sydney heat confounds him. There is no escaping it by slipping into the water whenever he wants as he would do at home. And the smoke from the fires has made it even more brutal; he worries about the smoke weakening Vailea's lungs. Everything would be easier if there were midday napping, so common on the island, but here there is no slowing down at all, everyone pounds on, paying no attention. Surely inattention will make them sick.

Analu believes in paying attention. Shouldn't everyone? But today paying attention got him in trouble. He was raking up blossoms from the jacaranda tree when Mrs. Martin came out of her unit onto her small patio area. She is one of the more active residents of the Sweethome Retirement Community, wiry and strong for a woman in her eighties. Analu often sees her outside in her wide-brimmed hat, fussing over her plants while he mows or prunes nearby. She always waves to him, and she has asked his name and given him hers, so now she calls out to him, *Good morning, Analu,* sometimes embarrassing him with the beam of her enthusiasm.

Today she wanted help with moving a potted ficus plant inside. Its leaves were getting scorched by the direct afternoon sunlight, she said, it needed a rest. He stood on the other side of her gate as she told him this. He wasn't supposed to enter the residents' units unless his manager told him to. His job was on the grounds. He wasn't even supposed to talk to the residents. In the ten months he'd been working there, two groundskeepers had been fired for stealing. One of them Analu is quite sure *did* steal some things, jewelry and cash; the other one Analu isn't sure about. That guy, Hien, was from Vietnam and his English wasn't good, but he was a gentle soul who didn't possess a thieving spirit.

Mrs. Martin pleaded with him. "It will just take a moment," she said. The plant was much too heavy for her to move by herself, he could see that, so he passed through the gate and hefted the heavy pot inside. Mrs. Martin tried to give him some money, but he said no. Only when he got outside again, and found himself face to face with his manager, Mr. Riley, did he notice there were bills hanging from his pocket. He understood it looked suspicious. Nothing he could say sounded right. He was fired on the spot. His ten months of reliable service meant nothing.

As he was leaving he glanced back toward Mrs. Martin, but she'd gone inside. She waved gaily through the sliding glass door. She would have defended him if he'd explained the situation, he thinks, but she had no idea what was happening.

He thinks of his mother and dreads breaking the news. He has always been a good boy who fixed things and made others happy. When he was only eight years old he rescued his older sister Mahina from drowning. She was knocked off a rock by a strong wave, and her leg was broken so she couldn't swim, and she began to sink. He swam out to her, dragged her to shore, keeping her head above water. After that he could do no wrong. Sometimes he wonders if he was encouraged to believe in himself too much. He should never have insisted on bringing his mother to Australia when she didn't want to come. He thought she would like it here—the modern conveniences, the good doctors, the plentiful food—but nothing here has made her happy. She rarely goes out, instead sits on the patio, sad and still, but uncomplaining, even about the smoke. Now she's lost teeth, and he has lost his job.

Halfway home he steps into a corner store and buys himself a beer with the money Mrs. Martin slipped into his pocket. It's strange that Riley fired him but didn't try to take the money away. He drinks the beer fast, and in the unforgiving January sun it goes to his head quickly. He'll find another job, but will he find another job outdoors? The idea of working inside all day, behind closed doors, staring out glass windows at weather he can't feel on his skin—well, he's never done that, and he's quite sure it would make him crazy. He resumes walking, thinking of Mrs. Martin. They liked each other. He should have handled the situation differently, stood up for himself and asserted his innocence. He's fairly sure she would have supported him.

Feeling sorry for himself, he buys another beer and drinks it on a bus stop bench two blocks from the apartment. It is early afternoon, one of those long hot days designed to make you question everything. He can picture his mother dozing on the patio. He does not share his mother's talent for dozing, even after two beers. He will go home and tell his mother what has happened. She will not rebuke him, but he will feel rebuked.

He steps inside the front door and calls out quietly. Vailea does not respond to the greeting. She's probably asleep. The apartment is dark and quiet, but for the neighbors' young children shouting and laughing in adjacent yards. Analu collapses on the couch in the room that doubles as kitchen and living room. It isn't cool, but it's cooler than outside. A wave of sleepiness clambers over him and begins to nestle in. He makes himself stand and peers through the kitchen window out to the patio.

Vailea is not in her chair. He hurries out. She lies on her side on the flagstones, her eyes closed. He kneels, lowers his ear to listen for her breath, her heartbeat. The snake lies a few feet away in a circle of sunlight, sleeping.

Something moves, but is it her pulse or his own? She opens her eyes. "What happened?" he asks.

She shakes her head. "I don't know."

"Did you faint? Did you hit your head? Are you all right?"

The snake stirs, lifts its head. Did the snake scare her? He always thought the snake was looking after her, keeping dangers at bay, but he knows his mother isn't fond of the snake; it isn't an animal she recognizes.

He helps her inside, to the bedroom she shares with Penina.

"Beer," she says, sniffing as he settles her in.

He does not say yes or no. He does not tell her he lost his job. He wants to say, *Tomorrow I will take you home,* but how can he make such a promise now, with no savings, no job. Instead he says, "Tomorrow I will take you to the doctor."

She shakes her head firmly, no, then falls asleep.

He goes out to the patio and sits in her chair. He should probably take her to the doctor right now, but he isn't sure where to go and, woozy with beer, doesn't have the will. Tomorrow will be soon enough. The snake is still lying there, coiled tightly again, asleep or pretending to be. Maybe his mother is right, maybe the snake does not belong here loitering in their midst like a spy. He's crowding them, bringing bad luck.

Analu feels a flash of hatred for this animal intruding on his family, acting as if it lives here. He goes to the kitchen and finds the biggest knife, tiptoes back out.

With all his stealth he inches toward the snake who lifts its head and whispers something. Analu doesn't pause to listen, doesn't want to hear. He severs the snake's muttering head with a quick chop, and watches the animal rear up, electric, skating over the flagstones, headless and shocked, oozing wrath and indignation. *Take that,* Analu thinks, as the snake's petulant spirit grows listless then fades into the heat like a fume. *Things change.*

14

This morning's call from Elena, Felipe's agent, is most welcome and very surprising. She wants Felipe to come into her office, today, now. In the weeks since the theater closed she has been a huge disappointment to him. She expresses enthusiasm about Felipe's prospects and claims to be making phone calls on his behalf, but he questions the zeal she puts into those calls. He imagines she thinks he's past his prime, but he's only thirty-eight for God's sake, he still feels like a young man. He looks at least ten years younger than his age—everyone says so—and he's maintained his dancer's long lean muscles so he's fitter than most people twenty years younger.

He's not about to share with her the strange feelings he's been having of late. He's been awakening too early, wondering if he might be getting sick. His symptoms are vague and roving. Thrumming behind his eyes—not an ache but a pulse. Resistance in his knees. Trouble directing energy to the parts of his body where energy needs to be. Most disturbingly, he's been holding his breath. The incoming air seems to get hijacked on its way to his diaphragm, then it stops altogether. He can't be holding his breath—he knows better than that! Years ago he mastered the skill of deep breathing, allowing oxygen to suffuse his entire thoracic cavity, not only his upper chest. It's an essential skill for dancing, for acting, for anyone hoping to stay vibrantly alive.

Felipe pulls himself together and springs for a cab to take him downtown. Elena's fortunes have risen dramatically since Felipe first signed with her a decade ago when he was making the transition from dancing to acting. Back then she was working out of her modest apartment. But now she works on the twenty-second floor of a swanky glass office building.

Her young assistant brings coffee and tells him Elena will be delayed. She just now had to take an important call. No problem, he says.

The waiting room is tastefully sconce-lit and equipped with soft white leather armchairs fit for sleeping. Every wall is lined with head shots of Elena's clients. It's an elite group, and Felipe counts himself as fortunate to be among them. In fact he feels fortunate to have discovered acting in the first place. It was a fluke. An old friend from school was directing *Hamlet,* and the actor playing Horatio was seriously injured in a car accident. Could Felipe step in?

Felipe was hesitant at first—he had no acting experience and he'd never had to learn lines. But the director wasn't worried. "There aren't many lines. You'll do fine." So Felipe agreed. He still remembers the pleasure of those early rehearsals, watching the other actors leaving their own skins behind, transmuting themselves into people who weren't the least bit like their day-to-day selves. He tried to imitate them. He asked the lead actor for tips. Soon, he felt himself taking those same leaps, folding his concentration in on itself, leaving Felipe Delgado behind. Each night he became a burning ball of Horatio. Felipe concerns, Felipe heart, Felipe body—they ceased to exist. How good it felt. It wasn't work at all. It was cleansing. Humbling. As a dancer you were only yourself, always in the same set of muscles, always the same body type. Dance was all about adulation of body and self. But acting was about transformation.

Half an hour passes before Elena comes to get him, her brassy voice preceding her down the hallway. "Felipe!" She greets him like a long lost friend but he's not fooled. Her office has a magnificent view out over São Paulo's downtown, everything within view shiny, glassy, reflective. From up here it all appears clean and promising, not like a city blighted by drought.

Elena sits behind her shiny black desk and irons it with both palms. She regards Felipe assessingly, almost severely, for long enough to make him uncomfortable, before she begins to speak.

"I called you in here because I don't want you to take this wrongly. You mustn't be offended."

"You're dropping me?"

"No. Of course not. Don't be paranoid. This role. It's not *you*, you understand? There's no typecasting."

"Typecast all you want. I need a part."

"There's nothing you find unsavory?"

"What is it? Just say."

"They need some men at the Scorpion Club."

"The strip club?"

"Yes. First there's a little skit in drag, and then you strip. The contract is for six months. It's good money. It would be you and three others."

In the silence Elena's palms iron the desk again.

"Why me? I'm no drag queen."

"It's acting. You're an actor. And you have the dance experience which would be useful here."

"I'm not even gay."

"No one said you were gay, Felipe. You don't need to be gay. It's *acting*."

He opens his airways and visualizes his breath traveling up through his nasal passages, then down his trachea, into his lungs, his chest expanding, his belly bulging, his whole body weightless as a balloon.

The other three men on the job are all exhibitionistically gay, with fey gestures and high-pitched lisping voices. Felipe has no issue with gay men—he could not have been both a dancer and an actor if he were a homophobe—but he would prefer not to be seen as gay himself. Why? Because he is *not* gay. He's attracted to women, not men. But he's well aware that there is something about him that leads people to assume he might be gay, and men come onto him all the time. Is it his full lips perhaps? Is it the way he cants his head quizzically to one side? Is it the readiness of his smile, or the care he takes with his body, or his smart dressing style? Or is it possibly his unguarded enthusiasm for almost everything and everyone? He has stopped trying to guess what leads people on. Let them think what they think. No one knows or needs to know of his love of soft things. That he keeps exclusively to himself. None of his girlfriends have known. If he were to tell people, they would see it as pathological, and making it public would certainly taint the pleasure.

Each night, waiting in the wings for the show to begin, wigged and rouged and lipsticked, costumed in tutu and tights and tiara, Felipe peers around the black curtain at the suited businessmen sitting at round tables close to the stage. They are drinking, laughing, already raucous. When the lights dim a rueful hunger appears in their eyes, an implacable need to locate other human beings—even one human being—afflicted with a loneliness as deep as theirs.

15

Diane is supposed to be holding office hours, but she posted a sign on her door saying CANCELED and came home and filled the tub with lavender bubble bath and scalding water in which she now lies submerged. Marooned.

Diane, a fighter, has always adhered to the New England belief that depression is no more than a failure of will. She has never been depressed herself. There have inevitably been episodes of the blues, short-lived and situational, when she found her own solutions in hot baths and more baking than usual, but she's never had any long-term mental malaise that could have been diagnosed as chronic or idiopathic.

Now, however, she's lost enthusiasm for the things she's always found enjoyable. She's teaching so numbly her students scuttle out after class rather than hovering around the podium with questions. In the hallways and on the campus pathways she is ignored by other faculty which, for a social woman like her, is tantamount to being shunned. No one comes to office hours anymore, so she sits at her desk staring at numbers that no longer sizzle with pattern and meaning.

A thought keeps haunting her: There may be no more need for climate science research. Ice melt and sea level rise and carbon dioxide levels need to be monitored, and better predictive models need to be developed, but the brutal *fact* of a warming Earth has been more than adequately analyzed and catalogued. It has been announced to the public over and over again, with varying degrees of desperation, but the fundamental message of alarm is out there. There are nuances, of course. Which ice cap will melt first? Exactly how high will the oceans rise? How and where will the human species find itself most ravaged?

Where will the water scarcity refugees go? Which populations will die off first? It is bleak prognostication and, while based in science, in the end it is only speculation. There is no way of knowing these things for sure. There are too many factors involved and human beings are not entirely in charge.

She's kept this thought at arm's length for some time, wanting to be proactive and retain her optimism. But the warnings of science are falling on deaf ears. Politicians across the globe are paying only lip service to climate change. Business people are cleaving to old ways. Activists are deluding themselves—it is a matter of too little, too late.

In light of this, Bronwyn's disappearance, her adamant refusal to do anything with her skill has been particularly aggravating. There is so much she might do at this juncture that could, at the very least, buy the planet a little more human-habitable time. Bronwyn has been Diane's last hope because she can perform direct action as no one else can. She could probably learn, eventually, to scour carbon dioxide from the atmosphere and to deacidify the oceans. She could be an agent to restore balance. But, she's gone, and Diane has reluctantly begun to accept that she isn't coming back, a thought that arouses a cavernous internal ache. How she misses the days when she and Bronwyn were a dyad, brainstorming together about clouds and vapor and ice crystals and aerosols, the days before Bronwyn became a phenomenon.

Diane inspects her wrinkled red knees. They emerge from the bubbles like twin volcanoes. Lifting her feet, she rests her ankles on either side of the tub. It isn't often that she has the occasion to examine her legs, concealed as they usually are beneath pants and skirts. No one would call them attractive legs. They're pale—or would be but for the scalding water—and lumpy and, because she never shaves in winter, they're sprinkled with a fuzz of stridently black hair. The skin of her thighs has lost coherence and hangs from muscle and bone as if some interior latching has come undone.

She should be disgusted, but she isn't—she's perversely fascinated. Here is her body, a living thing, taking its natural course, largely immune to intervention. She could lose weight or exercise more, but it's doubtful her legs would look much different. For a moment the legs seem not to belong to her, rising as they do from the bubbles, not visibly connected to anything else. She wiggles her big toes to clarify that the legs are indeed hers. She's reminded of a radio report she heard recently about a rare condition in which the people it afflicts feel so strongly that one of their own body parts does not belong to them that they seek amputation. *Body integrity identity disorder.* Not unlike a trans person wanting to excise breasts or a penis. Diane wonders how many people this disorder afflicts, if she could ever come to be one of them.

The phone is ringing and she lets it ring, savoring the defiance, imagining it's the Dean calling to tell her she's fired.

When the phone stops ringing she lugs herself from the tub, accompanied by a satisfying operatic tohubohu of groaning and sighing. She robes her sweating flesh without drying off, and, still soggy, sits at her computer and composes an email to the Dean, cc'ing her department chair and the Provost. She will take a leave of absence of indeterminate length, she tells them, effective immediately.

16

The Wichita airport makes Patty nervous. This is only the second airline flight of her life. So many planes taking off at once—what keeps them from running into each other? She's not a traveler by nature, but looking around she sees she's the exception. For most of her life she was content to stay in Kansas. It amazes her to hear stories about the young people who go all over the world, as if it's nothing at all, as if the globe is only as big as a schoolyard. Bill and Cora's daughter, Eve, was in Mongolia not long ago. Why would anyone choose to go to Mongolia? Next she plans to go to Antarctica to run a marathon! Why don't people enjoy staying at home? Patty wonders. But not everyone lives in a beautiful place like Kansas—in that regard she's been lucky. She would stay in Kansas forever if it weren't for the tornados.

She's been back here for a month, getting her house ready to put on the market in preparation for finding her own place in LA. Figuring out what to get rid of was more challenging than she thought. She went from room to room, humming along with the radio's Country and Western station, putting things in the throw-out pile, then reclaiming them. Even Rand's clothes still spoke to her—his shirts faintly imbued with Mennen's musk scent and his body odor, his DNA really, fixed right there in the fibers, how could she toss out those last vestiges of him?

Every room was like this, packed with memories from their thirty-three years there. All the people who came for dinner, all the craft nights with her women friends, all the things she baked. Rand's cigars, his tools, his gun magazines. What an idiosyncratic man he was, the way he would have certain days of not talking much, claiming his mind was blank, that he had no thoughts at all. He had these spells even before she married him, so she was prewarned. "Everything is fine," he'd say when she asked him. "I just don't have anything to say." So she learned to accept that sometimes she had to be the solo juggler of the conversational ball.

The biggest challenge was her craft closet with yards of beautiful fabric she'd never gotten around to using. There were embroidery threads and beads and some tiles from her brief period of tiling. And her sewing machine—she couldn't get rid of that. She still expects to sew.

What astonished her was how two people could accumulate so many things, when they'd never been the types to go to Costco every week and load up on cases of pineapple juice, and ten-pound tubs of cashews, and frozen steaks for an army, as if nuclear Armageddon was right around the corner.

Bob and Cora drove her here, which was very generous of them, but now she's alone at the gate, trying hard not to think of that young pilot in Europe who intentionally crashed his plane into a mountainside a few years back. Everyone killed, the pilot included. It turned out he was mentally defective. Patty wonders, if she'd seen him beforehand would she have been able to tell he was off balance? You have to look closely, examine the face and the eyes. She's pretty sure she would have been able to tell. She has a sixth sense about people. She plans to give the pilot of this plane to California a very close look. Especially his eyes, the most candid of body parts.

In the row of seats facing her is a skinny girl with purple hair streaks and a ring in her nose. She holds a cased guitar between her knees and listens to something through lime green earbuds, head lightly marking a rhythm as she stares at the paisley carpet. How young she looks to be traveling on her own, though they all do these days, Patty is well aware of that. She is fascinated by this girl's boney frame, so different from the pillowy body she herself has always occupied. How different human beings can be. In the past she might have been scared by this girl's presentation—the nose ring, the purple hair, the snake tattoos running down both arms, the arms themselves bare despite it being winter—but studying her now Patty is overcome by a feeling of connection. The girl, she thinks, is not as bold as she looks—in fact Patty can see, even without looking into the girl's eyes that she's scared, maybe in pain. Patty suspects that if she had had a daughter maybe her daughter would look something like this. A wounded rebel. What an odd thought, but true. Bittersweet. She'd like to talk to the girl, but doesn't want to interrupt her. Surely a young girl like this wouldn't want to talk to Patty.

Two stewardesses glide by in demure tailored blue suits and hats like sailors, pulling their small rolling bags. Everything about them speaks of efficiency, not an extraneous movement, not a wasted second or penny. Not far behind are the two pilots, trousered legs scissoring. Patty wishes they would slow down so she could see more easily who they are and which one is in charge. She wonders if they feel like royalty, loathe to mingle with their subjects.

"Excuse me," she says loudly as they pass. "Captain?"

One of them hears her and turns his head, and now both of them walk more slowly, staring at Patty with questions in their eyes.

"Yes?" says the taller of the two.

His eyes, oh my heaven, his eyes. They're made of chamois, gentle serious eyes, the eyes of a man who concentrates intently and does his job well. Patty has stood without realizing it, and she sees the men are suspicious.

"I just—nothing. Nothing at all. But thank you for what you do."

"Yes, ma'am. Thank you."

She takes her seat again and they continue on, picking up speed, looking at each other and laughing a little. Patty doesn't mind, now that she knows what she knows.

"We're in good hands," she assures the people near her who look back blank-faced.

Much as leaving Kansas has made her sad, and settling for good in California still scares her, she can see it's high time for a change. It's funny how life teaches people to be afraid of change. She's no stranger to that fear. But long ago something happened that has helped her, over the years, to not fear change quite so much.

She was eight years old, and at the start of her third-grade year her hair began to fall out. It thinned slowly at first, but after a couple of months she had no hair at all, and by Christmas she was entirely bald. Her mother took her to the doctor, and she was given some medicines and a cream to apply to her scalp at night, but nothing worked, the hair would not grow back. She felt fine physically, there were no other symptoms, but the lack of hair did not do her mental health any good. Strangers assumed she had cancer, and her classmates were merciless, teasing her even after she got a Shirley Temple wig, especially then. She stopped wearing the wig. *Baldie, Goon, Tater-tot, Penis-head,* her classmates taunted, despite the teachers' warnings.

Her mother and father were kind, as were her older sister and her two older brothers, but she couldn't stay in their midst forever. The pretty dresses her mother bought her to compensate, the fancy patent leather shoes, the Barbie dolls, nothing helped. When she wasn't in school she went to her room with coloring books and Barbies whose heads she'd shaved so they'd look like her. At some point her mother began to teach her to bake. That she enjoyed, and still enjoys. Her mother truly was considerate. But what really changed things was when her father came home one day with a radio. A radio for her alone, to take to her room and play whenever she wanted. She played it all the time. She found the two or three stations she liked, and she switched between them. She discovered Country and Western singers like Patsy Cline and Emmylou Harris, and folk singers like Joan Baez and Judy Collins. She began to sing along with them, learning the words to certain songs. Her voice was good and the more she sang the better it got.

In the spring her mother signed her up for lessons, and she began to take singing seriously, practicing at home in her room for hours at a time. At the end of her third-grade year she got up at the final assembly and sang a solo, "Amazing Grace," hairless and proud. No one had a voice like she did. Everyone was astonished. They adored her singing. She understood she was one-of-a-kind. And that summer, her hair grew back, a darker shade of blonde, thick and wavy.

Would she have found singing if her hair hadn't fallen out? Maybe, maybe not. But she always says this to herself: *You might have to lose something you like if you want to find something better.* She thinks about this a lot these days, wondering why it is human beings hold on, putting on blinders, getting so terribly attached to how things are when change is the only rule.

She sits near the back of the plane, in a middle seat next to the same girl she was watching in the airport. What a coincidence. The girl hunkers against the airliner wall, staring out the window. It's quite obvious she doesn't want to chat. Patty settles in, glad she checked her bag, but wishing she herself weren't so large. Her dress and coat are overflowing onto the man in the aisle seat. She tries to tuck herself in, nodding apologies to the man, but he ignores her, already sunk into his laptop. Patty feels as if she's at a dinner table with strangers, everyone eating, no one bothering to say hello.

When the plane begins to move, Patty closes her eyes and grips the armrest. Once she's sure they're in the air she opens her eyes again. The girl has taken off her earbuds and is digging in her backpack.

"I think we're in good hands," Patty says. "Our pilot has very trustworthy eyes."

"Oh," says the girl, rising from her pack with a book. Her smile might as well be a grimace.

"I'm kind of a nervous flyer," Patty explains. "I don't travel much. Are you from Kansas?"

The girl nods.

"Me too. I think we're lucky. I live in LA now and it isn't nearly as nice. I've been living with my sister, but I'm going to look for a place of my own. What takes you to LA?"

"College."

"Oh, good for you. I never went that route. Maybe if I was coming up now."

The girl nods, fingers her book. "It's not really all it's cracked up to be. Best of times and all, like my parents say. Believe me, it isn't."

"Oh yes, I'm sure it's a great deal of work. What did you do with your guitar?"

"Overhead," the girl says. "It barely fits, but it freaks me out to check it."

"Things must rattle around terribly down there." Patty shakes her head. "I love to sing too."

"I don't sing."

"You don't sing along with your guitar?"

"I play classical."

"How nice. Classical guitar. You don't hear that every day."

Patty pauses and watches the girl's gaze flit to the window, her book, the aisle.

"I won't bother you anymore. I can tell you want to read."

"School stuff, you know."

"You looked lonely to me. I thought you might want to talk."

The girl frowns. "I'm fine." She opens her book. "Well—" She begins to read.

Patty understands she has said too much. Beyond the girl's bent head the tiny window features a square of cloudless blue. The pilot is telling them it should be a smooth flight to California. What a relief. If only more of human life involved smooth sailing. She wonders if the pilot with the chamois eyes thinks the same thing. Surely he's had his share of turbulent flying days on top of whatever other life sorrows he's known.

Patty reclines her seat and her elbow inadvertently bumps the girl's arm. "I'm so sorry," Patty says.

The girl recoils as if electrocuted, but says nothing and keeps reading. Her shock lingers for a moment in Patty's own arm. What has injured this girl so deeply already? A boy? Her mother? Maybe the girl will become more resilient as she gets older. Patty wonders if she herself has become more resilient over the years. In October she'll be sixty-one. Often it doesn't seem as if she feels things any less intensely than when she was sixteen. She remembers sobbing once over a boy she had a crush on who had no interest in her. It makes her laugh to remember. Maybe she recovers from setbacks a little more quickly now. Well, of course she does. After all, here she is making a new life for herself not long after her favorite people in the world died. She hopes this girl's tote bag of sorrows will be, like hers, only the ordinary load.

17

What Analu likes best about coming to the harbor is how Penina becomes a child again. Her shiny black hair—Nalani's hair—sails on the wind. She skips and laughs and doesn't care if her clothes become soiled. She teases Analu about walking slowly. On days like this it doesn't seem so long ago that he taught her to swim. Standing in the water, waist-deep, he would launch her from his belly with both hands, and she swam out a ways then paddled back to him, led by her grin, her long hair aswirl like the loose arms of an octopus.

It's a busy day at the harbor, motorboats hurtling past, the sails of yachts taut in the wind's grip, the water a roughened denim blue. The clouds travel quickly, passing the sun and making sudden blinking shadows that disappear as quickly as they arrive. The day is noisy as the island's feasting days, and they have to shout to make themselves heard.

Just this week Analu started as a dishwasher at an Indonesian restaurant called Pasar Malam. It doesn't pay well, but he couldn't stay out of work a day longer. There are so many questions ahead of him, decisions to be made. They line up in his brain like a firing squad—*pop, pop, boom.* How quickly will Vailea begin to weaken so much that he will have to stay with her all day long? The doctor says she'll live out the year, but probably not much longer. Her one wish, her only desire now, is to get back to the island to die where she was born, the land of sun and water where she bore her children, who bore her grandchildren, who are now giving birth to great-grandchildren. Can he ever obtain enough money in time to take her back to the island before she dies? It took him years to save the money to come here in the first place. Will he bring the whole family, or leave Nalani and Penina here? Bringing all four of them would be a huge expense. And if they get there how will they ever return? Sometimes he thinks they shouldn't come back to this place where, despite its modern conveniences, everyone seems headed for premature death.

Penina stands at a concrete wall intended to keep people away from the water and gazes out longingly. "Where can we go in?" she asks Analu.

"Not here. The water is dirty. And there are too many boats."

"It doesn't look dirty to me."

She is still young enough to believe everything of consequence can be seen. "How would you like one of those motorboats to run over you?"

"Can we get our own boat then?"

He smiles. He's always saying no to her these days. He hates saying no. She has no idea how much it would cost to own a boat. He doesn't really know either, but he knows it's a lot, much more than they can afford. It's hard enough meeting daily expenses. "Maybe someday."

"When Momu gets better? She'd love to go on a boat."

Analu laughs. "She hates boats."

"No, she doesn't."

Penina is braiding her hair to keep it out of her face. Eyes closed, she faces the wind, embracing the brusque way it handles her. A butterfly appears out of nowhere, flutters past, and lands on the back of Analu's hand.

"Penina," he says.

She opens her eyes and they watch the dainty indigo creature trying to maintain its balance.

"Little butterfly, you shouldn't be out in the wind." She smiles at Analu. "I guess you still have *mana*."

He's amazed she remembers what *mana* is. A certain power. His friends used to like to tell him he had *mana* when he was a kid. He laughed it off, but it's true. Animals have always been drawn to him. He would dive underwater and fish circled him. Even when he was on a boat they sensed his presence and surfaced. This made him a very good fisherman, the best on the island. Birds were drawn to him too, often perching on his canoe's bow or gunnel. When he relaxed in the sand they would land close by, regarding him with their curious eyes, quieting their nervous necks. Sometimes he woke at night to find geck-os on his chest or arm. It had to do with his talent for being still, his talent for listening. Now he launches the butterfly and it disappears into the wind.

"Penina, sweet, Momu is very sick. The doctor doesn't think she'll get better."

"But you do?"

"I don't know. No one knows."

"She could die?"

"Yes, she could die."

An elderly man and woman, both tall and white, pass by as he says this, and they shoot Analu hateful looks. He smiles and looks away.

"But she might not?" Penina persists.

"Well, she will definitely die—someday."

Penina begins to walk quickly toward the point, barefooted, san-dals dangling from her fingers. He doesn't have the heart to tell her to put the sandals back on. He follows her, allowing some space between them. Nalani and Vailea are still on the bench where they stopped to rest. He waves but they don't appear to see. They are so small at this distance they might be anyone, but still he recognizes their shapes as belonging to him.

Penina turns so quickly her braid slaps her cheek. "What does Momu think?"

"She wants to go back to the island."

"Will we?"

"I don't know. What do you think?"

"You said the island is sinking."

"It is, yes."

"Then why would we go back there?"

"Because it's our home where your aunts and cousins live."

"It *was* our home. Now this is our home."

"Momu isn't happy here."

They walk side by side now. Amorous couples are everywhere, en-twined, kissing, but Penina doesn't seem to notice.

"Will the island sink completely? So it won't even be there anymore?"

"We don't know how long it will take, but yes."

"Why can't they build a dyke or something? Like they have in the Netherlands."

He shrugs. "Surround the island with a wall? That would be ugly." He has imagined this plenty of times himself, but how could an island be walled securely enough to keep out the ocean and still retain its glorious island nature?

"Well, they could do *something*. Dinh says they're building cars that don't need drivers."

"Don't believe everything you hear."

"But I'm sure there's something. You could ask for help from the Fire Lady. If she could stop those huge forest fires, she can probably stop an island from sinking."

"Fire Lady?" Analu laughs. What an imaginative child he has spawned. This is what he gets for having transported her to a larger world.

18

Unmistakably scientists, they're bustling around the small Kangerlussuaq airport baggage claim area as if everyone else is in their way,
hefting their Pelican cases from the conveyor belt—obviously full of
equipment, not clothing—and assembling them in a staging area at
the corner of the room. They're all dressed in bright high-tech outdoor
gear, sunglasses parked sportily on top of their beanies, and their behavior is flock-like, one member dashing off for a moment then returning to the group of ten or twelve and bending in with great intensity
to share his information. Even the set of their faces—sudden bursts of
ersatz jocularity jetting past the determination—seems to mark them
as a group dedicated to a cause and suffused with the critical nature
of their mission.

Diane is riveted. They're all men. Did she ever, on all her data-gath-
ering missions, resemble them, so cheerless and self-important? She
fears she probably did. She's half tempted to talk to them and find
out who they are, another part of her wants to duck quickly away and
begin acting like the hermit she's come here to be. She's saved from
the choice, however, as they're speaking a language she doesn't know—
Danish, she thinks.

Of course she should have expected to run into researchers of her
own ilk here in Greenland, one of the meccas for scientists in her field.
Everyone wants to measure the melting ice sheet—in fact it's strange
she herself has never been here before, getting in on this particular
research action. But her plan to come here was made on such short
notice she didn't think about all she might encounter. As soon as she
finds her bag she skulks away.

The last few weeks were spent in a blind frenzy as she informed administrators, colleagues, grad student mentees, research partners around the globe that she was facing a "personal emergency" and could not be relied upon to fulfill teaching, mentoring, or research commitments until further notification. No one understood. To withdraw from everything so precipitously, without any advance notice, without a cancer or heart diagnosis everyone would understand, was unheard of in her world. It was tantamount to professional suicide, to permanently tainting her already very tarnished reputation. In the old days people might have said she was having a nervous breakdown, but that is far from the truth, as a breakdown implies a falling apart, whereas what she feels is the opposite, that some kind of convergence is happening, certain ideas coming together in a way that makes it impossible to continue in the usual way. But that is much too vague a notion to explain to people, so instead she has kept repeating the phrase "personal emergency" which she knows makes people imagine all sorts of lurid possibilities. Even Joe does not fully understand why she has had to ditch everything so abruptly, including him temporarily.

The rental house in Upernavik, on Greenland's west coast, arranged by a climate scientist friend who frequents Greenland, is small and bright red and quaint as a Lego creation, at least on the outside. Inside are two rooms, one for sleeping, one for living. The arrangement is austere and serviceable, and serviceable is exactly what she wants for the months of contemplation ahead. Her landlady, Aka Suersaq, lives next door, in a nearly identical bright blue house. Aka is a short, bespectacled Inuit woman in her thirties with a cheerful disposition despite being a mother of five and wife of a fisherman who, if Diane understood Aka correctly, is often gone.

This settlement of a little more than a thousand residents is built on a rocky, snowy hillside on the Western shore of Greenland above the Arctic Circle. Diane and Aka's houses are near the top of the hillside, reachable only by foot. One of Diane's windows has a view past dozens of primary color houses like her own, down to the harbor where the anchored fishing vessels appear tiny against the backdrop of icebergs. The entire town is mostly inaccessible to visitors, aside from the cruise lines that bring tourists up the shoreline in summer. To get here Diane had to book a private helicopter from Kangerlussuaq. It descended for landing on such a small rectangle of concrete she had to close her eyes against the vertigo. There are only a few roads in the town, and the cars can be counted on two hands. People travel mostly on foot or, when there's sufficient snow, on dog-powered sleds and snowmobiles. Rickety Rube Goldberg-like wooden staircases have been constructed to make traversing the steep rock faces easier.

When she wakes the first morning she's surprised to see she has slept past noon, and the light, an ethereal Arctic blue, already looks as if it might be slipping away. In late February, four months out from the solstice, the days are short and the light quality is entirely different from the clobbering light at the forty-second parallel. She wonders if much of her time here will be spent sleeping. If so, it will be a huge change. Since she was a teenager she's been an early riser, not because of a biological predisposition as from a psychological one, a drive to get up, get out, see what she might make of herself.

Something in the moody quality of the light brings on a clutch of dismay. What a mess she has made of her life. In sloughing her obligations she hasn't really sloughed anything, she has simply transported her concerns along with her in the suitcase of her own brain. It was easy to say back in Cambridge that she cared nothing about her reputation, that the mandate to explore the truth about Bronwyn's power outweighed her other involvements, but now, here, far from everything familiar, it seems as if her reputation is the only valuable thing she's ever had. Here no one has any idea who she is and what she has accomplished; even the scientists she saw in the airport ignored her, though that wasn't surprising—her name might mean something to them, but her face wouldn't. She thought such erasure was exactly what she sought, but she imagined she would confront it with more equanimity and a more tranquil brain. Her brain right now is as far from tranquil as it has ever been.

The situation is likely to be magnified by the spotty internet. She was told her rental cottage was equipped with internet service, but she arrived to find it on the blink, and while Aka says she can travel down the rocky hillside to the community center where two computers are available for public use, Diane is doubtful this situation will suit her needs.

She is usually in the habit of awakening early, her mind aswirl with thoughts about her research—most recently the PyroCb Project which is investigating the long-term effects of fire-caused high-rising pyrocumulonimbus clouds on the atmosphere and ozone—but this morning she woke to the scorched landscape of her professional relationships which she fears may already be damaged beyond repair.

A solitary person comes into view now, an elderly man mounting the staircase, step by labored step, a bag of groceries dangling from one mittened hand. He stops at a landing to catch his breath, perhaps fifty feet from Diane's house. She hurries to her suitcase to find her binoculars and, when she brings them back to the window, the man is still there, squinting down at the harbor. She fixes his face in her viewfinder. An Inuit face, once round, now lengthened by gravity, skin drowsing from a strong jawbone. There's a scruff of gray beard and a gray forelock poking out from beneath his fur cap. He chews on something, and every once in a while he retracts his lips to disclose several missing teeth.

She has never used her binoculars for watching people. Birds, yes, and deer and elk and foxes, and once in Montana, a bear. She's scanned tundra and mountainsides and cliffs to identify foliage and rock formations. But she's never studied people this way.

The man turns uphill again, about to resume climbing. Then he glances up, directly into her lens. His cheek twitches. Has he seen her? She lowers the binoculars, suddenly sweating. When did she become a person who spies on other humans? She needs to be a good citizen here in this tiny town where news, no doubt, travels fast. She refuses to let herself be another imperious white woman. Horrified by her own impulses, she buries the binoculars deep in a pocket of her suitcase.

She's reminded of an event from her middle school days, when it was discovered that the boys had punched a hole between their bathroom and the girls' bathroom. They had been spying regularly and reporting their findings. This girl had her period. Another girl had thunder thighs. Yet another squeezed her acne in the mirror after every class. All the girls were outraged. They found the hole and plugged it up with notebook paper and tape, and they elected Diane as their spokesperson. Diane took up the appointment gladly. She lambasted the leader first, a boy named Kevin who, to her surprise, cowered and apologized and told Diane he'd always admired her tits. After that Diane felt powerful and went to the principal to plead their case. It's painful now to remember that episode—once the spied upon, now the spy.

She layers herself in wool pants and fleece and sets about the business of the day. The immediate task is to clarify her purpose here, establish routines. She also needs to write a letter of apology to Joe. She left ignoring his objections, refuting his insistence that she was fleeing from things instead of facing them head-on which has been her usual style. "Can't you see you're not yourself?" he said, by which he meant she was acting strange, and he was worried. His worry is redundant—she's already worried for herself. She hopes she can explain to him that clearing her head wasn't possible in Cambridge.

The need to get outside overtakes her suddenly. She'd like to see where she is before night descends again. She hasn't had anything to eat since she arrived last night, and as she picks her way down to the harbor on wooden stairs and ice-clad rocks, keeping close track of her footing, she feels slightly dizzy, her brain a nullity, her skull hollow. Occasionally she disturbs small rodents who scurry away in haste. The whole town feels desperately empty, and the insistence of the brightly painted houses in the sere landscape makes her sad. *We are here, we are here,* their color seems to proclaim, the kind of claim one makes when one fears disappearance. Behind some of the houses sled dogs are chained to rocks, sleeping mostly, except for a few who eye her warily. Even they can tell she's a stranger.

She stops on a street that limns the harbor. There is more activity down here than she could see from above. A few fishermen have pulled up to a dock where they unload their catch, dumping it slowly into huge barrels that are being set on the back of a truck. There's the steady hum of generators, the huffing of boat motors, the chortle of ice floes knocking lightly against each other. Soft rock music floats in from somewhere, a woman singing in a Scandinavian language. Or is it Greenlandic—the Inuit dialect called *Kalaallisut*? On a beach just off to one side several young boys are roughhousing with a puppy. Two elderly women sit on a wall chatting as they keep track of the unloading catch. A delivery truck guns its way uphill to the supermarket.

The smell of fish and exhaust is almost annihilating. At the edge of the water, not far from where Diane stands, something floats, an eviscerated carcass, pink and bloody, only recently dead. She spots a paw and understands it's the pelt of a seal. Why would they discard such a pelt? Isn't sealskin a valuable commodity? She wants to ask someone why it's been left here, but her Greenlandic consists of only a few words, and everyone seems too busy to interrupt.

She has never been more acutely aware of being unnecessary. All her life she's had such purpose and drive. People have needed her. She's always thought she had skills with people, but has she really been good with people, or does she only know how to tell others what to do? If they follow her lead, she's a joy to work with—funny, flexible, lenient. But if they have their own ideas, if they cross her, defy her, suggest she's wrong, well, it's a different story. Then her social skills dissolve, and she has no idea how to proceed. For years Bronwyn followed her suggestions.

This is what dawns on her as she stands there, staring at the bloody seal pelt: She's here not because she's a pariah at work, not because the Dean has humiliated her, she's here because Bronwyn's independence has flummoxed her.

Pensive, she heads back up the hill. The light has already annexed the gray of twilight. She will be insomniac tonight after having slept so late. Nervousness strums her underlying lethargy. She stops for breath several times on the hike back up the hill to her house and decides not to make the detour for groceries.

Will she really survive here until May? It suddenly seems like a vast amount of time. There is only so much reflection even the most thoughtful human being can tolerate—and Diane would be the first to agree that, unlike Joe, she has limited capacity for self-reflection. She is already, one day in, too full of self-recrimination.

Someone is on her doorstep. Or does she have the wrong house? "Aka!" Diane calls out, surprising herself with her eagerness to connect.

Aka turns and waits, smile blazing. "For you." She thrusts a brown paper package at Diane. The unmistakable smell of fish bleeds through the greasy paper. Diane peers in. A whole fish is in there, head and all.

"My husband—today he catch."

"Oh heavens," Diane says. "You don't need to do this."

"For you," Aka insists. "You welcome. Enjoy!"

Aka, in her yellow European-style down jacket and fur-fringed red hat, eyes blinking beneath her round frameless glasses, smile still undiminished, withdraws to her house. Diane, left with the stinking fish, retreats inside.

19

Bronwyn knows Matt worries about her biking in the fog, but the island's traffic is so minimal in winter it hardly seems dangerous, and she loves the way the fog gloves her and beads on her skin as if it's confiding. She's in her element. She pedals hard, and her body begins to heat as it knifes through the wall of undulating gray.

It is one of those days when she fully appreciates her ability to see and hear and smell with her whole body. She has come to think of herself as a seismologist listening to the Earth's heart. Images rise up from the soles of her feet, insinuate themselves through the tips of her fingers. Sound enters through her chest and neck, funnels down the length of her spine to her coccyx. Scents arrive and twirl around her like scarves. Rain, blood, exhaust, pea soup. The legs of ants crawling through the grass. Tectonic plates creaking. The whoosh of oscillating tides. The celestial crooning of faraway whales. When she holds her coffee mug on such days, she sees beneath its glazed surface, the ceramic clay, the coffee's hydrogen and oxygen and ground Brazilian beans all distinct parts.

She has tried to explain this to Matt, the symphony of it all, the masterful design. How it sometimes overwhelms, but above all is beautiful. He listens like someone imperiled, desperate to understand; he cannot conceal the desertion he feels. *Take me with you*, his eyes plead. She would if she could.

Last night she didn't sleep. Biblical rains have been falling across the Midwest. She heard this at work yesterday, and Matt confirmed it last night. It's the kind of rain that makes roads impassable, kills crops, catalyzes mudslides, the kind of rain that is more enemy than friend. This morning it is still falling. Two full days now.

Knowledge of it runs in her blood. It can't be unknown. The *thing* in her has awakened and begun to rustle like a behemoth animal lumbering from its lair in early spring, squinting into the light, lurching, reluctant, curmudgeonly, but incapable of resisting the cyclical bodily mandate. Her pinky finger, too, has been more responsive of late, sending out brief trills of inchoate sensation.

This morning she felt feverish. Drinking her coffee, she could hardly breathe.

The fog has cleared at the island's center, and she locks her bike in front of the Dockside Café in sunlight feeling abruptly exposed. Wind kicks up from the harbor. One strong gust knocks a gull off the railing. From thousands of miles east the smell of rain reaches her, pirouetting through the countervailing wind, along with the stink of submerged decaying crops.

Jackie, her dreadlocked coworker, bounds up in greeting, her enthusiasm reminiscent of a Labrador pup, though she's pushing forty. She was hired in August, after years of surviving without a legal identity, evading the law, and she's still in the process of situating herself back on the grid. She squatted at several locations in California, Oregon, Washington, no amenities, sleeping in makeshift shelters without heat, water, phone, computer, bank account. Hand to mouth by choice. "After a while it kicks your butt," she told Bronwyn. "You get too old for living like that." Her face is weathered, but her energy is youthful. She fascinates Bronwyn. "I kept dreaming of a real bed."

Thirty minutes into the shift and there still isn't a single customer. Brad, the bartender, has turned on the TV news. *Must he?* A few weeks ago a ghastly snowstorm buried the eastern seaboard. By the time she learned about it, it was too late to intervene, and she was too far away anyway. She pushed it from mind as well as she could, made a point of avoiding newscasts. But avoiding news entirely isn't easy, even on this island, not when she works at a place with a giant TV. Now she knows what's coming and turns her back on the screen to face Jackie.

"Cataclysmic," says the newscaster.

"Sunset, Volcano, River, Tree." Jackie enumerates the names she's gone by. "Then there were the colors: Red, Blue, Green. At the time those single syllables seemed so strong. Jeesh. What a cliché, right?"

". . . a disaster for one of the nation's biggest agricultural regions . . ."

Blood in her legs pulses as if she's been running.

"I'm working on the bank stuff now. I never knew there were so many ways you're supposed to be legitimate . . ."

". . . stranded and homeless . . ."

The day has turned bright blue and blustery. The ocean's spindrift glitters like tinsel, and the vapor-sifted winter sunlight splinters the waves into hundreds of colors, hues of blue and green and silver and black. Gulls form a line along the railing. Behind them a fishing boat chugs into harbor.

The screen images seep everywhere, determined to reach her. There is no filtering peripheral vision when the things in that vision aren't peripheral. A long slow pan across the swelling Mississippi, rain dotting the camera's lens.

She turns to the window. Jaunty cumulus clouds march by with the rapidity of Morse code, swarming and transmuting themselves like spies. Seismic messages from the restaurant's foundation shimmy up her femurs. How is she supposed to sort these messages? If only her body could report a single thing.

"The new norm . . ." says the newscaster.

"Hella hard," says Jackie.

A membrane in her gut seems to tear, spills cold like a summons.

"Bronwyn, we have a customer!" sings Norma, the owner.

"Right." She turns to Jackie. "Would you mind . . . ?"

But Jackie has disappeared. There's only the too-big screen, featuring a farmer being interviewed, acres of brown water stretched out behind him. Humidity flares her nostrils. She is there with the farmer, alert, porous, ankle-deep in mud.

She approaches the customer in the corner. A thud snares her attention. A bird has hit the window and lies motionless on the deck, dead or stunned. "Excuse me, sir, I'll be back in a minute." She hands the man his menu and hurries out.

She lifts the bird carefully with two hands. On his way to death, he holds only the slightest trace of life's hum. She ferries him to the side yard and lays him in the grass. He's a pelagic cormorant, black with an iridescent head. In death he seems surprisingly delicate. Since she's been on the island she's been so attuned to birds. All wildlife—seals, otters, whales, deer—but especially birds. To study birds is an exercise in learning the deficits of humans. Swifts copulate in flight two thousand feet up. Arctic terns can fly up to fifty-six thousand miles per year. European robins navigate by *seeing* quantum entanglement. The lyrebird has such highly developed vocal chords it can mimic with perfect accuracy the sound of a chainsaw, a camera, a car alarm. What led this cormorant astray? In the months she's been working here this is the second bird who's hit a window. It isn't a sign, she tells herself, but it feels like one.

She lingers for a moment, eyes closed, letting the breeze drub her cheeks. She's always known the time would come when she would lose her lease on private citizenship and have to put her skill to work again. But she isn't ready, not quite yet. When does *can do* become *must do*? This is her question, hers alone. Regrouping, about to head back inside, she tries not to think of the acres of choking brown water.

A woman leans against the railing at the end of the row of gulls. The woman from the field, wearing a black tuxedo jacket and black pants, her hair cut boy-short. She rests her bottom on the railing so her languid body describes a sickle through whose curve fishing boats can be seen arriving at their moorings. Her look impales Bronwyn. *How long will it take you? How much damage will you ignore?*

The woman's arms rise overhead in slow deliberation, as if she's beginning a sun salutation, but instead of completing the posture she glances at Bronwyn again with another confrontational look, before striding down the deck stairs, past Bronwyn, and out of sight.

20

The tan, two-story stucco apartment building looks like a motel, not a place to live permanently. It's situated on a busy boulevard, adjacent to a Wendy's, a Chevron station across the street. Patty, trying to be game, follows Jean and the realtor, Bobbi, up the outdoor staircase to the available apartment on the second floor. The day has not turned out quite as Patty hoped it would, but she can't blame Jean. She's a retired schoolteacher, a friend of her sister Barb's who happens to love real estate; she certainly didn't *need* to spend the day driving Patty around to different parts of the city, showing her the options.

Patty surveys the living room. Would anyone want to live here? The dim light. The loud traffic. The flimsy walls. The paisley vinyl on the kitchen floor curling up at the edges. In some places the worn carpeting has been burned, and the textured bedroom wallpaper feels like plastic. No one could ever call Patty a snob, and she certainly doesn't need anything large and fancy, but this apartment simmers with quiet desperation. She wouldn't say so, but it suggests a place you might situate a recently released convict.

"It's certainly spacious," she says.

"And the price is right," Jean adds. She's practical and forthright, with a flat barrel chest, narrow hips and long legs made longer by the perma-press beige pants she wears. She seems to Patty almost sexless, from choice or birth who knows, but nevertheless a sharp contrast to the realtor, Bobbi, who is petite and blonde and moves around like a ping pong ball.

"You could make this little alcove into a study or a sewing area," Bobbi suggests. "It could be very cozy."

"Cozy," Patty says.

"My client has to think it over," Jean says.

Why she calls her a client, Patty has no idea. They have no professional relationship at all and only met this morning.

"Do you have any questions?" Bobbi asks.

She tries to think of something. To have no questions makes her appear dull, but truly she has no questions about a place she surely won't choose to live. "Not right now," she says brightly.

Back in Jean's boat-like pale yellow Impala, Jean says, "I know that place was a piece of crap, and I know you want to be closer to the ocean. But I'm all about options, because when we get closer to the ocean, you'll see, it's going to be sticker shock. Then you'll be happy to have seen some other places."

Patty has already felt sticker shock. This last place cost two to three times what a similar place would be in Kansas. "I'm happy to go smaller."

"There's only so small you can go." Jean lurches into the fast lane, wedging the Impala behind a silver Lexus, missing its bumper by inches. "I agree, that last place was a dump. But what didn't you like about the other places?"

How can she explain? It's not that she didn't like them exactly. They were all clean and had lovely palm trees and bright bougainvillea, most had swimming pools and utilities included. But was it too much to hope to live in a place that looked a little like you, in the way dogs and their owners resembled each other, in the way she felt her house in Kansas looked like her?

"They were all nice," Patty says, "but . . ."

"Cut the bullshit."

Patty chuckles. Jean has no trouble speaking her mind. What Patty wants to say is that Kansas has spoiled her. Surrounded by fields of wheat and corn and soy, the view from her house stretched straight to the horizon. The fields and sky reminded her of animated faces, constantly shifting in color and aspect. With wide open spaces it was easier to feel you were part of the land. Here in LA everything is submerged under concrete and asphalt. It's too much. But to say so would sound ungrateful.

Her sister Barb never minded leaving Kansas; as a teenager she couldn't wait to get out. Their brothers, too, left Kansas, though they all remained in the Midwest. What accounts for one person's fierce attachment to a place and another's disregard?

Jean is skeptical about Venice Beach, feels as Barb does that it's too full of drugs and marginal people, along with exorbitant prices, even by LA standards, but Patty wants to have a look. Earl might be easier to reach near the ocean.

Sure enough, Bobbi has found a place that could not be more perfect. It isn't large—a second-story apartment with one bedroom—but certainly adequate for one person. It has a luscious view of beach and water, and it's fully furnished which would makes things easy. It's perhaps a little more clean-lined and modern-looking than Patty would normally choose, but that's fine, she can work it into her own image. She can't believe her luck.

Bobbi announces a price that is at least five times what Patty can afford. Patty is flabberghasted, confused—Bobbi already knew her financial constraints.

"That's way out of our price range," Jean says, as if she herself plans to live with Patty.

"I'm showing you for comparison," Bobbi says, undaunted by Jean's disgust. "So you can see what the market bears." She looks at her clipboard. "I really only have one place near here that's within your reach. It's hardly what you'd call a *premium* property, more for student types, but maybe . . ."

They follow Bobbi in the car only a few blocks. They could easily have walked. Out of the car they turn from the sidewalk into a narrow alleyway erupting with foliage, short banana trees and some kind of gigantic red blossoms, almost pornographic, like that Southwestern painter whose name, beginning with a J or a G, Patty always forgets. A few open-mouth trash cans leak the scent of fermentation that mingles somewhat mysteriously with a white-flower scent whose source she can't identify—it's jasmine, or honeysuckle, or maybe gardenia.

Doors line both sides of the alley, mauve on one side, pale blue on the other, suggesting the possibility of secret gardens behind them. Bobbi stops in front of #8 and checks her clipboard then searches for the key on her comically large ring. "Drat. I don't have the key." She struts back down the alley in a snit, clearly fed up with low-rent Patty.

"Wait!" Jean calls. She has given the door a push and it opened.

Patty regards the open door, and a bolt of excitement passes through her. She and Jean go in without waiting for clearance.

Two rooms, kitchen and bedroom. Tiny, yes, but in a storybook way, like a dwelling for an elf, or a diminutive monk. It's a place for the basics, sleeping and eating, and yes, she could sew here. She wouldn't have much room for pacing or calisthenics, but she isn't a pacer or an exerciser. The windows are cracked, and grime is compressed into the creases of things. It cakes the kitchen and bathroom walls almost purposefully, like an element of design. The place is undeniably marginal and maybe too confining for a woman of Patty's size, but she's intrigued. A life here would mean stripping down to essentials. A life centered and given purpose.

In the bathroom Patty sits on the commode and her knees butt up against the sink cabinet. She laughs.

They step back outside to join Bobbi who is checking the broken lock, clucking. Jean holds up a syringe she found in the kitchen. Patty shrugs, walks away.

She can smell the ocean from here, maybe even hear it. It can't be too long a walk to get there. A kind of ecstasy fills her and, forging ahead of the other two, she makes her way to the street humming, banana leaves brushing her trousers, borne by certainty, knowing she's one step closer to where she's meant to be.

21

Matt is awakened by a clamorous northwest wind pawing at the cabin's windows. The clock says 2:30 a.m. Bronwyn is not beside him. He sits up and cocks his ear for movement beyond the bedroom, but the furious wind obscures everything. He gets out of bed.

The living room, bathroom, and kitchen, milky with the light from the proprietary full moon, are empty. He stands at the picture window that offers a view of beach and ocean and, when it's clear, the snowcapped mountains of the far peninsula. Wind whips twigs and bits of desiccated seaweed across the moon-whitened lawn and stirs the waves to a manic dance. Is she out there in this cold and chaos? Only half the beach is visible from where he stands, the nearest part obscured by rocks. She is nowhere in sight.

She's been restless for the last month, a subtle shift marked by moments in the midst of conversations when she seems to slip away and gazes out across the bay, listening intently as if someone is calling her from far away, her body suddenly still, her face slack. A few beats and then she's back, animated and fully present. When he questions her, she laughs it off, can never explain exactly where she has disappeared to. Coming from a family of inveterate sharers, these inexplicable absences disturb him, and make him acutely aware of having fallen for a woman completely different from himself.

Hardly a day passes when he doesn't wonder what it's like to be her, to see as she sees and feel the responsibility of her enormous power. There is so much she could do for the world. At first he tried to convince her that Diane was right, that the Earth is in trouble and she should be out there trying to fix its problems every day. But after almost a year of living with her out here on the island, just the two of them talking around and around these questions of what she owes the world and what she should do, he has come to understand her caution, her sense that tampering with the Earth holds dangers, that whatever she does might bring unexpected consequences. She gives the example of the cane toads, introduced in Australia to solve a problem with snakes. They killed the snakes, yes, but then the cane toads propagated and became a terrible menace on their own, worse than the snakes. If she was to act, she insists, she must do extensive thought experiments to be sure she's *acting wisely*.

The pressure put on her by Diane drove a rift between mentor and protégé—he was there to witness that after they returned from Siberia, and he could do nothing to stop it. He's not going to risk having her flee from him because of pressure *he* has brought to bear. And it's never far from his mind that there is personal peril in her interventions. The lost pinky tip is a reminder that a lost life could be next.

Still, it pains him to see her going off to work at the Dockside Café, acting as if she's another workaday rube like himself. It's like watching Picasso hang up his paintbrush to become a bricklayer—however noble, a colossal waste of talent. And then the feeling ricochets back to himself; he cannot help but feel diminished by the thought of how ordinary he is compared to her.

He's wide awake now. With difficulty he wedges open the sliding door to the deck and steps out. He can hardly stand straight against the maverick wind. One of the metal chairs has been knocked over, a chair he would have sworn was too heavy for wind to budge. It's not safe for her to be out on the beach in this weather with the tide coming in. He wishes she had a stronger sense of her own mortality.

He goes inside for a jacket and comes back out. A cloud wafts past the moon, dimming it briefly before moving on. The grass squishes underfoot. He stops abruptly halfway across the lawn.

The wind has not merely abated, it has stopped altogether. The few scrubby pines along the shoreline have ceased their swaying. The ocean is porcelain-flat. In the absolute calm the moon seems brighter, bigger. The speed of the change is telltale, her signature alone.

He holds his breath, fearful of something, he's not sure what. She rises into view, the crown of her head first, then her ivory face and long neck, the riotous helixes of her dye-darkened hair, torso clad in close-fitting spring-green parka, the burning radical presence of her, teeming with internal heat and light, moving up the stone steps from beach to lawn.

She sees him and stops momentarily, then continues toward him, the only movement in the stilled landscape. The moon loves her.

He holds her tight, knowing she's ready, which means he must ready himself.

22

Six bodybuilders on Venice Beach have gathered a small crowd. They stand in a row, angled away from the setting sun which sets their rippling backs agleam. They hold their Atlas pose for a minute or so, staring mid-distance, slack-faced, bodies remarkably similar but for their skin tones which range from light Caucasian tan to obsidian. Their torsos are upside down triangles, like replicas of Vitruvian man, their musculature so articulated they seem to have been skinned. What devotion it must have taken to develop such muscles. It's a kind of perfection Felipe admires, but does not aspire to. He wants to see them walk, curious to see if those dense muscles impede their grace.

Robed and barefoot, he is on his way down to the water to swim. In his two weeks in LA, staying with Isabella's friend Metcalf in an apartment right on the beach, he has only gone into the water once, but now he means to make it a daily event.

After he got over his jet lag, he spent time on the set of Metcalf's new movie. An Assistant Director for the first time, Metcalf is eager, proud, sure this is a big step forward for his career. He's up at five in the morning and rarely in bed before midnight. A lot rides on him, he tells Felipe, because he's managing many people. Before this he'd had what he called lowly jobs such as Production Assistant and Location Scout, but then he went through a training program and now he's on his way to a Big Career and lots of money.

Metcalf had to pull strings to get Felipe on the closed set. He implied that if Felipe hung out there he might land a job. At work Metcalf's personality seemed to change. He wore headphones and he barked orders and told people to shut up.

A week was enough. Felipe never aspired to be in the movies, and after what he's seen on the set he feels his instinct was right. There is no fluidity to this movie-making, no spontaneity, the very things he loves most about live theater and dance. How could an actor ever penetrate a character with all that stopping and starting? With so many others standing around how could focus be achieved? The movie was supposedly a comedy, but everyone involved seemed overly serious, even joyless. He has no use for art without joy. Even sad art should be infused with joy in its making.

So he will find other things here in this city that reminds him a little of São Paulo. They are both shameless, exhibitionistic cities. Both cities of extremes and excess. Both dry. LA may not have the shameful favelas of São Paulo, but it is not lacking poor people, angry people, scores of homeless.

He leaves the bodybuilders and makes his way across the wide beach to the water. Some young girls practice cartwheels in the sand. A fit elderly man in a straw hat walks along the water's margin, head bent in rumination. No one is swimming now, he'll have the water to himself.

He could like it here, he thinks, if he had satisfying work and a car. Though he didn't come with the idea of moving here, only exploring. Because, as Isabella pointed out so strenuously, traveling and exploring are what he needs to recharge himself. He is thinking now she was probably right.

A large, fully clothed woman has plunked herself in the wet sand, legs jutting into the water, small incoming waves frolicking around her. She's talking to herself so he moves away, not wanting to embarrass her.

This water is colder than the Atlantic. He lets his feet acclimate first, then he runs to the depths and dives under. The bolt of cold is awful, delicious. He comes up gasping, every cell shocked, swims a few strokes toward China, then drops his legs, treading water, catching a rope of kelp and whipping around it, remembering how long ago it was in the ocean, swimming with his family at Guaruja and Santos, that he first discovered his love of dance.

He swivels back towards shore, fully situated in the sudden happiness of unexpected change. The bodybuilders, like moving statues, are still at it. The woman who has planted herself in the sand is watching him, unusually attentive.

A wave rises over him, pushes him under. His eyes open to the refracted blue-green light. Beyond the roar of the water lies a profound silence. He is made for this, to be a body exulting in water, selfhood no more important than seaweed or sand.

A current drills through his shoulder, seethes down the length of his arm. A wire of pain rings his waist, then his thigh, then his other arm. Electrocution everywhere. Stinging, sharp.

He struggles to shore, stroking as hard as he can, running when his feet touch the sand. Out of the water, he inspects himself. A purplish-red track runs the length of his arm. Another circles half of his waist and down his upper thigh. Like the marks of a whipping. The pain throbs, rising and receding and rising again, fogging his thought. He groans quietly, looks for his towel and robe.

The woman who was sitting in the sand is beside him now, bending into him. "Are you all right, hon? Can I do something? That looks nasty."

He allows her to take his hand. She leads him slowly up the beach to a bench.

"Jellyfish. I heard people saying they're out there. I should have stopped you."

So that is the reason no one was swimming. He wonders how he could have known. Is it because of his deficient English?

They regard his arm. Bits of gelatinous tentacle remain here and there, like clear mucus sprung from his pores.

"I'm going to get help," she says.

She disappears, and he sits in a pain that's alive and devours his attention, a hot orange fluid streaming through him, inflamed by the setting sun, shuttering all else.

She returns with a helper, a man in an official red jacket. Docile, Felipe relinquishes his body to inspection, to tweezers pinching and plucking to remove remains of the embedded tentacles. The pain distracts from the other different pain which still throbs in rhythmic accord with the beat of his heart.

"You'll want to get into a hot shower. Helps the pain," the man says.

He turns his face to the man's and, seeing gentleness beneath the shell of the man's harsh tan, he tries to move his expression into the gratitude he feels.

"If it's not better in a week or two, you'll want to get to a doctor. Expect some scarring. You okay, man?"

He rallies, nods, thanks the man, who disappears back up the beach with his gear.

Felipe remains on the bench, shivering a little, still wearing his cloak of pain. What has he done with his robe? There, it's on his lap, the woman must have retrieved it. She's still here, he realizes, as she begins spreading the robe across his shoulders. She sits beside him in the twilight, a soft maternal presence, radiating heat.

23

The library seems to Analu like a palace with its cool air and vaulted ceilings, its shiny surfaces and marble floors. Around every corner light startles, but the only sounds are occasional footsteps, muted laughter from the children's room, and the hushed voices of the gentle library ladies. Everything about the place makes it seem as if he's floating through a dream.

Analu tries hard to feel he belongs here. When Penina first brought him she had no question about belonging. She passed through the front door as if it was her home, chatting nonchalantly, racing up the stairs to the second floor, swiping her library card into the device that activates the computer. But without Penina in the lead, Analu is always a bit nervous. Fortunately, there's one library lady who's always here and always recognizes him. She's buxom and blonde, chuckles pleasantly, and is very kind to him, helping him log on when he has trouble.

The clip is only four minutes long, but he never tires of watching it. He brings his face close to the screen, trying to see beyond the edges of the frame. Who is this red-headed woman with raised arms who appears to be stopping a raging forest fire? How can he learn more about her? She is human but more—perhaps a person with *mana* like him? Penina has said most people think the video is a trick, but Analu doesn't believe that. There is the woman, right there on the screen, commanding the fire to quiet itself. She reminds him of a parent, ordering a child to go to his room. He feels her energy radiating from the screen.

Watching the video several times in a row puts him into a trance. He travels with the fire lady to the island where, tiny and powerful, she goes to work, directing the ocean back from the shoreline, inch by inch, foot by foot, returning the island to the place he knew in his childhood. It's a silly fantasy, he knows. The ocean is huge. It covers the earth, surrounds all the continents. A single human being, even one with *mana*, could never lower all the earth's water.

He is only allowed on the computer for half an hour if others are waiting. When his session is over and the screen goes black, he drags himself back to the world his body inhabits. He pauses his soothing daydreams, to resurrect later when he is at Pasar Malam, hands immersed in soapy water, scrubbing the pots. It is tedious work and hot, but not difficult, and it gives him time to think. He smiles ruefully at the kindly library lady on his way out. His visits are their secret. He has not told Nalani or Vailea where he goes—or even Penina. Only the library lady knows.

Penina spots her father as soon as she enters the computer room. What the heck is he doing here, staring so fixedly at the monitor? She crosses to his table and stands directly across from him, but it takes him a moment to notice her. When he finally looks up, he's surprised, and also sheepish, and she understands, without asking, that he was watching the fire video.

"Penina," he whispers. "What are you doing here?"

"I could ask the same of you." She smiles, aware of taunting him with her own secret world. She's never imagined he might have secrets too.

"I'm looking for jobs," he says.

"But you already have a job."

"Better jobs." He stands. "Let me buy you a soda."

They go to the shaded library courtyard where they can speak without whispering. "I always dream of the island," he confesses. "Don't you? Wouldn't you like to go back?"

She dips her head and cranks her eyes at him as if peering up from beneath a table. "No, there's nothing there. You said so yourself. Soon it won't exist. That's what you said."

Her words are thorns. He closes his eyes.

"Dad? I'm sorry. But—"

He hushes her. "We don't need to talk about it." It is not a bad thing that she likes it here. He wanted that, didn't he? They came here for her. "I know what you're thinking. You're thinking that lady could do something, aren't you? The one on YouTube who put out the fire?"

He says nothing, sips his soda intently. Sweat parades down his face.

"Dad." He sees she feels sorry for him, as if she is older than he is, and more knowledgeable about the world. "That was *invented*. With, like, computers. Movies do that all the time. It isn't *real*."

It isn't only her words that gouge him. It's her eagerness to say *I'm not you, I don't even think like you.* Overlooking the barbs, or trying to, he kisses her and leaves for work. When he gets home late that night Nalani and Vailea are in the bedrooms, but Penina has fallen asleep on the living room couch. She is still dressed in a short magenta skirt and a deliberately tattered olive T-shirt. Her face in slumber is smooth and full and relaxed, as if she has never suffered. Her bare toes are vital island toes that know the sand intimately. Sleeping, she is someone he recognizes.

He eases into bed beside Nalani, and she stirs only slightly. Her hair is fragrant with the floral scent he loves. After an hour of fretting, he falls asleep, and his daydreams seep into his night dreams so, waking, he feels hopeful.

24

These days Patty awakens at first light in her nestlike apartment and heads to the beach for a walk. The light is a gauzy violet. The ocean whirs and croons like a prelude to something louder. A few people are out running, or biking, or doing Tai Chi. Bums snooze on some of the boardwalk benches, loaded shopping carts nearby. Here by the ocean dawn is less of a whisper than it was on the plains, more of a shout.

Since she moved to Venice Beach Barb has been worried for her, but she isn't scared, not of the overly bundled homeless with their shopping carts, not of the people slinking around in the alleyways who could be peddling drugs, not of the fact that she has no idea why she's here. Her old Chevrolet, the car she drove all the way from Kansas that is now parked on the street, was broken into one night, the passenger's window smashed. That was a bit of a shock, but nothing was taken, and but for the broken window, and the old chicken parts and KFC buckets strewn about, no harm was done. At night she sometimes wakes and listens for smashing glass, but she doesn't worry, doesn't believe it will happen again.

In the early morning it's easy to find an empty stretch of beach by the water where no one will notice her talking to Earl. She summons him with a song—*Oh, What a Beautiful Morning* or *Here Comes the Sun*—and once she feels he's listening, she tells him what's on her mind, how good it is to have moved out of Barb's into her own place, how unusually full of energy she feels, how she isn't certain what she should be doing next. *It'll come,* Earl says. *You sit with it and it'll come to you.*

The one thing that frightens her, just a tad, is the vast Pacific. On certain days its waves coalesce into walls that advance with the speed of oncoming trains, reminding her of the volume in all that water out there, of its power and of the possibility of tsunamis. It would be lovely to learn to swim, she thinks, if she weren't so afraid of the water, and now, after seeing what happened to that poor man stung by the jellyfish, well, she doesn't dare. *Would you swim here*, she asks Earl, and he just laughs.

She sees that poor swimmer with the foreign accent out walking on the boardwalk now and again, sometimes coming down to the water's edge to check for jellyfish. The scar on his arm is still there, not ugly, but certainly prominent, circling his arm, marking him as having endured something, like modern stigmata. Poor fellow. And yet he is not, she sees, a person to feel sorry for. He strolls around in his beautiful body with an expression of curiosity and engagement, as if he is one notch away from irrepressible laughter. He is on the beach often enough that she guesses he lives nearby.

She usually walks two miles north on the boardwalk, turns around and retraces her steps, and then, close to the end of her walk, she likes to buy a breakfast burrito from a stand called Taco Mike's. It's a few steps off the beach, run by a friendly family from Mexico. In the morning the three kids are there before school, learning to take orders and tend the cash register. She takes her mammoth burrito back to the beach and finds a place to sit and eats while watching the day's rising action: the late sleepers coming out for a run or a walk, one day a class of school children with jars coming down to take ocean samples for science class, another day a movie crew setting up for a shoot. It's never the same.

"Do you mind?" he says, gesturing to the space on the bench beside her. It's him, she sees, his beautiful long body, his dark hair, his swarthy complexion.

She has just taken the first bite of her burrito, and bits of its egg and sausage have spilled into her lap. Her mouth is stuffed. She's such a slob. Covering her mouth, deeply embarrassed, she nods, speaks when she finally can. "Of course," and he sits.

"I look all over for you. You are so kind the day I swim and get stinged. I am Felipe. You?"

"Patty." She rewraps her burrito, lays it down, holds out her hand. "I was hoping we'd meet again. How are you doing?"

"I'm good. Still the marks, you see, but not the pain. I buy you dinner? Yes?"

"You don't have to do that."

"I want. For thanks. I see you many times. You sing. You talk. I don't interrupt."

Her face heats and is probably pinkening. He's seen her talking to Earl. She isn't crazy, but to say so would only seem to prove she is. Silenced, she stares into her lap, sees at the edge of her vision, a pulse in the vein of his resting hand. The tendons form a webbing, the fingers are unusually long. She has never seen such lively beauty welling up from a hand.

She steals a glance at his face and finds him staring squarely back at her, unabashed, without judgment. There is something magnetic about him, a curiosity that wants to swallow the world in order to know it.

"Your voice, it is beautiful."

Right then she could cry. She had no idea she was lonely.

25

Fearlessness is Diane's most salient characteristic. As a child she was unfazed by the usual terrors: dark rooms, ghosts, snakes, mice, spiders, big black dogs, looming ocean waves. She was always the one to plunge ahead of her quailing companions into the unlit room or the raging river. As she moved into adulthood, she retained this intrepid aspect, becoming a gutsy scientist and an assured public speaker. The one thing that scares her is flying in airplanes, and she has mostly mastered that phobia—it has certainly never kept her from doing the things she has had to do.

Here in Greenland, it is another story altogether—here she has become acquainted with what it means to feel terror. The long nights percolate with unfamiliar sounds. The wolflike sled dogs howl unrelentingly. The icebergs in the bay crack like cannon shots, dumping thousands of tons of ice into the bay. In a nearby house, a man sings Greenlandic ballads late into the night, and even those mournful sounds make her heart clutch. She stays awake long past the hour when Aka and her husband and their five children have all gone to sleep. When their house is quiet, she realizes the safety she feels when they are awake; asleep they cannot save her.

Without the urban light pollution with which she is familiar, the darkness of night here is black and absolute, particularly on the nights with a cloud cover. Silence is more absolute too. When the dogs cease their yowling and the singer has gone to sleep and a period of time passes without any ice breaking apart, the silence engulfs her. When she speaks into that silence her voice sounds thin and weak, and she understands her force in the world is negligible. The loneliness the silence and the dark arouse in her is a call to existential contemplation that has never been her habit. She has always been a practical, ambitious woman, a let's-get-on-with-things type, but when, on clear nights, she sits in front of the window and sees the stars unmasked and spilling so much light, she seems to bear witness to their movement. Though she knows better, she imagines them hurtling towards the Earth and the unrelenting chaos of the universe overwhelms her.

Morning arrives slowly, the twilight-gray of the sky impossible to read, so she wakes, surprised she has slept, having no idea what time it is. The gray sky merges with the gray water, eliminating any horizon, and in this monochrome landscape it takes her several moments to remember where she is and why she is here.

The rudiments of staying alive are not prohibitive, but they bring into stark relief how much she has enjoyed her creature comforts: the commodious rooms in the Brattle Street house; the endless supply of running water, hot and cold at will; the stench-free plumbing. Here water is delivered once a week to a large tank in her kitchen; it has been harvested from icebergs—a dangerous task, Aka reports—then stored in a giant tank near the bay. Aka told her to monitor her water use carefully so she won't run out. Running out entails a trek down to the grocery store and ferrying gallon jugs of water back up the hill with her own muscle power. Water, Diane has learned the hard way, is very heavy.

A bigger challenge is the sewage system. A camper-style commode in the bathroom collects waste in a heavy black plastic bag. It is Diane's job to remove the bag, seal it, then leave it at a designated location near Aka's house for weekly pickup. She tries to take the task in stride, but finds herself being more squeamish than she'd like to be and, despite a bathroom ventilation system, keeping the small room stench-free is a definite challenge that requires air fresheners and no-doubt-toxic antibacterial products that were here when she arrived. She watches the buildup of sewage bags—her own and those from Aka's family—at the pickup station and wishes for less transparency.

Then there is the ongoing internet issue. The two computers at the community center are often occupied; their internet speed is dismal, and they, too, often go down altogether. This is primarily a problem for communicating with Joe, but it also makes it impossible to address the slew of outraged emails she's been getting from research colleagues on the PyroCb Project.

A few days into her stay, early one morning (or so it feels to Diane) when she is barely awake and not dressed, Aka appears on her doorstep. Diane answers the door, still in her sweats, knowing it would be rude to ignore the knocking when it's obvious she's here.

"For your coffee!" Aka says, holding up a six-pack of Hostess cupcakes. It quickly becomes apparent that Aka expects to be invited inside.

Diane sets about boiling water for coffee, acutely aware of the still uncooked fish Aka gave her a few days ago. At home Diane relies on Joe to cook such things, to cook *everything* really; she has no idea how to skin and debone a whole fish. Now its strong smell has colonized the refrigerator and begun to seep outside, and she fears Aka will think she's ungrateful.

They settle around the small kitchen table with mugs of Maxwell House coffee (the best to be found at the local market), Diane groggy from lack of sleep, Aka wearing her bright yellow jacket, stalwart and lively as the sun itself. Diane will learn over the months of her stay here that Aka faces each morning with an optimism that embodies the Greenlandic word *nuannarpunga*, which means, *I am full of the delirious joy of being alive.*

Aka tears open one of the two-packs of cupcakes and hands one to Diane. Accepting it Diane tries not to laugh. She can't remember the last time she ate a Hostess cupcake—probably back in middle school—but the memory of its essence persists: the slab of hard chocolate frosting on top, the moist cake, the creamy white filling at the center. Bad food, toxic food, but still surprisingly delicious even now, if she can prevent herself from thinking what it's composed of.

"And so—" Aka says. Maybe a question, maybe a statement. *And so, you are here. And so, what is next? And so, tell me about yourself.*

Diane is on the verge of asking Aka what she does for a living, such a standard question among her friends and colleagues, but she stops herself—the woman has five children which certainly is enough to occupy her. "Tell me about your children," Diane says, tonguing away a smear of frosting that has lodged at the base of one of her incisors. "I see you heading out with them in the morning."

Aka nods in her enthusiastic way and gives a rundown of her children. Her English is not perfect, but what she says is absolutely clear. Edel, her oldest child, is fifteen. She's a rebel who wants to leave Greenland as soon as possible, go to Denmark, become a musician. "Rock band," Aka says, strumming an air guitar, laughing. "Rock band!" As if it's the funniest thing in the world. Imanek, the second oldest, a boy of twelve, loves being outdoors, loves animals, loves his mama. Ten-year-old Kalaaq is a soccer player who wants to be a fisherman like his father. The youngest two, both girls, Bera, seven, and Ina, five: "Who knows about them?" Aka says. "Too soon to tell." She speaks of her children without judgment, amused by them and fond, surprisingly ready to let them choose their own paths. "And so—" she says, wrinkling her nose and adjusting her frameless glasses.

"Your English is good, by the way," Diane says.

"I learned in school, but I get better when the ships come. Summer, I lead expeditions from the ships."

"Tourists?"

"Yes, tourists. We take kayaks. With them I learn to speak better. I try to get some job for my daughter, Edel. To help her English."

"That sounds good. Would they hire a fifteen-year-old?"

"Maybe. We see. And so—" She smiles at Diane, a mixed-meaning smile, and shakes her head, crumpling the Hostess wrapper and pocketing it.

They drink their coffee, their mutual silence congenial.

"She must learn good English if she wants rock band," Aka says.

Diane nods, wondering if Edel could be in a rock band if she spoke only Greenlandic.

"She must leave here. Meet new people. Maybe rock band, maybe not. Our Upernavik is too small for her."

"Yes, teenagers get restless. Around the world they get restless."

"Here in Greenland, it is bad. Nothing to do. No work." She shakes her head. "Edel's friend, she die."

"That's terrible. How did she die?"

"She take her life. January. At night she walk on the ice and she fall in. That's it, gone. She knows this will happen. She wants this. A fisherman find her in the morning."

"How is your daughter doing? Is she all right?"

Aka's face is solemn now, but she has not entirely dropped all traces of a tight *what-can-you-do-life-goes-on* smile, a look whose DNA Diane recognizes from various stiff upper lip New Englanders she knows.

"Not so good," Aka says. "She don't want school. All day she walks around. You know—?"

Does Aka mean to say that Edel is also suicidal? This is entirely beyond Diane's area of expertise, and she has no idea what to say. Is Aka asking for comfort? For advice?

"Mad at everything. Her heart is broken."

Diane nods. "I'm sure."

"I say to her: It happen. It is life. Death and life hold hands, you know? But—here in Greenland—too much. Many teens. Adults too. Maybe not in your country." Aka shrugs, smiles, her smile now expressive as a moan that causes Diane's breath to catch. "And so—"

Diane considers saying something about Americans dying of opioid overdoses, but decides not to. Can the despair of Americans be compared to Greenlandic despair when Americans have so much?

"This must be so hard. For her and for you." Diane reaches out to touch Aka's hand, but the gesture feels alien and awkward, and it underscores her feeling of overall ineptitude, that she cannot rise to the most basic of human tasks, the comforting of another human being. But she is also aware that Aka does not seem to be asking for comfort. Her eyes are blinking quickly behind her thick lenses, as if to say: *Forget it, I'm fine. You, of all people, cannot help me.*

"For you, what is hard?" Aka asks.

What can Diane possibly say? She arrived in Greenland thinking so much about her life was hard, but out of context none of it seems hard in the least. Not possibly-suicidal-daughter hard. Not no-work-to-be-found hard. Not five-children-to-support-when-fish-are-becoming-more-scarce hard.

"Your children?" Aka prompts.

The assumption Diane has children. It's not an assumption Diane encounters often in the States. In fact, many people have assumed the opposite, that being a successful scientist as she is means she couldn't possibly have had the time to raise children.

"I never had children," Diane says.

Confusion riddles Aka's face. "Oh."

"I guess you could say I never had the mothering instinct. And the timing was off. When I finally found the right husband, someone who I could imagine having children with, I was too old."

"I'm sorry," Aka says.

"Oh, there's no need to be sorry. It wasn't what I was focused on. I have my students. There's one—" Her use of the word have silences her. She doesn't have anyone, least of all Bronwyn, who for many years she thought she did have. She wonders if that sense of ownership is exactly why Bronwyn has cut her off.

Glancing back at Aka's serene, attentive face, a well of unexpected emotion floods Diane. "I had a student for many years who was very dear to me. Like a daughter in many ways. She was very talented, a good scientist, but we have drifted apart."

Aka nods—and so?

Drifted is not the right word at all—drifting is much too mild to describe what has happened. She and Bronwyn have been wrenched apart, but the feeling of connection—at least on Diane's part—is still very much alive despite the rift.

Aka is waiting for her to elaborate. "You still feel you are her mother, but you lose her?"

"Yes. Exactly."

Cracked open, perilously close to tears, Diane swallows the last half of her cupcake without chewing. It sticks on the way down, and she tries to chase it with coffee. Aka waits for her coughing to subside then asks, "Why she go away?"

"Oh, Aka." How can she possibly explain what has happened? What would Aka have to say about Bronwyn's talent?

It feels cruel for her to be crying now in Aka's presence. Bronwyn is not suicidal, she is simply out of touch. Still, Diane hunches over her mug, forearms on the table, gaze on the dregs of her coffee, and gives herself over to quiet harrumphing. Aka does not try to intrude. Minutes pass. When Diane regains control of herself, she is deeply embarrassed then, looking ruefully at Aka, she realizes she is not embarrassed at all.

"I would like to meet your daughter," Diane says.

26

She has been driving slowly south from Memphis for hours now, over the flat flooded alluvial plain of the Mississippi Delta, following circuitous detours where roads have been washed out, always keeping the water in sight. It's more extreme than she expected. The floodwaters are deceptively still, stretching for miles past the eastern bank of the engorged Mississippi, smearing the landscape with desolation. She's filled with the foreboding she's been trying to fend off, pictures of the death and devastation ahead.

Human habitation appears to be an idyll of the past, only ghosts remaining. Houses and barns aproned with water. Drowned cars breaching the surface like blighted whales. Trees with branches flung wide as if praying for their sodden roots. A few survivors appear, floating grimly by in boats over their submerged croplands, standing erect like seafaring explorers hoping to spot land. Some dump trucks unload sandbags for makeshift levees. Too little, too late. A half-obscured road sign says *Dead*.

The water, brown and silt-filled, looks intractable, determined not to leave. The sky, too, covered with a potent armory of clouds, gives off a fuck-you glow. She knows better than to impute such motives to the landscape, but she's human too and rife with human impulses. There is no mistaking one thing: the Earth has spoken. Without an intervention, it could be weeks before the water subsides and life returns to normal. If there is such a thing as normal. Not in her life certainly.

The light is leaking away fast. She doesn't need light to work, but it helps. Already in a fugue state and stiff from gripping the wheel so tightly, she parks the red rental Ford Fiesta on a stretch of road with only a single stranded house in view. It looks abandoned, she hopes it is.

She faces west in the direction of the river's spine, though the river itself is miles away and not visible. Something drifts slowly into her vision—a pink Mickey Mouse raft. But for the mewing she wouldn't have been able to tell there were kittens aboard. She would try to rescue them, but they're too far away.

This time it will be different—it already is different. She has done the thought experiments, considered what damage might be wrought by waters subsiding too quickly. Working slowly is key, it could take a full day to coax the waters away as slowly as she'd like. A steady and sustained output of heat is required, hastening careful drainage, the right amount of evaporation, but not too quickly. It will be grueling, but she's prepared, rested, determined.

There are no witnesses, no fanfare, both of which bring complications.

Her pinky twitches. She thinks of Earl who wouldn't have died if she'd stayed in Kansas as he wanted her to. Guilt can be useful. There was something special about that man. She calls Matt, leaves a message. "I'm about to begin. Wish me luck." He wanted to come here with her, but she insisted on coming alone.

The departing sun haunts the clouds. A shiver slithers through her, the twins of chill and excitement. She is suited to doing this, and it's been too long since she's done something challenging.

She steps forward, ready. Her vision blurs, telescopes, so she sees the river's headwaters at Minnesota's Lake Itasca and south to its wide silty mouth in the Gulf of Mexico. Between them the myriad arterial tributaries. In her belly the nugget of heat begins to gain heft, rises to her chest, her head, condensing as it goes. When it turns white-hot, she thrusts it, feels herself elevate, losing strict boundaries of self, her atoms mingling with other atoms that are not usually hers. The risk is always there, a risk she chooses not to entertain, that one day it will be impossible to recompose herself.

The electrical grid is down, so night brings on an impenetrable darkness, the only sounds, the lapping of water, the occasional lowing of stranded cows in despair.

She is tiny, smaller than a house, a truck, a cow, smaller than a man. But size is irrelevant. What matters is the formidable heat of her imagination, the uncompromising molecular force of her will. What matters above all is doing what must be done.

Slowly, slowly, millimeter by millimeter, the water starts to withdraw. By the time the sun rises, houses, barns, trees, livestock, gawk down at mud.

27

Sorrow blows through the apartment like a hot soughing wind, and some days it settles there, refusing to move, becoming something heavy and willful, so when Penina comes home from school, jazzed by friends and music and future plans, the sorrow seats itself on top of her and pins her down so all the jazz leaks out of her. It is heavy, this sorrow, heavy as a sandbag—no, a car—and once she's under it there's no getting out. It's *Vailea-is-sick-and-dying* sorrow and *the-island-is-sinking* sorrow, and *never-enough-money* sorrow, and those sorrows scoop up other sorrows her parents knew before she was born.

Penina no longer goes home right after school. She knows Vailea misses their private hours together, and she feels bad about that, but still each day she comes home later and later. Sometimes she goes to get sodas with Dinh, other days she goes to Gillian's house because Gillian's parents don't get home until six, so the girls have the house to themselves. Even when the parents do arrive home, they get drunk so quickly they mostly ignore the girls. Penina and Gillian watch movies and listen to music and eat ice cream and Gillian talks about her crushes. They always spend some time in front of the mirror, applying lipstick and comparing their looks. Gillian's face is covered with freckles that migrate here and there like drifting islands, sometimes merging into entire continents. Her skin is moon-white, her curls the color of the palest sand. Gillian strokes Penina's long black hair, trails a finger down her brown arm. "Soft!" she coos. Penina's body is robust and firm, with burgeoning breasts; Gillian's is flat-chested and skeletal, so thin Penina can see bones poking out where she scarcely thought bones existed.

Penina would like to be pretty, but she knows she's only a little pretty, not very pretty, not pretty enough. Her hair is good, but her face is too round, and she's too short. She studies the faces of her classmates, staring so hard she insinuates herself under their skin like a ringworm until she feels what it's like to be that person, to have the wide nose of Ba, or the lipless mouth of Nguyen, or to see the world through Nicole's pellet eyes.

She has to do something. She knows it's up to her. She sits at a computer in the school library instead of going to lunch. Nobody goes to the library at lunch except a couple of kids with conditions. Lance, the stutterer, and Marin, who'd rather read than do anything else. Penina feels out of place, as if she and her computer are gigantic neon blowup toys everyone can see from miles away.

She keeps her eyes on the screen. When she looks away the librarian catches her eye as if to ask if something's wrong. It isn't her business.

Dear Fire Lady, she types. Fire Lady sounds dorky. The woman must have a name, but no one seems to know it. Can it be Eagle? The email address Dinh found is Eagle8@gmail.com. She deletes *Fire Lady* and types *Dear Eagle.* But that looks stupider.

Dear Fire Lady, I need help. How pleading and desperate that sounds. But she *is* a little desperate. Her whole family is desperate, Vailea most of all. Desperate enough that she is here writing this email when she only half believes. She doesn't *not* believe in the Fire Lady's ability, but she doesn't fully believe it either. If it were real wouldn't everyone in the world be asking for help?

Wording is so tricky. She doesn't want to insult the Fire Lady by saying she has doubts, but she has to be honest.

The bell rings, lunch is over. She's due at science class in three minutes. The other two students are clomping around, gathering their things.

Just write it, write something, what's the worst that could happen? Probably silence. Erased by silence, big deal. But silence, ugh, that's bad too.

28

Through the gauze curtain of Metcalf's living room, Felipe sees Patty standing on the bungalow's front stoop adjusting her clothing—brown knit pants and a balloony overblouse printed with large geometric shapes in yellow and orange. Her hair, a dyed goldish-brown, rises from her head in cresting waves. She is considerably older than he—sixty maybe—and not the kind of woman he would ever have imagined meeting in America, but she helped him out, and he feels he owes her. And there's something honest about her he really likes. Instead of taking her to a restaurant, which is too expensive, he has invited her to dine here. How strange, he now thinks, to be hosting a woman who talks to herself on the beach.

When he opens the door she laughs; she laughs as Metcalf shakes her hand and scoots out the door to his night shoot; she laughs as she surveys the mess Felipe has made in Metcalf's small kitchen.

"This is how Brazilians cook?" she says, laughing yet again.

"Only this Brazilian. You laugh—some Americans do not laugh."

"Oh? What do you mean? Who doesn't laugh?"

"The movie people, on Metcalf's set, they do not laugh."

"I wouldn't know about movie people. But don't people generally laugh everywhere? At least sometimes?"

"I have no like for people who do not laugh."

She laughs yet again. "I have no like for them either."

He urges her to sit and she relocates herself at the table, buttocks spilling over the side of the chair, breasts drooping onto the place mat with the heavy density of slumbering infants. Why should a body embarrass him, he asks himself, trying to work against the feeling.

She seems to read his mind. "Look at you," she says as he ferries the dishes from the kitchen and lays them on the table. "What a beautiful body you have. I've always wanted a body like yours."

"Oh," he says, "it—I dance, you know." He waves his hand to dismiss the subject.

"Don't be embarrassed. It's lovely. It really is. It was never in the cards for me to have a body like yours. But I don't mind. I've gotten used to it."

"My instrument."

He names the dishes for her: *feijoada* made with black beans and sausage, rice, kale, orange slices, toasted manioc flour. "Brazilian. I do not cook often though. I hope I do not kill us."

"It would be hard to kill me with food. I love food." With the first bite she closes her eyes and exhales with pleasure. "Delicious. Not like anything I've had. How wonderful that you thought to cook for me when I'm a complete stranger to you! You're from Brazil, you dance, that's all I know. What brought you here? Tell your story, will you?"

What is his story exactly? A story has an ending. He has no ending. He tells her about the troubles in São Paulo—the lack of water, the lack of work, his need for a change—and it occurs to him that in the month or so he's been in LA no one has asked him much about himself. Metcalf asked a little but listened distractedly. Sometimes, when he's buying coffee, a barista hears his accent and asks where he's from, but mostly he's kept his "story" to himself. Now it feels good to talk.

She tracks his eyes as he speaks, as if there is something specific to be found there. He isn't used to such attention. An immense reservoir of feeling trembles beneath her skin. It overwhelms him a little.

When he's done speaking tears sparkle in the corners of her eyes. "Oh dear, life is so hard, isn't it? But doesn't it also break your heart to think of the world ending?"

He laughs. She's right, the end of the world would be terrible, he's thought that often, but he wouldn't have attributed such a thought to someone like her. "Apocalypse," he says.

She leans toward him, suddenly serious, her sleeve dipping into the greasy beans, her face so close he sees flakes of makeup caked around the base of one nostril, her breasts tumbling forward and converging to make a black hole of her cleavage. He forces himself to not turn away.

"I'm going to tell you something," she says. "I hope you won't think less of me."

"Oh no," he says, but he isn't sure.

"I came here because I was scared of the tornados in Kansas. That's the truth. Kansas is heaven on earth, but those tornados—they're the worst, worse than terrorists. Have you been to Kansas?"

He's never heard of Kansas. He shakes his head, no.

"I hope you'll go sometime—it's very beautiful. Isn't it terrible that it's fear that brought me here? I don't think fear should rule people, but it's ruled me more than I like to admit." She shakes her head. "Earl tells me I'm going to do something important someday, but that's just Earl. He believes in everyone, whether he should or not."

"Earl is—?"

"My minister. Former minister—he's dead now. From a tornado, just like my husband. But we still talk. Oh, I know how that sounds. But he—I suppose you just have to take my word for it. Crazy Patty."

She looks into his eyes again in that gently assessing highly emotional way, and he feels the look pressing on the nerve endings of his cheeks, his forehead, even his eyes, as strongly as if she's reached out and touched his face with her hand. No one has ever seemed to him more kind, less crazy.

29

They sit on the couch in front of a fire with plates of cheesy spinach lasagna, salad, and hunks of warm buttered sourdough bread. Her lids droop. The flame cracks. The lasagna's spicy sauce inflames her tongue. Her exhaustion is overarching, but not unpleasant, as it shuts out any worry, allowing her to feel the pride of accomplishment. She has made herself useful. She could stay here forever in the shelter of Matt's nurturing presence; it would be fine with her if she never went out again.

"No one seems shocked," Matt says. "It isn't at all like the fires. The meteorologists seem surprised, but not shocked."

Insatiably curious, he's been watching the news. The prevailing mood is one of relief. Yes, the water receded more quickly than expected, but no one has suggested anything about it was abnormal. Relief has superseded shock.

"Do you think Diane might have noticed?" she says. "If anyone were to question what happened, she would be the one."

"Maybe it's time to get back in touch."

"But then she'd start telling me what to do again."

"You have the strength now to resist her if need be. And aren't you ready to do more? It seems as if—" He stops himself.

"Right now I'm too tired to think."

The bay is tranquil so before bed they walk to the water's edge which often eases them into sleep, the small waves narcotizing as a lullaby, suggesting rhythms for their bodies to borrow. Their landlady and her husband are just coming up from a walk on the beach and they all stop at the top of the stone steps, greeting each other and chatting briefly before bidding goodnight.

Ruth and Hal are exceptionally hardy for a couple in their seventies. They hike and kayak, and often ride their bikes into town. They bring to mind Matt's own parents, Ivan and Marie, far away in Rhode Island. They, too, are in their seventies, mostly well and independent, though not quite as stalwart as Ruth and Hal. Matt has always been the care-taking son, and a visit to see them is long overdue.

Beside him a shiver shuttles through Bronwyn like a tic, and she links her arm into his. She hasn't complained, but he can tell this recent intervention has wiped her out. When he picked her up at SeaTac this afternoon, her skin was blanched to near transparency; a web of tiny blue veins stood out at her temple somewhat alarmingly, but lovely too, suggesting an interlocking system of miniscule rivers. Her face seemed more chiseled than it was when she left, and throughout dinner she could scarcely stay awake. Every once in a while her eyes drowsed shut and the conversation ceased, then she sprang to life again as if nothing had happened. But, despite this clear evidence of exhaustion, the hot essence of her burns on, the thing he's come to think of as her pilot light is undiminished, and she seems not only content, but downright happy.

They stroll along the sand, allowing small waves to nip their bare feet. The moon is a thin crescent, deferential to the light of the stars and enough to illuminate the beach. Three otters pop from the wa-ter only a few yards away and scamper across the sand to the woods. The surprise rattles through her arm, prompting another full-body shiver. Her body is always taking measure, a human litmus strip and, while he understands her strength, he also feels a parallel fragility. Too many interventions like this could take a toll on her health. It's his job, self-appointed, to make sure she paces herself.

Back at the cabin she changes into a nightgown and follows Matt's lead in checking her email—reception tends to be good on a tranquil night like this. She sits in the dark living room, computer on her lap, listen-ing to Matt pad around in the bedroom, opening drawers, sitting on the bed. One final bounce of the bedsprings and quiet reigns.

The computer seems alive in the silence, its internal humming, its insistent glow, its messages from distant lives. Despite her background as a scientist, she never fails to be amazed by the apparent sentience of computers. She runs through her email, deleting most without even opening. A bunch of ads, promotional notices, a plea for money from her undergraduate college. Her coworker Jackie writes to say she has her first email address ever and is ecstatic to be on-line. Bronwyn doesn't recognize the sender of the next one and almost deletes it, but skims it first. Then she slows herself down, reads it several more times. The words pulse and enlarge and send up a voice that is young and female.

> Dear Fire Lady,
>   I am writing to you from Australia. I saw you on the internet. If you really stopped that fire it was awesome. I wish I could meet you. I hope that movie was real.
>
> I am writing for my dad but he doesn't know. He's not so good on the internet, but he has mana. If you can really do things like put out fires maybe you could do something to save our island. It's really small and it's sinking so we had to move to Australia. But my grandmother is sick and probably dying and she wants really bad to go back to die there. It's her home, she says. I don't know if it's my home anymore.
>
> My dad wouldn't dare say so, but I think he thinks you could maybe do something about it, unsink the island or something. I'm not sure myself. Can you? If you can, will you write back? My dad's name is Analu. I'm Penina. I'm twelve but I'll be thirteen in May. I hope you write back.
>
> Bye-bye,
> Penina

She bats away exhaustion, trying to understand. Who is this girl? The girl's words have leapt off the screen to tramp around in her head, stirring up trouble.

"Are you coming to bed?" Matt calls.

"Could you come here?" she calls back.

He stands behind her and leans over her shoulder, his warm, tooth-brushed breath raining on her ear and cheek. They read silently.

"Mana," Matt whispers. "I've heard of that." He consults his computer and reads aloud. "*From the South Pacific Islands. Power, effectiveness, prestige. Understood to be supernatural.* What do you suppose she means when she says he has mana?"

She shakes her head. She has no idea. In bed they hold each other tightly, more alert than ever before.

Weary as she is, she scarcely sleeps. The young girl stalks through her head all night, not rude, but assertive, staking her claim.

In the morning, despite shrouding fog, they take the kayaks into the bay. The tide is low, but the water beneath their keels lifts them with its muscularity, and they know to take care. Open ocean is not far away. They glide along close to shore, listening to invisible gulls, the clanging buoys, the dip and lift of their paddles. Occasionally a motor passes in the distance. All the while she thinks of the girl in Australia. How can she not help the girl? To intervene with a sinking island would be a challenge of huge magnitude, very likely beyond her ken.

"You'd go all the way to some South Pacific Island?" Matt said over coffee.

"I can't ignore her. How can I ignore her?"

"You don't have to decide now. First recover from the flood. If you go, I go too."

"Of course."

The sun is a peachy stain in the east, it will be hours before the fog clears. The day seems to match the hazed state of her brain. When they return to the cabin she'll try to log more sleep, though she doubts she'll sleep until she can banish thoughts of the girl. What has touched her so much? The dying grandmother? That the girl doesn't know where her home is? That she says her father has mana? That she's so young?

Penina. She pictures the girl's face, round at twelve, the face of a child, the eyes dark and proud, full of enterprise and longing. Penina.

She slips into bed while Matt showers and does last night's dishes, then silence prevails in the outer rooms. She dozes, dreams of the girl standing on an island no bigger than a rowboat, waving her arms to summon rescue.

She's awakened by the weight and warmth of Matt's gaze. Disoriented, she can't tell if it's day or night.

"I didn't mean to wake you."

"What time is it?"

"Almost three in the afternoon."

She smiles. "I think you did mean to wake me."

"No. Well, maybe. I did something—I hope you don't mind."

"What?"

"I wanted to read that email again—I thought it would be okay, and I noticed there was a new email from Diane, so I read that too."

She says nothing, closes her eyes, beckons sleep again, knowing full well it won't come. The mention of Diane precludes sleep. So much history, so much guilt. It's been months since Diane emailed, longer since Bronwyn answered one of her emails.

"Do you want me to say more? We can pretend I never saw it. You can delete it."

She sighs, sits up, is relieved to feel a little more rested. "Tell me."

"She's taken a leave of absence. She's in Greenland."

"You're kidding?"

"I'm not."

"Why a leave of absence? You mean a sabbatical?"

"I'm only reporting what she said. You have to read it yourself."

My Dear Bronwyn,

    I don't know if you and Joe have been in touch, but I hope so, and I hope he's told you of my intention to write. I meant to write sooner, but it's taken me a while to figure out what to say. First, I want to tell you that I am deeply sorry about our rift, and about the pressure I've put on you over the years to be different than you are. Who and what you are is unique and terrific, and not I, nor anyone else, should ever try to change you. I have been saddened that you've felt you had to cut off communication between us, though I think I understand why you have. I hope you might, after all this time, rethink things.

The last year has left me in grave doubt about so many things, about science and scientific research, about my beliefs in general. What you've shown me, of course, has been part of that. Word has spread around the university that I'm a kook and no longer worthy of respect. It's somewhat hard for me to trace the origins of this, but I have tried to tell a few people about you, and that has had consequences. I've been ostracized for some time now. I haven't responded well, to put it mildly. I'm a sociable woman. It's hard to have friends and colleagues turning away from me. After a terrible meeting with the Dean, I decided to take an indefinite leave of absence. I've come to Greenland for a good long think.

Joe isn't happy with me, I know, as I left very abruptly and without much explanation. (I should not bother you with this problem which I must resolve with him.) At any rate, coming here has been very clarifying. I've been living a somewhat monastic life, and getting to know some fantastic Greenlanders who are setting me straight about myself.

A scientist, as you know, should always begin each exploration from a position of not knowing and, though my reputation as a scientist is strong, or has been until recently, the truth is I haven't been the best of scientists, as I've often approached my research from a position of being pretty sure I *do* know certain things and setting out to prove I'm right. Oh my, there's so much about which I haven't been right. I'm overreaching at times, bossy. I know that. I've gone through much of my life trying to be cordial to people, trying to hear them out, but always assuming in my heart of hearts that I know best. Which brings me to you.

I've acted a lot as if you belong to me, as if it's my right to tell you what to do. You don't belong to me. Hah-hah, you will say—when did you figure that out? But let me continue. I know full well that I didn't create you. I can't take credit for your academic brilliance, or the unusual talent you've developed since leaving my tutelage. I hope you can forgive

me for these things and take me back into your heart. You've been such
an important part of my life for years. I've always loved you as I'd love
a daughter. I've always respected you as a thinker and a colleague. And
now I see the ways you've surpassed me in understanding what's important in the world.

I hope our work together isn't done. You've become a beacon for me,
showing me the ways a person can change for the better. I'm trying not
to fear change—I know I'm desperately in need of it.

I've been eating lots of musk ox sausage and reindeer stew and seal meat,
along with occasional halibut and too many Hostess cupcakes. There's
no question that I will return to the US—to Cambridge, to Joe, and
hopefully to you and Matt—changed in both body and soul. I hope to
hear from you soon, see you soon. I miss you.

Love,
Diane

Matt has gone outside, leaving her to read alone. She closes the email
and goes to the bathroom, shedding her clothes in preparation for a
shower. There's a relief in reading what Diane has written, and vin-
dication, but there's something else too. Maybe Diane was too bossy
at times, too sure of herself, but she was also the first person to ever
truly see Bronwyn and understand her strengths as a thinker and potential scientist. It pains her to think of Diane chiding herself alone
in Greenland.

   She stands in front of the bathroom mirror, naked, assessing herself
from the chest up. There's a thin wrinkle scrawled across her forehead,
a new spawn of freckles on her upper chest, her clavicle is more defined. She's not displeased to see these things. She's been through a lot
in the last few years and it should show. Under the carroty orange glow
of the bathroom light she sees sediments of former selves, one psyche
composed of innumerable, ineradicable layers, cloud lover, scientist,

meteorologist, presumed witch, and so much more, all compressed into the no-longer-timid—or much-less-timid—Bronwyn of now.

She steps into the shower and holds her face directly under the nozzle, thinking of Diane and Penina calling out to her at the same time. How she misses Diane, wishes she were here, embracing the fusion of her own multiple identities.

30

As California winter begins to tip toward spring Patty's mind fills with thoughts of the Kansas plains thousands of miles away. She knows what's happening there, sees snippets on TV: Monster tornados have been sweeping through, much bigger than usual and in swarms, some haven't quit for hundreds of miles. The images are pasted across her lids from memory, the cruel look of the sky when the storms gather. "Evil incarnate," Earl used to say. A bright day would turn almost as dark as night, but you could still see the charcoal silhouettes of the roistering clouds. The sky took over everything. Vicious. You could see so clearly how it wanted to inflict damage, delighted in taking lives, longed to destroy what human beings had spent so many years building.

She was right to have left and yet, she hasn't really left, not while her thoughts are so stitched there, not when her dreams take her back almost nightly. She sees the tornados, glares at them, even spits, but she sees other things too, the magical light in the fields, the rainbows, the furrowed rows of dark brown earth. And the people, of course, she thinks of them too. Cora and Bill in particular, but others too. Jobsville is a tight community. When she thinks of the people still there, she feels she was wrong to leave—everyone there is in jeopardy, some will die, and she deserted them to save her own skin.

She thinks of these things even in the happy warmth of a California day, the ocean sparkling like music, everyone on the boardwalk and beach stunningly alive. She sees, but doesn't fully receive what is right in front of her—this is what she tells Felipe. It is mid-afternoon and they're having coffee at their usual place, Figtree's Café by the boardwalk.

Felipe gapes at his new friend. How well she expresses herself, how openly. He might say the same thing if he had the expert command of English she does. His vision is always double here, the streets of São Paulo and its people never disappearing from a corner of his mind; he walks on the beach to rhythms of tamborazo and samba, even when the only truly audible sounds are sirens and skateboards and hustlers haggling; he worries for his city, imagines it blowing apart in his absence.

"Even Earl doesn't know what I should do," she says. "He keeps telling me to wait and see." She squints at Felipe. "You don't think much of Earl, do you?"

He laughs. "No, no, I love Earl. He talks to me too."

Patty eyes him. "You're not serious."

"Very serious."

She isn't sure what to make of him. He's probably baiting her. Their coffee cups are empty. He rises, smiles at the people at the adjacent table so they smile back as if they're friends. He does this everywhere, she's noticed, spreads goodwill and energy over situations as if he's dispensing diamond dust, making the ordinary suddenly better. That has certainly been her experience with him. He has a magnetism that goes beyond good looks. But it hasn't swollen his head.

"We walk," he says and she follows him out, proud to be his friend.

Metcalf—wiry, anxious, film-obsessed—has a few days off from his shoot and has driven them to Topanga Canyon to hike along a high ridgeline trail. What an odd trio they make. Felipe worried about bringing Patty, but despite the rugged terrain, the dust, the afternoon heat, she has surprising endurance. Her face has reddened and she is pumping out sweat, but she has no trouble keeping up, and she appears quite cheerful.

They're all talkers, but Metcalf predominates, telling gossipy tales about people in the film business, mostly stories about stars and directors who have suffered catastrophic decline due to overspending, or becoming arrogant, or falling prey to drugs. Occasionally he interrupts himself to name the vegetation. Live oaks, eucalyptus, sycamores, chickweed, yarrow, pampas grass, vetch, lupine, nettles. He seems to know them all, apparently learned them for a particular shoot on which he was a location scout, though it's clear he has no inherent interest in vegetation, is only showing off. Still, Felipe feels the shameful ignorance of an urban dweller. For all his love of homeland, he cannot name a single Brazilian tree. He wishes Metcalf would be quiet and, at the same time, he feels sorry for the guy—so ceaselessly anxious, so scared about the possibility he might not succeed in film. It's hard to understand Metcalf as a friend of Isabella's, but then she would probably think the same of him and Patty. And of course he's grateful to Metcalf for putting him up for free indefinitely, so he's not going to hush him.

They follow a dirt trail so narrow it necessitates stepping into the underbrush when people pass. Now Metcalf is talking about discovering the director of photography and the lead actress behind a car kissing. He was supposed to be summoning them back to the set, but he hated to interrupt such a moment. When they noticed him, they were horrified, and swore him to secrecy, so now Patty and Felipe must not tell a soul.

Felipe laughs, who would he tell? He pushes Metcalf's voice to the back of his brain to better admire the view. It is unlike any view he's seen, the Pacific spread before them, massive, silver-sequined, dwarfing the city of LA itself. He thinks of his ocean, the Atlantic, that he always viewed at eye level. It was a warm approachable ocean compared to this. But the vegetation here reminds him of *Sampa*'s vegetation, parched leaves tinged gray like moribund patients.

He is suddenly aware Patty is no longer behind him. She's stopped at an overlook. Without notifying Metcalf he circles back to join her, first yielding the path to another trio of hikers. He comes up behind Patty, then hesitates. She might be talking to Earl. But she notices him and turns. "Smell this. It's heavenly."

He takes the bit of crushed leaf and sniffs it. It's a scent he recognizes but cannot name.

"Bay," she says. "A bay leaf. You might use it in spaghetti sauce. But this is so much nicer than what you get in the store."

Metcalf is jogging toward them, his sneakers stirring up cyclones of dust, aluminum water bottle banging his hip, his narrow face aghast, so Felipe imagines he's seen a snake or a bobcat, maybe a bear.

"You won't believe this. You know who just passed? Lyndon Roos! Lyndon Fucking Roos!" He glances over his shoulder. "Should I go back and introduce myself?"

Felipe glances at Patty who shrugs back. Lyndon Roos?

"You guys don't know Lyndon Roos? The vampire movies? They were really big a few years back. She's a major actress. Fuck, I'm going back. Wait here."

Metcalf jogs out of sight again. They laugh, but say nothing as they move further off the path and find a place to sit on an outcropping of rock. Insects he can't name buzz up from the grasses. The heat seems to pulse. Patty's breathing is so slow he pictures her chest as a vast furnace.

"'Oh what a beautiful morning,'" she sings. "I know it's not morning anymore." She grins. "Do you know that song?"

"No."

"It's from a musical called *Oklahoma!*. Very American."

Patty's thin polyester tunic, pink and red paisley, is soaked with sweat and pasted to her bosom. She plucks it away in sections, as if skinning a reluctant persimmon. When she laughs he can't help joining. "Shameless," she says.

Metcalf is back, panting heavily. He takes a seat on the other side of Patty and draws a long slug from his water bottle. "I walked behind her for a while. But she was with two other women and I couldn't bring myself to interrupt. They were talking about women's things—you know relationships and stuff—and one of them seemed pretty upset. I couldn't do it."

"What would you say to a movie star?" Patty asks.

"What would I say? Oh my God, where to begin? She's not just any star. There's history between us. First, when I was a PA a few years back, I had to take a script to her house. She lives like right down there in the woods in Topanga. Amazing place. We could almost see her house from here if there weren't any trees. So she invites me in and gives me tea and all, and you know movie stars, there's like this aura. It was pretty amazing. She's not my type though—too woo-woo. Nothing ever came of it professionally.

"So, okay, you remember the bad fires we had a couple of years ago? Oh right, I keep forgetting you guys weren't here then. But there was one here in Topanga and another big one further east, and there was all this hoopla about how some woman supposedly stopped them, with magical powers or something. Go figure. Well, it turns out this woman that everyone was talking about was the girlfriend of my old college buddy, Matt. He happened to be staying with me at the time and he brought her to my place afterward to recover. I wasn't there, but, well, that's another story—Matt was totally gullible. Bought his girlfriend's story, hook, line, and sinker.

"Anyway, there was this video that went viral and it showed her stopping one of the fires—totally CGI'd, of course. But Lyndon Roos went on Twitter to vouch for this woman, saying she was for real. She claimed the woman had, like, come onto her property on the way to putting out to the Topanga fire. She said the woman was credible. So it caused a big uproar on social media for a while—people saying it's true, it's not true. I'm amazed you didn't hear about it." He shakes his head. "Damn, I wish I could've talked to her."

Patty's breath has become noticeably shallower. She glances at Felipe, her face slack, pale, her eyes engorged and struggling, everything about her disarranged. A heart attack? She's looking at Metcalf now, ejecting sounds, syllables, not words. *Ah. N. Fft.* Could it be a stroke?

Felipe leans into her, lays a hand on her thigh. "Are you okay . . . ?"

The words finally come out on a rush of air. "I know this person. I—"

"You know Lyndon? God, shit, you should have said something." Metcalf is frothing, almost angry.

"Let her speak."

"I know who she is, I think. The woman who stopped the fires."

"You saw the video?"

"No, no, I *know* her."

Patty closes her eyes. Felipe gestures across to Metcalf. *Quiet, please. Please be quiet.*

31

Everything is finally aligned. Metcalf has gone back to work, and Felipe and Patty are alone in Metcalf's bungalow. She knew they had to watch the video alone, without Metcalf's scornful, dismissive presence. They pull the living room blinds and settle on the sofa with cups of coffee, Felipe's computer on the table before them.

Patty feels short of breath, the way she used to feel before taking tests in school. *Relax, you have nothing to lose,* Earl told her, but she can't let go of the nervousness. She wants Felipe to see the kind of spectacle she's seen. She wants him to imagine things he's never imagined before. Most of all she wants to confirm that the Fire Lady really is Bronwyn. Felipe pushes play.

It's an aerial view of a hillside, the right half of the screen covered with fire that plumes and slithers. An unleashed army of snakes, she thinks with horror. The image is shaky, at times blurred, and the woman is only a tiny dot on the screen, but there's no mistaking her; the red hair, the commanding gestures, the tiny body, the ferocity, it's definitely Bronwyn. She appears to be shouting, but the only soundtrack is the chunk of the helicopter's motor and the voices of two pilots, rising and falling in volume. *What the hell is happening? Are you seeing this? There's a girl down there. She's got to be crazy.* Patty is borne away by rapture, a feeling that fills her chest and makes her want to sing and cry at the same time. It's exactly the way she felt watching Bronwyn in Kansas commanding the tornado away. The look of uncompromising dominance was slightly frightening, but it also made her inexplicably proud. As if it was her own daughter out there doing something truly remarkable, something no one else could do. The memories of that day crowd around her again and she wishes Earl were here to see this. If anyone should be proud, he's the one.

It's only four minutes long. When the screen goes to black Felipe says nothing. He presses play again. She can't look. She has already decided she must not try to convince him of anything, he must draw his own conclusions. He plays it a third time, and she gets up for a glass of water.

Inscrutable. The hilltop. The wall of flame. The girl or woman with hair that almost matches the flame. About thirty seconds into the four-minute segment, the blaze begins to retreat; by the time it ends, the flame has shrunk to near-nothingness. If only he could zoom in and see what she's really doing. Her arms are raised above her head, moving rhythmically, as if to conduct the fire like a maestro. He stands up for a moment and mimics her, raising his arms to see how her powerful gestures feel in his own body.

Can she really be quelling the fire? The segment could be computer-generated, but why would someone choose to create such crude footage? He has no idea what to think.

He plays it yet again, a fifth time, then a sixth. Patty has drifted off to another room. On the eighth viewing he keeps his eyes entirely on the woman. Something shifts a little. She almost seems to glow. There's a force at work here, he's not sure what, but glimpsing the glow, his perspective pivots. He sees a tiny opening into what might be happening.

He closes his eyes, wondering how to put all this together. A memory comes to mind of long ago when his life turned unexpectedly on a single night.

He was eleven years old and already fed up with his father's irrational brutality. Always a picky eater, he had not finished his evening meal of *cabidela*, rabbit cooked in its own blood, a food he hated to look at, let alone eat. After a shouting match—his father yelling at him to finish, Felipe refusing—his father yanked his arm, dragged him to the front door, and locked him out. He knew better than to pound and beg to be let back inside. That would only gratify his father. So he began to walk. It was a hot São Paulo night and people were out in the streets, jumpy, seeking distraction from the heat. He hugged the shadows, afraid of being seen. The neighborhood was known for its drug houses, its sketchy people, but being outside on his own was still better than being in his father's sightlines, under the vise of his father's rage, sure to be beaten before he went to bed.

Music streamed from open windows, dance music, snatches of songs. Beer bottles smashed and voices bit at each other like feasting hyenas. He wondered if he should go home after all, creep through his sisters' bedroom window and hide from his father under one of their beds.

From a window above him, two or three stories up, came the sound of a woman singing. It stopped him short, this music full of longing. It anointed him like warm rain, more beautiful than anything he'd ever heard in his life. It entered his body and filled his blood and made him sway and turn in slow circles. He ducked into an alleyway where he could move with no one noticing, no one telling him to stop. He was so used to being told he was in the wrong place, doing the wrong thing, everything about him was wrong. He fell asleep in the alleyway, drifting off to the sound of the woman's voice, and when he woke at dawn the tunes were still in his head, and as he walked he sang what he remembered, substituting the words: *I am Felipe, I am fine. I am Felipe, I am fine.* He stretched the words so they matched the melodies and he made his way home, knowing things would be different now. Having heard such beauty, his life had to change. It was shortly after that, he heard the call of dance.

He hears Patty seating herself on the cushion beside him. He opens his eyes. What can he say? He isn't sure what he saw, but he's eager to learn more.

32

The hours of day lengthen noticeably, connecting Diane to the Earth's orbit around the sun in a way she has rarely, if ever, experienced so viscerally. Of course she *understands* the way the Earth moves on its own axis and around the sun, but it has never appreciably affected the way she has lived her life until now.

She begins to rise earlier with the lengthening day so when Aka knocks for coffee, always with some donuts or cupcakes, Diane is dressed and the coffee is ready. It is not uncommon for two hours or more of chatting to elapse before Aka rises to attend to her duties. Her responsibilities are far-reaching in their scope, including not only the shopping and cooking and childcare duties Diane first imagined, but also meetings with a citizens group that is trying to improve the schools; plumbing and waste system repairs in her three rental houses, including Diane's; and, when needed, assistance to her husband in unloading his catch. Having noticed Diane's uneaten fish in the trash, she brought another freshly caught fish wrapped in newspaper and taught Diane how to debone it and cook it, using an *ulu,* a special Inuit knife used only by women. Twice she fixed a problem with Diane's bathroom ventilation system. She has taken Diane out kayaking on the bay and, in preparation for their expedition, she hefted the kayaks on her shoulders a hundred feet or so from their racks down to the waterside. Diane has also learned that Aka is one of the few people of Upernavik who speaks, in addition to Greenlandic, Danish, English, a little German, and she aspires to learn some French. Seeing Aka's multiple talents makes Diane feel her own skills to be appallingly narrow.

Since hearing about Edel, Diane has been eager to meet the girl.

Many times she's caught sight of her hurrying down the hill and disappearing quickly from view, a lean black-clad figure. One evening they encounter each other when delivering sewage bags to their pickup point at the same time. The girl drops her bag and retreats a few steps but remains there, watching Diane with curiosity or judgment, Diane can't say. The girl's clothing looks inadequate for the evening's chilly temperature. Diane, always cold here, wears down mittens and a heavy sweater beneath a long hooded down coat. The girl: tight black jeans, short black jacket yawning open on a T-shirt stamped with the image of a howling face, atop her head a flotsam of black green-tipped hair, bare hands.

"Hi," Diane says. "I'm Diane. You must be Edel?"

The girl nods. In the twilight it is impossible to discern her attitude, but whatever it is, it makes Diane nervous. She drops her bag hastily and the knot slips open, threatening to release the bag's content. "Eee gads!" Diane says, seizing the bag again to avert disaster, yanking off her mittens. Trying to reknot the heavy plastic with cold bare hands she is stupidly clumsy, made more so by Edel's unreadable gaze.

After a moment Edel steps forward to help and quickly seals Diane's bag with deftness born from years of practice.

"Thank you so much. I'm such a klutz."

Edel says nothing, but offers Diane a mixed-meaning smile taken directly from Aka's playbook. It is only when Diane is back in her cottage replaying this encounter does she remember that Edel does not speak much English.

The next day, out on the bay in kayaks, water smooth as mercury beneath their keels, Aka pulls alongside Diane's boat and takes hold of the gunnel. "And so—is this okay? You help Edel with English. You are professor."

"Well, I've never taught English before. But I could try."

"You make her laugh."

"I do? Why? Because I'm such a klutz?"

"Your coats. You wear so many coats, she says. She sees you go down the hill."

"Oh yes, I suppose I do look funny. I can't get used to this cold."

They bob there, gazing out to the mouth of the bay where ice floes circulate in an inscrutable pattern, bidden by currents beneath the surface. Diane is reminded of the ducks in the pool at the Boston Public Garden, how seeing them paddle here and there she always wonders about their governing intent.

Something alive glides into view a few feet from their boats. No, it's too inert to be alive. Aka extends her paddle to push it away. "Dead seal," she says. "Sick." This, Diane thinks, is a woman well acquainted with death.

No specific appointment is made. Edel simply arrives on Diane's doorstep one evening after dark. Diane was already hunkering down in her bedroom with a glass of wine for a night of reading and fending off the recurring existential terror, and she's already inserted earplugs to mute the howls of the dogs, so it takes her a while to hear the knocking. Fortunately, she is still clothed. She answers the door expecting Aka and is not entirely pleased to see Edel at this hour—she isn't prepared yet to teach English, let alone finesse a social interaction.

"You and me?" Edel says.

"Of course. Come in."

Edel steps into the kitchen and looks around.

"Can I get you something?" Diane asks.

Edel doesn't respond. She is considerably taller than Aka, Diane notes, and her tight black pants emphasize her height and relative leanness. A lavender sweatshirt hangs off one shoulder and is deliberately styled with holes around the waist to reveal bare skin, a fashion Diane recognizes, as it is *de rigeur* among her MIT students. Diane studies her, trying to understand what makes her so alluring. Her face is round and a smooth brown, like Aka's, her mouth full-lipped, her eyes inviting to those with the right password.

"Would you like something to drink?" Diane mimes drinking. "Coffee, tea, water. I don't have soda."

She opens the refrigerator as if she'll discover something she doesn't know she has. She has left the wine bottle, an acceptable red, on the kitchen table. Edel points. Wine? She's only fifteen. Diane is well aware that in these parts people drink at a young age whether or not they should. Alcoholism has become a big problem in Greenland, and Diane has seen evidence of this on her walks, men in various stages of inebriation yelling at each other down by the harbor. She wants to say to Edel *I must ask your mother,* but understands how this will set them on the wrong footing. She fetches a jelly glass from the cupboard and pours it half full, then she recovers her own goblet from the bedroom. When she returns to the kitchen Edel is already sitting at the table drinking her wine, peering out from the cave of her adolescence to see what the world holds.

Diane sits, feeling woefully unprepared not only for the teaching task she has taken on, but for how to approach this reticent green-haired girl. The undergraduates she teaches are young, but not this young, and they are more predictable, having chosen to go through the necessary hoops and hurdles an elite science education requires. Over the years most of them—there have been thousands certainly—have been largely pandering, wanting to enter the world of science but nervous about measuring up, seeing her as holding some kind of key. Diane does not know Edel, but her first impression is that she panders to no one, inhabits an island of her own, is unmoored to any world beyond Greenland, and possibly not even moored here. But Diane cannot begin to imagine how Edel spends the hours and days of her life now that she is not going to school.

Tomorrow, Diane decides, she will make up some kind of a teaching plan; for now chit-chat will have to suffice. Edel's glass is almost empty but Diane refrains from filling it.

"Aka tells me you like music. You're in a rock band?"

"Rock band," Edel echoes.

"What instrument do you play? Guitar?" Diane mimics Aka's air guitar.

"No guitar."

"Oh." Did she misunderstand Aka?

"Sing," Edel says.

"You sing? Wonderful. What kind of songs do you sing?"

Edel stares at Diane with a blank expression that makes Diane feel foolish. It is the rare person who has the capability to make Diane feel foolish. There is something uncanny about Edel.

"Greenlandic," Edel says.

"Greenlandic songs?"

Edel nods.

What would make this conversation easier? More English verbs would be useful. Pronouns. Prepositions. Diane once heard about a language teaching technique that relied largely on prepositions as a way of elucidating the relationships between things and people: between, around, about, during, within. Am I *on* Greenland now, or *in* Greenland, she wonders.

"Why you come?" Edel says. "Here."

Diane laughs. "Good question. Why did I come? It's hard to explain." She pauses. It is such a direct question, a perfect question really, but Diane is still asking it herself and failing to come up with an adequate answer.

Without thinking she pours them both more wine. Edel nods her thanks. Diane decides not to worry yet about what she'll say to Aka. "I guess you would say I had problems. Problems I needed to work out."

She searches Edel's placid face to see if she has made herself understood. The stillness of the girl's entire countenance is unnerving. Diane is accustomed to conversing with people whose faces are like slot machines, pinging with responses whenever a coin is inserted. As she watches Edel she gleans something she missed earlier, a thrumming beneath the stillness. Diane's understanding has been wrong, an error in the paradigm. Like not seeing the speed of the ice sheet's melting because most of it is happening beneath, while the surface remains more or less intact. Edel's mind is hard at work parsing what Diane has said. If they were conversing in Greenlandic she would probably have plenty to say.

"Problems. Now. Far. Away," Edel says, enunciating so each word retains its importance.

"Yes. Exactly! They're far away. That doesn't necessarily solve them, but I can maybe think about them more clearly when I'm away. Maybe." She pauses. "Is that too many words? Am I saying too many words?"

"No. I also. Go. Far. Away."

"For school?"

"No school. Only life."

"You would like to go to Denmark?"

"Denmark. Or America."

"To sing."

"Yes. Sing."

"I don't suppose you'd sing something for me now?"

"Sing now?"

Diane nods.

Without further prompting, as if this is precisely what she came here to do, Edel closes her eyes and, remaining seated, begins to transmute herself. Her torso expands, her neck elongates, she lifts her head and a voice issues forth in a song unlike anything Diane has heard. The lyrics are Greenlandic which Diane cannot begin to comprehend, but the emotions are nevertheless clear, swooping from sorrow to defiance back to sorrow. Occasionally Edel's voice is so deep and guttural it almost sounds male, and Diane realizes this is the haunting voice she's been hearing on sleepless nights. Every once in a while, Edel raises her elbows to her waist and extends her arms in a gesture of pleading, eyes still closed. Everything about the performance takes Diane by surprise, the display of emotion, the obvious talent, the fact that Edel is able to transform herself on a dime from rebellious teenager to soulful singer.

When the song is done Edel opens her eyes and Diane feels as if some kind of benediction is in order. As if Diane has channeled Bronwyn, a gust of wind rears up from the bay hammering the cabin and sending tremors through the walls. Pellets of hail follow, clacking loudly against the windowpanes. Edel and Diane both laugh—the timing could not be more perfect.

"Marvelous," Diane says. "Truly impressive."

Edel, fully acquainted with the vocabulary of praise, cracks a full-blown smile. "And so—" she says.

Diane watches as the girl heads home, ducking under the pummeling hail, cutting nimbly over the lobes of smooth icy rock separating the two houses. It's a relief to see her disappear safely inside.

Diane retreats to her bedroom, but is much too restless for sleep or even reading. Her mind is fraying, undone by the building storm and Edel's song which lingers as an enigmatic murmur in her blood. Snow has replaced the hail and it whirls at the windows, resembling radar images of cyclones. It is quieter than the hail was, but the volume of the moaning wind more than compensates, afflicting the entire house with a palsy so the front door creaks and the windows seem to be on the cusp of shattering; the table and chairs chatter, as do the glasses and mugs in the cupboard, along with the pots on the stove. The bedroom window usually allows for a view down to the harbor, but now it is a frenzy of white. The entire house offers no more protection than a tent.

She would be fine if it weren't for the sound. The wind's descant is indistinguishable from a woman's scream, but it doesn't mask the howling of the chained dogs, furious about being left outside to the vagaries of the weather. And intermittently, there's a rumbling, the lowest tone of all. Can it really be a calving iceberg, in such cold? It feels to her like a Greenlandic earthquake.

She wishes Edel hadn't left. Solitude doesn't suit her now, not with so many inexplicable sounds at large, and not in a dwelling that feels so temporary, so fragile. She tries to move Edel's song from her bloodstream to her vocal cords, without success. The wind ululates as if protesting something, the sound of someone wronged.

Diane thinks of Aka telling her about the *qivitoqs,* the half-dead creatures who are reputed to come stalking after dark, people who were abused or banished in life and are now seeking revenge. It's only folklore, Diane knows, but knowledge doesn't banish the fear.

The lights flicker, then expire. Blackness obliterates everything except for the hopped up dance of the snow. She fumbles around the house to see if she can see light coming from any of the other houses. Aka's house is dark, as is the house of the old man who lives above them. Has the whole town gone down?

She imagines Aka's family huddling together in one room, keeping each other warm and happy, chatting and singing, unafraid. If she were to go to their house she's fairly sure they'd welcome her, but she cannot possibly traverse the smooth icy boulders in this wind and snow. Furthermore, she would feel like an intruder. She misses Joe desperately. He may not be the bravest man himself, but his humor would be helpful. She misses Bronwyn too—Bronwyn would be able to call this storm off.

The storm continues for close to twenty-four hours. Diane does not sleep for more than an hour or two. She busies herself making guesses about the wind speed and temperature. She peruses her Greenlandic (*Kalaallit*) dictionary wondering which words the residents of Upernavik would use to describe this storm. Contrary to popular urban myth, there are not a hundred Inuit words for snow, but there are still quite a few. *Pirsuq* meaning "snowstorm," might be appropriate, or *qanik*, meaning "falling snow."

At nine the following morning, still dark, the storm still raging, Aka pays a visit to see if Diane is okay. She brings a container of musk ox stew and apologizes as if the storm is her fault. "You okay?" she says. "You are not freezing?"

Diane makes a show of laughing. "Not freezing yet."

When Aka leaves Diane calls out, "I'll call if I die," and Aka turns and gives her a puzzled look and Diane realizes her joke either didn't come across or was in terribly bad taste.

At close to 11:00 p.m. of the second night the snow dwindles then stops, and the wind recedes, and the sky clears. Stars flock the sky and a nearly full moon paints a wide swath of light down to the tranquil water of the harbor. A single dog barks then even she hushes. After the clamor of the storm the abrupt silence is dizzying. Diane listens, waits, incapable of moving from her perch at the window, vision glazed from sleeplessness, body numb, half expecting the wind and snow to resume.

At first she thinks she's dreaming. A band of green flares up from the horizon like a fast-growing fire. It streams across the landscape in plumes of red, pink, purple, fanning out like flowers bursting into bloom. Vectors of light stack up into spires, into multi-colored skyscrapers, pulsating, flickering, swirling. Patterns but not predictable ones. Solar winds disturbing the Earth's atmosphere.

The show continues for forty minutes and, tired as she is, she can't turn away. She has never witnessed this, for all her traveling. She has friends who have structured entire trips around seeing the Northern Lights, a reason for travel Diane always found frivolous. When she knew she was coming here the Northern Lights never crossed her mind.

How short-sighted she has been. The display is nothing short of spectacular. She feels like an early human hundreds of thousands of years ago, picturing this for the first time with no science to explain it, no understanding of solar flares and charged particles and atoms and electrons and photons, knowing only that there are mysterious forces in the world much larger than any human being, forces that must be noticed and honored. No wonder Greenlandic folklore explains that the Northern Lights are the souls of dead children playing ball with walrus skulls. *Arsarnerit,* the ones playing ball.

Only when the last flicker of green subsides does she give in to sleep.

33

The east coast has thawed, the snow has melted and, but for puddling in low-lying areas, there are few visible remnants of the punishing winter. Matt and Bronwyn have spent the last few days with Matt's parents in Rhode Island and now they're driving north to Cambridge, Massachusetts to see Joe, anguished Diane-less Joe, who solicited this visit. Bronwyn has never spent time with Joe without Diane present. He has always been in the background when Bronwyn's been around, playing the supportive, laid-back novelist spouse, the perfect companion for Diane and her opposite in so many ways. Bronwyn has always appreciated his humility, and felt great ease around him, but she doesn't know him very well, and it's hard to imagine how this visit will unfold.

But now, driving, Matt at the wheel, the visit with Ivan and Marie still occupies her mind. It was a fine visit by most measures, Ivan hearty and joke-cracking, he and Marie both delighted to finally be meeting Bronwyn. They took walks on the beach, prepared a number of memorable meals, listened to Ivan's favorite arias. Matt played the good son, happily following the conversational lead, but Bronwyn felt terribly awkward. There was so much she could not discuss. She reflected aloud on what it was like to live on an island in the Northwest, and about her job as a waitress at the Dockside, but she and Matt had agreed beforehand that she would not divulge anything about her most important characteristic. Matt thought it was ill-advised to tell his parents everything on a first meeting. *Hey Mom and Dad, meet my new girlfriend, and by the way, she can change the weather.* Once they got to know her a little, he said, then they'd say more.

As a result of this restriction she could not relax for the entire five days they were there. Her skill has become central to who she is; it is why they're living on the island; it is how she met Matt in the first place. It has become her organizing principle, an inseparable part of her identity. When Marie asked about what she did before they moved to the island, she floundered; she mentioned her PhD program and the meteorology job, but was unable to find a credible explanation for why she left them both. So many things currently preoccupying her mind were off limits for discussion: the flood, the emails from Diane and Penina, the disturbing climate conditions all over the world. For the entire visit she felt inarticulate as a novice speaker—and like a terrible fraud.

"If we go to the South Pacific to help Penina, will we tell your parents why we're going?"

Matt turns to look at her. "You want to go?"

Let me think about how I might help you, she wrote back to Penina, to keep the connection alive, not committing herself, but buying time. "I'm leaning that way, but I know it would be expensive."

"I can take care of it. My dad gave me a check. And maybe I could get the journal to give me an assignment there."

They drift again. The sound of her ringing phone, a monastic chime, is hard to recognize in the mayhem of Boston traffic. The chiming doesn't stop, and she rummages in her purse. She doesn't recognize the area code, wipes the call away. The only calls she answers routinely are those from Matt, and he's right here with her.

As soon as she restores the phone to her purse, it rings again. Same number. She cancels it again. The third time the chime starts up she stares at the screen—who is being so persistent? "Just ignore it," says Matt. But curious, she answers.

"Yes?"

"Bronwyn? This is Patty Birch. Do you remember me? It's been a long time. I'm Earl's friend."

Yes, she remembers. Of course she remembers. Rotund Patty who cried at the drop of a hat and worshipped Bronwyn in a way that was very unsettling. She's the person who called to inform Bronwyn of Earl's death. "What a surprise. How are you?"

"I've moved to California. I couldn't take another tornado season.

I'm fine, but it's not the same here, you know? I'm a Kansas girl and I miss it like crazy."

"You grew up there, didn't you? No wonder you miss it."

"But the reason I'm calling is because I saw you on the internet— that video of you putting out the fire. My friend from Brazil, we saw it together and we just couldn't believe it—I'm so impressed. Well, I *could* believe it because I saw you do the same thing with the tornado, but honestly, I— You know Earl has been telling me to get in touch with you for so long. Now here I am, finally."

"Earl? But I thought—wait, you mean Earl's not dead?"

Matt is gesturing at her to get off the phone. She raises a finger, just a minute.

"Oh no, honey, he's dead all right. Still dead. I miss him all the time. But we talk, you know? He's so supportive."

"Please," Matt says urgently, "I need directions."

"Oh, Patty, I have to go, I'm in the car. But I'll call you back, I promise." She disconnects, stirred by memories. A vivid picture comes to mind of Patty singing hymns in Earl's living room, emotions, like an effluent, swimming over her skin.

"Turn here," she tells Matt, "Memorial Drive."

To step into Joe and Diane's house is, for Bronwyn, to step back in time. She has always loved this old Colonial—or is it Georgian?—just off Brattle Street in Cambridge. For so long it was like her second home. Inside it is spacious, and rich with jewel colors and shabby elegance; outside there's a deck and a fenced backyard with lilac bushes and a single apple tree with a swing. Some of her best ideas have arrived on that swing. Back in college she was cowed by this house, its long history and urban gentility. She had trouble saying much at Diane's department parties, or even in smaller groups around the dining room table, but over the years she found a way to relax here (at least at times when Diane wasn't actively pressuring her), and now she's pleased to see not much about the house has changed.

Joe, tousled as ever, greets them with bear hugs, as if they're all intimates. He crows at Bronwyn's dyed-black tresses. He's made turkey sandwiches and broccoli soup, and he urges them to sit, and they take places at the dining room table where she has sat as a visitor so many times before. It is all so much the same and yet, without Diane, whose presence always commandeers a room, entirely different.

"So, Diane—" Bronwyn begins, but she's stopped by Joe's arresting palm.

"Not yet. I'm not ready yet." He looks down, directing the full force of his confusion and sadness into his green soup. So they speak of other things that also must be shared—of their new lives on the island, Matt's job, Joe's upcoming novel, and, as always, the violence and extremity of recent weather.

"We might go to the South Pacific," Matt says.

"Oh?"

"A girl wrote to me," Bronwyn says. "Her island is sinking. She wants me to do something to save it."

"Could you?"

"I don't know, it's definitely a different kind of challenge—much bigger. But I can't ignore her. She's only twelve. She saw the video."

"I'm glad to hear you'd consider it," says Joe.

Bronwyn grins. "Are you Diane's stand-in now?"

Joe grins. "No, I promise. No advice from this camp. I've always said it's your gift to use however you want."

After lunch Matt stays at the house to work remotely, while Bronwyn and Joe go out for a walk. They stroll along the Esplanade by the Charles River, absorbing the balmy weather. Spring is barreling down aggressively. The days of late March have been warm and the soil is loosening, the spines of the trees rediscovering their supple stretch and bend, their buds plumping and reddening. The birds have begun to trust the earth's beneficence, and their eyes have let go of glassy winter panic. Sculls skim silently by on the Charles as if powered by thought.

So many times Bronwyn and Diane have walked together on this same path brainstorming, Diane's red sneakers clomping loudly, like a metronome for her brain. She seems to be here now, ghosting the space between them, and Bronwyn tries to resist the feeling that this is some kind of memorial walk for someone they'll never see again.

"She wrote," Joe says. "An actual letter."

"She wrote to me too—an email. Just recently. She said she hoped you and I would be in touch."

"She's going through something I only partially understand."

"I think I'm responsible. I know I am. I shouldn't have cut her off as I did. But she's so forceful that I didn't know what else to do. I haven't answered her email. I wanted to find out more from you first."

"Don't beat yourself up. She had her role in it, I'm sure. It's always a two-way street. But she left so suddenly it's hard not to feel it has more to do with me. I still have no idea when she'll be back. I haven't written a single new thing since she's been gone."

She'd like to tell Joe that Diane's departure had nothing to do with him, but how could she possibly say this with assurance. They always appear to get along beautifully, but who really knows what goes on in private. "She won't say when she'll be back?"

"She hasn't so far. Things got bad at work. She doesn't even know if she wants to do science anymore."

"What else would she do? She's all about science."

"That's what she's wondering. I'll show you her letter. I haven't gotten a snail mail letter from her since—I don't know when, years ago. I love letters. The paper. The handwriting. They're such precious artifacts."

Starlings pass high overhead, silent as the sculls, filling the sky in raggedly elegant formation.

"What do you think of her idea that you could teach?" Joe says.

"What do you mean?"

"She didn't mention it to you?"

"No. Teach what? I never got my PhD."

"Not academic teaching, teaching what you do. Your skill."

The starlings are pinpricks now that quickly vanish to nothing, flying somewhere entirely beyond the reach of her retina, joining all the other things that exist but can't be seen. How could she ever teach what she can't even describe in words, something that was never taught to her in the first place? The only model she has for teaching is the university model, Diane's model, authorities professing, lecture-style, occasionally in seminars. She's a practitioner of something, but she's not an authority. Isn't authority always established through words? "Don't worry about it. Especially if she hasn't said anything to you. It's a new idea of hers. You know Diane and her ideas."

Back at the house Joe hands her the letter. "Let me know what you think." She takes it out to the deck to read, settling in one of the Adirondack chairs, touched by Joe's openness.

My Beloved,

I'm ashamed of myself. Please don't think that any of my rude selfish behavior in the last couple of months has anything to do with you. That couldn't be further from the truth. You must believe me. I've been thinking about you so much, rattling around in our big house, probably wondering whether I've lost my marbles, or if I'm filing for a divorce. It isn't that—well, maybe I've lost a few of my marbles, but I'm still essentially myself, and I'm definitely not filing for a divorce. And now that I've emerged from the worst of it, I had to get in touch with you. Guilt was getting the better of me. I adore you and I hope to be home soon and I hope you can forgive me for keeping you in the dark so long.

I've always wanted to save the world with science. I really believed I could, but now I don't know. We scientists live on our own little island and what we have to show the world, well, the world often just doesn't want to see or hear. Our facts, especially in climate science, lead to the unsettling conclusion that human beings are blind, or murderous—or both. I find myself frightened by the virulence of humans.

Being here where my life has been so stripped down, so simple and unbusy, I've begun to wonder if I have a life as a scientist anymore. Science discovers facts, but it doesn't hold answers as to what human beings should do with those facts. Human life is a muddled, complicated enterprise that we scientists don't always like to contemplate. Greenpeace, for example, thinks no one should be killing seals because they're heading for extinction (science), but hunting seals has been the Inuit way of life for years. Seals, reindeer, musk ox, polar bears—they're all central to survival here. And survival here isn't easy, it's an unbelievable challenge. When the killing of seals is restricted, the more people turn to Hostess cupcakes. You know the problems with that!

At any rate, being a scientist, at least in the way I have been, doesn't excite me as it used to (sometimes it even feels vaguely immoral). Maybe everyone gets to my age and loses a little career drive, I don't know. Of course Bronwyn discovering what she can do has prompted some of this self-searching—it's made me question my fundamental assumptions about how the world works—but I think it would have happened eventually even without her.

This is a bleak and beautiful place. I have coffee every morning with my landlady, Aka, and I'm teaching English to her fifteen-year-old daughter, not exactly my strong suit, but I'm trying. We've all become good friends. Remarkable people, I wish you could meet them. People here are expert listeners. They give their all to the art of listening without making you feel you're wasting their time. I've spent a lot of my adult life shouting—maybe not literally shouting, but I've done a lot to make sure my opinions have been heard. As a woman—a woman in science in particular—it's always seemed important. But I've done enough shouting—now it's time for me to learn to listen.

The long and the short of it is I have to find some new way to navigate the rest of my days. What it will be I can't say yet, but you must know I hope very fervently that it will include you. Can you forgive me for this recent spell of mine? The early years of my life don't begin to compare in joys and love to the years I've spent with you. I can't even imagine a life without you. You know I'm not given to overstating my emotions— believe me when I say I adore you. There I am, unvarnished!

I hope you're well and not too furious at me. Have you begun your next novel? Maybe you'll allow me to go on book tour with you in September? Please tell Bronwyn I'll be writing her too. I'm not ready to ask anything of her yet, except forgiveness, but I've been hoping she might consider trying to teach what she does. But that's another long discussion.

Take care of yourself, my dearest.

Passionate love,
Your humble servant,
Diane

She folds it up, moved and slightly embarrassed to be privy to such a personal document. There is such love between them, not just felt, but expressed. She's never seen this side of Diane, the lover, the contrite uncertain woman, the woman on the verge of disavowing science. The Diane she's always known has been defined by certainty, and unflagging commitment to the scientific method. The teaching—why didn't Diane mention that in her email?

They dine at the Harvest Restaurant so Joe won't have to cook, and again they avoid talk of Diane. There are too many questions about her that none of them can answer, and both Bronwyn and Joe are haunted by how they've hurt her. Instead Bronwyn tells about the flood, how she worked to get the water to recede, but slowly, so as not to draw attention.

As Matt talks about his parents, Bronwyn's mind wanders to Diane's letter and its suggestion that she teach. She isn't Diane's acolyte any more, she need not pay attention to what Diane thinks she should do. But she paid close attention to Diane for so many years the habit is hard to break. Diane's suggestions in the past were usually worthy of investigation. *The virulence of humans,* the letter said. Bronwyn has long thought poorly of humans, but Diane always seemed to think people were, on the whole, good. She appears to have changed.

She thinks of Patty Birch's peculiar phone call too. She remembers Patty clearly, but hasn't thought of her for a long time. Earl, on the other hand, often comes to mind. He was such an unlikely friend, religious man that he was, but he took her in and believed in her skill.

She wishes he were still alive. That Patty talks to him is enviable and completely crazy. She'll have to remember to call Patty back.

She and Matt bed down in the guest room. The last time they were here they were new lovers, fresh from Siberia, taking careful note of each other's habits, sexual preferences, favorite foods, keen on learning about each other from every possible source. The ease between them now is something she has never experienced with anyone, something she could never have imagined for herself when she was in her twenties. What a find he is: the gentle way he laughs at her when she's obsessed or overly serious; the talent for listening that makes him such a good journalist; his synthesizing intelligence; his nimble body and convoluted hair. So many men out there would have been scared away by her gift—she daily reminds herself she must never take him for granted.

Recently she has not been sleeping, beginning with her first sightings of the strange woman in the tuxedo. The woman was a hallucination maybe, but one bearing a message Bronwyn knows she can't ignore.

She slips out of bed so Matt doesn't notice. Outside the dark brings on a particular sentience. Her consciousness is corralled by the rustling of urban fauna, raccoons bushwhacking through back yards, the creeping of mice, birds hopping along branches. And more. Tires on asphalt, the ticking of clocks, the pinging of bedsprings all over Cambridge. She sits on the bottom stair of the deck, absolutely still and more sounds arrive, the distant flutter of wings and fins, the tapping of livestock hooves, vapors merging into clouds, currents of rivers, ocean gyres, beneath it all the roiling tumult of magma; above, the exploding sun. Some nights this receptivity brings cacophony, some nights music.

She crosses the yard to the swing, settles into its cradle, and pumps with the singular focus of a child, thrusting her feet forward, arcing head and neck back, wind whooshing past her cheeks as she rises and descends through darkness. The rhythmic movement carries thought, and each rise and fall of the swing hones the thought, and after a while the thought assumes a clear shape.

34

They're back on the deck in the morning with coffee, and she puts forth her proposal. It's another incomparable spring day, suspiciously warm for the calendar date, but impossible to revile. What if they were to go to Walden Pond, and she were to try to teach them? They could bring on a light shower perhaps. Or even snow. Just briefly. Under the radar. Nothing she couldn't quickly undo. The two men stare at her uncertainly.

"But I thought you said you had no idea how you'd teach anyone," Matt says.

"I don't, but I want to try."

Matt looks dubious under the dark cap of his sleep-rumpled hair. "But why? To what end? Just because Diane suggested it?"

"No, not that—I understand *why* she suggested it. I'm only one person. I can only be in one place at a time. If I could teach people . . ."

Joe remains silent, thoughtful, but Matt resists.

"You'd unleash a terrible power. Not everyone would be as responsible as you are. This is what you were thinking about when you weren't sleeping last night, isn't it?"

She doesn't answer, didn't think he'd noticed her absence, and definitely didn't expect this pushback. "Joe?" she says when his silence has gone on long enough to be notable.

He stares out to the shadows by the back fence and speaks quietly. "I wouldn't mind trying."

"Really?" Matt says. "I don't know. I really don't know."

"Well, let's all go," she says, "and you can try if you want and watch if you don't."

Joe says Walden Pond will be too crowded on such a sunny day, and suggests instead a drumlin not far from Walden, a glacial deposit that isn't high but offers an unobstructed view in all directions. By the time they park the car Matt is on board, loathe to be left out, she thinks, wanting to be as game as Joe.

They hike twenty minutes to the top and gaze out over the scrubby, rocky New England landscape, winter-brown meadows, deciduous trees with barren branches, spikey against the pale blue sky. It couldn't be a more perfect place to practice, especially since there isn't another soul in sight. The look of the landscape is wintry, but the feel of the day is that of languid East Coast summers, warm, high humidity, meandering cumulus clouds.

"One at a time," she says. "Who wants to go first?" Joe steps up. "Let's bring on a light shower."

Now what? What was she thinking last night? She has no strategy for teaching. "Face west," she tells him, without knowing why, except that it's morning and it would be unpleasant to face the sun.

He stares out, arms penciled by his sides like a first grader intent on doing things right. Matt has retreated behind her, and she tries to eliminate him from her mind.

"Now what?" Joe says, turning back to her, his blond hair riffling on the slight breeze, his serious face the picture of unusual innocence and frightening receptivity.

"It's mainly a matter of concentration. You're trying to move energy from inside your body to outside. First, get a picture of what you're trying to achieve—you need to keep that firmly in mind—then begin to generate heat, I can't say how exactly, but as I begin to do it maybe you can feel it and imitate me."

He nods as if she has said something useful and faces west again. She steps behind him. He is so much taller than she, broader and thicker, so all she can see is his back. She lays her hands on his shoulders, cautiously at first, aware of the intimacy of touch, aware of Matt watching somewhere nearby. She palpates the striations of muscle and bone pressing through Joe's corduroy shirt, feeling out of her depth. There is only instinct. She thinks of arctic terns migrating thousands of miles each season from one hemisphere to the other, often to places they've never been. There's a parallel instinct in herself.

She gathers her heat, inching it from stomach and chest to head. His body rumbles a little, an engine warming. When she places her ear on his back his breath is a roar. She encourages her heat across the fabric into his dense flesh and muscle. After a moment of resistance something softens, yields, allows her heat to flow through him. In unison they rock back and forth, symbiotic, pouring their pooled heat down over the hillside then up, up, up. He heaves with the effort. The sky's blue becomes gunmetal gray and, after a time she cannot measure, a light shower begins to fall.

His body goes still, his face slackens, his mouth hangs open. "Fuck no. Did I do that?" He turns to her, grinning, speechless. They embrace. He did it—they did it together. He hoots skyward, his call wolf-like. He opens his mouth to the rain.

Matt has sidled into view, shaking his head in Joe's direction. She sees anew how short and wiry Matt is beside Joe's larger, bulkier body. It should be easier to teach Matt, she thinks, since they are already conduits for each other's energy. "Are you ready?" she asks.

"Ready as I'll ever be. Shut up, Joe."

Sheepish, Joe hushes himself.

She intended this to be experimental and fun, but she knows no way to impose such an atmosphere. "Okay, let's stop this rain before we get soaked. You heard what I said to Joe? Concentrate and keep your intention firmly in mind. Think about generating as much internal heat as you can."

What passes through Matt is hard to name. A helix of fear, dread, jealousy. He'd like to back out, but pride prevents that, and part of him wants her to do with him whatever magic she wrought with Joe.

He steps up to where Joe was standing, turns west as Joe did, and feels her glide behind him, a wraith, her hands weightless on his shoulders. She is almost not there at all. No moment marks a beginning, and yet something is coming over him, a sudden heat that flows across his back, spreads to his buttocks, his neck. At first it feels cold, a second later it's brutally hot. He lurches, rights himself with a few quick steps.

She needs to give him more instruction—he has no idea what he's supposed to do.

The heat cuts through his jacket and shirt, singes his bare skin, hopping up all his systems. Could this kill him? Is this what she did to Joe? "What am I supposed to be doing?" he growls.

"Concentrate," she rasps, sounding not at all like herself.

He feels as if they're sparring animals. He tries to picture a clear sky, but his vision is blurred. A sharp pain cuts across his lower rib cage.

"Stay with it," she whispers.

The pain is almost unbearable. He sees nothing but gray, cannot begin to imagine blue sky. His chest breaks a sweat. Nausea softens his limbs. He bows his head. "I can't take this." He steps away from her, drenched with rain, drenched with the dizzying slop of failure.

She remains where she is, ignoring him, fully dedicated to the business at hand, concentration impermeable. The sky begins to lighten to its former eggshell blue, the rain ceases, and the lazy day resumes.

"Are you okay?" she asks, coming toward him, laying an arm on his shoulder, peering into his face.

"I feel like shit."

"Take a break. I know how exhausting it is. We can try some other time," she says.

Exhausting? He would use a stronger word, like *life-threatening*. "Good going," he says to Joe. He might be a failure, but he's not a poor sport.

Joe lies on his back in the grass, pale and obviously spent. "She did most of it."

"Some, but not all," she says. "Next time we'll see if you can do it on your own."

Next time. Matt knows there will be no next time for him. Maybe he could learn if he stuck with it, but he doesn't *want* to learn. What he felt was terrifying—it was as if he was offering himself up for a dismemberment from which he might not return. He isn't the same as she; his boundaries aren't so porous. Much as he loves her, he likes staying in his own skin.

Joe doesn't want to feel nervous, but he does. He was the one who insisted on trying again, despite his exhaustion from yesterday, despite his awareness that Matt is still in a funk. They have driven all the way to New Hampshire, to a beach she used to frequent and loves. He can't turn back now, despite his second thoughts. He thought he'd rid himself of this particular performance anxiety—he didn't feel it so acutely yesterday—but having one success under his belt makes the pressure worse. It's intruding on his bodily functions, shortening his breath and making his heart race as they walk to the point.

"The beach," she says, "is ideal for teaching, I think, because so many of the Earth's forces converge here. You see the rock and sand, the horizon, the water, the clouds, the sky. You feel the wind at work. You can see your whole canvas."

He isn't sure why he's so invested. Maybe he wants to prove something to Diane? At any rate, here he is, feeling the way he felt for the better part of his two years as a premed student. He was studying physics and chemistry and math and biology with geeks for whom the science was a snap, people who aced the tests without even studying. The knowledge they summoned stuck close at hand, like sand they might reach out to grab at any moment for a castle accruing height. For him it took real work, hours of cramming, sequential all-nighters to retain the moment's pertinent information, and even then he only pulled out low Bs and Cs. He was like Sisyphus, learning the same equations again and again, forgetting the elements, or one of the laws of thermodynamics, or a critical stage of the Krebs cycle. Finally he had to conclude that maybe medicine wasn't for him. Maybe his mind wasn't structured like a doctor's mind. But in laying that dream aside, hard as it was to give up, he was able to discard so much of his anxiety.

They walk until no one else is in sight. The offshore wind is ferocious, grabbing the collar of his jacket and scarf, abrading his eyes. They stand facing seaward.

"Shall we try doing something to soften this wind?" she suggests.

He'll do whatever she says.

They begin as they did the last time, Bronwyn behind him resting her palms lightly on his shoulders. "Remember, the clue is to concentrate," she says and he hears his high school chemistry teacher: *Memory is nothing more than concentration.*

Her heat enters him and floods his torso, traveling up his back and into his chest. The task feels so amorphous. He tries to concentrate, but what is he supposed to concentrate *on?* The entire landscape seems to be flogging him, the wind, the waves, even the seagulls sound assaultive. And the heat feels downright dangerous. What if he melts? Explodes? He feels a kernel of anger he knows is misplaced. It was *his* idea to be here, not hers. He understands why Matt has foresworn this.

Gradually, something shifts. The movement on the outside seeps in and takes hold of his interior, as if he himself has become the thunderous wind. His eyes close. When he tries to open them he can't. He's losing himself, being sucked into the atmosphere, into space, dispersing into billions of particles. But no, he feels certain body parts more acutely than ever, his feet planted in the cool sand, his knees about to buckle. Wavering, he thinks he might fall, but doesn't. When did the world become so loud?

Her hands are no longer on his shoulders.

"Joe?"

He opens his eyes. The air is dangerously still, the wind's invective absent and every other sound vacuumed away with it. He has never experienced such silence, such disorientation. Where are the gulls?

"You did it!"

"I did?"

"Yes. I did hardly anything to help. Now breathe deeply, get your energy flowing again." She places her arm on his back, exuding something he can't name. It is part heat, part encouragement, part sympathy, many things entwined, like one of those untranslatable words he loves—*saudade* from Portuguese, *goya* from Urdu, *kilig* from Tagalog. In this case it's the embodiment of all that is good and all that is unattainable. She could be a child or a crone. He tries to receive what she's offering.

"Next I want you to reset things as we found them—get the wind going again. This time entirely by yourself. Are you ready?"

She wears a look he can't decipher. Is she mocking him? Does she really think he can do this on his own? Without her hands on his shoulders, he hasn't the slightest idea how to start. He keeps expecting someone to round the bend, find them here as the culprits who are stirring up trouble. Would an officer of the law arrest them? Is changing the weather a criminal act?

She stands about fifty feet behind him, out of his sightlines. He has no idea where Matt has gone. He stares out over the sea, motionless as if embalmed. He locates a single point on the horizon. Is this concentration? He's no longer sure. His mind is certainly not at rest, not as it is when he writes. Perhaps that's the state he needs to summon, the writing state, a kind of trance. He waits, his vision clouding, trying to access his writing mind. His gut acids churn. His chest bulges. His entire body seems to enlarge, as if busting out of a sheath. Is that a touch of fledgling heat? Blood shoots past his arterial walls, his ganglia have never been so alive. He bears witness to every active molecule of his being. "Thrust!" she calls out, a command he intuits more than hears. He does his best rendition of thrusting, a propulsion that begins in his flanks, migrates to belly, sternum, throat, then fulfills itself in the tidal fissure behind his eyes. His whole body is gored by the effort. He can't continue. He drops forward, rolls to sitting. There she is, beside him.

"Look! You did it again! Feel!"

Following her example, he brushes his palm against the air where a light wind vamps. Inconstant, nothing at all like before, but still something. He should feel elated, he supposes, but he's mainly exhausted. He has never done such a difficult thing.

35

She's glad Matt sleeps for most of their flight home. She needs to gain some clarity about what happened in the last few days. Something has been set in motion, but is it good? Matt is depressed about himself, and they left Joe in a terrible state of exhaustion, too tired to get out of bed or even eat. She should have taken things more slowly with him—she would have if he hadn't been pushing so hard. Perhaps they should have postponed their flight, but Joe insisted he'd be fine on his own after a day or so of rest.

Despite these things, she knows something now she didn't know before. She was able to teach Joe. She *can* teach. He performed an intervention on the beach without her assistance, and this fact cracks things wide open. Diane was right: She can impart this skill, not to everyone, but to some. She wishes Matt hadn't gotten cold feet. But it makes some intuitive sense to her. He's more of a rationalist than Joe. Joe, as a novelist, passes much of his time in the labyrinths of his imagination.

The thought of others learning to do what she does ignites her with hope. If others could do interventions alongside her, she might not feel so alone, so uniquely responsible. Could she develop a team of people like herself who could judiciously begin to heal the Earth? Who would these people be? They'd have to be imaginative, fluid thinkers with loose boundaries and little stake in appearing rational. How could she locate such people?

She thinks of her awful meeting with Vince Carmichael, the meteorologist and tornado expert who was once her hero. He mentioned a Kickapoo woman who claimed to be able to influence natural forces. Could she be found? Bronwyn doesn't know the woman's name, and she's certainly not about to ask Vince—it's doubtful he would know anyway. But that woman doesn't need Bronwyn's teaching. Who else then? Who might help her locate such potentially teachable people?

The plane begins to descend over the snowfields of Mt. Rainier, awash in the saturated pink light of sunset that spills into the ravines, tinting the snow, the trees, even the rocks. It occurs to her in a flash—there's no need to look further, the people she needs have already come to her.

36

Diane's days begin to fill in ways she couldn't have expected when she arrived. For the first time in years she does not awaken with thoughts of science in her head. Most mornings start drinking coffee with Aka. After that, if the weather permits, she takes a kayak out, with or without Aka, for a spin around the bay, obeying Aka's stern command not to go too close to the icebergs which do not necessarily give warning when they are about to collapse. Diane has become a familiar figure to the fishermen and dock workers, and they always exchange waves and greetings. In the afternoon or evening Edel stops by, ostensibly for English conversation, but Diane senses she comes primarily for something else, prompted by a peripatetic curiosity, as if in visiting Diane she is making a claim on a new life for herself. She has moved beyond her initial shyness so she now moves freely around Diane's two rooms, picking up Diane's iPad, her notes, her books, examining them and asking questions. Diane is not offended by this as she would be at home—it seems absolutely right, especially for a curious girl of fifteen. Diane, having always been a responsible teacher, started to develop a "curriculum" for teaching Edel, but quickly abandoned it in favor of undirected conversation. Sometimes she jots a few notes for Edel to take home—the conjugations of various irregular verbs like *to be, to have, to get*—but has decided that written English is secondary to the conversational English Edel needs.

"Better than school," Edel said to Diane once, and Diane glowed with the unexpected flattery.

"I write a song," Edel tells Diane one day. "In English."

"Wonderful," Diane says.

"You hear band play my song?"

Diane takes the rickety staircase, icy since the snowfall, down the hill
to the town's center where Edel's rehearsal is being held in the concrete
block community building with an empty hall that resembles a shabby
school gymnasium. Edel and her three other band members are setting up, plugging in amplifiers, setting up microphones and a small
percussion section, including a snare, a xylophone, and a hand drum.
The two men and one woman, about Edel's age, possibly a little older,
are all dressed in the same uniform of black jeans and leather vests
over matching red and yellow T-shirts.

Edel nods to Diane in greeting and comes to stand beside her, suddenly shy in this new context and unwilling to engage in direct eye
contact. The other band members amble over too, friendly but also shy,
and names and handshakes are exchanged. Orfik, the most proficient
in English. Malik. Doru. Diane.

"Welcome," Orfik says. "We are glad you came. We like to sing for
you."

They return to their instruments and a long preamble of strumming and tuning and chatting in Greenlandic follows. Diane retreats
to a seat on the floor, back against the wall. Orfik sets down his guitar
and trots out of the room, returning with a folding chair which he
places directly in front of the group, beckoning to Diane. She must
seem elderly to them, she thinks, taking the chair gladly.

A few other people of various ages, relatives of the band members
perhaps, amble into the room, some carrying folding chairs, and they
assemble near Diane, greeting her with nods. It is good to have others
present, comprising an official audience so Diane does not have to be
the only one responding. She is not well-acquainted with contempo-
rary youth music and does not feel comfortable being placed in a position of judgment.

The informal nature of the occasion shifts suddenly, and the session begins with a nod from Orfik, the group's ostensible leader. The
first song begins with a solo guitar which becomes a guitar duet, then
adds the two vocalists, Edel and the percussionist, Malik. Their voic-

es are forceful, almost strident and, while Malik sits as he sings, Edel struts, lifting her knees, swinging her arms, raising her chest. Malik occasionally stops singing and focuses on his drums, ceding the melody to Edel. The polyphony of voices and guitars fills the hall with a sound Diane would have to call rock music, but it is not like any rock music she has heard in the US. The strong vocal line reminds her of a women's Slavic chorus she once heard in which every song seemed to be drawing a line in the sand, announcing the end of nonsense.

When the song ends, the motley audience claps, and the band members nod their thanks. Then the group segues into more serious performance mode, as if their audience numbers not eight but eight hundred and their venue is not the all-purpose room of a shabby community center, but Carnegie Hall itself. Orfik introduces the next song.

"A friend of ours died. Kunnana. She was not happy and she wanted to die. There are many like Kunnana—too many like her. And so— Edel and I, we write a song for her which we will now sing."

The song commences with a guitar duet, a contrapuntal call and response between the two instruments. They seem to be posing questions, limning a problem. This conversation gives way to a single legato guitar, an invitation. Picking up from a lone fading note Edel decants her song. Her voice soars through the room, engulfing everyone, ardent and forceful as a king tide.

> People say the quivitoq took you away
> But it is not the qivitoq, *not the qivitoq*
> It is your heavy heart.
> *Heavy heart. Heavy, heavy heart.*

It's a lament, a hymn with repeated spoken words interspersed, lending it a ferocious insistence.

> Hope squeezed away, dried up, drowned
> You know the ice will not hold, but still you go
> And it breaks like your heart
> It breaks under the weight of your heavy heart, heavy heart.

You go the way of the polar bear and the fish
The narwhal and the whale. Gone. Extinct.
Not a fairy tale, not the qivitoq
This is real—you are gone. *Gone. Gone.*

Edel, microphone in one hand, raises her broad face to the ceiling, a plea, a communication to the universe, to all departed souls. She is summoning spirits, and they arrive in numinous waves and oscillating currents that circle the small audience and raise goosebumps on Diane's neck, causing an involuntary shudder. Diane is unusually aware of herself in the act of listening, an activity that employs her entire body, not only ears, eardrums, brain, but the length of her spine, her ribcage, and abdomen, the muscles in her legs. It occurs to her that this is how Bronwyn has been listening all along.

Now Edel assesses her small audience, takes a few steps forward, and thrusts her arm out, gaze centered on Diane.

Come back. Come back. We miss you. Come back.
All the heavy hearts come back.
Bring the world back to life
Bring the animals back to life.
Let the people have light hearts
Bring back the light hearts

Come back. Come back. Come back.
Let the people be happy.

Song done, Edel retreats back to the group while the guitars strum a few final elegiac notes. She hangs her head through the clapping.

Diane is overcome. She already knew Edel was good, but she did not expect this, the direct words, the soaring music combining oceanic sadness with confrontational strength, the force of Edel's voice, and her confident stage presence. She has had intimations of Edel's talent, of an uncanny power in her, but she didn't expect to feel so bewitched. Hugging Edel, she knows whatever she says will be inadequate.

"Many people should hear this." There is so much more to be said, but she cannot, yet, begin to say it.

37

Penina arrives home after Analu has gone to work, guilty, knowing Vailea has missed their private hours together. Nalani pops to the door, and Vailea, usually glued to the sofa, hefts herself up to join them.

"You have a letter," Nalani says, holding it out.

"It has your name on it," Vailea says.

Penina turns the envelope over and over, examines the stamp. She's never gotten a letter before, but she knows who it must be from.

"It's from America," Nalani says. "Open it, please. We're dying to know what it is."

Penina examines the handwritten return address. Just as she expected: B. A. Bronwyn Artair, the Fire Lady. They've been exchanging emails, and Bronwyn asked for her address. She hasn't told her family—they wouldn't approve of her having email conversations with a stranger. She glances up at the expectant faces of her mother and grandmother. They lean in as they do on birthdays, as they do for all celebrations, their enthusiasm pressing too hard, like suffocating scarves. She jerks back from them, hugging the letter to her chest.

"It's private," she says. She has never invoked her right to privacy, not with her family. Heat sponges her face.

"Twelve years old. What private do you have?" says her mother.

"It's my letter. Addressed to me."

She drops her school bag and elbows past them to the patio where a single weak light bulb flouts the oncoming darkness. Her mother and grandmother are watching her through the kitchen window. White moths circle the bulb. They have no interest in Penina, but their disinterest seems like protection. She loves their soft wings, their love of flight.

She bends to the letter, wanting to savor the surprise of it, prolong the mystery. Whatever is in this letter could change her life. She coaxes the seal apart slowly, so as not to rip anything. She slides out the inside paper and unfolds it. Something slips to the ground. She reaches down, hand and heart fluttering. A check in US dollars made out to her. *This is to cover your airfare and your father's. We'll be in touch. We can't wait to meet you both and do some good work. Best, Bronwyn*

Her mother is gone from the window, but her grandmother is still there, her dying face tranquil as ever, waiting for news.

PART TWO

Emergence:

A process whereby larger patterns and regularities arise through interactions among smaller or simpler entities that themselves do not exhibit such properties, so that a system becomes more than the combination of its parts.

38

They caravan north over the rocky soil of New England, past glacial eskers, drumlins, monadnocks. The woods along the highway are not in full foliage, the pale greens still mingled with brown. It is an unassuming beauty here, scraggly, craggy, a beauty of reticence, folded in on itself, to some unspectacular.

Bronwyn Artair, Matt Vassily, Analu, and Penina Tuati ride in one car; Joe Donahue, Patty Birch, Felipe Delgado in the other.

Squantum, Merrimac, Massabesic. Shame from the past imbrues the landscape with apparitions.

In the back seat with his daughter, Analu remains quiet, watching the pale, green-eyed woman who has lured them here, wondering what will become of this long journey. He cannot picture where they are on the globe, or where they are headed. He has been in the United States for four days, staying with Penina in the big house with Joe and Bronwyn and Matt, and then Felipe and Patty arrived, but he is still spinning through space, dizzy with travel. What a leap of trust it took to get here. He would never have agreed to the trip if Nalani or Vailea had objected, but they wanted him to come, encouraged him. What did he have to lose? they said, they would be fine on their own. It was Penina who tipped the balance. Her glum mood had lifted. The check was made out to her! How could they *not* go? What if they really could save the island?

"Dad look," she says, and Analu follows her pointing finger to a carved totem pole. He nods, appreciating her ready enthusiasm, thinking that though she is his strong daughter, almost thirteen, she is still so young.

Pembroke, Winnesquam, Passaconaway.

They turn off for gas. Tumbledown cabin motels. VACANCY. KIDS WELCOME. Lawns splayed with disassembled motors. Wrecked cars. ANTIQUE MART 50% OFF. SENIOR DISCOUNTS.

Patty, in the front seat of Joe's car, cannot get enough of looking. She has never been to New England before, and it couldn't be more different from Kansas or Los Angeles. Strange as it is, it feels right to be here, the curving gray road ahead could be the Yellow Brick Road itself, transporting them all to something unknown, something they need. She is so happy Felipe agreed to come. He had no reason to trust in her belief in Bronwyn, but he was game. As it turns out, Bronwyn is even more intense than she remembered, even without her red hair, and she senses Felipe is registering that intensity too. She turns to him in the back seat and winks. When she faces forward again her voice produces spontaneous song that sails through the car and beyond, sowing the landscape with scraps of her yearning soul. *"This land is your land . . ."*

Joe smiles. Who knew she had such a voice?

Felipe had no idea there would be so much water here. Water appears around corners, in gullies. Streams, ponds, sudden lakes. Ponds called lakes. Lakes called ponds. Streams called rivers. It astounds him. Excitement flickers through all his limbs. If Bronwyn can do what Patty says she can do, it will be wonderful, but even if she can't he likes being away from LA, away from one-note Metcalf, here with these new people. Joe Donahue with the gentle smile, seething green-eyed Bronwyn and her wry boyfriend Matt, timid Analu and his fiery daughter. And, of course, his pal Patty. Isabella was right to urge him to travel. It's good to see new places, and if—when—he returns to São Paulo, it will be with invigorated eyes.

Arethusa, Attituash, Ammonoosic. They work their way north.

Penina squeezes her concentration and pitches into Bronwyn, trying to situate herself inside that small body. She expected Bronwyn to be bigger and bolder than she is, but it turns out she is small and shy. Her hair, red in the fire video, has been dyed a less-pretty black. Where does the magic live in this small person? Maybe in her bright green eyes? Penina has decided to watch Bronwyn carefully.

They exit onto the Kancamangus Highway for a picnic on the Swift

River. The river, true to its name, is full and fast from recent snowmelt. It thunders over boulders, cascades into deep pools, eddying, ricocheting, casting up a fine spray. Its roar makes talking difficult.

Bronwyn assesses the group she's assembled to teach as Matt and Joe lay out sandwiches and cookies and iced tea. Analu's watchful attention to his daughter. His sun-darkened face. The exhaustion he does his best to hide. The repose of his callused hands. Penina's labile energy, her long black hair, burgeoning breasts, skimpy skirt. On the cusp of womanhood, but still just a girl. Patty seems happier than when Bronwyn last saw her. Though she tears easily, her tears are less those of the sorrowful than those of the easily moved. And Felipe, what a find. Lean and fit, stretching and moving at every opportunity, he breathes deeply, at home in his body. She was not surprised to learn he's an actor—he possesses the necessary magnetism and dark good looks.

Penina and Felipe have scampered down to the river and are removing their shoes. Analu stands above them on the bank, eyeing his daughter, fisting his hands. Penina wades in, shrieks from the cold, and Analu hurries down. Something stops him abruptly—Felipe's gaze. The two men regard one another.

"I watch her," Felipe calls over the water's roar. "Okay?"

Analu hesitates, nods, says something Bronwyn can't quite hear, and retreats up the bank.

Camp Clearwater, owned by Joe's college acquaintance Robert Gorham, sits on the shores of Ponsett Lake, near the Maine border, not far from Canada, well north of the touristy part of New Hampshire. It is a shabby unreconstructed mid-twentieth century relic, no internet, no flush toilets, only the lodge and craft house wired for electricity. When they first visited over a month ago, the structures all looked aggrieved, dark and mildewed and calcified with a fabric of pine needles, spiderwebs, mouse droppings (which they've since cleaned), but the beauty of the location was irrefutable. The lake's clarity and serenity. The sandy bottom and rocky shoreline. The low blue mountains in the distance. The fragrant pines. It is an undomesticated beauty, a beauty without any evidence of human tampering. Even the structures—lodge, ten eight-person cabins, craft house, boathouse, outhouses—seem to vanish into the landscape. Bronwyn knew almost immediately it would be the perfect place to teach, a place of serenity and silence with little interposing itself between them and the Earth.

They told Robert—an overgrown Boy Scout of a man; not, Joe said, a fluid thinker—that they wanted the camp for a writer's conference, and he gave it to them for a small fee to use during the first two weeks of May, well ahead of the camp season.

At the end of the rutted dirt road the trees seem to part only for them, unveiling the lake as a secret. They peel themselves from the cars. The day has cooled and twilight has begun to ease in. The air is a tranquil pale purple, the water so still it mirrors trees and mountains. A lenticular cloud of textbook perfection is centered above the lake. Numinous stillness presides.

They amble to the water's edge, admiring the view. After a few minutes Bronwyn—hyperaware of this moment as a beginning—corrals them to action, unloading luggage, handing out flashlights, distributing linens and blankets for the guests, sleeping bags for herself, Matt, and Joe. She assigns cabins: Analu and Penina in one, Felipe with Joe, Patty in a cabin of her own. She and Matt will share another cabin. Organized, she surprises herself. Not since she was an on-air meteorologist has she been called upon to be so practical.

Matt and Joe, who will be in charge of the cooking, ferry bags of groceries to the lodge. Bronwyn leads the others along the path to the cabins. A simple pasta dinner will be served at six thirty.

Here they are. The task is clear. Though there is plenty of uncertainty, she feels an unexpected spike of confidence.

Penina insisted to her father that she's fine alone, so now she stands on the dock breathing in the peace. She's never seen an inland lake before, and she's never understood water could be so quiet. It's a stillness that has a distinct smell, different from the ocean. Blue mountains drowse like lazy cats in the distance beyond the far shore. How far across is it? One mile? Two? Could she swim it?

Small birds flit along the water's surface and disappear as if sucked into the air. Bugs draw circles, rippling the water like perfect little artists. A shadow of a large bird lofts overhead, but it's gone before she can see the bird itself. She could stay here forever watching the busyness beneath the quiet. The oval cloud that was centered in the sky earlier has grown lopsided and begun to melt into the darkening blue.

Her father has told her she's here only to witness—he's doing the learning, she's too young—but Bronwyn never said that. Penina doesn't see what being young has to do with anything. She's here, isn't she—and she's smart, a quick learner. If there's magic to be learned, she's going to learn it.

She likes the grownups. Felipe, Joe, and Matt. Patty who loves to talk and mysterious Bronwyn. Joe said he'd take her with him when he goes to the store for more food. She's glad she came, aware of her life taking an important turn just when she's about to celebrate her thirteenth birthday. As if to second her thought, a fish pops up briefly, snags a bug, and flops back underwater. For a moment she's hijacked by a memory of the island at nightfall, quiet like this, but a different kind of quiet. Her father keeps asking her if she misses the island, but she doesn't think of it very often, not when there's so much else right in front of her.

The single bunks are narrow so Bronwyn and Matt bed down across from each other, a lacuna of dark air between them. She buries deeper into her sleeping bag so only eyes and nose are exposed to the chill. She needs sleep. Exhaustion has been her companion for weeks, along with insomnia, but how can she sleep now, on the verge of so much?

The night is vigorous with sound: bats under the cabin's eaves, raccoons crashing through the undergrowth summoned by the smell of human refuse. There are deer out there and moose and maybe bears, Robert told them. She finds it comforting to be in a place with so many animals.

All her life she has found human engagement to be the most challenging aspect of her life, but the interactions involved in arranging this gathering have been surprisingly rewarding. She has enjoyed communicating with Penina and Analu and Patty, explaining what she hopes to do and enlisting their involvement. Perhaps she is finally evolving into a more social person.

Still, fatigue and the lizard-brain of night are nibbling at her boldness. Has she promised too much? Trying to teach Joe and Matt was hardly a raging success—both have sworn off attempting any more interventions. What if, having brought Analu and Penina and Patty and Felipe from so far away, the results are no more successful?

A pressure on her shoulder. Matt's arm has bridged the dark and his hand kneads her arm lightly through the sleeping bag. "I know you're worried, but try not to be. It's going to be fine, whatever happens. Even if it doesn't work."

How well he reads her. "I wish Diane were here. She's the real teacher."

"You don't need her."

But she does need Diane. For over a decade Diane has been present at the major junctures of her life, including the death of her mother. Diane always has good advice—Bronwyn might not have gathered these people to teach them if Diane hadn't suggested it. What would Diane say now? She'd say a scientist must forge ahead with the work and not be focused on outcomes. She'd say that the desire for a particular outcome taints the investigation.

She pictures the others bedding down in their cabins nearby and hopes they aren't too cold, too scared of the dark, too disgusted by the primitive latrines. An owl hoots. The same species—Great Horned— she used to hear at her cabin on the Squamscott River further south.

"He followed us," she whispers.

Matt's smile scythes a path through the dark. What an unpredictable turn his life has taken since he met Bronwyn. Mostly good, though not entirely. He adores Bronwyn, and they are suited as partners in so many ways, but being with someone who possesses such an exceptional talent isn't easy. It makes him question the value of what he has to offer. This must be how the spouses of celebrities feel. He has not, for most of his life, suffered from lack of self-confidence. He knows his strengths—his gift with words, his ability to listen to and draw out his interview subjects, his talent for loving—but these are the talents of a normal human being, whereas Bronwyn's talent is truly exceptional. She is, so far, one of a kind. Joe has told Matt he feels somewhat the same in relation to Diane, who is such a star in her own world. Joe is a very good writer, but he's not nearly as well-known in his field as Diane is in hers. Over the years he has had to learn how to maintain his self-respect while also being a supportive husband. He does a remarkably good job, but he's been working at it for years. It helps Matt having Joe to confide in.

. He gets out of his narrow bunk and slides in beside the wand of Bronwyn's slight body. All her nerves are astir. "No worries," he says, stroking her hair. "It's going to be fine. You're going to do exactly what you came here to do. And everyone is already getting along, which is great. Penina's a hoot, isn't she?"

"I wish I'd been as brave as she is when I was her age."

"I bet you were in your own way." He has often wondered what Bronwyn was like as a child, whether her difference from others would have been visible. She has no pictures of herself—not like his childhood which was recorded by Ivan and Marie ad nauseum—but he can easily imagine her at Penina's age. Quiet and receptive and glowing, a smaller version of what she is now.

"It's so interesting to see Patty again. When I saw her at Earl's house almost two years ago, it was kind of awkward, because she wanted to, you know, almost worship me."

Matt pinches Bronwyn's cheek. "Like me, you mean?"

Bronwyn chuckles. "But really, she seems different now. More down to earth or something. Anyway, I like her. Felipe too—what a lucky find."

"Are you worried about Analu? He seems somewhat—anxious?"

"I think he's just shy. Like me in a way. I think he'll be receptive to being taught, if anyone is."

"Receptive to being taught. You probably thought that about me too—before you tried."

"I wish you'd stop being so hard on yourself. It isn't like riding a bicycle. And everyone doesn't need to know how to do it." She pauses, and he feels her adroit irises investigating him through the dark. "Maybe you'll try again?"

Something flares in him. "No." He withdraws his arm. "Don't." The edge of something ugly gruffs his voice. He cuts it off, falls silent. "I'm sorry. It's just—" More silence. "Look, remember how you always resisted Diane's pressure to act. You've resisted my pressure too. And I've stopped pressuring you, haven't I?" He's no longer harsh, only firm. "Please return that favor."

She sits up and palms his cheeks with both hands. "I'm so sorry. You're absolutely right."

"We all have our paths and this isn't mine."

"Of course. Of course." She brings her face within inches of his. Her fingertips travel through his scalp, quivering with contrition. He could never be mad at her for long.

Chilly, Analu draws the blanket up to his chin and listens to his daughter's light snoring. He thought she might be afraid of the dark here, but she fell asleep immediately. He envies her easy access to sleep, her quick adjustment to this new place and new people. His own body, after being transported so quickly over so many miles to so many different places, is too disrupted for sleep.

The night is scribbled with animal sounds. An owl hoots at regular intervals, and twigs snap under the strutting hooves of a deer. It soothes him to listen, to sense the close proximity of creatures, even unfamiliar ones.

He has loved traveling with his daughter for the last few days, hearing her speak on and off of school and friends, the talent show they'll be putting up soon. He tries not to say anything that will close her up and turn her back into the little scorpion she's been of late. Once, in the airplane, when all the lights were dimmed and everyone around them was sleeping, she had her head on his shoulder, and she lifted it and whispered, *Dad, do you think I'm good enough? Good enough for what?* he said. A stretch of silence passed. *Never mind.* She lowered her head again, closing her eyes. *Of course you're good enough,* he said quickly, but it was too late. As she reclined there sleeping—or probably not sleeping—he went over and over the exchange, realizing he should never have said *Good enough for what?* which implied there *were* things she wasn't good enough for. When the lights went on again and she sat up, he went overboard reassuring her. She turned her head to the window, not wanting to hear. It made him terribly sad. She is so beautiful, so passionate, so capable of anything.

Today driving up here, he knew she wanted to shed him and be here with these people by herself. The thought of losing her to the world this way is unbearable—not the way he lost Heni and Ipo, their bodies gone, but their essences and love still belonging to him. With Penina it is her spirit that seems to be drifting away, her love evaporating. It's too much: his mother dying, the island sinking, Penina turning away.

At the bottom of his bed something moves, and he shifts his feet, and a mouse creeps up the length of his body to greet him, and its soft inquisitive nose and thread-like whiskers bring him solace through the dark.

39

Bronwyn, happy to have slept well, stands alone on the dock, veiled by a cool mist. There is no up or down, only the encompassing sac of gray, and she loses herself for several minutes, merging with the vapor, forgetting for a moment who she is and why she's here. Awareness returns slowly, plucking from the mist a spectral sense of the dead: her mother, Earl, and others too, strangers who have lived near here, all bringing obscure messages, their meaning indecipherable as the silent blinking of stars.

She turns and finds her students gathered around her as if sprung from the mist, Patty in a folding chair, Felipe and Penina dangling legs in the water, Analu on his haunches. A mourning dove coos from the roof of the lodge where Matt and Joe are cleaning up breakfast. She wishes for sun and warmth, but the wish alone does nothing, and right now an intervention is premature.

"You slept well?" she asks.

Maybe tonight, Analu thinks.

"Oh yes," says Patty.

"Can we go swimming?" Penina asks. "Felipe and I want to go swimming, right Felipe?"

"Well, we like to swim, yes. Sometime. Maybe not now?"

"Yes, now!"

"Penina," Analu warns.

Bronwyn hesitates. Should she let them swim or keep to her plan? She glances toward the lodge, wishing Matt were here to weigh in. "It's very cold."

"I like cold," Penina says.

"Okay, why not," Bronwyn decides impulsively. "I'll get some towels."
Felipe hurries off to his cabin to fetch his trunks.

"No towel for me," Patty says. "I won't be swimming."

"Why not?" Penina demands. "It's fun."

"Well, I'm ashamed to admit I don't know how to swim. I just never learned. There wasn't much water near where I grew up and well—"

"My dad can teach you. He taught me, right Dad?"

"Oh," Analu says. "It takes time. Maybe later?"

"Thank you, Analu. I might just take you up on it."

"I'll show you, Patty." Penina plucks off her tiny skirt, rolls her halter top up over her luscious brown belly, and dives in. Hooting at the chill, she strokes out, oblivious to the wreaths of mist. "See Patty!" she calls out. "This is how!"

Patty laughs. "I see!" She turns to Analu, who is clearly not happy with what he has witnessed. "Your daughter is delightful. Kids always help us sort out what's what, don't they?"

"She doesn't like to obey these days."

"Some days I'd prefer not to obey too," Patty says.

Bronwyn goes to the lodge for towels, slightly alarmed that things have so soon left her control. When she returns to the dock Felipe is there in tiny orange Rio-style trunks, his clothes in a pile on the grass. He stands at the edge of the dock, tall and lean and perfectly proportioned as Adonis, readying. His dive slices the water without the slightest splash or sound, and he strokes out, long arms wasting no energy, to where Penina treads water. She splashes him and he splashes back and soon they are trying to dunk each other, screaming and hooting. Both nimble, expert swimmers, neither prevails.

"It's okay," Bronwyn reassures Analu. "We have time. And she has energy to burn."

Felipe and Penina swim back to the dock after ten minutes, and Patty helps Penina dry off. "You'd better put a sweater on or you'll catch your death."

Penina laughs. "Catch death. I'm going to catch death? Is death like a ball?" She can't stop laughing.

"A figure of speech," Patty says.

Analu is ready with some dry clothing for Penina and the purple down jacket Joe purchased for her in Cambridge when he saw she didn't have anything warm. Felipe goes behind the boathouse to change back into his clothes, adding a fleece on top. Bronwyn has the strange sense that all this human movement and cooperation is being orchestrated by some force outside herself. She is reminded of Matt's parents moving about their kitchen, preparing a meal in perfect concert with each other, and she suddenly realizes that this spontaneity is the perfect prelude to what she has planned.

"So, let's begin." She clears her throat. "Welcome. Again. I've been thinking of you all as potential doctors of the Earth. Healers." She pauses, shrugging off a flicker of self-consciousness, the words sounding too ponderous after the earlier playfulness. Then she forges on. "You all have specific local weather and climate issues we're going to address, but . . ."

She hesitates again, imagining people in the houses and cabins along the shore listening in. She could so easily be seen as a heretic. This gathering already feels subversive; it started to feel that way when they didn't tell Robert, the camp owner, of their true intent. Her gaze roves across the faces. Analu still looks tense. Felipe hugs his knees to his chest, chilled but receptive. Patty nods. Bronwyn has no idea what they know and don't know about climate and science. They're here because of their sensitivity and intuition, not their knowledge.

"These first few days we'll be doing various things to prepare for the hands-on work that will come later. First, we'll introduce ourselves and do some exercises in order to find ways to tune into what the Earth is telling us. You'll learn to listen with your body. Think with your body." A wire of cold, beginning in her pinky, expands to electrify a meridian from neck to heel. "Are you all warm enough?"

Nods all around so she forges on. "We tend to think thoughts that are regulated by the culture we live in, its demands and expectations. But our bodies aren't so acculturated. They're more linked to the Earth, and it's been my experience that my body is more capable than my mind of reading the Earth and knowing it and responding to it . . .

that's the kind of reading I hope to teach you . . . a kind of listening really. Corporeal listening. Listening with the body."

She and Matt have discussed these things a little, but primarily she has thought about them. Spoken aloud they sound different. Are they true? "Does this make sense?"

"Oh, yes," says Patty.

Analu nods. Felipe nods. Even Penina nods. A flock of geese tunnels through the mist, a sudden disruption, their wings pumping the air, their calls urgent and loud, their bodies mostly invisible, but for a faint oscillation of gray. Remember the Earth's insistent spin, they call, remember time is passing, remember change and entropy are the rule.

She waits until silence is restored. "We'll also be doing what I call 'thought experiments.' This is a time-honored practice among scientists. A scenario is played out in the mind and all its possible consequences are explored through the imagination. It's a way to test out a hypothesis. You'll use this technique to think about the repercussions of any interventions you might undertake. Not just short term and local effects, but also longer term and global effects. We want to avoid harming people—and animals, and the Earth itself.

"But I'm getting ahead of myself. First, we need to know each other better. Let's go around and each of you say a little bit about yourself, where you're from and what brought you here. Maybe tell us when you became aware of what's unique about you."

No one speaks. They gaze at the water, embroidered with insects. They look at the cabins, sequestered under the trees. They look at the ashen fog that seems determined not to move. Felipe cracks his knuckles. Penina picks at a cuticle. Patty buttons the top button of her sweater.

Felipe releases his knees and stands. "Maybe we breathe first? Get the—the air in flow. In theater, in dance, we start with the breathing. It help the work."

Yes, of course, she should have thought of that. Breath is such essential fuel. She nods and follows him to the grass, Patty and Penina in tow, Analu hesitating for only a moment.

Felipe has flung down his fleece jacket and cap so in his tight black jeans and black turtleneck his body resembles a supple wire that bends willingly in any direction. The others form a loose circle and follow his lead, breathing in to a slow six counts, filling and expanding their bellies, taking another six counts for the exhalation. Felipe raises his arms overhead on the in-breath, allows them to fall on the release. They all follow suit.

Matt stands at the window of the lodge watching the proceedings, riding a strange rollercoaster of thought. Only a few years ago, when he was working for a tabloid called *The Meteor* (a crappy job he hates to admit he ever held), he would have dismissed Bronwyn, this group, this entire effort, as absurd. Now he thinks otherwise. And yet, grounded as he is in the conventional world of his job as a reporter for a respectable online publication, and having spent the better part of his first three decades as an avowed skeptic, he can still inhabit that point of view. It bothers him that he hasn't been able to tell his parents about Bronwyn. On certain days he wants to shout aloud to the world about her exceptional talent, other days he wishes it would all go away so they could live a life that might be called normal.

The morning fog partly obscures the people on the grass so they're stripped of their individuality, still identifiable by the sizes and shapes of their bodies, but more alike from where he stands than they would appear up close. The obfuscation seems to reveal a truth. They *are* alike in many ways. Alike in their openness. Their sensitivity. They're more like Bronwyn than he is. This is why she's assembled them. He thought he'd made peace with the ways he and Bronwyn differ, but watching her work with these students, the thought still niggles him.

Bronwyn, small as she is, is hardest to see. Every once in a while, fog blankets her completely, as if she's been vaporized, giving shape to one of his fears—that one day she will disappear completely, simply dissolve into the atmosphere, and his life will never be the same.

The memory of Bronwyn trying to teach him on that drumlin still pains him. Part of what tortured him was his jealousy of Joe, the way Joe appeared to work so synchronously with Bronwyn and was able to bring on rain, something he, Matt, failed to do. The more humiliating part of the memory is the fear that engulfed him, not only fear of the wrenching physical pain, but worse, the terror of being peeled open so completely he felt in danger of losing his mind. Each time Bronwyn does an intervention there is an accompanying disorientation that she describes as a temporary loss of self. So far, she has been able to reconstruct herself afterwards, but what if sometime she can't recover? He has thought of this too often, and that day she tried to teach him he worried about the same thing for himself. He is sure his own loss of self would be far more extreme, that he wouldn't return from it, that he'd be rendered insane.

Out on the lawn they reach for their toes in unison, only Analu exhibiting slight reluctance. Analu the quiet one. Patty and Penina the talkers. Felipe's a talker too, but he'd probably prefer to communicate through his body. Matt chuckles at himself. He hardly knows these people and he's already categorizing them, a journalist's habit he can't break.

Joe stands beside him now. The jealousy of Joe has abated, thank God. He and Joe have forged a bond, arising from their status as outsiders, facilitators yes, but still on the periphery of the main action. "It makes me nervous to watch," Matt says.

Joe nods. "She seems to know what she's doing. Analu and Felipe and Patty are not us—I think it's going to be easier for them."

"Let's hope."

They shake their heads and share rueful smiles.

"By the way," Joe says, "I know what you're thinking, but you and I, we have our own things, we just don't know what they are yet. I'm working on my sense of smell so when I stop writing novels I can be an oenologist—one of those people who gets paid a shit-ton for smelling wine."

"Hah. Good plan."

"Another thing. If you ever start to feel like an albatross with Bronwyn—something I've sometimes felt with Diane—well, those birds, the albatrosses, can fly six hundred miles in a single day. So they're no slouches."

"I'll remember that." Matt laughs. "Hey, man, sorry Diane isn't here." Although a part of him is glad she's not, as it would disturb his alliance with Joe.

Joe, who misses Diane acutely, makes a face and turns away.

Bronwyn has already revised her plan. She understands it's difficult to speak about yourself publicly, it has never been her strong suit. Writing first might help loosen them. She hands out the notebooks she brought for them to use as journals and instructs them to write for a while then they'll reconvene in an hour to talk. Penina wants to stay on the dock which is fine with Bronwyn. Patty and Felipe, arm in arm, head up to the lodge for warmth. What an unusual friendship. "Portuguese!" Felipe calls out, waggling his notebook overhead. "I write in Portuguese!"

Analu hesitates before taking the notebook. Beyond contact information on job applications, he rarely writes. He has no interest in writing. His education did not go beyond seventh grade. "I can't write," he tells her.

"That's fine. You don't have to write. But take the notebook anyway. You can use it for drawing."

He doesn't draw either. Penina is at the far end of the dock, already bent over her notebook, her pen whipping across the page, black hair streaming from her pink hat and across the purple jacket. What is she writing about so avidly? Bronwyn is watching too. Does she see the same thing he does, he wonders, the diligence of his daughter, her eagerness to participate?

He takes the notebook. He wants to say something more than *thank you*, wants to tell Bronwyn about his worries for his daughter, wants to ask if she is close to her own father. But now is the wrong time, so he only smiles and goes to sit at the edge of the trees, far from Penina while keeping her in view.

Bronwyn joins Matt and Joe in the kitchen. They set aside lunch preparation to join her on high stools at the butcher block counter, bringing fresh cups of coffee for all. In the large room beyond, Felipe and Patty sit companionably in adjacent wicker chairs near the fireplace, writing in their journals. Matt and Joe, both sporting the rumpled appeal of backwoods dudes, watch Bronwyn expectantly, waiting for her report on how things are going. How lucky she is to have the support of these two uncommon men.

"You saw them swimming?" she says.

"We saw." Matt shakes his head. "It must have been freezing."

"They're both fearless."

"It looked to me like a good icebreaker," Joe says.

"It was. There's a synergy building among them. But it's nothing I can control, and all my plans are ..." She shrugs. "I feel like I'm winging it."

Joe laughs. "Because you're not following the curriculum someone gave you? Of course you're winging it—this has never been done before. You're the first."

"You've always wung it," Matt says. "Kansas, California, Siberia. You're super good at winging it."

"It's just odd how—I don't know—how life grabs you and takes you miles from where you started without you realizing it."

"That pretty much sums up life as I've known it for most of my forty-eight years on the planet," Joe says.

They reassemble on the dock in the late morning. The air is still chilly but the mist has cleared, and the sun has begun to assert itself. She must go first with self-revelation, she understands, to set the example.

Her story begins in a small house in working-class New Jersey, dark, claustrophobic, yardless. No known father and a single mother afflicted with crippling anxiety. The curious young girl will combust if she doesn't get out. She first escapes to the square of fenced concrete behind the house, lies on her back and levitates into the clouds. There, dreaming as young girls do, she grows in the only direction she can, and the seeds of the woman who speaks with sky and Earth are sown.

Lying on that patch of concrete whose discomfort she scarcely noticed, she studied clouds endlessly, savoring their myriad shapes—cats and cows and rollercoasters and Christmas trees and candy. Her cells began to know things she had no idea they knew, her body storing knowledge for later. Wanting to understand more, she assembled a cloud collection—all the clouds she'd seen, described as well as she could—and she learned how to make certain crude meteorological instruments. Eventually the pursuit of clouds and atmosphere and weather became a career.

Through all this she was a timid girl, a reticent young woman, never sure if she knew anything of value. Her mother told her she mustn't expect much from the world as the world rarely delivered. When the young woman's mother died, she took her mother's words to heart. Without an aggressive mentor who took a strong interest in her—without Diane—she would have foundered. But Diane saw something in her, recognized her passion and intellect, drew her out. For a while, she thrived.

Later came a collapse. She began to doubt her career in science, was jilted by her boyfriend, knew failure and humiliation and deep self-doubt. But that collapse turned out to be a second beginning, without that and its attendant pulverizing of ego, she might never have discovered this wonderful thing, this communication with natural forces, with air and water and fire and Earth.

She pauses. The day has thrown off its cover. A brassy sun has rebuffed the mist, and a slight breeze makes the water choppy. Across the lake to the northeast even the mountains seem to shimmy. Patty and Penina and Analu and Felipe are all angled toward her in keen attention.

"That's you?" Penina says. "That girl is you?"

Bronwyn nods.

"Was she happy or unhappy?"

"A little of both maybe. No more unhappy than anyone else."

"A bad thing, then a good thing," Felipe says. "Many times life is like that. With me my father, the bad thing, then the good thing, the dance. Without my father maybe not the dance. I am nothing without this body. Dancing, acting." His torso sways to interior music.

"Yes," Bronwyn says. "Will you say more?"

He closes his eyes and lifts his face to the crowning sun and tells of his father's rages, the terror he and his mother and sisters felt as plates flew, glasses broke, full tables were overturned. He tells of the beatings which left suppurating gashes on his arms and legs that he covered with clothing for school, the bruises on his face he could never hide.

His mother was a beautiful woman, it was inconceivable anyone could hit her, but hit her his father did, in the face usually, bloodying and cracking her nose, breaking the skin beneath her eyes. He can still recapture the look that came over his father before those episodes: His eyes receded under the hood of his brow, his shoulders rounded, a hump like a backpack of venom rose on his upper back. Felipe could do nothing to stop his father, nothing to save his mother and sisters. Remembering, he still feels shame.

Then, he discovered the miracle of his own body. Who knew a body could do so much. It stretched and bent and leaped and pretzeled. He learned to stand on a single leg and spin on the tips of his toes. Blood dashed along his spine, feeding his limbs, feeding his soul, and he knew he was saved, his body had saved him.

Done speaking, he bends at the waist and kisses the dock in a kind of benediction. He is stripped open. He has never told this story to anyone. To Isabella, yes, but no one else. Certainly not to strangers. But already he feels he knows these people. He can't thank Patty enough for bringing him here. This is what he has needed for so long, to be with collaborators as in the theater, working for something larger than himself. He is so grateful to Isabella for pushing him to travel beyond his own city, his own country. How can he ever cram into a text everything that lives in his heart?

Patty was preparing herself for speaking next, but now, having heard Felipe's heartbreaking story, she's overwhelmed and can't imagine saying anything. It's not that she doesn't think she's unique, special even, but she has no story to match Felipe's, none of that terrible pain and shame and helplessness. Not that this is Queen for a Day, but whatever she has to say will sound so trivial. Why did he not share this story about his father earlier, during one of their many walks in LA? She fights the urge to get up and embrace him. She and Analu regard one another apprehensively: *Who's next?*

Felipe, raising his head, sees the reaction his story has wrought. He waves his hand, laughs lightly. "Long ago now. I send this away. I dance. I act. Arts save me. It is gone. Zing. Only a memory and I am fine." He laughs again. "Please. Later I dance for you. Thank you. I am here."

Bronwyn holds her breath. Is this what she expected when she asked for stories? Stories of such pain?

"I guess it's the same for me with singing," says Patty. "I got to it from a bad period. But it's nothing like what you went through, Felipe. How awful that sounds."

"It make me Felipe. Like Bronwyn be Bronwyn."

"Yes," says Patty. "I suppose you're right. It's different for everyone."

On a wave of bravery, she dives in and tells the story of her long-ago baldness, the inexplicable loss of her hair that shaped so much of who she's become. The long afternoons and evenings holed up in her room with coloring books and Barbies, sometimes assessing herself in the mirror and wondering if her head really did resemble a penis as her classmates teased. At the age of eight she'd never laid eyes on a penis.

"Now, thinking back, I suppose I was depressed, but in those days no one talked about depression. No one went into therapy. Something else had to happen."

The radio turned out to be better than therapy, she says. The radio led to the singing that got better and better until she was able to stand in front of the whole school and perform, a little girl of eight, belting out "Amazing Grace."

"Maybe that girl was braver than I am now."

Penina looks stricken. "Are you wearing a wig?"

"Oh no, this is my hair"—she runs a hand through it punishing-ly—"not at its best this morning. The hair grew back that summer and I've had hair ever since. No one could ever say why I lost it in the first place, but in some ways I look at it now as the best thing that ever happened to me, you know?"

"I would *die* if I lost my hair," Penina says, bunching her tresses and hugging them into her chest as if someone is threatening her with scissors.

At least Patty's story is not quite so soul-shattering, Bronwyn thinks.

Analu is relieved to see it's time for lunch. Joe is ringing a bell outside the lodge and waving at them to come inside.

"After lunch?" Bronwyn says to him.

"What about me?" Penina says.

"If you like. But you don't *have* to say anything."

"I *want* to. I have things to say."

"Good. We want to hear them."

How outspoken his daughter has turned out to be, so different from him. Analu isn't used to thinking much about what has made him the way he is. He has always thought he was the same as everyone else, more or less. A man who can boat and fish and swim and take good care of his family. At least that's who he was on the island. When he got to Australia, then he began to see how he was given to silence more than others, how he liked to be outside more than most, and how maybe he wasn't as good a provider as he thought he was. If anything has made him who he is it is simply having been born on the island and learning to do island things.

He eats his turkey and cheese sandwich slowly, thinking about what he'll say. Perhaps some sad things have happened to him in his life, but they're over now and he has no need to revisit them, certainly not publicly. He would be happier simply watching and listening to the others.

"I would hide in a closet until it grew back," Penina says to Patty.

Patty laughs. "I don't think so, honey. It's amazing what you find you can do." She is aware of not having said a word about Earl which seems like a big oversight since Earl is really the reason she's here. What could be said about Earl though, when these people can never meet him? Words don't fit easily around Earl.

Having bared his soul, Felipe's exhilaration makes him ravenous. He eats two sandwiches. He loves everyone at this table. How is it possible that life seemed so dire only a short time ago, but now he glimpses a bright future? He is still poor, still jobless, still without an official home, but he's at a turning point and new possibilities will surely unfold. Perhaps Bronwyn really can do what she professes to do. Maybe she'll teach him. If not, that's fine too, something else will happen. The sun is out in full force and the day is heating up. He would like to embrace them all, dance to Patty's singing, swim with Penina, chat quietly with Analu. He tries to contain his exuberance, knowing his tendency to overwhelm.

He never loses sight of Joe, steady Joe, presiding at one end of the long table.

When the others return to the dock, Penina is already there, limbs splayed, basking in the sun. She wears another outfit, yellow shorts and a red tank top, exposing her sleek legs and a band of alluring almond belly. Her eyes are closed and her black hair is flung everywhere. Seeing her, Analu catches his breath. For a brief second, mature and seductive as she looks, he doesn't recognize her as his daughter.

"Penina," he says, a little too sharply.

She sits up, dazed, blinking. "What?"

He answers with a headshake and sits himself on the dock where he was earlier, eager to get this storytelling over with. He watches Felipe settling into a cross-legged position and wishes he lived in his own body as comfortably as Felipe does. He feels Bronwyn's nod, feels Penina's eyes on him too. He must acquit himself well.

"My only story is this: I was born on an island that is disappearing and soon it will be completely gone. Ten years, twenty, I don't know exactly. Maybe less. I want to save our island. I want to take my mother there so she can die where she was born. It is her home. It is my home. It is Penina's home. I have come here to learn how maybe I could save our home. That is all."

In the silence it is quite apparent they want him to say more. He shakes his head. "That's all I have to say." He stares down at the gray fissures in the splintering dock. How he would love to possess the talent for talk.

Bronwyn watches him, she watches his frowning daughter watch him. Of all those assembled she feels most like Analu. They are both people with little use for words, though she has had to make peace with a world that has expected her to speak. She cannot push him to keep talking, much as she'd like to hear more.

"Wait, Dad. Don't be crazy. There's so much else to say. You have to tell about your *mana*. That's, like, a kind of power, you know. Some people on the island have it. Not everyone, just some people. With my dad it's about animals. Animals love you, right Dad? They come to him.

When we were still on the island all the fish would come around him when he went out in a boat and so obviously he was the best fisherman. And other animals too, birds, and geckos, and butterflies. You'll see— it happens wherever he goes. He's special. So . . ."

Special. Analu can't look up—tears will fall if he does.

"Really?" Felipe says. "You show us? You teach us?"

"You can't teach it, can you, Dad? It's just something you're born with."

Analu looks up at Bronwyn. He feels trapped by so many stares, but proud too. He shrugs, smiles. Penina isn't done.

"And there's something else. What *I* was going to say is why we left the island. I wanted to tell you about my sisters. We had lots of storms and floods. The water would come up into the houses and stay there, all brown and stinky. And people would get sick. Like my two sisters, Heni and Ipo. They got sick with diarrhea, so sick they died. Heni was older than me and Ipo was younger, but I never got to know either of them very well because I was only about two when they died. I think about what they'd be like now and what we'd do together. Sisters, you know, they're always there for you, always your friend. Ipo was just a baby when she died. And Heni was only three. I don't have any other sisters but them. And now I don't have them. I have cousins, but it isn't the same."

Penina pauses. Her father is looking at her snake-eyed, as if she's said something she wasn't supposed to say. But it's true, her sisters are dead, why can't she say so? Patty and Felipe and Bronwyn are all wear- ing crunched up *We-feel-sorry-for-you* faces that make her feel a little guilty. Her sisters *did* die, but she hardly remembers them now. The sadness is more *idea-sad* than *feeling-sad*. Still, other than leaving the island—and the trip here—it's the biggest thing that's ever happened to her. She would be another person, a person with sisters, if Heni and Ipo hadn't died.

"It's okay," she says to Bronwyn, ignoring her father. "You don't have to feel sorry for me. I got over it. I'm like Felipe—I'm good."

After dinner Matt and Bronwyn stand arm in arm on the lawn in deep twilight watching Felipe and Penina swimming for the second time that day. They've been in the water for at least half an hour, impervious to its cold. It doesn't bother them that most people wouldn't dream of swimming in mid-May in northern New England.

"What a surprise this day has been," says Bronwyn. "People said so much—much more than I thought they would. I'm a little over-whelmed. I'm thinking we should move on from talking and get to the hands-on teaching, skip the days of silence and maybe even the thought experiments."

"But isn't the silence a critical part of the overall plan? That's what you've been telling me."

"Yes, but—"

"If I were you, I'd stick with the plan. Then, if things change, go with it. But now it seems a bit too early to switch gears."

He's right. She shouldn't second-guess herself. The days of silence have always been the most critical element of her plan.

Penina and Felipe hoist themselves onto the dock and dive for their towels. The bats have come out, and they swoop low to the insect-rich water and rise again in elegant parabolas. Penina squeals. Another sound, a single low note, threads its way through the twilight from the deck of the lodge, a human voice, open-throated and sonorous. The note lingers, then seamlessly flows into new notes, a sequence from which a pattern emerges, a wordless melody they all recognize. "Amazing Grace."

Joe, the last left in the lodge, scrubs down the industrial-sized, black, twelve-burner stove which has a way of snagging food and clenching it like some giant Velcro'ing parasite. He can imagine bits of food lodged here from years ago, perhaps decades, tenacious baked beans, gummy tuna casserole, drooly mac and cheese, all now unrecognizable pellets on their way to becoming fossils.

He doesn't mind cleaning, he actually enjoys it, but being here has made him miss Diane unspeakably. The windows are dark, and he can hear Patty singing and the distant melancholy trilling of loons, all these sounds that speak to him of Diane's absence. Ever since he got her letter he's been longing to talk, longing to have her home, longing to find out about Greenland and what the place has done to her. Most of all he longs to hold her. He misses her smell—some herbal product she uses in her hair—her plush body in his arms, the warmth of her hip against his as they sleep. So many things he misses he would not have thought to name when she's around, but when she's gone, they pop into his mind as suddenly distinct. The way she talks to him at night while she's brushing her teeth, garbling the words but still expecting him to understand. The habit she has of chuckling at everything, from things she likes to examples of egregious stupidity. He won't get traction on another novel until she returns, so he might as well be here, keeping Matt company while witnessing this experiment and helping out.

He tries to envision her now on her rocky Greenland promontory in the tiny house above the harbor. It's hard to imagine Greenland fully, though he's searched out pictures on the internet, and found the very town she's in. He saw the bright houses, the fishing boats, the icebergs, the asperity of the landscape, but an internet search isn't the same as being there, and what he can't imagine is the feel of the place, the air, the people, the isolation.

She said in her letter she's coming home soon. *Soon? When is soon?* he asked in his return letter to her. But no answer has come.

Patty lies in bed needing to pee but not wanting to pick her way through the dark woods to the stinky outhouse. She's trying to be game in this outdoor life, but the outhouses are a definite challenge. Debating the trip through the dark, she thinks of all the things she could have said today but didn't. In not mentioning Earl she was aware of holding something back, and it felt akin to keeping a shameful secret.

What an effort it is to go out. First finding the flashlight, then dragging herself off the bunk and rummaging around for her coat and shoes. Finally, she's got everything together, and she goes out the creaky door and galumphing along the path in the dark, flashlight jerking, feeling clumsy and out of place as the woods rustle and crack with fleeing critters. She hums tunelessly to dim the fear. She's never been a camper, and these woods they come down tight around you, so different from Kansas. The outdoor spot from the lodge leaks just enough light through the trees to create a pied mob of shadows, leaf shadows and shadows of tree trunks, kinetic in the light breeze. The swooping bats scare her the most, as she's heard stories about them getting tangled in people's hair. *Come on now, Patty.* She stops for a moment, braves on again, stops once more. Something is frozen on the path ahead of her, but the flashlight exposes nothing. A bear? Joe said it was unlikely they'd run into a bear, but if they did, they shouldn't run, they should make noise and show the bear who's boss.

This bear isn't moving.

Patty sings. "Sometimes . . . in the country . . . dah, dah, dah, in the town . . ." Distracted, she forgets the words and hums. ". . . duh, duh, duh, duh-duh . . . jump in the river and drown." She backsteps slowly, still singing, "Irene . . . goodnight . . . Irene . . ."

"Patty? Is that you?"

She shines the flashlight on Analu, who is coming toward her on the path.

"I didn't want to scare you," he says.

"Oh, my heavens, I thought you were a bear."

"I'm not a bear."

"I see you're not a bear. Are there any bears between here and the outhouse?"

"None that I've seen. But I can come with you, if that would make you feel better."

"Oh, would you? That would be so nice."

He accompanies her to the outhouse, their two lights pooling to illuminate more of the path.

"I'll wait for you," he says.

"Oh, I'll be fine, you don't have to wait." She doesn't want him to hear her peeing—the sound amplifying as it travels the depth of the hole so you can't help picturing the nasty pile it's falling on—but then she also doesn't want to walk back in the dark alone. She steps into the outhouse not knowing if he's staying or going. Bottom hovering inches above the wooden seat, she hears nothing beyond the torrent of her own stream, and she has to struggle to make sure the hem of her coat doesn't dip down into the hole.

When she comes out Analu is still there, bless him. But oh my heavens! There's an owl on his shoulder, a big yellow-eyed owl, the two of them standing there, still as statues, but for the owl's head that rotates to look at her. The owl's eyes are huge and, frankly, a little scary.

"Oh—my—God," she whispers, not meaning to swear.

He shoos the owl away. "I'm sorry," he says, and he shepherds her back to the cabin without another word. What a surprising man!

Inside, she collapses on the bed, coat still on.

Analu turns off his flashlight and stands still in the cool darkness outside Patty's cabin. He is finally beginning to feel grounded in this new place, not quite a sense of belonging, but no longer not-belonging. The chill plucks at his skin not unpleasantly, bringing with it an awareness of his limbs, flesh against cloth, bone against flesh. He feels the shape of himself, his feet chafing against the press of his shoes. Of course he's been cold at various times, every human is sometimes cold, but heat has been the norm he has lived in, and his body has been calibrated for it. He thinks of his wife and mother alone back in Australia, wonders if they're as okay as they said they'd be.

An owl, the owl from earlier, alights on his shoulder again, and they peer into each other's eyes, the owl's look softly inquiring, the eyes a warm liquid, yellow and dimensional, with crenellations around the irises that remind him of coral formations. They unfurl a pathway that ushers him back through centuries, millennia, to a time before human existence. It seems as if there might have been an owl witnessing the creation, a memory that was handed down to all other owls, taking up residence in the rods and cones of their enormous eyes. Thinking these things and feeling the accepting presence of this bird on his shoulder, he is overcome by a flood of remorse for the snake he killed back in Australia. There was no call for such an act of violence, despite his disturbance at the time, and he hopes every creature does not now see in him a potential murderer.

A sound, Patty's voice, issues from the cabin, and he and the owl both turn toward it. He listens for distress, but hears nothing alarming in the rising and falling cadences . . . *if I could do . . . if you were . . . such a good idea . . .*

He chides himself for thinking poorly of Patty when he first met her. She seemed to talk too much, eat too much. She dresses in loud floppy clothing. Most of all she appeared to him distastefully American. But he cannot blame her for where she was born, any more than he can blame the snake for coming onto his back patio, any more than he would like to be blamed for his lack of education and funds. Maybe the snake he killed had a heart as warm as Patty's.

40

Today's project is fears and nightmares. Patty, who loves to go first, leaps in.

"My nightmare is death by a tornado. Tornados are bullies." She stands on the dock, rocking from foot to foot, speaking in a voice that does not sound like her own. "When my husband Rand went I watched the tornado pick up his whole truck. I knew it was over for him, but I couldn't do a thing. If I'd been Bronwyn, of course, it would have been a different story." She hesitates. "There are so many forces out there we know nothing about."

A long silence follows. No one dares say a thing. They look at her. They look down. They look out to the far side of the lake. She knows they're uncomfortable, but right now she can't worry about that.

"Death turns everything inside out. After Death, nothing's the same, for the living or the dead. Body, mind—nothing. When Earl went—Earl was our minister and he went only a few months after Rand—then I saw Death clearly. It breaks your heart, it does. I knew Earl so well I still talk to him. I know that sounds silly. But I hear him every bit as well as if he were alive."

There, she said it. Speaking of Earl infuses her with a bolt of strength and she speaks louder, as if Earl himself is lodged in her larynx.

A tornado is sinister, she tells them. It taunts and mocks and seeks to destroy everything human. It gallops across the landscape, tractoring everything in its path.

It is unpredictable, unchaseable, unstoppable.

Its sound is satanic. While it roars and gnashes and hisses, it is hurling cars, smashing houses, uprooting trees. It hates anything alive and whole, loves debris.

It is your swashbuckling cowboy, your stink-eyed pirate, your raping marauder. Godzilla.

There is no kindness about a tornado, it has no mercy. It is a killer, sociopathic and unashamed.

Patty windmills her arms so her blouse is lifted and her stomach is exposed, her crimped bellybutton disgorging lint fairies, all there for anyone to see and poke fun at. She knows she must look terrible, but she doesn't care. An alien wildness has entered her, it has to come out.

What does she want more than anything? She wants to stare into the brutal eyes of a tornado, grab it by the balls and squeeze until it begs her to stop. But she won't stop, she'll kill that sucker. There is no need for tornados to exist. They don't serve people, they don't serve the Earth. The only good tornado is a dead one.

Done speaking, Patty remains standing. Her vehement words sizzle through the air. The eyes of her audience seem to roll like marbles. If she knows how to read anything it's eyes, and can see she's shocked these people without meaning to. But she's never been so honest. She has always sugarcoated anything slightly negative. It's just the way she was brought up. *Be nice. Watch your words.* But oh my heavens, what has she gone and done now? *I'll kill that sucker*—did she really say that?! But she won't take the words back. She means them. She's here because of those killer tornados. They're the thing she fears most in the world. Earl, she is quite sure would approve of her rant. She lifts her spine, tugs at her clothing.

"My dream is," she says, feeling her eyes as flares, "to arrest every single tornado I can. Just like you did, Bronwyn. I want to do that. I *will* do that, if you teach me how." She resumes her seat in the folding chair. "And this man, Analu, I believe he can do whatever he wants. I saw him last night with an owl on his shoulder. I've never seen anything like it in my life. He's going to do amazing things, this man."

Analu smiles, amused by Patty's change, a little embarrassed by her self-exposure, a little envious she's capable of that. He understands, however, that his problem is of an entirely different order than Patty's. He's been thinking about it incessantly since Bronwyn got in touch. He's no scientist, but he is a practical man and an astute observer of nature. A tornado is a discrete thing, and an arrested tornado is certainly a town preserved, many lives saved. As for his biggest fear, the sinking island . . .

He lays things out as he sees them. He is calm and logical. It is easier for him to talk when he isn't discussing himself. All the oceans are connected, they ring the earth, so there could be no lowering of one ocean while leaving the rest alone—the amount of energy that would take, well it seems impossible . . . could any individual, even remarkable Bronwyn, be capable of that? Even if all the oceans could be lowered, what of the excess water? If it evaporated into the atmosphere, it would only come down again as rain, heavy flooding rain, creating so many other problems. The water would have to be frozen again, restored to the icecaps, but what of the Herculean effort that would take. Many people would be needed, it seems to him, in many locations. It is, he's quite sure, beyond the capability of a single individual.

He hesitates. The faces before him are thoughtful, pondering what he has said. Except for Penina who points to the lake. A family of ducks is swimming in, fluffy newborns in tow. Everyone turns to appreciate the sight, welcoming the uncomplicated distraction—*Aw, babies!*—and the ducks cozy up to the dock, as if they've come expressly to listen.

He continues. Maybe if he were to use his energy to raise the land itself, the earth's crust. Could it be done? he asks. Could Bronwyn do it herself?

"One more thing," he says.

He tells them of the day the fish washed up on the beach. At first all they could see from the island's center was an undulant purple-tinted silver sheet covering the sand like Mylar. As they moved closer they saw it was fish, hundreds of blue-headed fairy wrasse, thousands, flipping and twitching. Their scales caught the sunlight, an iridescent dance, suggestive of tinkling chimes. Truly magnificent.

Closer still, he spotted the bottomless panic in their black eyes. Hundreds of hardening kernels of despair. Little by little their movement slowed, shrank; one by one, they flopped heavily onto one another and into the sand. Inert. Dead.

By the end of the day the stench was impossible to bear. The villagers, masking their noses with scarves, dug a pit on the beach, shoveled the fish in, and covered them with sand. The few that remained they threw back into the water, hoping the tide would do its work. No one asked why this had happened. They all knew.

A terrible day that was, but he does not tell them how sometimes he dreams of it and wakes in a panic, feeling the black eyes of the fish as his own eyes, thousands of them adhering to his body, on his legs and arms and rump and chest, watching from every angle, at all hours of the day, seeing more than anyone wants to see, the multitudinous ways the end is near.

In the silence that follows Analu's description of the dead fish, Bronwyn feels humbled by everyone. Analu's appraisal is astute. His challenge is huge, possibly insurmountable. If anything were to be done many people would be needed. And Patty, too, has raised good questions. Is there any way tornados are necessary? Does the energy of a tornado do anything to maintain the Earth's balance? Does a "dead tornado," as Patty puts it, do the Earth any harm? Maybe she's right that tornados have no critical role to play. If they do have a role, what would it be?

"We'll return to these questions later," she assures them, "after you've had some practical instruction."

Felipe's turn. He looks at the small group assembled before him, suddenly cowed by their passion and intelligence. He isn't used to putting big ideas into words, especially English words. For several years now he has kept his waking nightmares to himself. In his mind the unfolding disaster has been clear, but he told himself it couldn't possibly happen in the apocalyptic way he pictured it. A modern city like São Paulo, filled with inventive people, would surely find ways to rescue itself. Nevertheless, he worried, and images propagated in his mind with horrifying specificity. He pictured the day when the only water to be found would be so rife with industrial chemicals, and human waste, and algae bloom, and deadly bacteria, it would be undrinkable. He saw the day when turning any faucet would be futile, it would only produce an asthmatic gasp. He saw the browning of the city parks, and the scabbing of buildings, shops windows, restaurant tables, with sediments of calcified dust and dirt. He saw the closing of businesses, slow at first, then a quick tumbling. He saw the thirsty desperation that would erupt into water wars. He saw new pandemics arriving, leaving bodies littered in the streets, water scarcity collateral. He saw a mass exodus of those with means, for others less fortunate, slow death from dehydration.

He sighs, shakes his head. It hasn't happened yet, but it could. He himself is already a kind of refugee.

"It is very bad, this drought in my city," he begins. "It is big city. Lively city. Many arts. Many culture. But this drought, it kills everyone. Water flow a few hours, not every day. Everyone fight for the water. People get mean. Violent.

"We are nothing without the water, you know? We drink. We cook. We clean. No water, everything break. No water, no work. Especially for actor like me. No water, no art."

He pauses, overcome, and suppresses an urge to dive in the lake. It's so serene, so clear. If only he could transport it back to his São Paulo.

"This here—so much beautiful water. Like magic." He kneels, bends over the dock, dips the cup of his hand to drink, then splashes another palmful on his face. When he looks back at the group Analu is nodding, Bronwyn and Patty too. He wants to say: *Come with me to São Paulo. See what you think. Help me out.* Having wrapped words around the disaster he has brought it to life again, and in his mind it is worse than when he left. He wonders if he was wrong to leave. He did not leave with the intent to rescue his city, only to escape, and that knowledge shames him. His entire body flushes and tenses with memories of São Paulo. "We are nothing without water. Nothing."

Penina has checked out. There's nothing for her to add to this discussion. It's too big to think about. Too much impersonal talk bores her. She liked it yesterday when people were talking about themselves. She tickles the water with her bare toes and watches a chickadee that is picking its way along the dock to her father. It jumps on his leg and everyone laughs.

Penina liked what Patty said about the tornados. She liked how riled Patty got, how angry. If Penina lived near tornados she's quite sure they'd make her mad too. She'd love to watch Patty kill a tornado. Come to think of it, she'd like to kill one herself. But there aren't any tornados in Australia, at least she doesn't think so, or on the island either. Are they only in Kansas? Mean as they are, she'd like to see one, at least from a distance.

"The only nightmare I have," she blurts, "is everyone getting so sad."

Bronwyn is taken aback by the discussion. They've already thought of so much, pinpointed where the problems lie. The questions they've posed have no ready answers. She yearns for Diane's assistance. Diane has the admirable ability to think of the long game when approaching a hypothetical problem, so essential to successful thought experiments. Bronwyn knows she can't be expected to find solutions for everything right away. Still, her gut hosts a burgeoning node of inadequacy.

After lunch, tabling her plan yet again, she suggests they take out canoes. The discussion can continue with less pressure while they paddle. Analu, the most experienced boater, shares a canoe with Patty, a novice. Bronwyn, Felipe, and Penina launch another canoe, Bronwyn as passenger since Penina wants to paddle.

The day has flip-flopped from chilly to summery hot, everything throbbing and pulsing, a polyphony of swarming insects, throaty frogs, the spank of aluminum against the water, paddles thunking the canoes' gunnels. They follow the rocky shoreline, the two boats close enough that they can talk.

"Many climate scientists," Bronwyn muses, "think we're well past the time where we can keep the Earth habitable for humans. They see how quickly the arctic ice is melting and the oceans are acidifying, and they understand feedback loops that accelerate those things. And there's only one conclusion: We've already gone too far. We'll never come back from the damage we've done, it's irreparable. So, these scientists think that, eventually, it's likely that human beings will become extinct. No one knows exactly when. But almost every good scientist believes, essentially, that unless something really radical in human behavior changes now . . . we're fucked."

Analu stops paddling. Patty glances back at him and stops paddling too. Following some homing instinct, Felipe draws his canoe alongside Analu's, and Bronwyn takes hold of the gunnel so they drift together as a flotilla. Penina lays down her paddle and lies back on the canoe's bow, hair cascading into the water. A pair of loons swims up to Analu.

Bronwyn's decanted words replay in everyone's ears and chests. They echo out over the tranquil lake, suckling the water's surface, rising up into the febrile atmosphere, drifting lazily to the bank and quivering the leaves. *Fucked, fucked, fucked.* The words, mere sound waves now, dissolve into the throbbing afternoon, stripped of meaning, only energy nudging air, lodging in the crannies of bark, under rock and pebbles, sinking down into the water where they seep into the lake bed mud, sequestered, hidden, disassembled, a fossilized human utterance. *Fucked. Fucked. Fucked.*

After a long time, Patty says, "I don't like to use the F word, but do you really believe that? Are we really—" She whispers, "Fucked?"

Bronwyn submerges the hand that is not holding onto the other canoe. The water's cold distracts her, but only momentarily. What possessed her? Why has she said these things? It was not part of her plan. She doesn't want to depress them, and yet—given their mission here was it really an option not to share this frightening knowledge?

"Probably." Then, "Yes, I believe that. Unless—"

Felipe nods. Analu sighs. Recognition runs deep. They might not have articulated this to themselves, but it's obvious they, too, already knew how dire the situation is, problems propagating and piling into an inextricable heap.

Patty resists. "But people are doing things now, aren't they? Solar panels and such. What do they call that thing where you scrape the air clean? All those things? Don't those things show that people are taking it seriously?"

"Not seriously enough. If we really want things to change significantly we have to learn to think differently. Think not in a way that is always *more, bigger,* but think about how much is enough. Businesses would have to stop trying to grow. People would have to limit their consumption, their driving, stop trying to get richer and richer. And it would have to happen fast, very fast, and we're human and humans tend to change very slowly."

"So why—?" Patty's makeup has worn off and her hair has been mashed down on one side.

"Why did I ask you to come here? Because together we might do some things that will buy us time until everyone is on board. Maybe. I don't know for sure. If we could save an island, or a drought-ridden city, or hundreds of people who might otherwise die in tornados—isn't that worth it? It's something. Enough? Maybe not, but it's something. I'm not as pessimistic as I may sound."

Penina sits up suddenly. "I have an idea. We could all just kill ourselves now, and then no one would have to be sad, we'd just be dead."

Bronwyn's vision flickers, goes white. She closes her eyes. A child is present. What was she thinking? What stupidity. She forces her eyes open and touches Penina's knee, the new skin, smooth and moist and sun-warmed. Is this the kind of girl who would take her life? "Do you really mean that?"

Penina shrugs. "It's just an idea. Hey, look."

Bronwyn stares back at the shore where Penina is pointing. Two people stand on the lawn, one of them a shape so familiar to Bronwyn, even at this distance, that she's derailed. It can't be. It isn't possible. How can she have gotten herself from Greenland to here in so little time? And how has she found her way to the camp?

"Who is it?" asks Penina.

"Let's paddle," Bronwyn says. "I'll introduce you."

Her mind is a miasma, full of Penina's dire suggestion, riven with what a misstep it was to convey such pessimism. What a bad time for Diane to appear. Or wonderful. She cannot get to shore quickly enough. She'll take Penina aside later, try to reassure her.

When they hit the dock, *bam,* Bronwyn hurtles out of the boat. "Excuse me. I'm sorry. I'll be back in a minute to help with the boats."

The dock bounces under her determined footfalls. The heat empties her. It's preposterous. Only hours ago she was wishing Diane were here and now she is here. Truly preposterous. At the end of the dock, she breaks into a run and flings herself at Diane, the safe haven of the body that is Diane. "You're back, you're home."

Diane answers with her rusty rumbling chuckle—*My God, your hair!*—and a hug that levitates Bronwyn from the ground. Together they drown in a chorus of *oh-my-Gods*.

Wrapped up in Diane, Bronwyn is slow to remember that someone else has also arrived. A young girl. A teenager. Round face. Short black hair tipped in green. A stillness about her. A reticence.

"This is Edel, my friend from Greenland. Edel, this is Bronwyn, my former colleague. Future colleague perhaps? I hope—" Diane raises her eyebrows at Bronwyn. "I'm sorry I didn't warn you we were coming."

Bronwyn waves an arm, dismissing Diane's concern, though it's true their arrival will complicate things.

Matt and Joe take charge of rearranging the cabins. Felipe will move to his own cabin so Diane can move in with Joe. And Patty is happy to have Edel join her.

As soon as Diane heard about this project from Joe, there was no way she could stay away. She is not generally in the habit of being impulsive—her escape to Greenland notwithstanding—but she definitely decided to come here impulsively, without asking any of them if she was welcome. It was not her finest moment of decision-making, to voyage here uninvited. Still, she's pleased—relieved—that they seem to be welcoming her. Joe is ecstatic—*You rascal! You nut-job! You rat!* he said as he slapped her into a rough bear hug—but Bronwyn and Matt also seemed pleased to see her. She vows to stay on the sidelines and let this be Bronwyn's show. She did not come here to interfere, only to watch—and to expose Edel to some new things. It has astonished her to discover how easily she and Edel traveled together. Though Edel says very little, the silences between them are not awkward, and when Edel does speak, Diane finds her observations fasci-

nating. Edel, standing out as one of the few people her age unequipped
with earbuds, turns out to have extremely acute hearing; everywhere
they've been she has commented on the sounds, cocking her head
each time the airplane call buttons sounded, startled by the roar of
an airport espresso machine, clapping her ears against a jackhammer
they passed on the streets of Cambridge. The single night they spent
in the house on Brattle Street—a street Diane has always thought of
as relatively peaceful—Edel was alert to honking horns and sirens and
the clatter of garbage pickup. Diane wonders if she'll ever return to
thinking her home is quiet.

She walks Edel to Patty's cabin to help her settle in.

"Is this all right?" she asks Edel. "You'll be fine here?"

"Yes. All right." Edel nods, her face in repose, a person whose
thoughts and feelings are slow to surface. The proverbial iceberg really, ninety percent underwater. Unlike Aka who divulges her thinking
much more readily.

At dinner Diane has a chance to observe the others—Analu and his
firecracker of a daughter, Penina; cheerful Midwestern Patty; Brazilian Felipe with the restless energy. How did Bronwyn find these lovely lively people? Well, here is yet another of her talents, yet another
way that Diane has underestimated her. It seems to Diane that she will
spend the rest of her life being astonished by the unexpected gifts of
those around her.

To sit at the dinner table with Diane is to feel electrified by her intelligence, her interest in people, her extroverted personality. It is to
sit in the presence of power. Almost everyone, upon meeting her, is a
little smitten, and that appears to be true now as everyone listens to
her hold forth. She comments on everything—the shabby state of the
camp, the beauty of the location, the unseasonably warm spring—and
she already knows everyone's names. Bronwyn willingly takes a back
seat, watching as Diane engages each person and draws them out a
little. And she shares her observations about Greenland: the unusual
blue of the Arctic light, the towering icebergs, the country's sere beauty, and the difficulty of surviving there.

"Am I right, Edel?"

Edel nods. She sits next to Diane as if in her own silo, occasionally casting a glance at Penina, but saying nothing.

"Edel sings in a rock band at home. In Upernavik. Her voice is terrific. Breathtaking."

Edel smiles into her lap.

Bronwyn's mind is in whiplash, pleased and surprised by Diane's arrival—her apprehension about their rift dissolving—but still concerned about Penina who just this afternoon suggested they all commit suicide and who is now shooting *go-away* looks at Edel, and concerned about Edel, too, an unknown quantity joining this group that has already come to resemble a family. Diane is easy to integrate, as she is well known to Bronwyn and Matt and Joe, and the others are already warming to her. Why has Diane brought Edel? Bronwyn doesn't exactly want to exclude the girl, but she wishes Diane had given them some warning.

Tomorrow the three days of silence are supposed to begin. Should she postpone for a day or two until Diane and Edel are settled in and all the necessary conversations have been had? She needs to decide soon, tonight, and meanwhile there is still the cleanup, and they need to rescue Diane's car from where she ran out of gas on the dirt road. And, most importantly, she needs to talk to Penina about what was said this afternoon, apologize for sounding so bleak, probe Penina's thoughts about suicide.

Halfway through the meal—chicken chili with cornbread and salad—Bronwyn notices something different in Diane. It's hard to pinpoint. She's lost weight—not that she's thin, she'll never be thin, but there are angles in her face that weren't there before. The main difference, however, is in her manner. While she's talking a lot, she's also listening attentively to everyone at the table instead of a chosen few which is usually her habit. She isn't interrupting or marking time until others finish speaking. She seems more cautious than Bronwyn remembers her being, and Bronwyn might even, if she didn't know Diane as well as she does, think she's lacking confidence. Confidence has always been Diane's hallmark. Often she employs the endearing humor of self-deprecation—*Sieve-brain that I am . . . Fat as I am . . . Since I'm only a woman*—but the things she derides about herself are inconsequential—or downright wrong—so they never undermine the sense that this is a woman with a rock-solid belief in herself.

Penina wants to know if Diane can swim, and Diane laughs. "I *love* to swim, but I'm not very good, and I hardly ever get a chance to do it. I imagine you're an expert swimmer, having grown up where you did."

"Yeah, I'm very good."

"Excellent. Maybe you can help me improve." She chuckles and shakes her head. "I could use some tips." She catches Bronwyn's eye and winks.

Well-being bubbles up in Bronwyn like a fresh underground spring. How she has missed Diane. How satisfying it is to see her and Penina talking. It seems insane—foolish and immature—that she felt a need to keep her distance from Diane for so long, when to be with Diane has always made her feel that life, for all its problems, is well worth living.

Leaving the others to clean up, Bronwyn invites Penina to walk with her to the Craft Center, which is set apart from the other buildings, the perfect private place to talk.

"Did I do something wrong?" Penina asks on the short walk there.

It seems to Bronwyn so long ago that she was as young as Penina, attention flapping about in search of a perch. The worry about being wrong though—that she remembers. "Not at all. I just wanted to talk. We haven't talked much, just you and me."

She unlocks the door and turns on the light, feeble like all the other lights on the premises. Dust curdles in the air as if someone has recently visited with a smoke machine.

Penina sets about opening cabinets, pulling out supplies. She is so much bolder than Bronwyn was at this age. Her restless energy jettisons forward then suddenly retreats. A characteristic of youth, perhaps, but Bronwyn doesn't remember being like that. The counter is now covered with dusty spools of gimp, bunches of brittle raffia, plastic bags full of heavy dried clay, watercolors sets with cracked paint cubes, hardened tubes of acrylic paint, bags of sparkly beads.

"Who uses this stuff?" Penina says, peeling cobwebs from her fingers.

"I doubt if anyone uses it anymore. It looks ancient."

"Can I take some of it?"

"I don't see why not."

"I could make some things." Penina sits on the pottery wheel stool and spins, hair a kite behind her. Despair is nowhere in evidence, though it is the nature of despair to come and go, and she might be adept at hiding it.

"Why did that other girl come here?"

"Well, Diane is a good friend of mine, and I think she thought Edel belonged with us too. Maybe you and she will become friends."

"I liked being the only kid. Besides, I'm already friends with Felipe and Patty."

"You can never have too many friends."

"I don't think she's good with English. It's hard to make friends if you can't talk to the person. Hey, do we really have to not speak for three days?"

"Unless there's an emergency."

"What counts as an emergency?"

"Well, if you get hurt or—I think you'll know. Do you think you can do it?"

"I'll try, but I'm not like my dad—I like talking." She has dumped a bag of beads onto the table, and now she chooses the ones she likes best and lays them in a row. "Are you mad about today when I said we could kill ourselves?"

Would she raise the topic again if she were truly considering it? Still, the question startles Bronwyn. "No, of course not. But I hope you don't *want* to kill yourself."

"I say things sometimes I don't always mean. You know?"

"We all do." Words as ping-pong balls, or marbles, or cannonballs for that matter, objects for tossing back and forth and scoring points. She's always thought that.

Penina pauses to look up at Bronwyn. "Do you ever wanna be a pig? *Feed me, fatten me, kill me, eat me.* Then you wouldn't have to get old."

Bronwyn laughs. What an unusual mind. "Growing old isn't so bad."

"How would you know, you're not old? You should see my grandmother. She got really old. Can you really do magic?"

"It's not magic."

"What is it then?"

"It's harnessing energy and using it—differently."

"When are you gonna teach us?"

"Soon. Try to be patient."

"I'm never patient. My dad is always telling me to calm down and wait for things, but I can't be that way, I've told him a million times. I like my dad and all, but sometimes I wish he'd go away."

"He loves you and so he worries."

Penina strings her selected beads onto a strand of white gimp. "That's why it's better not to have kids. Why have kids anyway, if the world is just gonna end?"

Precisely what she has thought innumerable times. "Yes, I know. But the world isn't going to end tomorrow. I know I made it sound that way today."

"Yeah, but soon."

"Not before your birthday."

Penina grins. "Thirteen. You're going to let me try to learn the energy thing, right? I want to learn to kill tornados with Patty. Dad says I'm too young, but I think he's wrong."

"It's a big responsibility."

"But I'll be alive longer than anyone else here, so I should definitely learn. People might need me to rescue them."

"True," Bronwyn says. "We'll see."

"Grownups always say that—*we'll see*. It usually means no. Anyway, I'll be a teenager soon, so I'm not all that young."

"True."

"Is Edel a teenager?"

"I think so, yes."

"I need scissors." Penina opens drawer after drawer and finally locates a pair of blunt kindergarten-style scissors. With effort she cuts the gimp. "Turn around." She circles Bronwyn's neck with the beaded strand and ties it. "There, a necklace."

Bronwyn fingers it, sensing Penina's boldness in the warm beads. "Thank you. It's nice."

"Hey, if I get bored while we're not talking, can I come and hang out with you?"

"I'd be honored."

"I might paint toenails with Patty. She brought toenail polish and said we could do it together."

"Can you paint toenails without talking?"

"You know what? I think you're gonna say yes, I am old enough. That's what I think."

The girl swaggers her spine to erectness. Her eyes blaze. Her gaze is a truncheon that moves in on Bronwyn's soul, calling her to something, testing her. She can't recall anyone ever giving her such a look. A little frightening, but refreshing, too, in someone so young. Penina may be a child, but that doesn't make her simple.

"Also, because you like me." Penina grins.

"You're right about that," says Bronwyn.

Penina is still regarding her intently. "You should make your hair red again, it's more dramatic."

Bronwyn shrugs, loathe to discuss the evasive impulse behind her change in hair color, a timidity and shucking of responsibility that shames her.

"Let's leave this stuff out 'cause I might come back here."

They turn off the light and, hooking elbows, head companionably into the gathering dark.

Car rescued, dishes and ablutions done, people retire to their cabins. The night settles around them as a long emptying exhalation.

Patty is on her way back to the cabin with Edel, wondering where she can now go to talk to Earl. She really needs to talk to Earl. So much has happened today. She needs to sort things out. It embarrasses her to remember how she held forth earlier today, standing up there on the dock in front of everyone, loud and agitated. She used language she doesn't usually use, swearing and talking about killing. She shocked herself. And yet, she's also proud. She does hate tornados, they make her furious, so why shouldn't she say so? Wasn't that what Bronwyn wanted them to do, speak of their nightmares? Still, she might have gone a little overboard.

Then, the discussion this afternoon—that was surely unnerving. She has no reason to disbelieve Bronwyn, a woman of her background and education, but is the whole human race really going to become extinct? Can they really do nothing to fix things? It's honestly a little too much to wrap her mind around.

"Edel, honey, do you mind if I join you in a bit? I'd like to step out to the water alone for a moment."

"It's okay," Edel says. Lifting her hand in a wave, she walks on.

Patty bushwhacks through some low vegetation to the water's edge where she stands on a rock and looks across the glassy, gray-blue lake. Everything is a different shade of blue, the water, the mountains, the sky. She has no names for all these different blues, wonders how the Arctic blue that Diane was discussing is different from what she sees here. What a vague word blue turns out to be. Maybe in a place like this she could get over her fear of the water and learn to swim. This lake water looks as if it would hold you up, unlike the raging water of the Pacific. Maybe, with help from Analu or Felipe—or even Penina— she really could learn to swim here.

I'm sure you could, Earl says before she's even posed the question. True to himself, he's there when she needs him. How he locates her— first in LA and now in New Hampshire—she'll never rightly know. *Why not? You can do anything you put your mind to, as I've said before.*

"Do you really think the world will end like she says?"

As I understand it she said people *will end, not the world itself. Not the Earth.*

"But what's the point of the world without people?"

What's the point even with *people? I've come and gone. It's not much different for me or the world one way or the other.*

"I don't understand you. I honestly have no idea what you're saying. Did I make a fool of myself today?"

I was a fool my whole life—surely you saw that. There's a place in the world for fools.

"You might be right. I guess you are right. By the way, I might not be talking to you as much for a little while because I'm going to have a roommate. But don't desert me."

He goes silent, which she takes to mean he wants her to think about things before he says more. He likes to be mysterious sometimes. It forces her to figure things out on her own. Well, she will certainly have a great deal of time to think about things in the silent days ahead. So many things to think about: her ferocious thoroughly honest new self, swimming, the point of the world.

Sleep is unavailable to Bronwyn and Diane until they have talked. They stroll down to the dock. With no moon the stars prevail, and they seem to have descended closer to Earth as if, with a very long arm or a pointer, they might be touched.

"I'm so glad you're here," Bronwyn says. "I need to apologize for being out of touch for so long. I don't know what I was thinking."

"Let's dispense with apologies, because if anyone is apologizing it should be me. Bygones."

"I disagree, but okay. Bygones."

They step onto the dock and its boards creak and sway under their weight. In the scant light the gray wood appears white. Bronwyn leads them down one axis of the square that forms a shallow pool for beginning swimmers, then down one of the two lengths of dock that stretch from the square further into the lake. At one end is a diving board and they stop there, looking out and up, Bronwyn feeling the force of Diane beside her, and the flicker of expectation, the old insecurities she thought she'd retired. A mosquito lands on her neck but she leaves it there and feels its threadlike proboscis puncture the skin.

"Silence for three days. An interesting idea. What do you expect to come out of it?"

Bronwyn cringes. Diane's inquisitions are so familiar from the past; they were an essential part of her training, a crucible she always emerged from with flying colors, but sweated through nonetheless.

What *does* she expect from these days of silence? The truth is, she isn't sure. She wants people to pay attention, to listen to the natural world, to note what they see and hear, but are three days really enough to learn these skills? Listening, true deep mindfulness, results from years of practice and meditating, developing habits of attention. Buddhist monks spend entire lifetimes learning to be present, does she really believe that her students here will arrive at anything useful after a mere three days? She can never forget that she herself did not arrive at her skill through a conscious practice of listening. If she thinks back to her own development, she would say she was born listening. And she believes these people are special, already attuned in certain ways, just as she has been.

"Honestly," Bronwyn says slowly. "I really don't know—or at least I'm not sure. I want to get them listening closely, but I know three days isn't enough." She fixes her gaze on the Pleiades, the clustered sisters.

Diane nods, a movement Bronwyn senses rather than sees. "I have not, as you know, been a big practitioner of silence myself. Well, of course when I'm working out problems and writing papers and such, but I haven't pursued silence as any kind of discipline or practice by itself. But these last few months in Greenland it was thrust on me, because I was alone with myself for long stretches of time without anything in particular to do. No deadlines. No classes to teach. And it did something to be. A self-clarification, if you will. I can't say I'm happy about all the things I saw about myself. I'm surprised you've tolerated me for so many years."

"Tolerated? Don't be crazy."

"Do you remember the time you told me, very politely, to stop finishing your sentences?"

"I remember I had to coach myself for a long time before I said that!"

"I never meant to step on you. Over the years I just developed a narrow focus regarding what I needed to do and what I wanted everyone around me to do. Short-sighted, I now see in hindsight. Perhaps the little modicum of power I've had caused me to overreact. It's a terrible thought that power always seems to have that effect on people.

"The other thing is—and I'm not trying to justify myself here, but

I admired your talent so much that I wanted you to learn to be tough. Ready to face life among the Big Boys."

"You were right about that—I'm not inherently tough."

"Life in the sciences for a woman, even when she reaches the top as I have, can be a bear, so to speak. I've tried to let it roll off me, because you can't hold onto that kind of humiliation and anger or it will prevent you from moving forward. But if I were to tell you the number of times I've wanted to clock my male colleagues—men at my level, full professors with labs, but not nearly as many publications and citations as I have—well, I don't think you'd believe me."

"I think I would. Now."

"I'm not talking about the all-too-common dismissive comments, but about the concrete disparities between men and women at the same level, like access to funding and lab space and hiring of postdocs. It goes on and on."

"I didn't realize you—You've always seemed—"

"Oh yes, I've made a practice of holding my head high and my gaze forward—you know *acting as if*—and of course keeping a sense of humor about it all, but I've archived it all here," she thumps her chest, "a kind of scarring or grudge I try not to think about too much."

"I had no idea."

"I wasn't consciously keeping these things from you, but I didn't want to scare you away either."

"You must have sensed I'm too easily scared."

"If you weren't ultrasensitive I doubt you'd be able to do this—whatever it is." She gestures out to the lake and mountains as if to say *your canvas*. Bronwyn feels Diane's soft adjacent shoulder, the slow rise and fall of her breath. Diane has never been so candid. Bronwyn has never felt so close to her mentor, so comfortable with the silence that now cradles them.

"I can see something is afoot here," Diane says. "Trust your instincts and keep charging forward. All you can do is shoot from the hip."

Shoot from the hip? That has hardly been an approach Diane has relied on herself. Not as far as Bronwyn has observed. Diane has always been planful, always projected an array of possible outcomes from her teaching exercises and research efforts.

"Tell me about Edel."

"Edel. Oh my." Diane shakes her head. "She's the daughter of my landlady in Greenland. She's been through a tough time. A friend of hers committed suicide in January."

"Really? That's awful. Just this afternoon Penina suggested we all commit suicide since the world is going to end anyway."

"Did she mean it?"

"I don't know. It was my fault for speaking too openly about how many climate scientists feel despair."

"You were being honest."

"Should you be honest with a twelve-almost-thirteen-year-old? I don't know. But I spoke to her just now and she didn't appear to be suicidal. Not that I'm an expert."

"I'm so glad I'm not growing up now. How does anyone resist pessimism? As for Edel. Aka, her mother, got me to help Edel with English and we developed a good rapport. She's not always as reticent as she was tonight. She's in a rock band, as I said, and she and her friend wrote a song in English about their friend's suicide. They invited me to hear them play it. This girl, my God, she has amazing talent. Her voice is, well—I hope she'll sing for us here. Maybe when she's relaxed a little. She's formidable."

"Did you bring her here thinking I'd teach her too?"

"No, I wasn't thinking of that. I had no idea what you were really doing here. Joe told me only the broad strokes but I knew I had to see for myself. I hope it wasn't too forward of me to arrive unannounced."

"It was pretty forward." Shocked by her own candor, she pauses to search Diane's face, finds what she takes to be matching surprise. "No worries, I'm glad you're here."

They both laugh.

"Bringing Edel was a very last-minute thing. I thought she needed to get out of Greenland and see more of the world and when I suggested it she was immediately enthusiastic. Maybe she can watch?"

"Sure. Unless the others object. As I've said, I'm improvising every-thing here."

"Of course."

"No syllabus."

Diane laughs. "Of course not—the best way to learn, I'm discover-ing."

"The three people I've brought here are already very attuned," Bron-wyn says. "Analu definitely, but also Felipe and Patty."

"I saw that at dinner."

"You could tell?"

Diane chuckles. "Maybe you underestimate me. Maybe I could be your best student."

Diane is a wonderful woman, there is no doubt about that, and Felipe would never say aloud that he wishes she hadn't come, but that is ex-actly how he feels. He has moved to a new cabin where he sleeps alone. It was only natural that Diane and Joe should be in a cabin together, especially after so much time apart. But Felipe, who has for as long as he can remember lived alone, has liked the recent nights of bed-ding down with someone else in the same room. It was how his sisters used to sleep growing up, all in the same room, chatting until the pull of dreams silenced them. That's how it has been with Joe. The nights they've been here they've been sharing impressions of the others, dis-cussing the next day, discussing everything really. Felipe, who has a tendency to be over-amped, has been getting to sleep more easily and earlier with Joe nearby. He's begun to wonder if Joe likes it too. Is it possible, Felipe has asked himself, that he's falling a little in love with Joe? Is it possible that the assumptions people have always made about him are true? But if he was made to love men, wouldn't he have been aware of it long before this?

Whatever he feels for Joe is deep. And now, with Diane here, he's been cast out, and he feels a surge of loneliness. He can't help thinking about Joe and Diane in the next cabin over. Are they sharing the same narrow bed? What would it be like to lie next to Joe's body, a husky broad body but not the least bit fat, their legs rustling beneath the sheets, their heat mingling, finding Joe's head in the dark, ruffling his blond hair, tracing his features?

It does no harm to wonder about these things. Hasn't every man entertained such thoughts at one time or another? He will try not to hold it against Diane for taking Joe away. He can see she's a wonderful woman, it isn't her fault. Still, it doesn't stop him from wishing.

Patty hears Edel flipping and flopping on the narrow lower bunk a few feet away. Side to back to belly to side. Poor girl, she can't sleep. Patty can almost hear the girl's mind, electrified with thoughts Patty can't begin to imagine. Patty herself, distracted as she is by Edel's presence, can't sleep either. She wonders if this is how mothers feel, aware of every move of their infants, worried they're not comfortable, or not happy, or afraid they might suddenly die. Not that she thinks Edel is going to die, but she must be destabilized by all the recent traveling she's done. Patty herself never knows if she's coming or going after a plane flight.

She lies as still as she can, listening to the water lap the shoreline like a dog wanting to make friends. The lake has a tranquil vigilance she loves. It seems privy to ancient knowledge, a lure Patty finds irresistible.

"Edel?" she whispers. Then, a little louder, "Edel?"

"Yes."

"Would you like to take a little walk down to the dock?"

"Yes," Edel says, so quickly it's as if she was waiting to be asked.

Patty throws on a robe. Edel is already fully clothed, has gone to bed that way. Both holding flashlights, Patty takes the lead, the beam of Edel's light flicking between Patty's legs. In the short time Patty has been here she has become quite familiar with this path and she feels remarkably confident despite the dark.

"Hey!" Penina hails them with a loud whisper. She stands in front of the cabin she shares with Analu. "Where're you guys going?"

"Oh, you surprised me!" Patty says. "We couldn't sleep so we're going down to the dock."

"I can't sleep either. Can I come with you?"

"Maybe you should you check with your father?"

"He's asleep."

"Sure. Come along."

Penina slips back inside for her flashlight then falls in behind Edel, and the three make their way through the trees, across the lawn, and down to the dock, Patty feeling like the Pied Piper. The girls are silent and Patty remembers Penina's moodiness at the dinner table, her apparent dissatisfaction with the new arrivals.

At the edge of the dock Patty hesitates. The gray arms of wood stretch out over the black water, swaying a little with the water's movement. She suddenly realizes she shouldn't lead the girls onto the dock when she herself can't swim.

"Come on, let's go," Penina says, scooting past Patty and skipping down the dock, impervious to danger.

"Wait," Patty cautions. "Edel, do you know how to swim?"

"No swim."

"I don't swim either. Penina, we shouldn't go out there. Edel and I can't swim so if something happened . . ."

"I can swim. If something happened, I could rescue you. Well, maybe not you, but I could rescue Edel. But we won't fall in, I promise." Penina has double-backed to them to plead her case. "Please."

Patty wishes she hadn't proposed this expedition. It's almost midnight and they should all be back in bed trying to sleep.

Penina has shifted gears. She scans Edel, head to toe. "Why can't you swim, Edel?" Curious more than confrontational.

Edel shrugs. "Cold."

"She comes from a land of snow and ice—the water there is much too cold for swimming."

"I'm gonna teach you. You and Patty and Diane. Okay?"

Edel nods.

"We'll see," Patty says. "I think it's cold here too. Maybe not as cold as Greenland, but still pretty cold."

"Can't we go out there for a minute? We won't run. We'll walk slow. Just for a minute."

"Oh dear," Patty says. "I guess so. But very carefully."

Penina takes the lead now and Edel follows. Patty falls in behind, tightening the belt on her robe, hoping that Penina will rein in her headstrong spirit. But Penina, true to her promise, advances slowly, their footsteps quiet on the weather-beaten wood. The whine of the planks. The knocking of metal hinges. At a gap between two sections of the dock Penina reaches back to grab Edel's hand. "Careful here. Take a giant step." They cross the gap hand-in-hand. Patty follows.

They reach the dock's end and stare out, Penina and Edel standing beside each other, shoulder to shoulder, Patty hovering just behind. The water and sky are smeared with stars. The night sounds crescendo around them: the chanting peepers, the occasional burp of a bullfrog, overhead the pump and flutter of wings.

"Isn't it gorgeous?" Patty says.

"Many stars," Edel says.

"Let's eat them," Penina suggests.

Edel chuckles. "Too many."

"What's your animal?" Penina asks Edel.

Edel regards Penina curiously. "Animal?"

"You know—what animal are you most like? My dad—he's a fish. Me, I'm some animal I haven't met yet." She growls and makes a face.

Edel laughs. "I don't know."

"How old are you, anyway?"

"Fifteen."

"My birthday's coming up in a few days. I'll be thirteen."

Edel nods, absorbing it all, accepting it all. Two island girls from different hemispheres converging here so unexpectedly, so randomly, tiptoeing toward friendship at the end of this lakeside dock in New Hampshire. What an unlikelihood, Patty thinks, what a wonderful serendipitous unlikelihood. She wishes Earl could see.

41

All night long Bronwyn rattles with questions. She has always sought silence—the silence of pre-dawn while most are still asleep, the hush of museums and churches and libraries, the active silence of forests—but it wasn't until she reached college that she began to understand that the unrelenting racket prevailing nearly everywhere in modern cities is actually dangerous. It blunts the senses, interferes with concentration, curtails thought. She suddenly became aware of noise as a source of stress in her own life and, as she researched a paper about noise pollution for an Environmental Studies class she was taking, she learned that a surfeit of sound, especially prolonged exposure to loud sound, could affect human immunity and cause a variety of health problems. She was lucky to receive a small grant that enabled her to travel to Minneapolis to visit the anechoic chamber at Orfield Laboratories, a soundproof room that blocks 99.9 percent of all sound. She was eager to experience what she thought would be as close to pure silence as possible.

The room was devoid of the usual clamor of human life, of course, but it was hardly silent. The blare and squall of her own body took center stage: eyelids scraping like snowplows over her eyeballs, tendons and bones snapping when she reached out an arm, hair rustling over her shoulders like crinkling wrapping paper. Each intake of breath rattled down her trachea, and her gut churned and boiled as energetically as magma. When she turned her head, even slightly, her scalp moved over her skull with the sound of a stretching tarp. Who knew her own body produced such a carnival of sound?! She left the chamber understanding something she'd never known before: A person's hearing could, under the right circumstances, be trained to be more acute.

In the months and years following that astonishing experience, she learned how to spin a chrysalis of protective silence around herself while going about her daily business, a sheath that sealed out the assault of horns and jackhammers and jets, even the lower decibel incursions of cell phones and voices. Eventually this capability allowed her to hear—and then alter—the deep rhythms of the Earth.

But how can she teach these foundational skills to others? Quiet Analu seems to possibly already be on the path to deep listening, but what about Felipe and Patty who are both avid talkers, especially Patty? Chatty Patty. Can one be as social as Patty is—and Penina too— and also be a supreme listener?

Who knows what is teachable? She can only try. On the precipice of sleep she makes her decision: Yes, they will observe the days of silence, as planned. The hooting owl affirms her decision and guides her into sleep.

She awakens early, pulls on trousers and a fleece, and creeps quietly out of the cabin, leaving Matt asleep. The morning is cool, but she can already feel that by midday it will be summery-hot, despite solstice being over a month away. She makes her way down the forest path past the other cabins, happy to be the first person up. After breakfast, she'll call a short meeting to clarify the importance of the upcoming days of silence.

A surprise/not-surprise to see Felipe stretching on the dock. He waves to her and she crosses the dewy grass to join him on the dock. "Good morning. You're up early." Her voice is a sacrilege in the vast quiet.

"I may speak?"

"Oh yes. No silence just yet. Breakfast first. Then a meeting."

"I don't sleep much here. Something says: *Get up.* The air? The water?"

"Yes, me too."

They contemplate the lake. The water, graduating from black to gray, is unfathomably still, the sun a mere wink between the trees on the Eastern shore. In the static air the smallest of sounds are amplified. The domestic rustle of waking birds. Evaporating dew.

"Everything is okay with you?" she asks.

"Very okay. Very excellent."

"Good. Don't let me interrupt. There will be coffee in the lodge soon."

She leaves him to make a pot of coffee in the lodge kitchen, then brings a cup out to the deck to watch the sun ripen, feeling resolute and strong.

After scrambled eggs and toast and subdued conversation—people have apparently already prepared themselves for silence—the expanded group gathers on the deck, Patty and Diane in chairs, Analu, Felipe, Edel, and Penina perched on the stone wall that forms the deck's perimeter, Joe and Matt standing. How willingly they listen to her. How ready they appear to follow her lead. She knows this is not the teaching norm. She's attended numerous classes over the years in which a few students have taken on the role of provocateur, bent on challenging whatever ideas are offered as authority or wisdom. Her own opposition in the classroom has never emerged visibly; if she felt resistant she kept it to herself.

"So today we begin three days of silence. It might be challenging at first, but I think, in the end, you'll like it."

Penina's hand shoots up immediately. "What if we can't do it? What if we forget and talk anyway? We might *have* to talk—I mean, isn't talking sort of like breathing, like if you don't do it you'll die?"

Bronwyn laughs. Gorgeous outspoken Penina. "I don't think you'll die. But you don't have to worry—there's no punishment if you accidentally speak. Still, I want you to *try* to be as silent as much as you can. Here's why . . ."

She explains what she has learned about herself, how silence has become the precursor for deep listening. She tells them about how sound blunts the senses and interferes with focus, about the anechoic chamber, about how she has learned there is always more to be heard if you've made the space for listening. Analu is blinking rapidly. She sees she has said enough—the rest they must discover for themselves.

"Feel free to go anywhere you wish. Write things down if you like. We'll ring the bell for lunch at twelve thirty and dinner at six thirty.

And when the three days are over we'll talk about what it's been like. And, of course, we'll celebrate Penina's thirteenth birthday. Then we'll be ready for the hands-on work."

They stand and look about uncertainly, ready but not ready, unsure where to situate themselves.

"Wait!" Penina again. "Is it okay if we do things together? Patty and I were going to paint our toenails. Edel too, if she wants. And Felipe and I might want to swim, right Felipe?"

"You can do things with each other. But try to spend a good deal of time alone. If you're communicating with other people you're communicating less with the Earth."

"Are we allowed to sing?" asks Patty.

Bronwyn has not considered singing. It is certainly a form of human communication. But she can only constrain them so much. "If you need to sing go ahead."

Diane squeezes Patty's arm. "When we're allowed to speak again, we'll have a good chat, you and I."

"I'd love that! Now—where do we all go?" Patty gives voice to everyone's question.

"It's up to you," Bronwyn says. "Completely up to you. The trail around the lake is not a bad place to begin."

She rings the lodge bell and they begin to disperse, Analu to the boathouse, Felipe across the lawn to pick up the trail along the Eastern shore, Penina heading up the path to the craft house. Patty ambles to the dock to watch Analu launch a canoe. Bronwyn keeps her eye on Edel, worrying a little. What an odd experience to arrive in the US and immediately be brought to this camp full of strangers and thrust into silence. But what can Bronwyn do? Nothing at this point. Edel follows in Patty's wake, keeping a distance. She'll be fine, Bronwyn tells herself.

Matt, Bronwyn, Joe, and Diane remain on the patio. "I guess we're part of this too," Diane says.

"If you don't want to . . ." Bronwyn says.

"No, no, I'm all on board." Diane jogs in place to demonstrate her commitment.

"Group hug." Joe spreads his arms wide, summoning the others. Their faces come within inches of each other, their heat merging.

42

Matt and Joe return to the lodge for cleanup, and Diane descends the lawn and follows the path along the western shore. Bronwyn, alone on the deck and suddenly adrift, closes her eyes and senses all the others, just out of sight, sliding into the morning's hush, silent as fish, turning their senses inside out. The day opens to them: the lake a glassy rotunda; the trees with their fresh spring pinafores; the thickening grass crisscrossed, lacelike; the rocks along the shore stacked and tumbling like ancient ruins.

They listen with fingers, with tongues, with newly calibrated hearts.

Patty senses, in the quick passing of other bodies, intimations of sadness and joy.

Felipe, stopping at a sandy beach, moves to the rhythm of the dolorous song in his gut, lifts a leg, sweeps an arm into the air, spins with his eyes closed, his muscles gathering knowledge. A cricket clicks under a bush, leaps. Water licks the rocks.

Analu, in his canoe, picks up a floating stick, brings it to his nose to sniff, remembering the floral scent of Nalani's hair, draws the stick across his lips, notices the family of loons trailing in his wake.

Joe presses his palms into a ball of dough, labile, granular, smooth, the warmth of his hands pouring into it. The joy of Joe seeps into everything he touches, everything he regards. Diane is back.

Matt, after Bronwyn has disappeared, comes out to the deck of the lodge and sits on the wall. He makes a few notes in his journal, hearing the scratch of his pen merging with the scratch of a scampering chipmunk, merging with the flapping wing of a passing hawk. A woodpecker drills. Someone crunches along the gravel path. He is acutely aware of being an outsider here, but the journalist is always an outsider so he must learn to live with that, must be comfortable with always shining the light on the activities and accomplishments of others. Envy is unproductive; it gets in the way. But it's comforting to think that Bronwyn is also an outsider. In this way they are alike.

Penina spends an hour cutting lengths of gimp and stringing beads, wondering what she might do with all the raffia. She steps outside and the sun blinds her; she sees auras, vapors. She stands alert, something's about to happen. Where is Edel? Where is Patty? Songs race through her bloodstream.

Edel lies on her back on the lawn with her eyes closed, the sun pressing warmth into her cheeks. There is nothing to do. What freedom in having nothing to do, in doing nothing. She hears voices from far away that are buried in her skin, her dead friend Kunnana singing.

Diane walks for a while along the rocky bank, trying to expunge the fatigue of travel. In a cuneal space between rocks she sits and watches as light swoons over the lake and marks the passage of time. The geyserlike energy she has always had—physical energy, intellectual energy—is hard to locate. Now she wants to be quiet and thoughtful as she learned to be in Greenland. More like Joe. She hears Aka's voice: *And so . . .*

Let go, Bronwyn tells herself. *In silence, things happen.* She settles on a bed of fragrant needles under a white pine, bony spine against bony bark, face shaded, bare legs outstretched to the sun. She opens her pores, letting her "I" slip away.

When Penina sits beside her they hold hands and stroke each other's hair, Bronwyn's a jungle of feral curls, Penina's glossy and black, storing the sun's heat. Penina lays her head in Bronwyn's lap and smiles up, surprising Bronwyn with her radiance. Sun and moon converge in that smile. It occurs to Bronwyn that people sometimes—maybe not often enough—match the magnificence of the natural world.

Joe rings the bell and they converge like a flock. Around the table they navigate easily in silence, embracing the discipline, already acclimated, a slow minuet of bodies. Brief exchanges of glances and quick smiles, lovers grazing shoulders, nothing more. They take food outside on paper plates and scatter again.

Penina lies in the grass at the edge of the deck, savoring the last of an oatmeal cookie, and studying a whorl of high white cloud, thinking of the way Bronwyn described herself as a young girl. A car drives up. She sits abruptly. A man gets out. He's big and bearded, in shorts and a wide-brimmed floppy gray hat that dips down over his neck.

"Hey there, how's it going?"

Penina stares at the man's red face, thinking of tomato sauce. She blinks.

"Hon? Are you all right?"

"Is this an emergency?" she says. "I'm not allowed to talk unless it's an emergency."

"Are you Australian?"

Penina nods. Maybe she is.

"You came all the way from Australia to write?"

Penina blinks.

"Where's Joe?"

She points to the lodge.

Joe looks up. The sight of Robert is jarring.

"Hey there, Joe. Didn't realize you had kids here."

"Just one. Well, two."

"You don't let them talk?"

"It's—an exercise."

Robert shrugs, looks around. "I came by to see if you need anything."

"We're fine thanks."

"Getting things done then?"

"Yup."

"Hey, I forgot to ask—what's the name of your operation?"

"We don't have a name yet."

"No name? How do you do any marketing without a name?"

"We're working on it."

"All right then. Write up a storm." Turning to go, he peers out the
window and sees Felipe twirling on the dock. "Strangest way to write
I've ever seen. Give a call if you need anything."

"Thanks." Joe hesitates then calls out before Robert gets through the
door. "One thing though. What we're doing here, it's private. Surprise
visits—they interrupt the flow, you know?"

Robert frowns. "Butt out then, is that what you're saying?" He
laughs. "You creative types. Whatever you say, Joe. See you around."

Joe watches Robert drive off then he closes his eyes and allows the
silence to reenter him.

The day waxes hot, as Bronwyn anticipated, and passes through every
color, concluding once again in blue. With anticipation of the oncoming darkness the urge to speak becomes more insistent: a scream, a
groan, a song, some utterance, any utterance, meaningful or not. But
twilight completes itself in darkness, and night sounds rise around
them, and the urge ebbs.

Not everyone sleeps.

Joe has pulled two mattresses from the bunks and smooshed them next
to each other on the cabin's limited floor space and covered them with
unzipped sleeping bags and blankets. It isn't the most elegant sleeping
arrangement, but it enables him and Diane to bed down together more
comfortably than if they were jammed into one of the narrow bunks.
Matt and Bronwyn may be able to fit on one of those bunks, but he and
Diane need more space.

What a relief it is to hold her again. It is cold enough that they've worn sweats to bed and he has to poke around a bit until he unearths a swath of her bare flesh which gives him access to the perpetual vitality she exudes. It is what he fell for in her and what he has so desperately missed while she's been in Greenland. She is doing the same with him, spelunking toward his bare belly, his crotch, where cool air and warm skin collide. They remain silent for a while as they reacquaint themselves with each other's bodies, undeterred by the lumpy mattresses and the chaos of sleeping bags and blankets and clothing and the cabin dust they've stirred up and the chilly air. When they have both come, they laugh.

"Well, silence is good for something," Diane says.

"Deprivation doesn't hurt either. I'm so glad you came. Am I mad, you ask. Only a little. Not nearly as much as I was." He makes his sad face, to tell her he's mostly kidding.

"Oh, Bucky, don't be mad. You know my leaving had nothing to do with you."

"It *felt* as if it had everything to do with me."

"You have every right to be mad. I can only say it won't happen again. Does that help? By the way, are we exempt from the silence rule at night? The others must be talking."

"It doesn't matter for us. We're not her students."

"I think I am her student now. But she'd understand—we have so much to catch up on, you and I. I'd put money down that she and Matt are talking too."

"So what was your idea in bringing Edel here?"

"That sounds like a challenge."

"No, just curiosity."

"I saw how badly she needed to get out of there. It's a beautiful place, but so cut off from the rest of the world. Something about her touched me. When she sings—it's so powerful and passionate. And her curiosity. She's so ready for experience. Also, there's something about her that reminds me a little of Bronwyn—how Bronwyn used to be when I first met her. How can you not love young women?"

"What about women your own age?"

"Sure, I like them, but, as you know, I'm not usually around many women my own age." She pauses. "Oh, you're thinking of Patty. She's refreshing. I look forward to talking more to her."

"She's quite wonderful. More candid than you would expect. And somehow more powerful too."

Diane's head is resting on his arm so he feels her nodding through his bicep. "Do I seem different to you?" she asks.

He hesitates, wondering if there is some answer she hopes for. There *is* something slightly different about her—he sees it now that she asks. A very subtle difference. Greater repose perhaps. Lower decibels of certainty. But mostly she is the same woman he loves.

"Yes, maybe. Some new strains among the old?" he says.

She laughs. "New strains. That's it exactly, new strains."

Penina listens for her father's deep breathing. It takes forever for him to fall asleep, but he doesn't say a word to her, still bound by the silence. The silence is a relief to her, in a way, because it means he can't chide her or pelt her with questions. He has never asked her as many questions as he has on this trip. It's as if there's something he wants to know about her that even *she* doesn't know.

At last his breath moves like the tide, long and slow. She bunches up her blanket and shoulders it, finds her shoes and flashlight, and ever-so-quietly heads outside. It's cool out here, but the purple jacket keeps her warm. If she were another kind of girl the dark might scare her, but she's not scared—she has always been the last to get scared.

The other cabin is right next door, a short walk. She pokes her head in the doorway, aiming her flashlight beam down, expecting Edel and Patty to be awake as they were the night before. They're both conked out, still as rocks, Patty's breathing making a bug-like whir, Edel's silent as the stars. Penina enters, trying not to wake them, though she wouldn't mind if she did, and she fumbles her way to one of the empty bottom bunks. She turns off her light and sheds her shoes and climbs onto the mattress, drawing her blanket close, jacket still on, kept wide awake by the sound of her fluttering heart.

"Penina?"

It's Edel. "Yeah, it's me. I wanted to be in here with you guys."
"Yeah. Good. I like. Happy sleep."
"Happy sleep."

They awaken to rain, drumming, dripping, the air sodden with moisture. The heightened smells: mildew, decay, fresh growth. Sitting up in bed Penina wonders, is this an emergency? Maybe it isn't, she decides. Patty and Edel sleep on.

The downpour makes of the woods a bower. Umbrellas. Toads by the path. Worms everywhere. Wet sneakers.

At the main house Joe wads newspaper, arranges kindling, stacks dry logs that tumble from one another with a hollow clunk. The sulphury scent of the igniting match. Flame lurching, reaching. The warm acrid scent of the smoke, the scent of danger—and safety. Steam rises, phantom-like, from the wet shoes by the hearth.

On the lake raindrops fall like tiny explosions. Thousands of silver circles. Fish surface, mouths spread wide.

Felipe and Analu go outside and raise their faces, open their mouths like the fish, taste.

The plentiful water of this place, Felipe thinks.

The different water of this place, Analu thinks.

When they smile at each other it feels like speech.

They cluster at the lodge window, watching a moose who ambles over the grass as if he owns the camp, his gait arthritic, his jowly face dissatisfied. The height of him, the power, the thuggish insolence. Diane emerges from the woods, umbrella spread, sees the moose, stops. They are eye to eye, moose to woman, an uneasy standoff. An interminable minute passes. Diane lowers her umbrella as if arming herself. The rain shouts on the roof. The group's collective held breath grows heavy. The animal spreads his jaws, releases a hoarse, imperious bray. Diane inches backwards.

Analu pushes through the lodge's heavy front door onto the deck. He descends to the lawn. The moose turns to him. Analu advances within arm's length of the animal. The moose shifts his weight and the loose skin of his flank ripples. He stares at Analu. Analu now seems to have four legs—they all see it—and when he ambles into the woods on the far side of the lawn, the moose follows.

Diane, soaked, panting with relief, comes through lodge door, and everyone breathes freely again.

Rain, confining them inside, lengthens the day. Matt has brought a boom box and he puts in a CD. Classical guitar, deft, quick, sometimes mournful, each piece a different counterpoint to the plunking rain. He watches Bronwyn draw a finger pensively across her clavicle. He hardens, resists the urge to seize her.

Patty remembers the wounded, purple-haired girl on the plane traveling with her guitar. A bit like Edel, she thinks. She would love to sing now, but decides the time is not right. Instead, she brings out the toenail polish she brought from the cabin. Red, pink, gold. The girls crowd around her. Penina chooses the red, Edel the gold. Patty takes the pink. Patty paints Penina's toes. Penina paints Edel's toes. Edel paints Patty's toes. They work the tiny brushes with the slow deliberation of artists.

Analu inches closer to the crackling fire, feeling alone, not like the others here. He tries to keep his gaze away from Penina, as he knows she doesn't like to be watched. What panic he felt when he woke this morning to find she was not in her bed, only to see her moments later exiting with Edel from Patty's cabin. How can a daughter he is so proud of bring him such pain? Bound by silence, he has not been able to ask her why she left, but he knows why. He knows she is doing what many people say children must do, break away from their parents to learn who they are. But is that really necessary? Can't you learn who you are while remaining close to your family? He never disavowed his own parents. His father is dead, but he is still close to his mother. He can't remember ever pushing either of them away. Would Penina be different if they were all back on the island? Maybe, but how can he tell? Anyway, it's too late. He made a decision to leave the island and he can't take it back, and now things are happening to his daughter that even love can't prevent. He knows Nalani would tell him it's fine, but what if it's not fine?

Bronwyn thinks of the rain, how it's plastering them all with melancholy. How easy it would be to call up sun. She won't though. She sits on her hands, catches Matt's eye, smiles knowingly.

At night the rain drums on the cabin roof with a subtle syncopation that delights Felipe. It brings back memories of dancing with Isabella to a similar beat. Coordinating their two bodies to that beat was like finding the answer to a riddle no one else had ever been able to solve. This day of rain has transformed him. While the others settled in the lodge in front of a fire, he spent much of the day walking, fully centered in his body, hearing the power of his muscles at work stretching and contracting, much as Bronwyn described hearing her body in the soundproof chamber. He walked clear around the lake, his shoes squishing, his jacket soaked, inhaling the scent of wet pine trees, and the exercise cleansed him inside and the rain cleansed him outside, and he realized something about himself. For most of his adult life he has thought of himself as a free person, doing exactly what he chose, but in fact all his life he's been holding something back. Why shouldn't he love men and women both? Others are free with their love, why not him? Long ago he broke off communication with his father, but he now sees that his father's mark has remained on him, judging him, dictating what he could or couldn't do. But now, thousands of miles from home, in this rainstorm amidst this new tribe of people, he has become the Felipe he is meant to be, loving whoever he wants. Loving everyone.

He pulls the extra blanket over him. The rain seems to croon. No, it's a human voice crooning. He turns his ear toward the sound. It's Patty's voice, soaring into a high soprano melody whose words he can't make out. Tears spring to his eyes. Why is it that his friend Patty has so much power to move him? There's another voice there too, lower, throatier. He gets up and shawls himself in a blanket and steps barefooted into the rain.

He squishes down the path until he arrives at Patty's cabin. She and Penina and Edel are perched on the edge of their bunks, a flashlight on the floor, Patty and Edel singing as if for a huge audience. Penina listens. She spots Felipe and beckons him inside, patting the space on the mattress beside her.

The voices surround him, rich with the ache of human longing. He listens according to Bronwyn's instructions, as if listening to the Earth.

As Matt and Bronwyn bed down in the narrow bunk, Matt wants to talk, but he can tell Bronwyn might be too absorbed in thought. The silence was not designed for him, but it has brought him an unexpected peace. He has always enjoyed talking, since he was a young child and, as the youngest, held the job of keeping the family entertained. He has never considered before how talking can be a form of stress. But reflecting on it in the last two days he realizes how often he has worried about what he would say next, or has worried he'd said the wrong thing. Conversations can be fraught with so many interpersonal landmines, even with people you know well, like Joe and Bronwyn. Over the last two days he's found himself enjoying time in the kitchen working wordlessly around Joe. After the cleanup they have parted ways and Matt has chopped wood, restocked the latrine with toilet paper, then taken walks or short runs, returning in time to prepare meals. He's made a few notes in his journal, but mostly has found he doesn't want to write much. The first day Joe drove into town for gas and a few extra grocery items, but beyond that Matt has no idea what Joe has been doing.

The silent days don't seem to have relaxed Bronwyn. Sandwiched against her back he feels bolts of cognition streaking up and down her spine.

"Will you sleep?" he whispers.

"I hope so. But probably not." She turns to face him. "I was good for a while, but today it hit me that I'm in over my head."

"No, you're not."

"What if I can't teach them and have to send them home with nothing?"

"So big deal. That wouldn't make anything worse than it was."

"*I* would be worse. I would have failed."

"Bronwyn, listen to yourself. You had a bold idea and if it doesn't pan out, so be it—isn't that much of the history of human endeavor? You don't have to think of it as failure."

"I guess having Diane here makes me nervous. It makes me feel as if I'm performing."

"Tell her to go away."

"I can't do that. You know I can't."

"A few days ago you were wishing she was here."

"Oh, I know. I know. I'm just confused. I'll get over it."

He palms the back of her neck, turns her head, and pulls her face so close their noses touch. His eyes have adjusted to the dark, but still she appears to him in shades of gray. "I'd worry if you weren't confused." He finds her foreshortened pinky and holds it up. "Don't you agree, Lube?" He kisses the pinky tip and her lips, then he wriggles out from under the blanket and sleeping bag and tucks their edges more tightly around her. "I'm going to the other bunk so we can both get a good sleep."

"Wait. Listen." She sits up.

He pauses, kneels beside her bunk. Voices, singing voices, thread through the rain.

"Patty," he says.

"And someone else."

They listen. "Can it be Edel?" she says.

"See what you've already done? You're halfway there."

The third day of silence dawns clear. It's bound to be hot again. A spontaneous plan emerges. They prepare a picnic, take four canoes from the boathouse. Joe and Felipe. Penina and Edel and Patty. Analu and Diane. Bronwyn and Matt. They paddle across the lake where a strand of tawny beach lures them.

She paddles and thinks. Should she do the hands-on teaching with them as a group, or take them one by one? They might learn from watching each other, but she doesn't want them to become self-conscious or competitive. She tries to situate herself back in the present again, open-pored, resilient, only the sound of the paddles dipping, the aluminum keel parting the water, a plane buzzing overhead, the whir of proximate human breath and blood.

The truth of Matt's words: *You're halfway there.* He's right, something is working here. A few days ago these nine people could not have launched an expedition without speaking as they did today. Such accord. Such entrainment. Messages traveling between them with the speed of thought. They have learned things through silence, she thinks. It's up to her to trust their learning. And trust herself.

Penina's thirteenth birthday. They are free to talk and everyone talks ceaselessly all day long, exercising their vocal chords again—high, low, loud, soft, what freedom there is in speech! Even Analu is a chatterbox. They discuss what they saw, things they'd never seen before. The subtle noises they heard. What they dreamed about. The voices they heard from the past. Silence has uncovered so much. It has been like draining water from a lake to reveal furrows and rocks long buried.

Penina has made necklaces and she presents them proudly, one for each person except Bronwyn who already has one. And she has woven four raffia baskets, one for Patty, one for Edel, one for Bronwyn, one for her father. She cups them in her hands so they resemble bristly bird nests.

Joe has made a chocolate cake with pink frosting and decorated it with candles and an arrangement of leaves that say: PENINA—13! They all sing, Penina along with them. "Happy Birthday to *me!*" she shouts at the end and they all clap. Then they present her with gifts.

From Analu, a red and purple scarf he brought from Australia.

From Patty, a pink lipstick Penina has admired.

From Felipe, a stone in the shape of a heart he found on the beach.

From Diane, an "ice bear" tooth she smuggled in from Greenland.

From Joe, three gourmet chocolate bars and some maple sugar he bought in town.

From Matt, his own pocketknife.

From Edel, a blue-green iridescent feather she found in the woods.

From Bronwyn, a laminated map of the world she bought in Cambridge when she learned of Penina's birthday, along with a pair of lavender jellies, and a bar of verbena soap.

Thirteen, thirteen, thirteen, Penina says over and over, knowing she'll remember this birthday as long as she lives.

43

Bronwyn and Matt are up before dawn, alert as ravens, ready for anything. Matt makes coffee, Bronwyn arranges folding chairs on the lawn, facing the lake, just shy of the dock. There's a theatrical quality to what they're about to do, the dock and the lake their proscenium. She will take each student one by one, but she has decided they all can watch. The communal nature of this venture has never been clearer. There are so many ways they might help each other.

The day promises to be hot. She feels it even before the sunball breaches the horizon. This exceptionally warm spring is no surprise to her.

At eight thirty she stands before them, dressed in black jeans and black titanium jacket, hair tied back, feeling more rested than usual and indomitable. Her clothes are too warm for the day, but they'll help preserve her energy which will be in great demand. How fond she is of this tribe assembled before her—Matt and Joe have come down from the lodge too, the cooking can wait—and she's pleased, if somewhat surprised, that Diane and even Edel have blended with the others so easily. She's even more surprised that she no longer feels awkward taking charge in Diane's presence. She's rarely felt so sure of herself.

"We'll be feeling our way through this, as we have with everything else so far. Teaching this is as new to me as learning it is to you, so we all need to keep open minds. What I want you to do when it's your turn, is think of the awareness you've developed over the last few days, and try to use it to increase your concentration.

"There is energy all around us, much of which is never harnessed. What we're going to be doing is a very focused energy transfer. The first step involves corralling the energy in your gut, your internal energy, and condensing it into a ball. It requires deep, really directed concentration. You have to stay focused on your intention. The second part is shifting the energy to your chest and head and thrusting it outward, while keeping your intention in mind. Without strong directed intention, picturing the outcome, nothing is likely to happen."

She listens to herself, amazed she's found words to describe what she does.

"I'll talk you through the process quietly as you go, and I'll put my hands on your shoulders or back so you can feel my energy to help you build your own. For our initial efforts I'd like you all to try bringing on a light rain. We'll take it slowly. Maybe later in the week we'll get more ambitious."

She's about to summon Analu when it occurs to her that she should demonstrate. Patty has seen her doing interventions with tornados, and Matt and Joe and Diane have seen her at work, but Analu and Penina and Felipe haven't, apart from the fire video. Nor has Edel.

"Shall I go first?" she asks and everyone nods.

Remaining on the grass but turning to the water, she concentrates on the far shore, then elevates her gaze to the cloudless sky, envisioning clouds, picturing their vapor condensing into rain. She musters the heat and allows it to permeate her belly where it condenses to a white-hot ball. With minimal effort—an economy learned over time—she boosts the heat ball to her chest and lobs it forward, rocking slightly, lobs it again, lobs a third time—and rain falls.

Behind her, gasps, applause, but she doesn't turn, doesn't want the heat to dissipate. She centers her intention on stopping the shower and launches the heat again, three powerful thrusts. The rain stops.

She turns to them, panting a little, nowhere near as exhausted as she used to be. Patty and Penina are beside themselves. "Isn't it exciting," Patty says. "I forgot how dazzling it is."

"You have to let me try, Dad."

His daughter's voice disintegrates into the maw of his astonishment. The ground beneath his feet gives way as if the Earth has softened. This

woman standing before him, a woman who has seemed relatively ordinary until now, now he's sure she must be a goddess. She can't be
fully human. Who else could do what she has done? She darkened the
sky, brought on clouds, summoned rain, then she cleared it away, all in
minutes. She stands there smiling as if what she has done is perfectly
normal. Did he doubt she could do such a thing? Now he sees he must
have harbored doubt, at least a little. Seeing her perform in front of
him, it is nothing like watching the video, nothing at all like the fanta-
sies he worked up in his mind. He could almost see her energy on the
move, shuttling out from her body in waves. She looked to him like a
streak of lightning.

His notions about the world have always been indistinct, a haphaz-
ard composite of ideas from his ancestors, Biblical stories, folk wisdom,
all of which he has only half believed. There has been no call for him to
say this or that is true, he has simply gone about the business of living
and living has sometimes shown certain things to be more true than
others. The rest has remained uncertain, but uncertainty hasn't both-
ered him. It has seemed as much a part of life as truth. He has accepted
the world as it is, a world in which some things are known and others
might never be known. But now an uncertainty has resolved itself into
truth. This woman really can change the Earth.

In the grip of astonishment his body fills with island memories,
the sound of the murmuring ocean, the snorting of pigs, the scratch of
chickens, the scent of the island's hundreds of strands of life. For the
first time in months, he feels a rush of hope. He closes his eyes. *Thank
you. Thank you.*

Until this moment Felipe doubted. He wouldn't have said so to Patty,
but the video was finally proof of nothing. He came east with Patty out
of curiosity, and to support Patty who had become a good friend, and
because, as Isabella said, it was his job to see new things. But he never
expected to be turned inside out like this. Long ago he rejected his
family's—his entire culture's—Catholicism and its silly miracle stories.
He was always too old for the magic of childhood. He believed he was

too old for life to surprise him—or perhaps only bad things could surprise him, death and disaster.

Now there is only one thing to be done—endorse this big leap and
follow it as far as it leads him. He glances at Analu whose eyes are
shut as if in prayer. When Analu opens his eyes they share a smile of
incredulity.

The tears spring warm in Diane's eyes and carve salty rivulets down
her cheeks. They don't stop. She has always prided herself on being a
woman who, despite feeling strongly about many things, could always
control her tear ducts. But recently that has changed. She cried with
Aka and was surprised to see she felt no shame, and now she couldn't
be happier to let the tears flow as long as they must. It's been more than
a year and a half since Diane first saw Bronwyn in action, during the
remarkable walk at Walden Pond when Bronwyn brought on snow. A
pivotal moment in Diane's life. A moment that catalyzed such a radical
upheaval in her belief system that nothing has been the same since.
But, in the intervening time, when Bronwyn was absent and inaccessible, doubt crept in again. She never allowed it to rule her, but it made
her yearn to see more, eager to discover the range of Bronwyn's talent.

She could never not be astounded to watch Bronwyn in action.
She could never not be moved. Now, in deference to the others, some
of whom are seeing Bronwyn in action for the first time, she has to
hold herself back from locking Bronwyn in a fervid embrace and
squirreling her away. She can't help but feel proprietary. Nor can she
help thinking briefly of the Dean and all her mean-spirited colleagues,
and gloating a little about what she knows that they don't know. She's
proud of her own ability to stand strong when she's been ostracized.

Edel wonders if her eyes are playing tricks. It's happened before. A
week after Kunnana died, a blizzard came in. It went on for three
days, with monstrous winds and blinding snow, and Aka kept them
all inside, huddled around the stove. Her younger siblings kept busy
with games, but Edel was restless after only a few hours. She missed
her friends, missed her band; most of all she missed Kunnana. On

the third day, Edel sneaked outside. She bent into the onslaught and managed to travel a few paces out from the house. Nothing looked familiar. Everything spun around her until she herself seemed to be spinning. It was the time of year when it would have been dark without the snow, but the snow made everything darker. Her feet sank so deep they seemed to detach from her legs. Nothing resembled its usual self. When she turned to go back to the house it was gone from sight and she couldn't be sure which way to go. She stood still, calibrating, afraid to move too far in the wrong direction, afraid she might die. Her grandfather used to say Inuit people have perfect directional sense and never get lost—but here she was, lost. She blinked hard, as if clearing her vision would stop the snow. There was Kunnana, ten or twenty feet away, dancing like a thin wind-blown flame, receding into the snow then appearing again, laughing. Edel ran toward Kunnana, slipped, fell, got up, fell again. Was this how Kunnana herself had died? Was Kunnana urging her to come to the other side? Aka's call cut through the wind. *Edel! Edel!* Edel made herself rise and move in the direction of her mother's voice, refusing to look in Kunnana's direction though Kunnana was still there, still dancing and laughing at the edge of Edel's vision, as lively as she had always been in life. Back at the house Edel took Aka's chiding without a word of protest.

Was it the eyes or the mind that went crazy? Who was this Bronwyn who made rain? A sorceress? A witch? She was certainly someone extra-human. Edel wondered if she should be scared, but no one else appeared scared and neither was she exactly. Close to scared, but not. Excited. This wasn't what she'd expected America to be like, though now she realizes Diane was trying to prepare her.

Bronwyn wavers, stuck in some static pocket of time, shuttling along the paths she might take from here and those she's already taken. Before her their eyes flicker. She has their full attention and feels their deeper level of trust. Their need to learn is stark, it can't be hidden.

Heat flames in her hands, moving her forth.

"Line up," she says, pointing.

They form a row. Analu, Patty, Felipe. Penina gets up to join the grownups, but Analu shakes his head.

"Oh, Dad, come on. Please?"

"No." He turns to Bronwyn, seeking support.

"Just this part should be fine," she says. "It's only a short demonstration."

Father and daughter exchange excoriating looks then turn away from one another.

"Edel, would you like to join us?" Bronwyn asks.

Edel shakes her head, *no,* emphatic.

"Come on, Edel! It'll be fun," Penina begs.

"Let her be, Penina," Bronwyn says. "She has to want to."

Penina sighs and takes her place in line.

"I want you to know what this hot energy feels like in the body," she says. "Close your eyes."

She slides behind those who are standing and travels down the row, placing her hands on their shoulders, one by one, briefly, until she feels the tremor of skin beneath clothes, the successful transfer of heat. Analu remains still, Patty gasps, Felipe's shoulders twitch. She hesitates at Penina, stares at the white sheen of sunlight in the shawl of black hair. The girl stands in a state beyond still, waiting. No harm, she thinks, and she touches the girl's shoulders, feels a twinge, and withdraws quickly.

Penina ejects a growling laugh. "Got it. I got it!"

She sits them down again where Diane, Matt, Joe, and Edel have remained, a staunch and supportive audience. "That gives you a taste. Now we'll begin in earnest. Analu, let's start with you. We'll go to the end of the dock."

Analu nods, face slack, brown eyes rimmed with gold light. He follows her to the end of the dock near the diving board. "There's no need to worry, this isn't a performance," she says quietly. But clearly it is.

He says nothing, his concentration already doming, tensile. He stands with his feet apart and she slips behind him. His shoulders are hard, the dense muscles of a man who has spent a lifetime using his body for work. She touches them lightly. He isn't tall, maybe three or four inches taller than she, but his carriage is sturdy and vigorous. She can already feel his titanic focus, his burgeoning cache of heat, though she hasn't done a thing to help him.

"Okay," she whispers. "Gather it, let it rise. When you're ready, pitch it out there."

She hushes herself. He needs nothing more. He's alone with himself, churning, self-sufficient. She removes her hands from his shoulders, but remains behind him.

Almost immediately the sky darkens and rain falls, drops the size of coffee beans pelting the dock and lake, a downpour that has come on so heavily and in so little time that even she is astounded. Drenched, she resists the urge to laugh. Pandemonium sweeps across the lawn, shouts from Penina. Bronwyn and Analu do not turn.

"Now, arrest it," she whispers.

He shimmies from foot to foot. His breath buzzes. He widens his stance, hinges his neck back, stretches his arms to the sides like a raptor, then sweeps them overhead. She can't tell if he's in distress. She isn't strong enough to catch him should he need to be caught.

The rain ceases as quickly as it began and the sky regains its former clarity. He lowers his arms, turning to her with the purest expression of delight she's ever seen on a human face. She embraces him. The group cheers. He shakes his head in self-amazement. Elbows linked, they head back to the others who gather around, hugging and high-fiving Analu, their first Olympian.

For the first time since their arrival in the United States, Analu's doubt is erased. He wishes Vailea and Nalani had been here to see him. Never in his life has he felt so powerful. He made rain. He stopped rain. He wants to do this again and again, feel the swelling of heat in his chest, feel his will sweeping over the landscape and up to the sky.

Penina bounds toward him, hopping and hooting, her face painted with pride. She leaps up, clasping his neck, circling his hips with her legs. She may be drifting from him, but not entirely, she's here with him now. He returns her embrace, reeling with happiness.

Felipe will go next, but first Bronwyn proclaims a break. Everyone needs it, she in particular. They assemble in the lodge where Joe has laid out coffee and tea, lemonade, fruit slices, oatmeal cookies. Everyone is elated by Analu's prowess. They crowd around him, everyone but Edel, who keeps her distance.

"What did it feel like?" Diane asks. "I mean *inside* your body?"

Analu frowns, searching for words.

"Was it painful?"

He shakes his head. "Hot. Very hot."

Matt laughs "You're not kidding. She tried to teach me but I couldn't take the heat. Joe, however, was a real pro."

"No I wasn't. It wiped me out. I could hardly speak for days."

"Which is to say, we were both failures."

"Are you exhausted, Analu?" Patty asks.

"I'm fine. I feel fine." He grins winningly.

"I knew he'd be good at this," says Penina. "It's because he has *mana*. Maybe that means I could be good too."

Felipe has separated himself from the group. On the far side of the room near the fireplace he moves through a sequence of stretches. Bronwyn wanders over.

"There's no pressure to do this if you don't want."

"I want. I do want. I only have the stage fright. I always have the stage fright when I dance, when I act. You know?"

She nods. She worried about this, that pressure to perform would cramp them. She knows such pressure well—it haunted her in school, has haunted her with Diane. She always thought performers like Felipe had ways of banishing such anxiety. "I can tell the others not to watch if you'd like."

"Oh no, I get over it. I just breathe. It help to breathe." He takes an exaggerated breath and holds it, smiling, bent on reassuring her.

"Take as much time as you need. Let me know when you're ready— but no pressure at all. If you decide not to do it, that's perfectly all right."

Patty can't ever remember being so excited. Who ever thought life could turn in such a different direction after the age of sixty? She thought she was done with learning new things. She's so impressed with Analu, so impressed with Bronwyn. She hopes she'll meet with the same success. She thinks she will. Her whole body has been preparing unconsciously for weeks. But she wants to make notes before she has her turn. There were certain details about Analu's and Bronwyn's bodies that might help her out—the erect way they held their spines, chests lifted, the way Analu arched back his neck and raised his arms. She wants to photograph Felipe to better analyze these moves. She hopes her own body is strong enough to do what needs to be done.

She heads to her cabin for her notebook and phone, and hurries back, not wanting to be separated from the group for long, wanting to celebrate with them. As she emerges from the woods something at the far end of the lake nabs her attention. A rumbling. Tremulous light. A familiar insolent swagger. It cannot be. But yes.

She never knew she could fly so fast. She moves with the superhuman speed one knows only in dreams. By the time she reaches the dock the tornado is halfway down the lake advancing swiftly toward them, leering, jitterbugging, smaller than some tornados, but no less mean. Later she'll wonder why she didn't go to find Bronwyn, but now it doesn't occur to her. Her consciousness has narrowed to include only herself and the tornado; they're face to face, glare to glare, my power or yours. She's rehearsed this in her mind: visualizing her intention, harvesting energy, condensing the energy, then lifting and propelling it forth.

She squints. The squalling deafens her. Darkness bears down. The heat is present, but it's dense and heavy, nearly impossible to thrust. A sucking spin butts up against her, lifts, whirls.

Someone is hauling her from the water. *Patty? Patty?* She coughs. Spits. Gasps for air. Her eyelids flap. She lies collapsed on the dock, the men crouched around her.

On the couch in the lodge the clamor of agitated voices, their words nonsensical. She sorts her memories, but they're a mishmash, defying order and causality. The tornado's surly eyeless face. The unnatural urine-brown light. The fear. The nearly irresistible urge to flee. But she stayed, asserting herself, corralling heat. She can't remember the tornado ripping the boathouse, doesn't remember falling into the water. Most sadly, she doesn't remember the tornado collapsing to its knees, vanquished. Though this, she knows, did happen. If only she'd been aware at that moment. Next time, she thinks.

The voices gain clarity. "Who ever heard of a tornado in these parts?" Joe asks. Bronwyn and Diane say they've known of tornados in New Jersey, but not in New England. Though why should New England be exempt, Diane points out, tornados have no reason to respect state borders. Should they call Robert, or mend the boathouse themselves? Joe feels responsible to let Robert know what has happened—the place is his, after all—but he's not thrilled about having that man poking around.

Patty drifts again, pleased with herself, but so spent. When she opens her eyes she finds Penina on the floor beside the couch, knees hunkered to her chest, forking her fingers down a long lock of hair.

"I'm sorry," Penina whispers.

"Oh, don't you worry about me. I'll be all right."

"But I could have killed you," Penina whispers. "I didn't want to kill anyone."

Patty says nothing. Penina stares at the floor, lips retracted into her mouth, biting down.

"Don't tell my dad. He'll be so mad."

Patty waits a long time. It doesn't seem possible. "You did that?"

Penina blinks quickly. "I saw my dad do it and I just wanted to see . . . I've never seen a tornado before . . . I was going to stop it sooner, but . . ."

They weigh in together. Bronwyn and Matt, Joe and Diane. Matt and Joe say they can repair the boathouse themselves. There's only one side and part of the roof involved; once they get hold of the lumber it won't take long. Two days tops. Joe is ambivalent about not informing Robert, but agrees it could be worse to quit what they've started, especially now after such a near catastrophe. Diane doesn't weigh in. When has Bronwyn ever seen Diane choosing not to voice her opinion?

Maybe they should quit, she thinks. Isn't an incident like this the reason she gave up interventions in the first place? Should they risk calling Robert, having him come by and possibly put a stop to everything? Not that he would conclude that the tornado had anything to do with them, but he would probably feel a need to clear them out, clean up, and fix the boathouse ASAP with the camp season looming.

Felipe still wants to learn, but she could teach him elsewhere.

What of Penina, rambunctious Penina? At thirteen capable of stirring up a tornado with next to no instruction. A mind-boggling feat. If only she had the judgment to go along with her skill. Analu has taken her off somewhere to give her a dressing down, but Bronwyn will have to say something too.

Penina curls into a blanket cave, flicking the flashlight's cone of twitchy yellow light here and there, trying to crush a mosquito that got in there with her. Her father hates her. He gave her the anvil look, black and heavy and almost as scary as the mean look of the tornado. Not a big talker, his looks are worse than words. Maybe she'll hibernate in this cave for the rest of the day. She can't go out and face him again—or all those others she almost killed. She wishes her father would yell instead of talking to her quietly as he did, not raising his voice even a teensy bit. He wanted her to know that what she did was *terrible-terrible*, like the worst thing a human being could do.

She didn't *mean* to do it. Not like that. She didn't even know she *could* do it. But she was curious to see what a tornado would look like, just a small one she could easily put out. She didn't confess to him how powerful she felt calling up that tornado. She told him she was sorry. She told him she'd never do it again. She told him she didn't mean to. She said: *At least no one died.* But nothing erased his *I-can't-believe-you-belong-to-me* look.

For a while she cried, but crying got old, and she didn't like the idea of giving in to crying on the day after her birthday.

She has no idea how much time has gone by. Bronwyn poked her head in once and so did Patty. They both said her name a few times, sounding worried more than mad, but she didn't answer. She wonders if they'll send everyone home. Her father will tell her mother and grandmother what she did, and everyone will be ashamed of her, instead of proud as they're supposed to be of a girl of thirteen.

She snaps off the flashlight and turns over in a sweaty tangle of sheets and hair. Peeking out from under the covers she can't tell the time. She only knows that yesterday was the best day of her life and today is the worst. Still, every once in a while, she's pricked by a sliver of pride. She has the power! But as soon as she allows herself to think this, shame wallops the pride.

She yanks the covers from the bed and takes the sheet and cowls it over her head and hugs it around her shoulders and belly, so she feels unrecognizable as a desert nomad. She steps out of the cabin, trying to read the light. Midafternoon? Late afternoon? Still too many hours of this wretched day to get through.

She plods along the path away from the lodge, sheet flogging the bushes and catching in them. With no plan in mind she detours into the craft building and turns on the light. She's the only one who uses this place so she's come to regard it as hers, but now there's a chipmunk on the work table staring at her from under the raffia, his tiny cheeks bulging in and out like a mechanized toy. She takes a step toward him, and he skitters over beads and short ends of gimp, and heads straight down the side of the table and across the floor and into a hole between flooring and wall.

She should clean this place up. But why? If people are mad at her, she can be mad back. She plugs in the pottery wheel and watches it spin, useless spinning, stupid as the spinning earth. The spinning tornado jumps to mind, the rush of its killer wind, and the memory converts her anger to shame again. She unplugs the wheel and it whines to a slow halt. She doesn't care if they never go back to the island. She doesn't belong there anyway.

She stares at the ridiculous rounded kindergarten scissors on the table. Just looking at them makes her feel like a dumb kid, too young for anything sharp or fun. For grownup things like sex and love.

She sheds the sheet, and picks up the scissors, and tries them out on a lock of hair. It succumbs to the blades better than the gimp did, better than the raffia. The long strand, two feet or more, falls to the floor and lies there, a loose dark curve. One by one lengths of rope-like hair land by her feet, splayed like pathetic maidens waiting for princes to carry them off.

She looks up from the floor to see Edel just inside the door.

"You cut?"

"I was sick of it anyway." But the truth is, she wasn't sick of it—she has always loved her hair. She fluffs what remains, wishing she had a mirror.

"Now like me," Edel says, moving into the cabin and perching on a stool.

Penina gathers her hair and lays it on the table, strokes it. "That was stupid."

"You have much power," Edel says calmly. Although Edel is fifteen Penina has thought of her as younger, maybe because she's so shy, but now she seems her real age.

"My dad is really mad at me."

"Scary?"

"What? You mean was it scary? Not really. It was so fast. I wasn't really thinking about anything like being scared."

"For me—I be scared."

"Don't you even want to try? It was fun. It would still be fun if everyone wasn't so pissed off at me. You should try."

"No." Edel shakes her head hard, as if she's trying to convince herself of something.

"But if you did, you could do stuff in Greenland, right? Freeze all that ice again. Don't they need to do that?"

"You do that. I do—other things."

"What things?" Penina unravels the red gimp spool and begins cutting off short lengths of it. She has no plan, but the cutting is satisfying.

Edel shrugs. "Sing."

"Singing is good, but—I don't know, don't you want to, like, *affect* things? Me, I always want to affect things."

"Affect?"

"You know, like, *influence* things." Snip, snip. The gimp strands are growing into a small pile.

"With singing maybe. Influence the hearts."

Penina stops cutting and regards Edel who has placed a palm on her heart. What is she trying to say? Penina has the distinct feeling that Edel's heart is different from other hearts, bigger and more passionate in the way it pumps blood. Maybe Edel's blood is redder than other people's blood, and with a heart and blood like that she really could affect people with her singing. In fact, Edel's heart seems to be singing right now, singing of a feeling without any words or sound. Respect and sympathy. Friendship. Penina feels herself pitching into Edel's unusual mind.

Matt and Joe have gone to town for lumber and Bronwyn sits in a corner of the lodge ruminating, hand opening and closing as if beckoning herself. The others have scattered, she has no idea where. They're on their own for a while, recovering from the morning's shock. There are decisions to be made, but the most pressing one—what to do about the boathouse—has already been made. They're keeping it quiet and forging on.

Still, Bronwyn feels an acute sense of danger, not Penina herself, but the dangerous underbelly of this skill. Anyone can misuse it and, in a moment of thoughtlessness, endanger others. Which puts Bronwyn back in precisely the place where she was when she began this project. Can any intervention be executed without imperiling so much?

She fingers the beads of the necklace Penina gave her, feeling in them the girl's vast electric charge. Outside the deck grouses, and Diane's ample torso passes the window, then takes a seat in one of the Adirondack chairs so only part of her back is visible. Who is she to Diane now? Who is Diane to her? The friction between them has dissolved, but the altered relationship has not clarified itself. There's been so little opportunity for time and privacy with so many people around, and so much has happened.

The door opens and Diane peers in, face obscured in shadow, silhouette investigative, ursine. She steps inside and looks around, but it takes a number of seconds before she spots Bronwyn. When she does, she drags a chair to the corner and sets it down.

"I thought I might find you here."

Bronwyn nods.

"Hard to absorb, isn't it? Good that our mates are doers."

"You're a doer too," Bronwyn points out.

"Not in that way." Diane sighs. "Not anymore. In the old days I would have been in your face hours ago, telling you what to do." She chuckles.

"And I would have been begging you to tell me."

They both laugh. Diane's presence is a balm.

"I'm a woman powered by a different consciousness," Diane says. "Thanks to you. And Aka and Edel."

"I didn't set out to change you."

"Oh I know that. And I don't resent it—I didn't mean to imply that. Although, as you know, I find it challenging to live with so much uncertainty. But I'm getting better at it."

"At this moment I'm finding it pretty excruciating myself."

"You've done a good job here. I think you're a better teacher than I've ever been. And you're powering on. That takes guts."

"I'm having serious second thoughts. I feel like I'm unleashing so much danger." In the ensuing silence she inspects herself. Is she issuing a plea for advice? Perhaps, but not a desperate plea as it might have been in the past.

"When I was in Greenland I thought a lot about—well, I thought a lot about a lot of things. For a woman who was essentially getting paid to think, I discovered my life in Cambridge wasn't allowing me to think much. Not deep thinking. Anyway, one of the things I thought about was this article I read a few years back that stuck with me. It was about a man, a psychologist, who was having acute anxiety attacks—PTSD symptoms from some past trauma—and he found he was terrified to go to work and talk to patients. So he underwent an experimental therapy that involved taking some sort of hallucinogen—LSD, I believe—and going through a guided 'trip' with a professional, under controlled circumstances. It completely changed his life. He realized the only thing that was important was, in his words, to *show up and be open. Show up and be open*—isn't that wonderful?"

"Show up and be open." Bronwyn repeats the words several times in her head. It's exactly what Diane has been doing since she appeared here. It's what she herself has tried to do, though she's succeeded only intermittently.

"So that's my mantra these days. Dr. Diane Fenwick has a mantra, can you believe it? Every morning I say to myself: *Okay, Diane, just show up and be open.*"

"Do you mind if I borrow it?"

"I'd be honored."

Diane reaches out and touches Bronwyn's thigh and Bronwyn does the same. They are so immersed in one another they scarcely notice the door opening, a sheeted figure coming toward them.

The sheet drops to the floor. Penina's hair has been roughly shorn just below her ears. It thistles out in all directions, addled and forbidding, chic and wounded, reminding Bronwyn of a woman she once saw in Cambridge with tattoos up and down her throat. Bronwyn tries not to gasp, and senses Diane doing the same.

Penina extends her forearms—her thick black braid dangles across them, tied on both ends with purple gimp. "I'm really sorry. Do you know how sorry I am? You know I won't ever, ever, ever do it again?"

Edel is there too, Bronwyn realizes, just inside the doorway, watching them all.

The four men repair the boathouse. Felipe stands on a ladder and hammers away as anxiety trundles in again. How did he make it through all those years on stage—it seems incomprehensible to him now. But not much ever rode on a single stage performance. If he missed a few steps, or blew his lines, there was always another performance during which he could redeem himself. Now it feels as if the next big era of his life rides on his success or failure at learning this new skill and handling it with supreme wisdom. He has an image of himself as the prodigal son of São Paulo, returning to save the city with rain. But what if he can't learn to do it? What if he's afraid like Matt was, or finds it too exhausting like Joe? Or worse—does something unwitting-ly destructive like Penina? This day of construction has opened up too much time to think.

The women have gone into town, Bronwyn and Diane slightly sheep-ish about not lending a hand with the repair effort—they're perfectly able-bodied, after all, such work needn't be the sole province of men—but Joe and Matt insisted the men are more experienced and would be more efficient on their own.

So Bronwyn, Diane, Patty, Penina, and Edel are sightseeing. The two older women, the two younger women, and Bronwyn. They visit the site of an old mine rich with mineral deposits of feldspar, beryl, and mica. The formations date back to the Devonian period before which time the entire state of New Hampshire was underwater. They wander through the cavernous old shafts fingering the ancient meta-morphic rock, admiring the crystals. Penina and Edel collect sheets of mica almost as big as their palms.

They lunch on BLTs at Pop's diner, then browse in a gift shop selling whittled totem poles, hand-sewn dolls, ropes of black licorice and lumps of maple sugar. The aimless wandering soothes and restores them.

In the evening everyone convenes in the lodge for pizza. The day has exhausted the men, but the work is complete and everyone is relieved and mostly renewed, if more somber than before.

Felipe washes the dishes, offering Joe some relief from kitchen work. Diane dries. But Joe, tired as he is, can't leave the kitchen; he hovers behind them, chatting about what a skillful job everyone did on the boathouse, what a great contracting company they could create if they wanted.

Felipe feels the discomfort of Diane's keen attention. "There's no humiliation in not succeeding, Felipe. If you can't do it, you can't do it. We're all your friends, right Joe?"

"Yeah," Felipe says, thinking it's strange for Diane to call him a friend when they've only known each other a few days. But it occurs to him that she's right, they *are* friends. All the people here have become friends and will be forever, even if they never see each other again.

"I've said this before," Joe says, "but it bears repeating. Bronwyn tried to teach me and I found that I'm not cut out for it. What Analu did, what Penina and Patty did—it's just not for me. And I'm okay with that. And if it doesn't work out for you, we're here to tell you that it's really okay."

Joe comes up behind Felipe and kneads his shoulders, and he stiffens, but after a moment Joe's kneading compels him to relax, and his hands go limp in the soapy water, and his chin falls to his chest, and he drops the utensils he was cleaning and savors whatever it is that flows through Joe's hands, allowing himself to be the complicated person he is.

When they head to their cabins for bed they see an elation of stars, a billion trillion of them slung haphazardly across the sky, the gauzy swath of the Milky Way pulsing. Who would think that filmy-looking scarf is composed of so many stars? How human beings flatter themselves in thinking they know so much.

44

At dawn Felipe is on the dock in his soft slippers skimming through yoga poses. Against the pale pink sky his body appears meaningful as a Chinese character. When the chairs are set Bronwyn sits to watch.

His yoga has morphed into dance now, his feet tapping the wood lightly, giving context to the morning's encompassing quiet. He raises his long arms skyward, delicate bendable wands, then buckles suddenly at the waist, crumples to a rag-like heap that flourishes again in a leap that lands him eight feet across the dock. Sometimes his body ripples like wind or water, then it detonates as thunder. She's never seen a body change so readily into so many different shapes and sizes. For a retired dancer, he still appears to be at the top of his game.

In one of his turns he spots her and, as if part of his choreography, he glides down the dock. "Now!" he says. "I'm ready. I have no fear. Please, now?"

She hesitates. Only Matt is awake and up as far as she knows. The others are still in their cabins, but Felipe's insistence is hard to resist. He holds her wrist and tugs her gently to the end of the dock.

"Here," he says.

"So near the water? After what happened with Patty?"

"I want here," he says. He turns and waits.

When she stands behind him he knows he's ready. Her hands on his shoulders leak a powerful heat, but their weight is a mere whisper. His body is already smoldering. He thinks of Joe's hands last night kneading, coaxing him to relax. Remembering, he does relax.

All the corporeal energy he has poured into dancing and acting over the years, the innumerable times his cells and muscles have fired, all that colossal output floods back to him, fusing with his love and longing, with the wounding of his eight-year-old self, the legacy of his father's destructive ire, spiraling into a helix of joy and pain, a moil he captures and zips into his belly. He compacts it all to a shot-put of heat and, with characteristic muscular ease, he elevates the heat to his chest and flings it out, never stronger, never more sure. He flings again, astonished by his own force.

And there it is—rain tumbling from pink sky, soaking the dawn, the dock, his shirt and shoes, and Bronwyn too, all awash. He would be content to let this rain fall indefinitely, to strip naked and feel it nourish his bare skin. He has never felt such joy. The fear is gone, all the anxiety that preceded this moment cleansed by this gift of falling water and newfound power. He *will* be the hero of São Paulo, he will. Water collects in his cupped hands.

Aware of the sudden rain, knowing exactly what it means, Analu and Patty and Penina are hastening down the path, shouting, laughing, clapping. Matt and Joe run down from the lodge.

"Rain dance!" calls Felipe and he strips naked, right there in the grass in front of them all, and he dances with abandon, limbs soaring, penis and scrotum flapping.

After a moment of disbelief, they all join in, still clothed but dancing with their own customized wiggling and gyrating. Penina and Edel gawk at Felipe's perfect body. Matt spins Bronwyn and she returns the spin. Joe grabs Diane and dips her backwards. Patty leans forward and wags her broad bottom, Analu claps. The rain continues to fall.

"What the *hell* is going on here?" Who knows how many minutes Robert has been there watching when he blunders down on them.

Bronwyn instinctively turns to the lake and sets about stopping the rain, though later she will wonder why—rain is not incriminating in and of itself, but at the time it seems so. Distracted, it takes her longer than usual. When she is done and the sky is clear and only the soaked wood of the dock and the wet grass give testimony, Joe and Matt are already in a deep conversational tussle with Robert. The others, heads bowed, are folding the chairs and ferrying them back to the deck of the lodge, eager to escape the notice and wrath of Robert, who's clearly unhinged.

"So *this* is why you tell me you need privacy—you're a bunch of *nudists*! Honestly, Joe, I came down here to see if the tornado I heard about on the Weather Service Station had come in here, figuring of course it didn't, you'd call if it did. And *this* is what I find?!"

Joe tries to answer, but Robert is beyond hearing. "I want you people out of here. I'll be here at ten tomorrow and if you're not gone, there'll be hell to pay."

Joe raises his palms in submission. "We'll be gone, Robert, I promise. Full disclosure. A tornado *did* come through here and it clipped part of the roof and the side of the boathouse. But it was relatively minor damage and we fixed it ourselves."

"Oh, for fuck's sake, a tornado hits my boathouse and you don't even *tell me*?!" Robert strides to the boathouse and Joe follows.

Everyone else, without need for instruction, heads back to the cabins to begin to pack up.

"Walk with me," Diane says to Bronwyn later, on the cusp of twilight, after they've spent the day packing and cleaning. "No agenda, just a walk."

They follow the path that circles the lake, though it's too far to circumnavigate the entire distance before nightfall. It feels good to walk together, something they've done as long as they've known each other, though not in the last couple of years. Holes have sprouted in the toes of the red sneakers Diane has been wearing for years, marking the length of their friendship. One would never take her to be a college professor, or an esteemed scientist.

"I hope you don't take any of today's events personally," Diane says. "I still think you made the right choice to stay."

"I hope so. But now what? Analu and Penina have another ten days before they fly back and I hate to send Patty and Felipe home on such short notice."

"We have room at our place. It'll be fine. And there are plenty of parks and preserves around the Boston area where you can do more teaching."

The path emerges from the woods onto a small crescent beach. They stop and reach down to sift the sand which is white and soft and still retains some of the day's heat.

"It reminds me of Caribbean sand," Diane says. "Surprising to find such fine sand like this so far from the ocean. We'll have to go to the Caribbean sometime, you and me. The clarity of that water is unparalleled."

Bronwyn, having never been to the Caribbean, cannot weigh in. She'd prefer not to talk anyway. The silence is prodigious, as if all human enterprises everywhere have abruptly ceased. The evening light is a tease, breathtaking, but already fading. "How can things be so beautiful," she says, "when we know how damaged everything is? Shouldn't damaged things be more ugly? To alert us that something's wrong? That's the way I always feel when I see space photos. All those gorgeous patterns that speak to worrisome changes."

"Greenland was like that. Full of damaged beauty. Glaciers that should never have been calving, but were stunning to look at."

Bronwyn removes her shoes and wades in. The water is cool and transparent and the bottom appears to remain sandy quite a ways out. It's too perfect not to swim. "Do you mind?" she asks Diane.

"Be my guest. It's too cold for me."

She has never undressed in front of Diane, odd as that seems for the length of time they've known each other, but now she does so with ease. She slips into the water quickly, trying to embrace its chill, then strokes out, her lean arms strong and decisive, the water parting beneath them and shimmying like silk. She treads water, appreciating how different the shoreline looks from this angle. A few cabins she hasn't seen before appear from behind the trees like stage set structures, pure illusion, ready to be dismantled at a moment's notice. She hates to leave the camp, but they have no choice, and she is satisfied that something useful has emerged. In only a week they've become close, and they've experimented successfully with interventions. But the question remains: Can they continue to work in concert, first in Boston then flung to distant parts of the globe? Diane waves and she waves back. How she loves Diane.

She swims back to shore and stands on the beach dripping, enjoy-

ing the stimulating tingle of shocked dendrites, before patting herself
dry with a sock. Diane, at the water's edge, staring out, has evaporated
into her own world. The new Diane thinking thoughts Bronwyn can
no longer fully imagine. Dressed but for her shoes, Bronwyn stands
beside her.

"Knowledge is only a rumor until it lives in the muscle," Diane says.
"Have you heard that expression? From a tribe in Papua New Guinea,
I think. I've been meaning to ask Analu if he knows it. He certainly
seems to practice it."

"I haven't heard it, but for me it's absolutely true. It's why—it's why
everything."

Diane thinks back to early Bronwyn, naïve untrained Bronwyn of
the sad background. It would have been impossible to predict back
then what she would become. But then, it would also have been impossible to predict what Diane herself has become. Still, aren't the seeds
always there, kernels of future selves, embedded in earlier selves? She
thinks of her trip to Mexico, years ago, with her ex-husband. In Cu-
ernavaca they saw a small boy, a toddler, dash into the street. He was
immediately hit by a van and disappeared beneath it. A man, the father
Diane assumed, came out of nowhere, completely beside himself. He
tore into the street and, with superhuman brawn, lifted the van from
the boy, an inconceivable feat for a man of any size, any strength. He
ran off, cradling the child. Numerous times over the years she has re-
visited that moment, wondering how the man could possibly summon
such strength. Defying physics. No known algorithm to explain it. The
answer, she now understands, is so obvious: he was powered by the
magnitude of his grief and love.

A mourning dove coos. "It's time, I think," Diane whispers.

Bronwyn is not receiving.

"Bronwyn, I'm ready."

The musculature of Bronwyn's face mimics the time-lapse photography of a drying lakebed or a melting icecap, and understanding arrives. "You . . . ?"

Diane nods. "I'm the only one except Edel who hasn't tried." Her feet are bare and she situates them deeper into the sand. She urges Bronwyn's featherweight hands to her shoulders.

They stand still as heat germinates, flourishes, journeys slowly from Bronwyn's hands through Diane's skin and bone and through her vessels, displacing the blood until she seems to float. The sun has dipped. The trees, pleased with their invisibility, no longer genuflect; they sigh and stretch themselves differently over the Earth's crust.

Time shrinks and expands and abandons its linear march.

Diane's thought exceeds the speed of light, visits and plunders all she's known, the dross and joy, failures and disappointments, all her victories and loves, the sum total of everything she's been and known; these chips of memory ignite, become a vortex, churning and gaseous as the sun. No longer bound by human senses, dwelling in neither mind nor body, no longer earthbound, she cedes herself to the galaxy, to star dust and planetary motion, to red giants and black holes, nothing and everything.

Millennia seem to have passed. The two women gaze out at the rain-splattered landscape, never so united.

PART THREE

Hiraeth:

(Welch) Longing, nostalgia, wistfulness; a homesickness for a
home you cannot return to, or that never was.

45

Patty stares out the plane's tiny window at the place she calls home, acre after acre of greening wheat and sorghum and corn, sectioned into perfectly rectangular fields. From where she sits everything appears flat, flat, flat, though she knows there are plenty of dips and rises. How random it is that this is the particular place she was born and raised and to which she has become attached, a mere pinpoint on the earth. Would she have become attached to some other place if she'd been born elsewhere? To Felipe's São Paulo or Analu's island? Though she knows she would have, it's hard for her to imagine. For most human beings you love what's familiar.

This is only the fifth airline flight she's ever taken, the second descent into Wichita, and the excitement she now feels matches any she's known in sixty years. She is so relieved her house hasn't sold yet. For the first time in her life her purpose is clear. For so many years she was at the beck and call of others. As an elementary school secretary it was the principal whose orders she jumped to, as well as teachers, parents, and students. At home it was Rand who called the shots. He didn't command her in any nasty way, he wasn't that type, but he made it perfectly clear how he wanted things and what he expected her to do. She was always glad to be of service to these people (if sometimes aggravated by their requests), but now it feels so delicious to be in charge of herself.

She glances around at the other passengers, wondering whether these people are going home, or if they're visitors to Kansas. Perhaps they're just passing through on their way to other destinations. It tickles her to realize they have no idea who she is and how important she may turn out be. Who would ever guess this aging woman would have much to offer, and while one part of her is dying to shout out about what she can do, who she's become, how she's been chosen, another part of her is content to remain completely below the radar.

She wonders if Felipe and Analu and Penina will feel this way—so excited and hopeful and important—when they return to their homes. Of course they will. Like she, they've been selected to make a difference, and they know how to do things no one else knows how to do. In a few weeks' time all of their lives have changed. She's so glad she listened to Earl.

It's late May and the tornado season is in full swing. Each year it has been starting earlier and earlier, and lasting well into the summer and fall. A few EF3s swept through Oklahoma while she was gone. An EF4 destroyed parts of Louisiana. Patty is on high alert. What is most disturbing is that the tornados seem to be coming in clusters. She sidles around her mostly empty house with eyes on the windows. She steps out onto the lawn, trawling the sky for suspicious signs, sniffing for wind. Attuned as a prairie dog. Ears cocked. Is that a touch of quivering saffron light on the horizon? Are the livestock acting strange, huddling more closely than usual?

Inspired by Felipe, she's become newly aware of how her body parts connect to one another, rump to leg, armpit to ribs, neck to shoulders. Around the house she goes barefoot and watches how her toes grip the floorboards like a chimp. Remembering Felipe's rain dance she laughs to herself. It all starts in the body. Vince Carmichael, the tornado pundit on TV, he uses his body too, but she wonders if he knows as much as he's reputed to know.

Every half hour throughout the night she awakens and sits upright, listening. The land is definitely unsettled. She hears it quivering, sweating, as if a birth is imminent—or is it death? She feels the pull to do something, but what? She hasn't worked out the specifics. She should have thought more about that. While the others have the thought experiments to do, working out the possible aftermaths of their actions, her thought experiments must be focused on where she can best situate herself before any tornado action begins. Is she supposed to become a storm chaser, driving around to potentially afflicted regions across several states at all hours of the day and night? She's only one person—what a limitation that turns out to be!

During the day, as she continues to box Rand's clothing and tools, she sees things in the landscape she's never seen before: black striations across the pastures; pleats in the trees; crops with closed fists, clutching secrets. She blinks repeatedly, worrying about her eyesight. Things didn't look this way before she went to California—or was it this way all along and she's only now begun to see it? She notices there's a curious absence of undomesticated animals, even the odd squirrel or bird.

Cora wants to get together, but Patty's been putting her off. *I'm too tired,* she says, but tired does not describe her even remotely—she's more aware and awake than she's ever been in her life.

Rand used to work in insurance. People bought crop protection policies, earthquake insurance, tornado and fire insurance. They hoped to shield themselves from disaster. If you don't have fire insurance a fire is more likely to happen, human beings tend to think. They said that to Rand all the time. Toss a little money—or these days a lot of money—in the right direction and then you'll be safe. What wishful thinking. Things would not be all right if you were dead. If you lost your home or your family, those things could never be restored, no matter how much money you'd spent. *Don't you mean you sell assurance?* she kidded him.

Knowing all the bad things that can happen, how do people keep living? But amazingly most people do. They carry on, go to work, come home and eat dinner, make babies. Astonishing really.

Some things help. Not thinking too much, thinking can paralyze. You begin to picture how your house will look as rubble, how your whole town will look; you wonder how you'll find the strength and resources to go on living.

She's glad she sings. Singing helps. Dancing helps Felipe, she could see that.

But what of the people who don't sing or dance? There are puzzles and crafts. Baking. There's all the traveling and trekking Cora's daughter does. Church, she supposes, helps some people; though for her, church in itself, without Earl or singing, doesn't really amount to much.

She tries to remember Earl's Commandments for Good Living. Every week he would include that as part of the service. He would laugh at himself as he said it: *And here is this week's Commandment for Good Living.* Always self-mocking like he was Garrison Keillor. He would say such silly things. *Enjoy pudding.* Or: *Wear warm socks.* The things he said were more like motherly advice than what you'd expect from a minister. He wasn't much for moral righteousness. His commandments weren't commandments as much as reassurances. *It doesn't matter,* he used to say. *Everyone is loveable,* he used to say. *Do the best you can.*

After insistent hounding from Cora, she agrees to lunch. "I'm a little distracted," she warns Cora, but Cora is a good friend, and she owes her an explanation. They meet at the Aurora Café downtown. Downtown is a lofty name for the single main street, two blocks long, in this simple, unpretentious town. Laundromat, cafe, bar, bank, drug store, gas station. For groceries you have to go at least twenty miles north or south. Having been decimated by tornados five times in the last eighty years, the town understands its temporary nature, the ease and speed with which it can be wiped out. Each time it's been destroyed it has rebuilt itself, but without succumbing to fortress mentality. Comprised largely of farmers, and spouses and children of farmers, the community understands that the Earth often provides bountifully, but just as easily grabs back that bounty. This is not a town that expects reprieve.

Walking to the café from her car, Patty eyes the overactive sky, its posse of nimbus clouds powered by a stiff wind. The air is moist and warm, perfect tornado fodder. But is the necessary cooler air descending from Canada? Is the jet stream aligned to produce mayhem? Bronwyn would know. She wishes Bronwyn were here now.

They sit in a booth by the window and order patty melts. They always have patty melts here, for the humor of it, and because they like them, and because Delphine, their waitress, now expects it of them.

Patty intends to tell Cora where she's been, what she's done, what she intends to do from now on. It isn't like telling just anyone, as Cora is not only a long-time friend, she also witnessed Bronwyn at work over two years ago now. She attended the church Earl led, she appreciates Earl almost as much as Patty does. There's no reason for Cora to doubt Patty—or vice versa. But the time that has elapsed since Bronwyn was here stopping tornados is long enough to have altered memory, long enough to have rewritten the narrative of Bronwyn, long enough for Cora to question and reject what she saw back then.

Cora and Patty could almost be sisters, both with big frosted hair-dos and shelf-like bosoms and a taste for geometric-patterned clothing, but their moods today could not be more different, Cora relaxed and talkative, Patty on edge. They dive into their drippy patty melts and Cora talks of her daughter's Mongolian trekking adventures, how she stayed with a family for two weeks in their yurt, and ate *aaruul*, chunks of curdled dehydrated milk. "Can you believe it?" Cora says.

It has begun to rain, heavy drops that bounce off the hot sidewalk. Cora is smiling too frequently, which seems like a sign she isn't going to believe what Patty has to say. Patty lays down her sandwich, suddenly unhungry, queasy even. The yurt family didn't speak English, Cora says. And her daughter didn't speak their Mongolian dialect. They used sign language and lots of laughter.

The air crackles with a charge. Patty wipes the cheesy grease from her fingers. In the booth across from them, a man stuffs his mouth with a handful of fries as if they're insulation. Patty blinks hard to clear her vision.

Delphine is coming toward them with two mugs of coffee. The rain has turned to hail the size of gumdrops. Patty needs to get outside. Her body feels light, full of air, as if she might levitate. Cars drift down Main Street in slow motion. Delphine lays down the coffee mugs. The agitated coffee sloshes from side to side. Cora and Delphine exchange smiles. She has to warn them, but can't speak. The light has darkened outside, yellowed. This is not business-as-usual. How can it be that she's the only one noticing?

She squeezes out from the booth, pats Cora's hand, Delphine's shoulder.

"Patty?" Cora says, but Patty continues out the front door into the street, quick, focused, devouring the pavement with the strapping stride of a holstered cowboy, grounded and ready, eyes in full rotation, scraping the horizon. She has entered a new dialogue, hears only amassing fronts of warm air, congealing water vapor, the powerhouse of colliding heat and cold. Pellets of hail nest in her hair, melting gradually. Patty is oblivious to the frail mosquito calls of Cora and Delphine.

She's alone on the street. Everyone else has taken cover. The wind hoots and lashes. She struggles to keep her eyes open. She is inside something enormous, a giant churning washing machine; yet an underlying calm rules her blood and seeps through her skin to the air around her.

As she arrives at the end of the block the wall cloud appears, exactly where she thought it would be, and its comrade is there too, the funnel cloud, skinny, descending, a cyclone of spiraling energy, magnetic, irresistible, sucking everything. It glares, advances, its gyrating core powered by murderous intent. For a fraction of a second she is terrified. Then the terror dissolves inexplicably. At the edge of town she stares out past the road to the left, across the flat field of fledgling corn where the beast hunkers.

She stops, firms her resolve, remembers how spontaneously she responded at the lake, and earlier, as a bald eight-year-old, how it felt to find her voice and realize she could control it, push it up from her belly and chest far out to the very back row of the school auditorium.

Earl is with her. Eyes open, body porous, will steely, she harvests heat. She condenses and raises it, jettisons it forth.

The hellion swaggers.

She launches again.

It resists, jerks abruptly, switches directions and advances towards her.

Again she hurls. And again.

It staggers, stumbles.

Enjoy pudding. Do your best.

On all fours she shudders. It's too much. Her confidence was misplaced. She lugs herself to her feet, heaves the load once more, gasping. *Everyone is loveable.* There is no reprieve.

The quiet is voluminous. Sepia light pulses in regular intervals over the cornfield, weak as a dying TV signal. Is she the Earth's last inhabitant? Is she dead?

She collapses onto her bottom on the road's warm wet asphalt. There's no equilibrium. Her head spins. The Earth spins. They aren't synchronized and the result is crazy-making. She's alive. She's the only human insane enough to be out now.

The quiet itself is dizzying, but slowly things normalize and her focus returns. Something is altered. She looks around the empty field, the traffic-less road. No signs of recent disturbance but the deafening quiet, the emptiness and the eerie quality of the light.

She's won, but not won. Where does the energy of a dashed tornado go? It will have to return, won't it? Maybe not soon, but sometime. It can only be held at bay so long. When it does return she might be ready—but maybe she won't be. She's that poor man doomed to pushing his rock up the hill with all his weight, again and again, never outwitting the force of gravity. A life sentence.

She has the skill, but she'll never be in charge. Earth calls the shots.

Her skin fizzes, happily electric. She centers herself. Patty Birch. Her voice is pale and thin, but still it's a voice, a singing human voice, and she sends a few low wordless notes, *ooh, ooh, ooh,* out over the cowering rescued corn to remind herself of what she has done.

46

The captain announces they're flying over Brazil now, and Felipe stares out the small window at the miles of dark green rain forest below, not a dwelling in sight, not a road. Wedges of brown clearcut come into view. Felipe has never visited this part of Brazil, so central to the country's reputation and livelihood. Coffee. Sugar. Cocoa. Once a thriving rubber industry. He should really go there sometime. Having traveled to the US it now feels shameful that he hasn't seen more of his own country.

There is the Amazon River itself, an undulant brown coil snaking through the wilderness, a sight he slept through on his way north, and now it makes him teary with national pride. At this height, the landscape looks noble, with its majestic river and large swath of trees, and he understands the Earth as ancient, heedless to the rise and fall of human civilizations, unmoved by the extinction of species, responsive only to its imperative to orbit the sun, until the sun itself burns out. This thought is comforting and scary. These days nothing is singular, a thought that wouldn't have occurred to him before these last months away.

He closes his eyes and drifts into sleep and dreams he's swimming from one body of water to another, the lake in New Hampshire, the ocean of his childhood near the Port of Santos, the Charles River where he and Patty and Penina and Analu walked daily when they were in Cambridge, all of them merging, one into the other, all calm waters and so clean he drinks as he swims, so clear he can see to the rocks and sandy ridges and declivities on the bottom and in a few places there are holes, long tunnels through bedrock at the end of which orange magma glows.

He buses from Cumbica to Isabella's apartment in Bom Retiro, gazing out with incredulity at the size and speed of the city he calls home. It can't have grown much in the time he's been gone, but it appears gargantuan. He gets out at the Luz station and drags his rolling suitcase the rest of the way. The neighborhood has been undergoing renewal efforts for several years, but it has a long way to go; the reek of urine wallops him; he dodges panhandlers, makes a wide arc around a collapsed bum.

He has given up his own apartment, having no income and no idea what will happen next, and Isabella has graciously agreed to put him up for as long as he needs. When she opens her apartment door, her smile resplendent, a gauzy saffron outfit drifting like smoke around her slim figure, making her body appear weightless as it was when she was a dancer, he finally finds something recognizable from the home he left. They collapse into an embrace. What a relief to be face-to-face again; texting can only convey so much.

He's exhausted from overnight travel, but conversation is impossible to resist, so he joins her in the kitchen where she bustles about heating up a dish of coconut shrimp and rice.

"Tell me everything."

He laughs. "Everything. You first."

"For me, there's nothing to tell. Pedro and I broke up, but I knew that was coming. What a relief. He was a blimp—all hot air. So full of himself. So what did you think of LA?"

He tries to describe his days in LA, walking on Venice Beach and watching the exhibitionistic circus unfolding around him, swimming, meeting Patty. He shows off his jellyfish scars which Isabella finds impressive. He describes how he and Patty became friends and began to meet regularly. What a surprising friendship it was. "There was something special about her," he says.

"Yes, I see," Isabella agrees when he shows her a closeup of Patty, billowing hair and broad smile, an icon of good cheer.

"She took me with her to New Hampshire where she had been invited, and we spent time with a group of people on a lake." He stops. What can he possibly say? She watches him over the rim of her wine glass.

"And what?" she says. "Something happened?"

He hesitates. "I'm so tired."

"You and Patty fell in love?"

"Oh no, nothing like that. We're good friends—good friends only. But this group of people from all over the world—we became a team, I guess you'd say. It's hard to explain."

Isabella nods. "We have time."

This is one of the things he has always loved about her; she doesn't pressure him—*You must tell*—as others might. She respects timing and rhythm, a dancer's understanding.

"Was I right to urge you to travel?"

"Oh yes. I think I love the world more now. But—"

"But what?"

"I'm more scared for it."

She urges him to wash up and get some sleep and ushers him to her spare room where he finally allows himself to give in to fatigue. The bathroom door is closed and when he opens it he understands why. The toilet has not been flushed for some time and a sign above it says: DO NOT FLUSH UNLESS ABSOLUTELY NECESSARY. The smell is nearly overpowering. Another sign on the door says: PLEASE CLOSE DOOR TIGHTLY. A spouted plastic jug holding a couple of gallons of water has been nestled into the sink, clearly a replacement for what might have come out of the tap in better days. He drips a little into the cup of his hands and splashes his face, lets it sit there for a moment before he towels it off.

The next morning he sleeps late, and when he rises Isabella has been gone for hours. He bounces around in the empty apartment feeling inconsequential as a dust mote. He would prefer not to be alone, but solitude may be required to work out a plan.

His limbs take to the pavement gladly as if they haven't moved in years—the rest of him is dazed by the city's skidding wildness. Everything rushes at him, refuses to be organized. *Sampa,* his city. Eleven million people, or nineteen million, depending on how you count.

Terra Da Garoa, it has been called, *Land of Drizzle.* Now that name seems almost comedic. *Non ducor, duco* is the city's motto. *I am not led, I lead.*

The rhythm of bodies, fast, slow, subways howling up through grates, a wild throbbing symphony. A patina of dust powders everything. A hydrant gushes. He's forgotten how a city this size seeps inside a person, instructs the blood how to move. A car passes, pounding out favela funk. A woman with a wheelbarrow transports water jugs across the street. The side of a building is tarred with the bold black slashes of *pichacao.* He is that car, that woman, those fierce black runes.

The buildings at the city's center shine silver and pink in the afternoon sun, reflecting each other in their mirrored glass. Shadows are peppered everywhere, despite the sun being almost overhead. A woman in red stilettos adjusts her décolletage in a storefront window. A suited businessman jogs through the crowd like an athlete, tie sailing. In front of the *Teatro Municipal* a group of youths practices *capoeira* to the beat of a drum. He borrows the beat and merges it with the rhythms already in him. His legs tingle with exhaustion, his mouth is dry, everything claims his attention equally.

He sends Isabella a text, offering to make dinner, but she says no, she wants to take him out (and she will pay). They sit across from each other at a sidewalk table, scarcely able to hear themselves speak over the traffic. He can't relax. They've sat across from each other like this hundreds of times before, but now there's only a superficial ease. He's aware of all he's withholding, and she seems aware of it too. But how can he begin to tell her what happened in New Hampshire? Why would she believe him if he were to tell her how many times he brought on rain then stopped it? Even after he saw the fire video, he wasn't a believer in Bronwyn's skill until he saw in person what she could do. How he wishes Isabella had been there with him.

"The city is so different," he says, "in just two months."

"Not so different."

"It seems much drier. And angrier."

"It's always been angry. You forget. There's joy here too." Isabella's face pleats a little, becoming more lopsided than usual. "But you're right, the water situation is very bad. The reservoirs are at less than seven percent now." She shrugs.

"Someday we'll have no water at all."

"No. Something will happen. Someone will figure it out."

"And if they don't?"

"With all these people? Someone always does."

"Maybe. But that person is going to have to step up soon. I walked all over today and it felt to me like a city in crisis."

"Perhaps I can't see it. I'm always here, the boiling frog."

That night sleep evades him. The room's air is stagnant, despite the open window. Night has a way of raising the city's volume and now it's impossibly loud. The clanging construction across the street has stopped, but it's been replaced by a clamorous party spilling into the street, bottles smashing, the doleful wail of sirens, taggers armed with spray cans combusting into the night.

It all washes over him as a haranguing lullaby, unleashing a cache of memories of a time when he surrounded himself with a tribe of artists and none of them were shackled with worry. Remembering, he wonders if he could find such a life here again, or is it lost to him now? He rides a wave of insatiable longing, along with a primal terror he's never felt before. On his way home he imagined being able to help these ten million Paulistanos, but he could ruin them just as easily.

If he were to replenish the reservoirs—the Cantareira system, the Guarapiranga basin, the Billings reservoir—a big if—how far would that go to solving the problem? Does he really possess the necessary skill to fill the water basins slowly, bringing on rain in defined areas so it isn't lost to runoff and doesn't cause flooding throughout the city, especially in the favelas? He and Bronwyn discussed this issue at length, and she supervised him in the summoning of light rain after they left New Hampshire. And Diane gave him formulas about soil absorption and drainage; he understood them at the time, but now he cannot understand how to apply what he learned. In this giant city of the southern hemisphere, the stakes are much higher, and he doubts his skill is adequately nuanced.

He already misses his US family: Patty, Bronwyn and Matt, Diane and Joe, Analu and Penina and Edel. He can email and text them, and even talk with them on the phone, but it isn't the same as having them beside him in the flesh, talking face-to-face.

Lying there, splashed with streetlight, he feels like an overgrown baby. He rises, goes to the window, peers out. *Sampa*, the New York of Brazil, never sleeps. The night air is pleasantly cool, but still so dry and dust-filled it scuffs his face. He closes his eyes, trying to parse the individual sounds that make up the harangue. Laughter, engines, horns, sirens, air conditioners, and much subtler sounds he can't name, objects colliding with other objects, hissing and huffing, the multitude of energy outputs from humans and machines.

Above all he must listen, Bronwyn instructed. This is his first and only task.

He's up early to drink espresso with Isabella, and he promises to make her dinner. After she leaves, he wipes his pits with tissue and forgoes a sponge bath, as the water jug in the sink is only a quarter full. Fastidious as he is with his body, he wants to be a team player.

A city that embraces night wakes slowly. In the morning light everything seems to creak and groan and object to waking, like a not-so-young woman who has danced for hours and upon rising is surprised to find her joints ache.

From Bom Retiro he heads north to the Tiete. Sun claws through the streets and alleys, exposing the night's excesses. Vials, needles, broken bottles, a few bodies collapsed here and there, given over to stuporous sleep. He learned at an early age how to navigate such neighborhoods with purpose, not too fast, avoiding eye contact. His childhood neighborhood was not so different.

Today he looks around more than usual, cognizant of his purpose, to watch and listen and learn anew the city he mistakenly thought he knew. He thinks of the days of silence at the camp. Then there was only nature speaking, the birds, the rustling creatures of the earth, the lapping lake water, the blue mountains, the unmasked stars. Here it's a different kind of listening. How does one listen to the Earth with so much asphalt and steel and concrete and glass intervening? How do you even *find* the Earth with so much in the way?

Where does the soul of any city reside? In the land on which the city is built, its particular place on the planet? Can't it also be found in the people who live there, the people who built it? It's all so linked, he thinks. But Bronwyn never mentioned the human element in her teaching. For her, listening was all about the Earth alone.

The Tiete River, passing through the northernmost section of the city, is not the river Felipe considered *his* river for most of his life. His river, the Pinheiros, is further south. Like the Pinheiros, the Tiete announces itself well in advance of seeing it. The stink of industrial filth and sewage. The sight bears out the promise of the smell. A suppurating trash-filled brown gash. He stands on the bank, mouth-breathing into his forearm. Around him the city's din has crescendoed into a blue hum, mostly ignorable.

What at a distance looked like ice floes turns out to be chunks of white foam, bouncing a little as they float past, sculpted into peaks like beaten egg whites, speckled with bits of debris. Purulent, phosphate-filled, soapy effluvia. Innominate industrial waste coming from the hydro-electric plants and factories upriver, intermingled with all manner of plastic and aluminum, shopping bags, soda bottles, beer cans. The water itself is viscous-looking, a cesspool curdled with human waste, and who knows what else, dying or already dead. To gaze at this river is to feel unclean. He's the only one here on the river bank. Why would anyone come here? Not to enjoy the ordinary pleasures of a river. Not to fish or swim or picnic. Can this river be salvaged, or is it already too far gone?

He turns away. How could he have lived here so long and thought so little of the shameful state of the city's rivers? Certainly they were already bad before he left. How can anyone see this sight daily—smell it—and continue to do nothing?

He remembers something from a long ago dance he did, performed to a soundtrack of readings from the Tao Te Ching. One should try to be like water, it said, nourishing without competing, being unafraid to flow to low places.

Later that day. The favela called Paradise City. The streets unpaved,
human life wherever you look. Sun electrifies the murals on the walls
of the shacks. Gigantic faces, caricatures of joy, caricatures of anger.
Tamborzao rhythms, electronic drums, hip-hop. Life in sound. Life
as long as the heart will beat. Life beginning in rhythm, ending in
rhythm. A window chunked out in a crumbling wall in the shape of a
ragged heart. Behind it a woman, naked from the waist up, bent over
a washbasin. She turns to his stare and he moves on. A shirtless man,
back aglisten with sweat, crouches beside a hibachi with skewers of
roasting meat, talking to his friend who pisses into a wall. Done pissing, the friend fills a pot with water from a blue PVC pipe that twists up
and down the street. Their only water source? Felipe wonders. Bathing,
cooking, pissing, privacy turned inside out.

A *catadore* picks delicately through a heap of trash. Lifting pieces
of chrome, wire, dropping them, not so desperate he doesn't discrim-
inate. Treasure will come. He smiles at Felipe and brings his fingers to
his mouth around an invisible cigarette. Felipe paws his back pocket
and hands over the pack from the airport he shouldn't have bought in
the first place. The man nods, returns to his picking. It wouldn't take
much rain to bury this entire fragile hillside neighborhood in mud.

He has water on the brain, dreams of water in his mouth, its ineffable
taste, water in the belly, water in each of his cells, making energy, releasing it. Powered by water. Water cascading over his skin, a warm
shower, a cool one, a hot bath, a foot soak, an electric dip in a gelid lake.
The way it felt to dance naked in the rain in New Hampshire. The way
it felt as a boy to immerse himself in the sea, where he came alive, in
water, the place he discovered dance.

The whims of water, the way it plummets from a cliff, breaks surface tension and overflows the lip of a glass, seeps stealthily into dirt
or asphalt, flows gladly to the lowest place. Water evades human grasp,
drips through fingers, refuses capture. The spirit of water is untamable.
A glacier melting, a cresting tsunami, a soupy river. The volume of the

Amazon—two hundred thousand cubic meters per second. Why isn't everyone, in the midst of such scarcity, obsessed with water as he is?

It soothes him to cook. He keeps his hands busy, making Isabella's favorite dishes, *acaraje,* black-eyed pea fritters, and tomato salad. He has splurged on a good red wine. He wants to live outside his mission, at least for an evening, and he hopes to dissolve the scrim that has grown up between him and Isabella. He misses the intimacy that has always characterized their friendship, and he knows it's his fault.

The dishes are on the table when she arrives home from work and, delighted with his efforts, she takes the conversational ball. Did he hear about the riot in front of the home of a city official who has been siphoning extra water to irrigate the elaborate landscaping of his garden? She slaps down a copy of the *Rio Times* with a picture of this residence in the toney Alto Pinheiros neighborhood. A gleaming swimming pool surrounded by flourishing bougainvillea. A three-tiered waterfall and a koi pond. It makes her think about her own work, which pays well, but often involves defending large corporations against charges of wrongdoing.

"My firm is often on the wrong side of justice. That means me too."

They shake their heads, sharing each other's horror at how the world works these days, bending not toward, but away from justice. A silence ensues, the perfect opening for him to say more, but instead he turns to his plate of food and fills his mouth, making himself un-reachable. They are occupying opposite sides of a Mobius strip with a puzzling distance to travel before they'll arrive at the same place.

"When I urged you to go away I think I was speaking to myself. I'm the one who needs to get out."

The next day Rafael, his director friend, calls. He has heard Felipe is back and could use work—would he consider stage managing a Pinter play? What a good friend Rafael is. But Pinter—now, here, why? And *stage managing*? It is no small job—herding actors, calling rehears-als, communicating with set and costume designers, coordinating the stage crew, along with all the record-keeping—and while he's done it before, early in his theater career, he has no particular talent for it. It's

certainly not his métier, and Rafael could easily find a far more quali-
fied person. But Felipe needs work. He promises to tell Rafael one way
or another before the week is out.

Needing to assess the water scarcity close up, he rents a car to visit one
of the reservoirs, Guarapiranga. The water has receded dozens of yards
from the old shoreline, and the sandy soil of its bed has cracked into
polygons separated by deep fissures. Its friable surface crumbles under
his feet, and with each step he sinks as he makes his way slowly to
the water. He passes an ancient-looking car without windows, its nose
inexplicably jackknifed into the dirt. A couple of small birds skitter in
front of him, searching for possible sustenance before they wing off for
better hunting grounds.

He can see it must have once been beautiful; viewed through a certain lens it is still beautiful, if you don't think of the favelas encroach-
ing not far away, leaching toxic wastewater and sewage. Human beings
are programmed to see most water as beautiful, he thinks, as a promise of bounty and fertility, the malignancies of water often hidden to
the human eye. This reservoir is no exception. It has never been deep,
but it covers a wide area of this flat basin not far from the ocean, and
there are still birds in abundance and plenty of greenery around the
periphery.

By the time he arrives at the water itself his feet are sinking almost
ankle-deep with each step. The water's color is unlike any water he
has seen, rippling in the slight breeze from brown to neon-green. He
knows exploding algae bloom accounts for this color, growth brought
on by excessive nutrients, and it doesn't take a hydrologist to understand it isn't good. He looks around for other people, wanting to share
his shock, but also half-expecting an official will yell at him to move
away. He passed no gates, showed no ID to get here. Shouldn't this
place, a public water supply to millions, be fenced and protected? What
if he were a person given to criminal acts? What if he were to dump
cyanide? The water's ability to clean and replenish itself—especially
in this country, home to so much of the earth's fresh water—has been
taken for granted for too long.

He retreats to his rental car and returns to the city in harrowing traffic. He's an infrequent and tense driver, has never owned a car, and behind the hermetic seal of this Honda Fit he feels incompetent and vulnerable. People honk at his hesitancy and sudden lane changes, and he curses them. What a fool he was to have imagined a triumphant homecoming, Paulistanos celebrating him and ferrying him through the streets on their shoulders at Carnival.

He sits in Isabella's living room in the late afternoon, about to begin fixing dinner, but stuck in thought, sifting through a bowl of polished stones, smooth and cool across his fingers. *Sampa* is to him like an old lover now, like Isabella, curtained off, refusing to show him the face whose every curve and line he once knew so well. *Why have you changed so profoundly in so few months?* The landmarks are the same in objective ways, but they appear older, feebler, closer to crumbling. Collapse feels imminent. And when people flee, where will they go? *Saudade.* Never has he understood that Portuguese word so well. *An amalgam of longing, melancholy, and nostalgia that is said to be part of the Brazilian temperament.*

He is thinking about calling Bronwyn and asking for advice about where to begin his work. His biggest fear is causing floods. They discussed this potential problem in Cambridge, but never drew a definitive conclusion regarding how he could avoid it. Do Patty and Analu feel as confused as he?

Isabella's living room, with its modern furnishings—sage leather sofa, black and brown rug with a geometric design, Calder-like mobile in one corner—feels like the wrong place for him to be. He should be outside, listening for messages from the Earth.

The apartment door opens and Isabella storms into the living room, home from work early. Urgency eddies around her. She drops her briefcase, casts off her lawyer's pumps and prim gray jacket, pulls the clips from her bun so hair slides down her shoulders, glossy strands of it glinting red in the setting sun. She sits beside him, a warren of intensity. "We need to talk."

She holds him in her gaze, her nose leading the investigation, hound-sharp, her eyes with their low thick brows following. There is no escaping her, no pretending. He has never felt so exposed. She sees to his heart, sees everything he has kept from her. A momentary flight carries him back to New Hampshire, the tranquil lake, the electrified feeling in his body as he moved past the edges of himself, the arbitrary boundary of his skin, to bring on rain. The mobile begins to spin, though the room appears to be still.

Isabella is not still. She unbuttons her blouse. "We both knew this would happen," she says. She unhooks her bra and reaches for his hands to bring them to rest on her firm breasts, perfectly matched to the size of his palms. "Yes?" she says.

Yes, but. He has always wanted her—to dance with her, to fuck her—but they have agreed for a long time that the stability of their friendship is paramount. So why? But the answer, even as he asks himself, is obvious. She is done pretending, and he should be too. She can't stand the distance between them. Sometimes sex is the only way through.

With her dancer's arched foot and pointed toes she shoves the coffee table out of their way and positions herself on the carpet, naked from the waist up, addressing the zipper of her skirt and her lawyer's pantyhose.

The simplicity of it all. The familiarity. The pleasure of Isabella's unabashed expression of lust, a trait of hers he has always loved. Immersed in her strong body, dancing with her again in this way—it hasn't happened for several years—he knows what to do. He knows her preferences, the way she loves to come with his fingers inside her, instead of his cock. Entangled with her, his questions disperse, at least for the moment. What satisfaction there is in knowing what to do.

Afterwards they lie on their backs, her thigh over his, his arm curved over her head, the day ceding to twilight, his mind in hiatus, pleasantly blank, the growl of the city both present and distant, neither of them needing to question what this interlude means as they might have in years past. He would be happy to die now and thereby attenuate this moment for eternity.

"No more hiding," she says. "Tell me."

Everything roars back. He stands with a suddenness that surprises even him. He dresses on the stage of her bewilderment. "Get dressed and come with me," he says.

Trusting him, she dresses quickly, in a loose tunic and lightweight linen trousers, and follows him outside. Their bodies move down the sidewalk as a single unit, not touching, but cohering, as if the space between them is magnetized. They take each other's lead, instinctive as shadows, comprising their own city of two, the cacophony around them impotent. They walk in silence, gliding, hips swaying, left, right, left, right, other pedestrians stepping out of their way as if they're celebrities, demanding space and respect.

They arrive at the *Praca da Se,* considered the city's center, near the *Catedral Metropolitana.* The pedestrian promenade is lined with tall coconut palms and fig trees. An olfactory feast of jasmine dampens the exhaust. They come to an empty bench where he sits. She sits too, alert, attentive to his every move.

He sniffs. Dry air. Dust. Exhaust. White flowers. Pedestrians streaming down the promenade laughing, the sound hollow, elongated like the soundtrack of a slow-motion movie. Their eyes are wet, the only moisture in this city. He opens to those eyes of his fellow city-dwellers.

He stands. Beneath his feet the Earth sighs. Isabella is saying something, but he can't hear. Her voice and all the syncopated rhythms around him—the footsteps, the voices, the traffic, the cathedral's ringing bells—are drowned out by an elemental whir. *Show up and be open,* Diane and Bronwyn told him, again and again.

His spine elongates as if he's growing a dorsal fin. Its fibers are hot, charged, shooting currents through his torso. *Show up and be open. Do what you can.* It's never uncomplicated, never one thing. Prying intention from his gut where it was threatening to atrophy, he compresses it into the cone of heat, raising his arms, vision blurred. The voice of something infinite summons him to service, and, as he pitches forth heat, a light rain begins to fall.

Gradually, he returns to himself, or some version of himself, and he looks for her, finds her still on the bench, not aghast but laughing,

her uplifted face awash with fresh rain, *his* rain, indistinguishable
from tears.

47

The pastor, Maru, finds Analu on the beach one morning when he is about to go out for fish. "You seem upset, Analu. Are you upset?"

Analu forces a smile. Maru is a kind old man, but he seems to believe his role as pastor gives him permission to intrude on anyone at any time. He deepens his voice and makes it creamy as if he's trying to bewitch people, and he laces his sentences with informal references to his good friends Jesus and God.

"I'm fine, Maru."

"You seem to be restless, if you don't mind my saying so." Maru strokes the shell that dangles from his neck. "Are you right with Jesus?"

Analu leans down to examine the motor of his small skiff, thinking of starting it to silence Maru. He doesn't like discussing religion. He has his own ways of praying that have nothing to do with Jesus. But Maru means well.

"It's challenging to come home," Analu says. "After so much time away."

"Yes, of course," Maru says. "God bless."

Analu had not prepared himself for the strangeness of coming home. The homecoming itself was a celebration that could not have been sweeter, almost all of the island's 523 residents gathered at the airstrip to greet them, singing, dancing, decorating their necks with garlands. Penina's cousins pounced on her, exclaiming about her beauty. Analu's sisters guided Vailea gently into a wheelchair. They all formed a rowdy procession back to the island's center where most of the houses cluster. The grin that overtook Vailea's weary face is a memory Analu will cherish for the rest of his life.

For several days the celebration has not abated. There has been non-stop visiting and eating and drinking and music. Vailea is staying with Analu's sister, Mahina, in one of the island's most substantial houses of concrete block. They arranged her bed near the window where she can look out past the trunks of the palms to the water. He and Nalani and Penina have taken up residence in one of the sleeping huts, open to the elements. If they decide to stay on after Vailea's death, Analu will build them something more protective.

The island is a small coral reef, six miles long, half a mile wide at its broadest. It curves gently into the shape of a sickle moon, a lagoon at its bosom, undeniably the island's heart. All his life Analu has been a student of the island, attuned to its changes, to the way the daily tides sculpt the shoreline differently, to the health of the trees, to the state of the small patches of arable land. He has always taken informal inventory of the wildlife, the birds visiting the island, those that reside here, the fish populating the surrounding waters.

Now his eyes are more than ever groomed to spot changes, but he's aware of the inaccuracies of his memory. Was the water always such a violent turquoise? Was the sand always such a blistering white? And what of the vegetation that he remembered as bright green, but now appears more gray than green? The water seems to have risen noticeably, narrowing the beaches, but the only place he can conclude this for sure is on the south side of the island at Dung's abandoned resort. At low tide the water on the concrete platform used to wash over his feet, but now it comes partway up his calves.

At the island's center there is plenty of evidence of change. Everyone is proud of the recently completed corrugated tin house built for Tamati's family. A couple of new generators have been installed near the church, and the office in the community building boasts two new computers with internet. Land has been cleared for a new primary school building; the old building was flooded during a king tide that caused an inland upwelling, an upwelling that also left some of the arable land too salty for cultivation. It seems to Analu that there are more chickens roaming free. Yes, things have changed in various ways.

But he also sees an underlying sameness, mostly in the people. There's the same resignation to being an impotent people on a small island that's disappearing. There's the same sense that nothing is urgent. There's the same unquestioned belief that God will work things out.

Analu takes his brother-in-law Kimo aside. Kimo, who is on the island council, is a brawny man who has grown a little bombastic with his modicum of power. What is the council planning to do in the long run? Analu asks. Kimo assures him they're on top of things. There are some larger islands not far away they can migrate to, if it comes to that. And they're considering asking New Zealand if the island's residents would be welcome there. But when Analu pushes for more details, he realizes no agreements have been made at all. No conversations have even begun. The council's plans are only talk, no action. And the talk is laced with false optimism.

He sometimes wishes he were a boy again. When he was a boy he was always the deepest and longest diver. He could stay underwater so long he worried his friends, and when he surfaced he would hear them cheering with relief. Underwater was a place he escaped to when his friends were bickering, when his mother expected too much from him, when he couldn't stand to hear more demands or arguments. It was a place with its own rules, unknowable to most humans. When he was underwater sound fell away, so all he heard was the pulsing of his own blood, as if diving was a portal into his own body; the intricacies of the coral, its tubes and minarets, its crenulated surfaces were like his own organs and arteries. The water refracted the sunlight into hues never found on land, and the fish, emerging from secret precincts of coral, flocked around him, loyal as shadows, occasionally nibbling his legs and feet.

Now diving is more difficult. He can no longer stay under for such lengths of time and he comes up gasping. The colors below are more muted, the fish fewer, the coral bleached and broken. He dives anyway, and when he comes up he collapses on the sand with his eyes closed, trying to remember what it felt like to be a boy, wishing he could be a boy still, with nothing in particular to do.

The sand is warm and so is the breeze, and Penina closes her eyes and falls into the pleasure of her cousin Kali's fingers raking her hair into short braids. Every once in a while Kali reaches down for a shell strung on a piece of twine, and she weaves the twine and its shell into the braid. Kali is slightly older than Penina, loud and sexy and madly in love with a boy named Fetu, and she has chosen Penina to be her confidante and constant companion, not noticing or caring that Penina is so withdrawn. Kali talks enough for both of them. All Penina's earlier conversational impulses and conflicting ideas are now trapped inside her head, dozens of gabbling Peninas with strong opinions. *This is your home. You don't belong here. You're nothing like your cousins. You and your cousins are exactly alike. You belong back in Australia. You belong in America. You will never belong anywhere. You will grow up to be like Bronwyn. You will never be like Bronwyn no matter how hard you try.* Do most people have all these warring voices in their heads?

Fetu is unpredictable, Kali is saying. Some days he brings her candies and asks her to go on walks. Other days he ignores her entirely, doesn't even appear to see her. Kali is going crazy. What should she do?

Penina has no idea. She's only thirteen and has never had a boyfriend, how can she possibly offer advice? She opens her eyes. Her father is launching his skiff at the far end of the beach. Since they arrived here a week ago her father has been quietly stewing. She hopes she won't ever become the insatiable worrier he is.

"There," Kali says. "I'm done."

Penina takes out the cell phone Bronwyn gave her as a parting gift so they could stay in touch (one of Bronwyn and Matt and Joe and Diane's many parting gifts, another being a big chunk of money to get them back to the island). The phone doesn't get the internet, but if she's close to the center of the island she can text and call, and she can always take pictures, and it has made her the envy of all her cousins. She pats her headful of shell-studded braids, so short compared to her old braids, then she leans into Kali, extends her arm, and snaps a photo of the two of them. Seconds later, she texts the photo to Bronwyn, and seconds after that a text comes back: *Gorgeous. You and the beach both! So far away. Hope you're well. Bronwyn will call soon. Love to you and Analu. M & B.* The text was obviously written by Matt. She hopes Bronwyn really will call.

That night three escaped pigs come to their sleeping hut. She hears the grunting first, then feels a cloud of hot breath on her face. She opens her eyes on a bristly snout and yelps. Her father is already up, ushering the three pigs away from their cots and outside. Her mother laughs, but Penina doesn't find it funny. She's used to sleeping inside. It isn't right to be awakened by the raunchy breath of a pig.

Her father doesn't return to bed right away. She listens for noises, wondering where he's gone, what he's doing, but the night's silence has closed around them again, not a sniffle of a breeze bothering the trees, not a rooster crowing. Only the sound of her mother snoring lightly.

Does her father feel filled up with this new power as she does? Penina can't stop thinking of how it felt to see the tornado advancing toward them from the other end of the lake, the bolt of power that exploded in her chest like a popped water balloon. What pride of accomplishment she felt for a moment, until fear took over and later shame when the grownups came down on her. Later, in the woods around Boston, Bronwyn taught her to do other interventions, despite Analu's disapproval, and those moments of accomplishment keep coming back to her, making her feel there's something good in her future, though she knows, from her father's stern looks, that she mustn't tell her friends and cousins of their shared secret. Only her mother and grandmother know.

Vailea's heart and breath move to new rhythms here, instructed by moon and tides, or perhaps the wind. Sometimes her heartbeat seems quick as a hummingbird's and then, for seconds at a time, it stops altogether and her vision flickers and, after a quick dart of pain, piercing but fleet, it starts again. At those times she thinks the end is near and she readies herself and prays, but then here she is again, Penina stroking her hand, behind Penina's shoulder the brindled pattern of sun vexing the sea, the women cackling in the other room—how she loves the noise of them all back together; in Australia four was never enough of a family, everyone gone much of the time, making each day long and lonesome.

Her sense of smell is weak, but she remembers perfectly the way the sea smells, the salt and brine, along with the indescribable smell of water itself, so irreducible, like the smell of your own blood. If she could choose where to be after she's dead, it would be in the warm clutch of the lagoon, feet touching the sandy bottom, head tipped back to drink up the sun.

Every day she praises Analu for doing all he did to return her here. Dear, dear Analu. She cherishes all her children, but Analu has a special place in her heart. Along with Penina, who squeezes out love masterfully through her stroking hands. What will become of Analu and Penina after she's gone, after her cells have rejoined the sea? They've always been restless souls, those two, and now, equipped since their travels with new power, who knows where their restlessness will take them. They, too, are lovers of water and sun. She trusts they both know what is worth saving and what can be tossed away.

Kimo has called a meeting at the community center to meet the esteemed visitor who is coming from New Zealand. The visitor, Dr. Hector Cox, a professor, will talk to them about water, how to collect and conserve more rainwater for drinking, and how to construct self-composting toilets so floodwater will not spread human waste.

Analu plans to attend, and he wants Nalani and Penina to go with him, his sisters too. It's important for everyone to understand how to conserve water, how to keep the island clean. Penina agrees to go, but Nalani and his sisters say they have other things to do, and it is not in Analu's nature to bend others to his desires.

A group of twelve gathers, mostly men Analu's age, Penina the only woman and young person present—not a great showing, but these people can disseminate what they learn.

Dr. Hector Cox is a New Zealander in his early thirties, an ectomorph with a red beard and a sunburned face and a righteousness about water. He begins by telling them what they already know: Because the island is a coral reef there is no way to dig wells, so the only source of fresh water is rain. The system for rain collection needs to be more efficient, he tells them, with stronger gutters connected more firmly to houses so the water can flow smoothly into the tanks that are also more steadfastly attached.

"You're losing thirty to forty percent of your water to the ground because of malfunctioning gutters."

He has a slide show with examples of the right and wrong ways to do things. His point is easily understood, but he repeats himself too much, as if the assembled group is composed of slow learners. Analu sees the other men getting bored. He himself is restless. But on the other side of the room Penina sits on her knees, still as Buddha, gaze on Hector. She is impossible for Analu to read these days. Her short braided hair, decorated with shells, appears childish, but there's no mistaking her for a child. Her eyes are sharp tentacles; they stick on things and pierce them. Is this from Bronwyn teaching her about focus, or was she always going to develop this way? He has never fathered a child who grew as old as thirteen. He thought he would understand any offspring of his own, but she seems to be entirely different from both him and Nalani. Is all human development so unpredictable? He wants to talk to her, but what would he say? Words would only reduce his love to something common.

She senses him watching and turns her head, her mouth hinting a smile.

Hector is on to self-composting toilets now. They've been built on the Big Island, he reports. They're a huge success. The king tides no longer come in and spread the sewage as they did with the flush toilets. Slide after slide appears, some showing the filthy aftermath of the king tides, others featuring a variety of life-changing toilets. "See how the leaves are used for composting," says Hector, "a certain percentage of dry leaves, a certain percentage of wet ones."

Some of the men have lost interest entirely and are talking among themselves. Some are wandering off. Hector tries to call them back. "This is important stuff here. You'll want to know this."

"Guys!" Kimo chimes in. "Come back!"

But the ones who have wandered off do not come back.

"What, am I talking to myself?" Hector says. "This is for your own good."

Kimo stands to one side of Hector's table, pacing a little, wondering what to do. Having called this meeting, he feels invested in its success. "Maybe we should take a break?" he suggests.

Hector ignores Kimo. He looks around at those remaining, spots Penina. "See, this young woman understands. She knows it's important."

Maru, the peacemaking pastor, goes to the front of the room and stands beside Hector. Hector seems dismayed. He assesses Maru, taking note of his slight limp, his missing front tooth, the threads of gray fringing his hairline.

"We must respect our visitor," Maru says, his voice especially creamy. "God has sent him."

"God has nothing to do with it," Hector snaps.

"You mustn't say that, Mister Doctor Hector. We are friends with God here. We believe he likes us and will protect us."

"Yes, I know all that. But that doesn't mean you shouldn't also try to conserve water and learn to use self-composting toilets."

"Some will and some won't," Maru says.

"And meanwhile you're happy to have sewage cover your island? You're okay with being desperate for clean drinking water? Having your children get sick?"

"We're used to such things. We've made peace with our lives, with God's help."

Some of the men who were talking are listening again. "Amen," they say, nodding in Maru's direction.

"Oh, for Christ's sake," Hector says.

Maru pats his shoulder. "Please. You must calm down. Thank you for coming. We have learned a great deal."

Hector is dismantling his slide show, boxing his projector, folding up the screen. He moves with a quick mechanical precision born of anger. Analu wonders how a man with such a short fuse has made this

his business. Perhaps he's new to it. Analu is suddenly eager to talk to Penina, learn her thoughts.

"You will eat with us?" Kimo whispers to Analu. "Help calm him down?"

Analu hesitates, turns to Penina, but she's already gone. He's inclined to track her down, but they have time, their conversation can wait. Now Kimo needs his help.

Penina has slipped out to her new favorite place on the southwest end of the island where no one else seems to visit but the sand crabs. She settles high on the beach in the shade of a copse of palms. She has been coming here a lot since their return to the island; she needs solitude more than she used to, and this is a good place to think. She thinks about all the things that happened on the trip to America, the days on the lake in New Hampshire, the days afterwards in Cambridge when they all stayed in Diane and Joe's big house and took daily "field trips" to surrounding lakes and woods and the ocean to practice more complex interventions. They became like a family, and Penina misses them, the older women Patty and Diane who were like extra mothers, the men Felipe and Joe and Matt who were so much more carefree than her father, and Edel who, despite her shyness, became a great friend. And Bronwyn herself, magical Bronwyn, how Penina yearns to be like Bronwyn. Sometimes, when she was in Bronwyn's presence, she experienced Bronwyn as if she was air, all the cells of her—the atoms or whatever—floating around in space, not contained by a body. It was weird because of course Bronwyn had a body. Still, sometimes Penina had the feeling that the atoms of Bronwyn were surrounding her like a loose blanket. It occurred to her that Diane might be surrounding Bronwyn in the same way. A crazy thought, but Penina saw it when the two women walked side by side, leaning into each other. Influence maybe? Something crazy.

In the evenings after dinner they would all sit around the huge living room on the soft sofas, or in nests of pillows on the floor, and when Penina got bored with the discussion about thought experiments, she would move from person to person offering to massage feet or shoulders and neck and scalp. She would feel the unique crackle of each person emerging under her fingertips, their concerns bursting up like kernels of exploding popcorn. They loved her and she loved them and she misses that feast of love. She thinks of the whole big planet, all its different countries, and wonders how many other people there are out there who could join the feast and learn the skill. It occurs to her there must be lots.

How full of himself Dr. Hector was at that meeting. How sure he seems to be that he's the only one who knows the right thing to do and the right way to do it. She can't stand know-it-all adults. She's glad her own parents aren't like that. Still there are problems. Her father has become too caught up in his worries. As soon as one worry starts to fade, he trades it in for another. But his worry doesn't need to hold her back. He still thinks she's too young to understand the gravity and responsibility of their skill, even though he watched her do amazing things on those field trips. She was right in there with everyone else—once, on a very hot day, she brought on snow, and she was the only one among them who was able to do that! But her father keeps cautioning her that skill isn't everything; there are things she doesn't fully understand, he says, certain human things she'll only learn through life experience. F*%* that! She knows as much as she needs to know: Everywhere you go, the world and its people are hurting. Pop, pop, crackle. If you listen closely, you can hear it.

Analu is terrified—that she hears loud and clear. He doesn't like being as powerful as he is. Why are so many adults so scared? It isn't necessary. We all die in the end anyway, and her father has witnessed death before. Death is just a thing that happens to every human being. Vailea doesn't seem to be scared of her own death, and Penina is pretty sure she'll meet her own death in the same accepting way.

Penina used to think she and her father were alike—but now she knows they're not. She doesn't feel scared at all—she loves being powerful. There's a Greenlandic phrase Edel told her about: *Immaatinngilanga nipaartiinngilanga. I will not be silent. I will not be quiet.* That phrase inspires Edel's songs.

It's time to step up. She can almost feel Bronwyn telling her this from afar.

A coconut plummets from above and lands three feet in front of her, the sound muted by the sand. It's Bronwyn! Penina laughs and pulls out her phone and photographs the coconut and texts the picture to Bronwyn. *Is that you?* ☺ *I think I'm ready!* Immediately Bronwyn texts back: *Remember to listen. Remember the heat. Good luck! Tell me what happens. I'm thinking of you!* ♥

Dusk on the lagoon. She stands with bare feet buried in the warm sand, looking across the water to the setting sun. Behind her the comforting sounds of people preparing to eat and sleep. The sky has purpled so the petrels fly in silhouette, beaks like daggers. *Imingnarpoq: The air is so clear sounds can be heard from afar. Nuannarpunga: I am full of delirious joy at being alive.* The last few hours Penina has spent in solitude, gathering intention, focusing it.

Someone creeps up behind her. She turns. Her father. Yes, of course he would find her here.

"You're not going to do anything, are you?" she says.

He hesitates. "It's too dangerous."

"You mean it's too hard."

"There are other things we should do now. Like work on those water projects Hector talked about. We need to make sure we all stay healthy."

"That won't save the island."

"It's still important."

"You've given up."

"No."

"I'm too young to give up."

"Penina . . ."

His voice becomes a single note sailing off with the birds. She turns her back to the lagoon, cupping the needy darkening island in her gaze, its scuttling evening sounds, the pricks of light igniting here and there like low-lying stars, and she feels the thing inside her, the fierce spirit that is now an essential part of her, which sends up a vision of what the island could be. The vision turns to white-heat and disassembles her body. The lightest touch of her father's shoulder against hers, telling her he, too, is ready. She surrounds him with her own air, her atoms, her willful spirit, coaxing him, teaching him.

There is a low rumble, like a tuning orchestra, and she feels trembling beneath her feet, the sand shifting, spilling to new places. Once, thousands of years ago, a volcano erupted here and gave birth to the island. Now its memory echoes up through her soles. Things can fall from view, or memory, but nothing is ever entirely gone. Something always remains: a shiver, an atom, a smudge of DNA.

Waves of silver light engulf her. A cascading silence. Her eyes are expanding funnels, watching polyps of coral bloom, thousands of bright promises, branching, plate-shaped, globular, sculpting themselves into minarets, spindles, ravines, grottos, castles. A pulsing citadel, tinted with pale hues reminiscent of frescoes, pressing up and out, insisting on life.

Then: fish. Gliding, darting, present and elusive, here then gone. Viridian, azure, yellow, pink and purple and blood red. Colors so vivid they break your heart. Speckles and stripes. She remembers such fish from when she was little, her father naming them when they swam. Butterflyfish, parrotfish, unicornfish, goatfish, angelfish, wrasse and damsels. Triggerfish, bannerfish, grouper and chromis. Hogfish, hawkfish. She would giggle at the names, believing he'd made them up. And here they are again, all at once, in stunning variety. How can life be so colorful, so varied, so full of humor?

She wishes Edel were here to see. No one moves more fluidly than fish. In and out of the coral they go, changing direction quickly with a slight flick of the fin. They travel as light does, she thinks, undeterred by obstacles, taking things as they come, exploring what is. None of the clumsy collisions you see with mammals.

Without interruption she directs her energy to the coral, the plankton, the fish. A shimmering encases her, an undulation of fading sunlight, of rising moonlight and starlight. Penina, Penina, Penina, dissolving, who are you? She must have grown gills, she thinks—how else could she see what she's seeing, this broad swath of ocean above and beneath. Where is her father? She senses him nearby, but he's gone from view.

Time later to think of these things: gills, father, selfhood. Now there's only the task at hand, to bestow and restore what she can.

The island shudders, takes the deepest breath of its life, and Penina remembers long ago being a fish, nimble, graceful, powerful and humble. A creature of the water. A creature of the Earth.

THE END

ACKNOWLEDGMENTS

When I finished writing *Weather Woman*, the forerunner of *Sinking Islands*, I never imagined writing a sequel. I tend to think of my novels as one-off narratives with sequels played out only in the imaginations of readers. But Bronwyn and her mentor Diane lingered in my brain more than my characters usually do; soon, I realized I wasn't done with them. Their continuing story poured out quickly, as if it had been there all along.

In bringing the novel to fruition I'm grateful to so many people. To early readers Char and Don McElroy, Dave and Becky Dusseau, Andrea Schwartz-Feit. To my tiny dear writing group—or is it a therapy group?—Miriam Gershow and Debra Gwartney. Huge hugs to Kate Gale, Mark Cull, and Tobi Harper of Red Hen Press, and their stellar team, especially Monica Fernandez, Natasha McClellan, Rebeccah Sanhueza, and Tansica Sunkamaneevongse. And what would I do without my beloved agent and friend, Deborah Schneider, who has supported me with her wisdom, kindness, and encouragement for years?

It must be said: eternal love and gratitude to Paul Calandrino and Ben Howorth, who sustain my days with their love.

With the completion of this novel something became clear that should have been clear years ago: I must extend my thanks to everyone I've known throughout my entire lifetime, casual acquaintances as well as close friends and family, because in those cumulative interactions, observing and emoting with a variety of people over the years, I have become the particular writer I am.

Biographical Note

Cai Emmons is the author of three novels—*His Mother's Son*, *The Stylist*, *Weather Woman*—and a story collection, *Vanishing*. She holds a BA from Yale University and two MFAs from New York University in film and from the University of Oregon in fiction. Before turning to fiction, Emmons wrote plays and screenplays. Winner of a Student Academy Award, an Oregon Book Award, and the Leapfrog Fiction Prize, and a finalist for the *Narrative Magazine* and *Missouri Review* fiction prizes, she has taught at a variety of institutions, most recently in the Creative Writing Program at the University of Oregon. She lives in Eugene, Oregon.